Neil started his investment career in the City in the mid-1990s and has worked at various fund management houses in London and Frankfurt. He is a chartered surveyor and chartered financial analyst.

Following his retirement in 2016, he has spent his time writing fiction. *Pass the Parcel* is the first of a series of financial thrillers that Neil has been working on.

He lives in Woodbridge, Suffolk, with his wife, Michelle; twin boys, Tom and Charlie; and a black Lab – rapidly approaching middle age – called Barney.

For Michelle, Tom and Charlie.

Neil Turner

PASS THE PARCEL

AUSTIN MACAULEY PUBLISHERS™

LONDON * CAMBRIDGE * NEW YORK * SHARJAH

A CIP catalogue record for this title is available from the British Library.

ISBN 9781398421233 (Paperback)
ISBN 9781398421240 (ePub e-book)

www.austinmacauley.com

First Published 2021
Austin Macauley Publishers Ltd®
1 Canada Square
Canary Wharf
London
E14 5AA

A special thanks to Jim Kelly, who encouraged me to write a work of fiction – that happened to have finance floating around in the background – rather than a non-fiction textbook about finance.

Chapter One

When the lift doors opened, Chuck JK Whiteman II stepped out, ready to have his breath taken away. The sixty-foot-high panoramic windows of the lobby area of his hotel framed Jackson Lake in the foreground and the snow-capped peaks of the Teton Mountains beyond. The manner in which the windows captured the stark beauty of the Rockies reminded him of a perfectly composed landscape masterpiece. Then it got even better: it came to life. As he watched, kites and hawks were circling in the cloudless sky over the grasslands surrounding the lake and the tall pine trees shimmered like emerald tinsel in the gentle summer breeze.

He recalled trekking in those forests in pursuit of the Timber wolf – the iconic predator of the Jackson Hole National Park. He reached for the binoculars that were hanging from the paw of a stuffed black bear next to him and scanned the boundary between the trees and the valley floor. He felt the muscles in the nape of his neck contract and his hairs rose causing an involuntary shudder.

As he brought the binoculars into focus, he found himself back in those very mountains. It was over two years ago on a freezing cold wintry afternoon, alone in a small forest clearing. The trees seemed to lean into one another – the snow burdening the branches, as they frowned their disapproval at his presence. That's where he was stood when he noticed them in the half-light of dusk. He could see the lights of their eyes, white-silver fur bristling with frost and the canine teeth exposed as a sign of inevitable attack. Their breath froze the moment the vapour left their bodies – adding that silvery glint to their dark snouts.

He'd found them no more than three miles from where he was stood right now. The leader was just thirty yards ahead, a movement around the base of a tree stump; then a second off to the right and a third a few moments later to the left. He couldn't see the rest of the pack, but furtive movements in the undergrowth confirmed their presence. They had formed a semi-circle around him, an arc of collaboration between members of a pack working in partnership. The alpha male stepped out and moved closer to Whiteman, a low growl and the snout twitching to reveal the jagged set of teeth – the others followed their leader, closing in to entrap him.

As the wolf moved, it dawned on Whiteman what he'd done – interrupted lunch. Behind it and partly obscured by the tree stump was a fresh kill; a large deer from what he could make out. The leader was moving closer and a knot of fear tightened in the pit of his stomach, but he had no intention of taking the deer's place on the menu. Whiteman slipped the rifle – a Ruger No 1 – off his shoulder in one, quiet seamless movement and aimed. Through the sights, he could see the eyes of the alpha male, but he lowered the barrel and instead picked out the space just in front of his paws and squeezed the trigger. Thankfully, the sound and the splaying dirt was enough; the leader span away, quickly followed by the rest of the pack.

Whiteman's fascination with the animal he revered had put him in danger; it had scared him, but at the same time, he'd felt electrifyingly alive. And it was a reminder that the world is divided between the hunters and the hunted, and he, like the Timber wolf, was a hunter.

He returned the binoculars and headed for the Explorer's room reminding himself of why he was here and that he had a job to do: the Federal Reserve's annual shindig at Jackson Hole, Wyoming. This year's topic was The Greenspan era: lessons for the future was in honour of the outgoing Chairman – Alan Greenspan. For Whiteman's money, the Chairman of the Fed was one of the most powerful people on planet earth – setting interest rates for the world's largest economy. He could put money in people's pockets by lowering rates or take it away by increasing them, and he could do all this independently and away from the political shenanigans of Washington. He was retiring and handing over the reins to Ben Bernanke. Greenspan's tenure had been long – eighteen years – and a glittering success. It had been one of the most benign economic periods in history and Chuck Whiteman, of course, had contributed to that triumph.

As CEO of Silvermans investment bank, Whiteman had more than anyone else, promoted the use of derivatives that had delivered the economic stability that everyone enjoyed: the world of modern business and finance was now unimaginable without them. As he made his way through the hotel, he considered their mechanics. They were actually very straightforward; it was the mystifying terminology that the bankers deliberately wrapped them in that intimidated people. He smiled to himself. A derivative was simply a financial instrument with a value 'derived' from the movement in agreed-upon underlying assets, like oil, gas, agricultural products, interest rates or anything else for that matter.

In the real world, corporations had used derivatives for years to protect themselves from future raw material price movements. In order to 'hedge' its position, a company simply bought a derivative that increased in value if raw material prices moved against them. The increase in the derivative would offset the losses associated with the raw material price movements: simple.

In the financial world, things had moved on even further. Billions of dollars of derivatives were traded daily as banks and other organisations hedged-their-bets against movements in stock prices, bond prices, interest rates and other portfolio positions. For Whiteman, the contribution to society of all this activity was enormous and unquestionable. The hedging of interest rate movements for example, allowed millions of Americans to enjoy cheap, fixed-rate mortgages. The reason so many of his fellow citizens owned their own home, had a job, drove nice cars, sailed in boats and benefitted from a booming stock market was because derivatives had delivered the stability that harnessed economic prosperity. Whiteman was in no doubt that the he'd made an important contribution to the 'years of plenty' on behalf of his compatriots.

He stopped just outside the conference room and picked up a coffee, barely acknowledging the cheerful young waitress who served him. He placed his cup on a chest-high table and scanned his blackberry; everything was fine, there were no more requests for information from the Chairman of Silvermans. He checked his appearance in a nearby mirror. Whiteman was a tall, elegant man with a baldhead and mottled skin across his forehead. His rimless glasses gave him an unjustified, studious appearance – in fact, he looked more like a professor than an investment banker, but nobody had ever felt the need to tell him.

He entered the conference room and joined the other delegates; one hundred and twenty-six of the most powerful men and women in global finance hand-picked by the Federal Reserve to attend Jackson Hole to discuss the important economic issues of the day. He chose a seat at the back. The round tables were set for eight and arranged so that everyone was facing the speaker's rostrum. The deer antler chandeliers hanging from the low ceiling continued the rustic theme of the furniture elsewhere in the hotel. The carpets were a dark green and brown combination and the walls wood panelled; drenched in accoutrements from the early fur traders that inhabited Jackson Hole in the nineteenth century: a knife, an axe, a pair of primitive ski shoes and a fur trapper's hat. The many paintings hanging on the walls depicted trackers in search of their prey. It was a fitting tribute to the early hunters of Wyoming, an appropriate setting for their twenty-first-century counterparts – and a stark reminder that it was not good to be the hunted in life.

He acknowledged a few acquaintances on his table. Sam Michael from Lehman Brothers and Rob Barnes from Merrils. He returned the nod that he received from a very relaxed-looking Greenspan on the other side of the room and took his seat as the moderator finished his introduction for the first speaker. He crossed his long legs and adjusted his glasses as he waited for Professor Raghuram Rajan to begin.

He picked up the professor's paper and turned it over to the blank, last page. He doodled on the empty space as his sleep-deprived body began to remind him about the early hours of the morning. One of the bank's private jets had flown him from New York but it hadn't landed until the early hours and, on just four hours' sleep, he'd been on conference calls with the bank's Chairman back on the east coast. The calls went well: the derivative products that Silvermans had developed may have been helping his fellow citizens, but they were also driving the bank's profits and Whiteman's name was all over them. The thought went someway to soothe his tired limbs.

He'd been drawing shapes aimlessly for a few moments as the dull professor plodded through his paper, when a large hand tapped him on the shoulder.

"Hey, Chuck, what time's tee-off this afternoon?" whispered the banker sat on the table next to him. Although he was hard to miss, Whiteman hadn't noticed Big Dave. He was at Deutsche Bank. A lousy banker – God knows how he'd got himself invited here – and, unfortunately, a good golfer. Nonetheless, Whiteman was delighted for the interruption and the reminder that he had something to look forward to do later in the day.

"Two pm on the dot; don't be late. What did you think of Woods last month at the Open?" added Whiteman, his mood lifting.

"All class. That's Tiger's tenth major. The way he's playing, he'll beat Nicklaus' record hands down. You gonna make Augusta in April?"

Whiteman was just about to reply, when the professor's tone changed. He'd moved up an octave and seemed to pause for effect.

"If bankers are paid on the short-term profit generated by derivatives but they do not share any of the pain if they go wrong, they are motivated to take on ever-higher levels of risk."

Whiteman looked at Big Dave: Big Dave looked back at Whiteman. Both had picked out the key words – bankers, derivatives, pay and risk. Both men moved a little awkwardly in their seats but continued their conversation.

"Yeh, we're going. We're taking a few clients down and playing the course after the event. What about you?"

"If these banks lose confidence in each other…the inter-bank market could freeze up, and one could well have a full-blown financial crisis," asserted Professor Rajan.

"Full-blown financial crisis? Who the fuck is this guy?" stammered Whiteman.

"He's some academic from the IMF," replied the Deutsche man.

"Well, he should stay in academia. We're here to celebrate Greenspan's contribution to economic stability, not piss on his parade."

Whiteman looked up again at Rajan and sneered; the blue-tinged veins that traversed his temples on either side of his face twitching.

The professor was asked to sum up by the moderator.

"There may also be a greater probability of a catastrophic meltdown. These risks could eventually destroy their own firms – or even the entire financial system."

Whiteman eyeballed Greenspan; his craggy, intelligent face wasn't giving anything away but he noticed that the Chairman of the Fed was tapping his fingers on the table in front of him. Whiteman could see conversations breaking out across the room, whispers behind hands, shaking of heads and the pulling of faces. He caught the eye of the moderator as he was asking for 'any questions'.

The moderator obliged and said, "Mr Whiteman, over to you."

The Silvermans' CEO staged a pause; it was a long one, to the extent that delegates began to look around the room to locate him. Big Dave tried to become invisible – not an easy task for a man of his size – looking at the floor and shrinking as far back into his seat as possible. Whiteman finally stood, tapped the end of the roving microphone and began.

"Apologies ladies and gentlemen," he said, wryly, as he took control of the room, "but I'm still recovering from our learned professor here telling us that the world is about to end." Playing to his audience, he simultaneously tapped furiously against the left-hand side of his chest, as he feigned heart palpitations. He'd read his fellow delegates well. To a man and a woman, they laughed – loudly – and with Whiteman. Rajan, who was now seated, looked out at them; he managed an anguished grin but nothing more. Greenspan's expression was still imperial, fingers continuing to beat out some rhythm on the table. Whiteman continued in his flat, nasal drawl; the consequence of formative years spent in the Windy City. As he addressed his audience, he didn't once look at Rajan.

"Professor, in my experience, and I think the evidence bears this out, the innovations you have questioned have reduced risk – not increased it. That's why we developed derivatives in the first place. They make the globe's financial system more flexible and allocate risk around it more efficiently. Why would you say that the risk has increased when there is no evidence for this?"

Professor Rajan looked out at the delegates. The symposium's etiquette ensured that nobody was blatantly rude. But the nods, the murmurs and the closed body language made it obvious; the room was with the Silvermans' CEO.

He cleared his throat.

"With respect, Mr Whiteman, you can't claim to have evidence that derivatives reduce risk. What if their growth coincided with a period of economic stability as opposed to creating it? I believe they can be dangerous and, in a less stable period, will exaggerate both an economic and financial downturn," argued Rajan.

Whiteman wasn't having it.

"Believe me, Professor, the last 18 years was no coincidence. We" – at this stage, he swung an inclusive arm out over the seated audience – "built a stable and robust economy based on derivatives not burdened by them. The only thing that's dangerous around here is your view, sir. You can't just dismiss the best part of 20 years of history to try to make a name for yourself. What you're talking about has never happened before – ever."

Some of the other delegates joined in the debate, and were overwhelmingly in favour of Whiteman and just as offended that someone had the audacity to argue that their contributions could end up causing and exaggerating a financial crisis rather than reducing the prospect of one. Professor Rajan defended his paper, but the room wasn't in the mood. This was Greenspan's party and they were going to enjoy it. As Whiteman filed out at the end of the session, he was pleased to hear the whispered comments from delegates.

"I think he's a little misguided" was one, and "He's bloody dangerous; a Luddite who'd clearly want to over regulate the banks" was another.

Whiteman was smiling to himself, as he strolled out of the room; he was thinking about his first tee shot at the Jackson Hole Golf Club when he became aware that Greenspan was watching him. The great man was sat in one of a pair of wing-backed chairs placed in an alcove just outside the main conference room. He summoned Whiteman to join him. After shaking hands, the banker lowered himself into the seat opposite; he heard the decrepit brown leather yield as he sank low into the chair. He crossed his legs and placed his arms on each of the elegant, but equally worn, scroll arms – his posture and self-assured smile radiating confidence.

Greenspan leaned forward, conspiratorially, elbows on his knees and made a steeple of his fingers as he studied Whiteman, as if gauging him in some way.

"What if he's right, Chuck?" asked Greenspan finally; his owlish eyes peering at Whiteman through his signature black-framed glasses.

Whiteman's smile slightly faltered.

"I'm not sure I know what you're getting at," he replied, completely understanding the question.

"Professor Rajan," said Greenspan pointing to the man from the IMF a few feet away, "what if he's right?"

"He's not," replied Whiteman instantly, his smile now completely gone. He uncrossed his legs and leaned into the sagging leather.

"That's not what I asked," said Greenspan immediately. "I asked what happens if he is."

A small group of delegates stood nearby shared a joke. Whiteman looked at them briefly and then faced Greenspan again. He couldn't answer the question – no one could in 2005. He resorted to asking one of his own.

"Do you think he's right?"

"As a matter of fact, Chuck, I think he made some very valid points."

"So, you think derivatives are dangerous?" asked the banker, who didn't bother hiding the cynicism in his voice. He casually pointed – as if he was thumbing a lift – towards the Professor and raised his eyebrows. "You actually believe this guy?"

"For your sake, Chuck, you better hope he's wrong."

Greenspan stood.

"You'll need to excuse me, I need to get on. But if I were you, I'd take the trouble to read that," he said, as he nodded to Rajan's rolled up paper that Whiteman was still holding.

The Chairman of the Federal Reserve moved away without saying another word. Whiteman was left alone, sitting in the chair watching Alan Greenspan shaking hands with Professor Raguran Rajan on the other side of the room. What was it, he said? *Derivatives could eventually destroy their own firms – or even the entire financial system.*

Bullshit! Whiteman got up, left the paper on the chair and headed for the golf course.

Chapter Two

"Excuse me sir, but I'm afraid you must wear a jacket as you walk through the club. You are, of course, welcome to take it off once seated in your dining area."

"Are you shitting me?" the voice held a gritty New York edge. "You Brits got a rule that says whilst walking, you must wear more clothes than when you're sitting down. I get hot when I walk and you want me to put a fucking jacket on! And anyway, I'm wearing a goddamn tie and pants!"

Bob Santini, the head of the Proprietary Trading desk at Allied English had arrived at the exclusive Century Club, in the heart of the City of London.

"My sincere apologies, sir, but the rule is that a gentleman must be wearing a jacket at all times whilst walking through the club. We do have to consider all our members and their guests. And if you could lower your voice, sir."

"Well, I think the management should take a run and—"

"Bob – great to see you."

Santini turned, recognised the cultured, modulated voice while the waiter took a half step back as if in acknowledgement that authority had been restored.

James Dickenson was the CEO of Allied English, and Santini's London-based boss.

"Forgive us our little eccentricities, Bob." Dickenson was completely at ease in his £3,000 suit, running an arm around Santini's shoulders while discreetly casting Harry – Dickenson's favourite waiter – a long-suffering look.

He led his guest towards their pre-booked private dining room seamlessly switching into a commentary of the Club's Queen Ann interior, the full-length casement windows looking out over St Stephen's Churchyard and the deep blue carpet emblazoned with the Royal Coat of Arms. Anyone hearing his voice would have guessed he was a product of an English public school, the son of a Lord and a graduate of an ancient University, and they'd have been right.

Santini's background was, in a way, even more remarkable and Dickenson had double-checked his file before leaving the office to make sure he had the details right. The son of an Italian immigrant with no formal education he'd started in the mailroom of Morgan Stanley in 1983, yet he'd become the most successful bond trader Wall Street had ever seen. Dickenson may have enjoyed a graceful ascent of the career ladder, but he knew just how talented Santini had to be to make it to the top from those humble beginnings. For the third time that day, he reminded himself not to underestimate the aggressive New Yorker.

The private dining room could seat eight comfortably, so Santini and Dickenson were at one end of the antique wooden dining table. At the other end of the room, there was an ornate Victorian room divider – the four panels of which were oil paintings depicting the seasons of the year.

Apart from a few other period chairs dotted around the perimeter of the room, it was sparse. But most of all, it fulfilled its role – as a discrete, impenetrable venue for private discussion. There wasn't an investment banker left on planet earth prepared to talk business on recorded telephone lines and God forbid anyone would want to commit financially and politically sensitive business strategies to email. What the two men were going to discuss needed to stay within these four walls.

Dickenson carefully folded his six-foot five-inch frame into one of the delicate-looking chairs. Santini collapsed into his, the wooden legs creaking under the pressure, as he looked longingly towards a drinks trolley set to one side, a bottle of champagne with a flush of condensation protruding from an ice bucket. Dickenson's view was of the small garden that belonged to, and was maintained by, the Church of St Stephen standing just a few feet away. It held a very personal memory for the CEO of Allied English.

Early on in his banking career, he had told his late father in those Gardens of his decision not to return to the family business in order to pursue his banking career. His father, although bitterly disappointed, had accepted his son's decision. Lady Dickenson had not. She had disowned him; had not met his children and had not spoken to her son in 25 years.

The waiters' arrival brought Dickenson back to the meeting and the salivating American sat opposite.

The wine waiter took the orders and served the drinks and then left the room. Harry did not make eye contact with Santini despite, or possibly because, the American smiled smugly as he took off his jacket.

"James, apologies that the email I sent was a little cryptic, but I appreciate your time today. What I'm about to tell you is a little sensitive hence the request for a face-to-face meeting somewhere private and discreet." Dickenson gave an unenthusiastic nod of the head as the American hung his jacket on the back of his chair. As he did so, his trademark gaudy braces – this time in navy blue and polka dot pink – slipped off one of his shoulders and Santini manoeuvred it back into position with a thumb and an overarm movement.

"I know your strategy in derivatives has been brilliant, James. Selling subprime mortgage bonds and CDOs has been hugely profitable – no question about that."

There was another unenthusiastic nod from the Englishman, as he waited for the 'but'.

"But some of these subprime mortgages are crap and at some point, they'll fail. I want the Prop Desk to be able to bet against them," said Santini. He tugged at a cufflink with a dollar sign emblazoned in the colours of the stars and stripes as he studied his boss' face for a reaction.

Dickenson thought about the negotiation a few months earlier. The man sat opposite had demanded to set up the bank's Global Proprietary Trading Group – the Prop Desk, as it was colloquially known. This was a private company – 50% owned by Santini and the small band of traders that could tolerate working with him – and 50% owned by Allied English, and it used the bank's own money to make investments. Santini, and his team, would also keep a large share of the profits that the Prop Desk was expected to generate. It was just about the only thing that the bank could do to persuade Santini to stay and not leave for any of the mind-numbingly high compensation packages that competitors had offered him.

Dickenson assumed that the conversation would go in this direction – the bank's grapevine was more efficient at disseminating information than the multi-million-pound IT system they'd installed the year before. Frankly, Dickenson welcomed it. He also thought large parts of the subprime mortgage market were suspect and he knew that the bank's star bond trader had a fantastic feel for successful trades. And if Santini made money – as he had done in every trading year since 1988 – the bank would make money. In fact, Dickenson quite liked the idea of his fixed income department doing one thing and the Prop Desk another – that way, whichever way the market moved, the bank would be in a good position. But first, he decided to have a little fun at Santini's expense.

"Bob," said Dickenson, raising a single eyebrow, "are you telling me, the CEO of the bank, that you want to bet against all our clients?" He let out a long breath – that rattled his lips – and gave his colleague a flat, deadpan gaze.

For the first time that day, the American seemed to hesitate – as if he was unsure what to make of the Brit's poker face that stared at him from across the table.

"Yes, well, not all of them obviously, but some, certainly," replied Santini, this time tugging his other cufflink.

"It's OK, Bob. I'm teasing," said Dickenson, as he released a wide grin and raised his palms. "That's why we set up the Prop Desk – if you have a different view to our clients, you need to be able to express it. Just keep me informed of what's going on and don't get in over your head."

A delicate finger of Dickenson's right hand pressed the red button on the discrete oak-cubed busser next to him, signalling to Harry and his team – who were patiently waiting in the kitchen – that they were ready for lunch. As the food was served in the Cheapside room, Dickenson thought through Santini's proposal and the bank's existing derivative positions.

Allied English had done what just about every other investment bank had. It had created hundreds of billions of pounds worth of derivatives called CDOs, or Collateralised Debt Obligations. The value of the CDO was 'derived' from the portfolio of subprime mortgages that were sitting underneath it – the underlying asset. Provided people continued to pay their mortgages, the cash flows produced an attractive yield for the investors that bought the CDOs. The complicated-sounding name mildly amused Dickenson, but it was almost obligatory – no self-respecting investment banker would have called them a 'subprime mortgage derivative' – that would have been far too simple – almost vulgar; much better to think of a name that confused anyone that wasn't familiar with the concept.

There were two other points about CDOs that Dickenson reminded himself. The first was that CDOs, like some other forms of derivatives, were unregulated and unreported. They didn't trade through a recognised exchange – like a straightforward interest rate swap – they were traded 'over-the-counter' and were private contracts between 'consenting adults'. This also meant they were relatively opaque by comparison so clients couldn't compare prices very easily and therefore they were hugely profitable for Allied English. This was why they had grown massively – which brought Dickenson to his second point.

Allied had gone from zero to producing several billion pounds worth of these things, and he knew every other investment bank had done the same. But nobody knew precisely how many derivatives were out there – because they were unregulated, the banks didn't need to report them. He had sympathy with Raghuram Rajan on this point. He'd met the Professor the previous month at Jackson Hole and tended to agree with his excellent paper – if the housing market turned, the derivatives would become very toxic, very quickly.

Santini's proposal was for the bank to use its own money to buy insurance contracts that would pay out if the CDOs it created for clients began to fall in value. Dickenson decided to have his cake and eat it. He'd let the fixed income department continue to sell the CDOs to clients – and pick up the fantastically lucrative fees for doing so – and in the background, Santini could make his trades against the very same CDOs using the bank's money. It would be a win/win for Allied English. Indeed, Dickenson was warming to the idea so much that he made a mental note to organise his private investment strategy around it. To implement it, he'd need to arrange a very confidential meeting himself.

Chapter Three

At the risk of upsetting Sam, Andrew Longmire was glad he'd spent all of his Saturday afternoon locked away in his private study ploughing through the material. It was a good piece of work, as it confirmed his own point of view – Longmire's favourite type of analysis. He relaxed into a satisfying stretch, as he looked up from the report and gazed outside. But the Suffolk daylight had faded fast, transforming the French doors into an effective one-way mirror. So instead of the beautiful vista of his manicured lawn – criss-crossed with box hedges and bordered with topiary – rolling down towards the shallow banks of the river Deben, his own unattractive reflection stared back at him.

Longmire was fully aware that his looks were not his forte – he'd come to terms with that a long time ago. He noticed his paunch and released his outstretched arms from above his head and patted it gently. He'd need to do something about that. He looked up at the glass again and studied the face staring back at him; globular eyes set in a mundane, oval-shaped face. Not much he could do about that. But although he recognised his physical shortcomings, Longmire certainly had no false modesty when it came to his other attributes. He was intelligent, funny, successful, rich and, most importantly, getting richer.

He glanced down at the company logo embossed on the top right-hand-corner of the report he was reading and smiled. About eighteen months earlier, Longmire had been appointed as the CEO of First Capital Solutions, often referred to as simply First Capital. It was a specialist bank that lent money to property companies and had been around since the early 1990s, having been created by a husband-and-wife team called Steve and Andrea White. Longmire had argued, successfully, to launch the business on the stock market and First Capital was now a publicly quoted company listed on the AIM market – where small companies are initially placed. It was beginning to grow rapidly and it was his job to make sure that continued, despite the reservations of the ageing, conservative old guard.

Squeaking footsteps on the parquet flooring outside his study brought him back to the present.

"Would you like a drink, Andrew?" asked Sam Longmire. His wife had just returned from her gym session.

He declined. He was still sat on the low-level settee next to a glass coffee table. He didn't look up from his report.

"Actually, I am nearly finished for the day. This report's spot on; it supports what I have been trying to tell the bloody Whites for months that we need to be more aggressive with our lending. It's the only way our profits will continue to improve," said Longmire. He heaved his stumpy frame up from the ridiculously low settee, cursed the interior designer that had persuaded him to buy it and walked over to his desk to check emails.

Sam Longmire leaned her slim, athletic figure against a large wooden bookcase, as she watched her husband shuffle across the room. She was wearing black Lycra gym-shorts and a bright-yellow crop top. At thirty-eight, she was three years younger than him and at five feet nine, three inches taller. She had short, naturally blond hair, and a petite face with bright-green eyes. Andrew and Sam Longmire were living proof that there was something in the idiom that 'opposites attract'.

"Do you think they'll agree to the changes?" she asked, taking a sip from her water bottle. Longmire arrived at his desk and threw himself into the soft leather chair. The seat squealed in protest under the weight and swivelled so that he had to throw out an arm to catch the desk. He took out a monogrammed handkerchief and mopped his brow.

"Of course not and I don't give a shit about what they think. They've lost the plot and haven't the appetite to make the changes that we need," he replied, looking at his wife for the first time since she'd entered the room. He clocked her attire; it corroborated his thoughts when he'd heard the squeaking trainers. The hair on the nape of his neck bristled involuntarily. He didn't mind her going to the gym – it was who she went with that annoyed him. He wiped his hands and then replaced the handkerchief, but didn't say anything.

Sam raised her eyebrows as if to acknowledge that he had finally registered her presence. She then asked him about the meeting that had been organised with their son's tutor.

"What meeting?" asked Longmire, as he returned to the screen.

"The meeting I told you about three weeks ago. We're due to see Mr Temple, Simon's form tutor. I tried bloody hard to get this arranged for the beginning of term, Andrew – they wanted to wait until after half term. It's at the end of this month," Sam replied. She took a step closer to his desk and placed her hands on her hips.

"Can't make it. We'll have a shit-load to get through regarding the new loan documentation that I want to introduce," he said, tapping the report next to him, "and it's always a stupid busy time of year for us – you know that," he replied, his eyes still locked onto the computer screen.

"Andrew, will you stop looking at that fucking computer and talk to me properly! That's why I gave you as much notice as I did and why I put it in your diary myself. We're always playing second fiddle to you and your bloody business! It really bugs the shit out of me when you promise Simon or me something and then business gets in the way."

Longmire's gaze flicked upwards towards his wife. *And it really bugs the shit out of me when you play that card*, he thought.

"Have a look around you, Sam. Look at the house you live in, the car you drive, where your son goes to school, the holidays that we have. Me and my fucking business pay for it. Don't you think you're being a little churlish?"

Sam's eyes tightened and a pinched expression commandeered her face.

"Andrew, there is more to being a husband and a father than just providing financially for your family. We also need time with you and there always seems to be a reason why you don't have it or can't find it. Yet we're always there for you," she replied.

"Don't give me that shit, Sam. You know I'm working 60 hours a week to provide for you and Simon. Do you think I enjoy doing this on a Saturday?" he asked, picking up the report.

She was glaring at her husband now; her arms folded in front of her with one of her training shoes tapping impatiently against the floor. "Yes, I think you do, Andrew. Even when you're at home, you spend time in here reading or invite guests to stay at the house and don't even bother to tell me."

"They're work colleagues, Sam, and they need to be here for meetings. Don't be so bloody petty," he said. He shook his head whilst he stared at her before looking down and returning his full attention to the report on his desk – a sign that he'd decided that the conversation was over.

Sam looked like she was considering escalating hostilities again. Eventually, she turned and left the study. "Fine, I'll do the bloody meeting myself."

Satisfied that he had added sufficient value to First Capital for one afternoon, Longmire got up from his desk and closed the study door firmly – it wasn't a slam, but it was sufficient to make a statement to his ungrateful wife. He then returned to his computer and closed all the First Capital files. His pulse quickened, his mouth dried and the usual sensation of butterflies developed in the pit of his stomach, as he set about his next task.

He opened 'D66' – his beloved spreadsheet file. It was saved in a particularly obscure part of his complex filing system on his hard drive and could only be opened once the user had gone through the elaborate password protection sequence that Longmire had established. He never opened the file in the presence of any other person – ever.

The sheet was linked to a number of different sites that brought in live financial data feeds; the last traded share price of First Capital, the closing balances of the Longmire's joint banks accounts, the closing balance of Andrew's secret bank account, a clever summation of their shareholdings and, finally, what Longmire had simply labelled 'assets' – which was a manually updated list of material objects such as the Longmire's house, boat and cars; the toys that Sam liked as much as he did.

Everything in the spreadsheet summed together neatly, culminating in one magical figure – TOTAL ASSETS – in an especially formatted cell – D66. He revered it: a private display of Longmire's wealth for him to enjoy at his leisure. He admired the simplicity of it – all that was most important to him reduced to one hypnotising number. There was nothing subjective about it – it was real, it was precise (to two decimal places) and it was a true measure of his success. He glanced at cell D66 for one more time before shutting down his computer for the day, GROSS ASSET VALUE – £5,552,600.54. *Sam has no cause for complaint,* he thought.

★

In Lombardy, northern Italy, Steve and Andrea White were sat at their table looking out from the cloistered walkway of their hotel. Through the archways formed by the sixteenth-century columns, they could see Lake Como below and the mountains gently pouring themselves into the crystal-clear water. The clinked their glasses – part-filled with equally clear champagne – as they toasted Andrew Longmire. They were delighted that he'd walked into their lives and was doing exactly what they needed him to do to effect their own business strategy; a strategy that Andrew Longmire knew nothing about.

Chapter Four

Ann looked at the man opposite her. He was sat in his favourite contemplative pose – podgy fingers interlinked around his generous girth and his feet planted together in front of him but toes turned inwards – a kind of ancient Caucasian Buddha with pigeon toe. The shock of long, misbehaving white hair and matching beard added years to his appearance. And in sharp contrast to many in his profession, he often left people with the impression that he was one of the financial community's meek who would certainly not be inheriting the earth. Ann didn't believe any of it – not for a single moment.

Lester FitzGerald was the CEO of Lambda – a secretive hedge fund manager that he had established a decade or so before. Formally, it was there to take advantage of 'unlikely events' in financial markets. Informally, at least from what she could work out, it was there to make fun out of investment bankers.

"So, why does Lambda exist?" he asked his new recruits in his mild, neutral voice. He smiled generously, and the crow's feet in the corner of his eyes revealed themselves fully.

Ann sneaked a look at Sally sat next to her. They'd joined Lambda on the same day three months earlier and had become firm friends. Apparently, they'd both made the short list of two and Lester, even after a second interview, had been unable to choose between them. He'd decided to employ both. Ann knew that Lester would want to answer his own question. She paused sufficiently to allow him to do so.

"In a nut shell, we don't believe that our raw data; house prices, stock market returns, bond price movements or any other financial data that you care to mention are symmetrical. These data ALL fail to occur in well-behaved bundles of normal distributions around an average. As a result, certain events have a much higher probability of occurring than most market participants believe. Since everyone else thinks certain events will never happen – especially if they haven't happened before – they become too cheap and so we develop investment strategies to take advantage of this."

Whenever Ann heard the CEO of Lambda talk, as passionately as he did, about the absence of symmetry in financial data, she was always struck by the role that it assumed in other aspects of his life. Although Lester hadn't had much say in the matter, his physical appearance for a start – he had well-proportioned regular features that provided one of the most uniform faces that she had ever seen. The way he was sitting right now may be more spherical than symmetrical, but she reminded herself that she had never seen him sat with crossed legs.

The few pictures that hung in his office were all forms of symmetrical art. His favourite, which appeared in a couple of locations in their Pont Street office in Knightsbridge, was Vitruvian Man by Leonardo De Vinci. The one with the man stood inside a circle and a square with outstretched arms. She'd Googled it – it was supposed to symbolise the essential symmetry of the human body for goodness' sake!

It was as if his devout adherence to asymmetry in finance was met by an equal and opposing force – one that caused him to deliberately pursue symmetry in other parts of his life.

The knock at the door interrupted her thoughts.

"Lester, I'm sorry to interrupt, but Mr Dickenson is here to see you. He's in reception," said Susan, Lester's secretary.

He turned and, simultaneously, glanced at his watch – never a good idea for a man whose hand-eye coordination was as poor as Lester's. His coffee mug and remnants of its contents went flying. Susan rolled her eyes, and calmly told the CEO to get out of the way.

Lester apologised and suggested to both Ann and Sally that they finish off either later in the day or tomorrow and asked Susan to book them another slot. He then left his office to meet the CEO of Allied English.

As he walked along the corridor to meet James Dickenson, Lester found himself smiling; they should, of course, have become sworn enemies and both men knew that. Had they not become firm friends as young men – before the prejudices of age and experience could get in the way – they almost certainly would have been.

James Dickenson, as the CEO of Allied English, represented an industry that relied on hugely complex quantitative techniques and the assumption that the financial data they gobbled up was perfectly symmetrical. This created the fancy charts and the Greek alphabet of formulas that dominated their power point presentations that they used to sell their wares: particularly derivatives.

Lester knew, first hand, that it was all academic and banking hubris. He'd watched the industry become over reliant on dubious mathematics; in fact, he'd resigned from an investment bank in protest over it a decade earlier. He was convinced there was money to be made out of proving the bankers wrong and Lambda often found itself on the opposite side of the trade to most banks – not something that generally endeared him to the finance community.

But in 1970, Dickenson had been the very first person that Lester had met at Cambridge University – literally bumping into him whilst making a cup of tea in the common room on the first day that they both arrived at their college. They studied different subjects – Lester mathematics and James the Classics, but found they had plenty in common. Lester had even been invited to the various Dickenson homes during university holidays.

"James, how wonderful to see you!"

"Thank you, Lester, it's been too long. I really appreciate your time."

Dickenson was dressed in a dark-blue suit, crisp white shirt and red tie – he looked every bit the purveyor of successful investment products. Lester FitzGerald looked like he'd just got up and was popping out on a Saturday morning to buy a pint of milk from the corner shop. He wore a blue pair of jeans, comfortable, soft leather shoes and a green polo shirt. His only sop to formal wear was his favourite, but decrepit, tweed jacket. The leather patches – designed to protect the fabric at the elbow – were now themselves threadbare thin and the cotton had managed to unstitch itself in places.

After a brief tour of the small office, the old friends walked back through the main reception area, down a narrow corridor and arrived at Lester's private office. Lester asked Susan for some refreshments and the men entered the room.

The old friends sat at the small round meeting table. James relaxed into his chair, his long legs crossed and rotated away from the table so that he had sufficient room. Lester was sat upright, feet together and hands clasped on the table in front of him. They talked for the first half an hour or so about their time at Cambridge and the occasional bits of business they had done with one another since. And then, Dickenson moved the conversation on.

"What do you know about US subprime mortgages, Lester?"

Lester withdrew – physically moving further back into his chair.

"What's the matter?" asked his friend.

A shit load, thought Lester. Aloud he said, "Nothing, nothing at all. It's just *you* asking *me* about subprime mortgages."

Lester cocked his head to one side; as if he couldn't quite believe he'd been asked the question, but the fluttery feeling in the pit of his stomach grew.

The question had spooked the CEO of Lambda because of the aggressive email he'd received yesterday – the one that had prevented him from sleeping last night. 'WE WILL NOT APPROVE ANY INVESTMENT AGAINST US SUBPRIME MORTGAGES' had been the email's heading. The Consortium had sent it; an eclectic bunch of investors in his hedge fund that were becoming increasingly hostile towards Lester's latest investment strategy. And today, presumably totally independent of that event, here was one of his oldest friends questioning him about exactly the same thing.

Gently stroking his beard, he continued. "Well, to answer your question, a great deal really. I've looked at that area over the years and here at Lambda, we're putting the finishing touches to an investment strategy around the subprime market. But James, why do you ask?"

Dickenson didn't flinch.

"I want to short the US subprime mortgage market." He looked directly at his old friend, like he was looking for a reaction.

He got one. Lester smiled; now that he knew his friend was humouring him, he playfully swatted Dickenson on the arm. He started to grin and the crew's feet reasserted themselves. Then the stubborn expression on Dickenson's face suddenly registered. The tight jaw, pressed lips and the piercing eyes fixed on Lester's. He knew that expression from old. Dickenson was deadly serious.

Lester's smile disappeared as quickly as it had arrived.

"Come on, James. You're one of the world's largest producers of subprime mortgage bonds, why would you want to bet against them?" asked Lester.

Dickenson paused and looked across the table. The banker swallowed, hard – his prominent Adam's apple lifting and then releasing his knotted red tie and buttoned collar, as it rolled down and then back up his throat.

"It's simple, Lester – there are two outcomes here. The subprime party goes on and on and the bank makes super profits in the next few years or it all blows up over a much shorter timeframe. Under scenario one, I walk away from the bank in a few years as a superstar and with lots of money. Under scenario two, I'm probably out of a job the moment this all goes to hell in a handcart."

Lester looked at Dickenson. Despite him being a banker, Lester considered his old friend to be one of the brightest people he knew. When Dickenson had backed him to bet against the dot com bubble in 1999, there were a great many sceptics. But Dickenson had immediately understood the arguments and backed the strategy. They'd both made lots of money that time around. But he wondered what it was that Dickenson thought he might be able to do this time.

"And what's the probability of one or two occurring, James?" asked Lester. He'd managed to recover a little and smiled at his friend; he had the expression of a mischievous schoolboy who had just asked his teacher an impossible question that everyone knew he wouldn't be able to answer.

Dickenson returned the playful grin. "Lester, that's why I'm sat here in front of you. You're the probability Wizard!"

Lester smiled again at the light-hearted reference to his appearance and asked, "So, how do you think Lambda can help you, James?"

"I'm not sure that it can, but on the basis that I can't predict when this whole thing might change direction, I'd like to buy some insurance. I want a very discrete, very large, private investment that will pay-off massively if the subprime market implodes. I don't want anyone to know about it except you and I, and I'll make the investment through an off-shore entity."

Lester took a further hour to explain the strategy that his latest fund would pursue, after which, Dickenson agreed to make a substantial private investment in *Credere*. When Lester told him the name of the fund, they smiled at each other and then giggled like the immature undergraduates they once were.

"I thought *you* might like the name." Lester had almost forgotten how quick his friend's mind worked.

Not many people appreciated the quirkiness of Lester FitzGerald's sense of humour, but James Dickenson was certainly one of them. As a Cambridge Classics graduate, Dickenson knew that 'credit' came from the Latin '*credere*' – meaning 'to have trust in'. Banking didn't work without faith, but too much of the stuff often led to bubbles that (almost) inevitably burst. Both men thought that the US subprime mortgage market was overinflating and, at some point, something was going to give. When it did, and the trust had vanished, *Credere* would be there to pick up the pieces.

When they'd stopped laughing, Lester remembered the overnight email and his investors' demands.

"Listen, James, I think you know this anyway. But if we make this trade, you know it will be *Credere* against the rest of the world, don't you? Investment bankers – present company excepted – will think we're wrong. They'll probably laugh at us and remind us that this has never happened before."

A knowing grin arranged itself across Dickenson's patrician face.

"I seem to remember most of them doing that in 1999 Lester."

Chapter Five

A little self-consciously, Marina Alfero looked around her kitchen. She was with her husband and a mortgage broker in the decrepit one-bedroom flat that they rented in the poor Tenderloin district of San Francisco. She was a little embarrassed that the kitchen's battered linoleum floor covering had chunks missing that revealed the fragile wooden floorboards beneath. The ancient cast-iron stove, with its thick walls, worn engravings and twisted flue gave the appearance of a gnarled old tree; similar to the one her and her little sister had climbed when they were children in Mexico.

The cheap, wooden kitchen cabinets were so old, that time seemed to have driven a wedge between the drawers and the carcasses and slamming them shut was the only way that she could operate them. Thank goodness Tina Scales had not needed the bathroom – well not yet anyway. A facecloth was currently plugged into the hole in the window to keep the elements at bay – she had almost given up chasing the landlord for the more permanent solution that he'd promised.

As the conversation turned inevitably to finance and mortgages, Marina focussed on Scales. She had warmed to the diminutive lady from the Globe Mortgage Company who, like her, was barely five feet tall. She dressed professionally, but certainly unpretentiously – she noted the pastel dress, flat sensible shoes and a baggy cardigan. Marina felt uncomfortable discussing finances with anyone other than Rodrigo, but Scales' gentle mannerisms had put her at ease almost immediately.

The three of them were perched at the table and chairs crammed into the corner of the kitchen hatching an escape route for the Alferos – not a new experience for the young Mexican couple. They had crossed the border into the US four years earlier, leaving behind levels of poverty that were unimaginable to most Americans. The small *Bandera de México* – the vertical tricolour of green, white and red with the national coat of arms positioned in the centre of the white stripe – was hanging on the wall in front of Marina. It caught her eye and she thought about family and the tree-climbing antics of her and her sister.

"Now then, Marina, tell me about your salary information," Scales asked, "and please don't be shy. The biggest problem I have with my clients is that they're too modest – they undersell themselves. Remember, Marina, Rodrigo" – Scales paused and her eyes alighted on each of them in turn – "I'm here to make your dream come true so give me every chance to be able to make this happen."

Scales' challenge brought Marina back and she pushed the thought of family to one side in order to concentrate. She took a deep breath – she was going to have to talk numbers (definitely not her forte) to an industry expert in her second language. Not a comfortable situation for a twenty-seven-year-old immigrant. But she was determined to make this work and Scales was patient and encouraged her, teasing out extra information where necessary. The broker swiftly entered the relevant data into the laptop in front of her as she manoeuvred effortlessly around the mortgage software.

Frustratingly for Marina, from where she was seated, she could only see part of the screen – the frightening part where various formulae and calculations were arranged. She was fighting the temptation to move in order to check the interesting part – the results section. Scales continued to tap away and flick between screens before finally looking up from her work and smiling.

"OK, I think we have enough for the moment."

Marina forced her fingers to rest on the table. She'd suddenly realised that the coffee cup in front of her had been grinding into the wood where she'd been frantically turning it. The broker produced a final, satisfying tap of the return key, as if she had played the concluding note of some complicated piano sonata. The sound snapped Marina's head towards the keyboard and her fingers reached for the cup once more.

"How much do you think we can borrow?" she asked, her pitch discernibly higher than a few moments before.

Scales cleared her throat and then slowly, almost ceremonially, swivelled the laptop around so that Marina could learn her fate.

Full Loan Amount – $350,000

The broker casually settled back into her chair, crossed her legs and waited.

Marina was wide-eyed. She started to verbalise everything that rushed into her head as she grabbed one of her husband's arms.

"But that's incredible. Rodrigo, we could buy a house…with a garden…we can leave Tenderloin." She checked the number again and then again.

Marina's thoughts were racing now. Sometimes it had seemed to her that leaving Mexico was easier than trying to escape this damn flat: the latter was certainly taking longer. This was their fifth attempt to secure a mortgage. Chequered credit history, irregular incomes (Marina had still been unemployed three weeks previously) or lack of deposit monies – there always seemed to be an obstacle that prevented them leaving this place behind. She had a very real sense that Tina Scales and the Globe Mortgage Company were about to change all that.

Rodrigo Alfero stared at the screen as if he was tolerating a film he had little interest in watching. He sat upright and his powerful arms remained folded. Beyond pleasantries, Rodrigo had said very little – until now.

"But what about the repayments – they must be high – can we afford them?" he asked. He gave Scales the same deadpan expression that he'd offered throughout the meeting. He didn't uncross his arms.

Marina turned to her husband. She squeezed his arm even tighter than before, and bit her bottom lip.

Scales was silent. Slowly, she unfurled her legs and leaned in. She gathered the loose papers in front of her and holding them in both hands, she repeatedly soft-dropped them against the surface of the table until they arranged themselves into order.

"Mr Alfero," she said finally, putting the papers down and offering a friendly smile, "I'm glad you raised such an important question. We have designed these loans to be as affordable as possible so, for the first two years, you'll enjoy a reduced interest payment. After that, there will be a modest increase in the monthly interest charge. I think no more than you currently pay in rent, so I am sure that you will be able to afford them. And those payments are two years away; plenty of time for you two hard-working people to win promotions and possibly even pay rises. House prices will be higher again by that point and you can always refinance and clear any back-payments in that way. You must remember, Mr Alfero, that it's not in our interest to lend money to people who won't be able to pay it back."

Rodrigo looked at the broker and then his wife and then back at the number on the screen. Slowly, he gave Marina a weak smile and a gentle nod before looking away.

A few other technicalities were briefly discussed, but Scales left no more than thirty-five minutes after she had arrived with the Alferos signed up to a Globe Mortgage.

Scales called the back-office to pick up the details of her next appointment.

"Hi, Mazy, I'll send in the paperwork overnight, but I have just left the Alferos' and they've signed up for $350,000. It's a great deal for them and a great deal for us, Mazy." She virtually skipped to her next meeting.

Tina Scales had done her job and created yet another US homeowner – God Bless America.

Chapter Six

Andrew Longmire had already showered and had forced his plump frame into the hotel's sleek logo-emblazoned dressing gown and his podgy feet into the similarly decorated towelled-slippers. It was about 7 pm and he was looking out over the still hectic streets of the City of London five floors below. He smirked, as he observed the spent London commuters dragging themselves home after another day of grind and felt gratitude: gratitude that his talents had raised *him* above *them*. The view, the incipient dusk falling over the city and, not least, the glass of Merlot in his hand had put Longmire in a reflective mood.

He congratulated himself on the progress he had made in two short years as he adopted his ridiculous power-stance. He peered out of the window, glass of wine in his right hand whilst the left was tucked behind his back – clutching his initialled linen handkerchief – as he planted his feet wide apart. When he joined First Capital in 2003, he had insisted on buying part of the business. It had consumed virtually all his personal wealth. He had re-mortgaged heavily against his house and since then borrowed against his First Capital shareholding to buy more shares – but wow, did he feel vindicated!

The price he had effectively paid to Steve and Andrea White for his slice of the company was 125p per share. He would have been prepared to pay over 155p but the Whites had rolled over in the early part of negotiations at the lower price – an absolute steal. Due to Longmire's leadership, the share price had since risen steadily. By the time of the IPO, following his marketing campaign and his first year in charge, the share price was at 158p and today he noticed that they traded at 165p.

"165p! How much further would that take *me* away from *them*?" he asked himself, as he looked down, imperiously, at the minions below. Scurrying around the pavements, they looked like worker-ants frantically undertaking their duties before heading home via a series of dark, dingy tunnels. He was glad he wasn't one of *them*. Longmire was curious about the answer to the question he'd just posed and walked over to the desk, fired-up his laptop to locate the file that would tell him. As the computer whirred into life, his body endured all the usual physiological experiences, but it was the excitement that was the overpowering sensation. He fanned himself with one hand – and the help of the flapping sleeve of the bathrobe – as he scrolled down to the cell containing the First Capital share price with the other. He typed 165p over the previously linked entry and hit return.

"You fucking genius," he said, slowly and deliberately to an empty room.

At that price, his First Capital stake was now worth over £4.2m – higher than it had ever been before and a cool profit of almost £1m on what he had paid for the shares. Longmire hadn't anticipated such an impact and he raced further down the screen, the adrenaline rush energising his fingers as they wrestled with the keyboard to locate the cell. Images of what the magic number in D66 might be flashed through his mind.

He sucked in a deep breath and exhaled slowly to savour the moment. There it was; the single, objective assessment of Longmire's accomplishments – £6,445,789.33 in total gross assets. After a few moments of staring at the number, he strolled back to the window, warmth now radiating through his thrust-out chest, as he looked out across the streets again.

Following his private self-indulgence session, Longmire set about preparing for the morning. It was the evening before the first Annual General Meeting for First Capital since the company had been listed on the stock exchange and he still had plenty of prep before he stood up tomorrow morning to present. He made sure that he knew where the revenues came from, the same for profits and even the company's market share. He also ensured that he could articulate all of this information in a way that underplayed the historical development of the company and embellished his own recent contribution.

He decided he needed a shower again before turning in for the night. Finally, he set his alarm for 4.30 am to give himself plenty of time to run through his slides again and again. He was determined that the audience would appreciate just how good Andrew Longmire was.

Chapter Seven

At about six o'clock in the evening, Lester, along with the other conference delegates, entered the Westchester Suite – the venue for the Gala dinner. He couldn't help but be impressed by its sheer size and opulence. Within this vast expanse, large circular tables set for ten people were stretched out as far as the eye could see. Each one decked in pristine white tablecloths, shining cutlery, an array of glasses for each guest, place names and a candelabra bejewelled the centre of every table.

He was beginning to realise where the $2,500 he paid for his conference ticket had gone and reminded himself why he was in New York attending a major conference on the US mortgage market: before he started betting against subprime mortgages, he wanted to see if he could meet anyone that could persuade him not to bet against subprime mortgages.

Immaculately dressed waiters and waitresses were patiently waiting for the moment when the guests would be called to take their seats; Lester estimated there were about one hundred of them, such was the size of the event. They had starch-white jackets with golden buttons, matching epaulettes and wore white cotton gloves. The waiters were wearing black trousers with a shiny golden stripe down the outside leg and the waitresses, simple black skirts – all wore highly polished black shoes. Lester thought it wasn't just their uniforms that lent them a military presence; they all stood to attention around the perimeter of the suite waiting for the headwaiter's instructions.

In the centre of the room was the *pièce de résistance* – a Champagne Tower the likes of which Lester had never seen before. It was over eight feet tall and the pinnacle was a precariously balanced single Champagne Coupe. Below the tower's summit were hundreds, maybe even thousands, of identical Coupes that were delicately resting on the lip of the Coupe that occupied their place in the tower immediately below. The slightest exogenous force looked like it would collapse the tower at any moment.

Lester made a mental note not to go anywhere near it; jetlag, innate clumsiness and a tower of glass were probably not a great combination.

To the left of the doorway as he entered, stood a large brash digital display that denoted at which table each delegate would be seated. He walked over and found his name – Lester FitzGerald, Hedge Fund Manager, London – and looked to the right-hand column. Table thirteen. He wasn't overly superstitious and checked who else would be joining him at the baker's dozen. There were two junior investment bankers – probably salespeople thought Lester – to be avoided at all costs. But one of the names immediately piqued his interest; Jerry Hill was, according to the electronic display, a Credit Analyst at True Score Credit Rating Agency. *Excellent,* thought Lester – he wanted to know a lot more about how these agencies rated the mortgage bonds, but particularly the CDOs.

He'd spoken to Dickenson about them. He couldn't quite remember what the acronym stood for; Collateralised Debt something – whatever that meant – but Lester actually took this as a positive. In his experience, the banks deliberately introduced products with difficult-to-understand names so that – surprise, surprise – clients couldn't understand them: that was the point. If clients did understand them, they wouldn't touch them with a barge pole, and that would never do.

But in Lester's experience, the more complicated the product, the more chance that the bankers would ultimately confuse themselves – and that often presented opportunities for Lambda. As he was reading various documents on the flight over, he'd began to consider that the CDO was a classic example: it had a fancy name; had a marketing brochure drenched in Greek letters and algorithms 'proving' that the clever, highly paid, bankers had transformed something that was once inherently risky (a bunch of subprime mortgages) into something that was now low risk. And finally, an independent, third party had given their stamp of approval – True Score Credit Rating Agency had declared that the bankers were right and the investment was, indeed, low risk.

Lester was intrigued as to how the banks had done it; having dinner with Jerry Hill might answer some of his questions.

The first to arrive at the table, Lester quickly re-arranged the place names to ensure his immediate neighbours around the large, white table for the evening would become Jerry Hill and a lawyer from Seattle. He hovered over his seat holding the back of the chair – following the etiquette of standing until all the table guests had arrived before seating. The two junior marketing guys stumbled up to the table next, found their re-arranged seats – by now as far away from Lester as possible – and immediately sat down laughing at some private joke. They barely acknowledged Lester who breathed a sigh of relief and returned their half-greeting with equal disdain.

A few minutes later, Lester was introducing himself to Jerry Hill from True Score with the verve of a man who had narrowly escaped an evening of painful hard selling. It wasn't reciprocated; it appeared to Lester that Hill was tense – like he was pre-occupied about something. His gaze seemed to flit around the room without settling. Lester wondered whether he was looking for somewhere else to sit. Perhaps he was disappointed about sitting next to a hedge fund manager from London.

Hill was a short, wiry man with owlish glasses and, rapidly thinning jet-black hair. Lester put him in his mid-thirties, but without a great deal of conviction: the dark circles and puffiness under his eyes and his hair line dragged Hill somewhat north of forty, but his skin, young man's clothing and snow-white teeth suggested more like thirty; so Lester split the difference.

As most of the guests were now hovering, they took their seats. The lawyer that Lester had placed on his other side was a no show and on the other side of Hill, two old college friends had hooked up at the conference after not seeing one another for a few years – it was obvious that they weren't going to be talking to anyone else. The waiters and waitresses were doing their attentive best to make sure that glasses were filled and delivered the starters to the tables with military precision. Hill had another glass of white wine and Lester decided to stick to the water.

Lambda's CEO tried to put the man sat next to him at ease and explained that he worked for a hedge fund that mainly focussed on the stock market and had been asked to attend the conference by a considerate boss who thought he should improve his cursory knowledge of mortgage bonds. He told Hill that his knowledge was probably less than cursory, but that he'd love to learn more about CDOs.

"Well actually, we don't have our own CDO models. We rely on the banks. They email us their model and I check it out for my *boss*," said Hill, almost spitting out the last word.

"They normally send it over and say, 'how does this look?' But what can I do? They're our biggest clients and I'm being told to rate the CDO. We don't even have all the mortgage data since my *boss* says that it's not necessary and insists nonetheless that we come up with the investment-grade rating. It's unbelievable."

A number of things struck Lester about Jerry Hill. The first was that he didn't like his boss – not that there was anything unusual about that in the financial services industry. The second was that he was almost babbling – like a man that had made his mind up to say something and was determined to get it off his chest before changing it. The third, and probably most important, was that he seemed wonderfully indiscreet.

"Wow, that must make your job really very difficult," sighed Lester. He took a sip of water and offered a thoughtful expression. "It must be tricky to rate the CDOs without knowing what's in the individual loans?"

Hill sipped his wine and gave Lester a 'tell-me-about-it' shrug, before responding. He seemed encouraged by Lester's indulgence.

"The bank provides us with averages for the entire pool – we just make sure the average credit score is over 645 before we award our investment grade ratings." Lester noticed that Hill had averted his gaze and completed his answer by talking to his Californian Chardonnay. The credit analyst himself didn't even look convinced – and he was the one undertaking the analysis.

Lambda's CEO gave Hill an understanding nod but thought through the implications of what he'd just been told. Focussing on the average was obviously meaningless. Any CDO could be stuffed full of lower-rated credit scores and the average cynically dragged up by a few higher-rated mortgages. But if the shit hit the fan, the CDO would be doomed to fail and here was Hill telling him that these things were rated investment grade.

Hill topped-up his own wine glass and gestured towards Lester with the bottle. Lambda's CEO nodded and thanked him. He didn't much care for wine, and very rarely drank, but was beginning to think that Hill could do with the moral support. And anyway, a little empathy might encourage even further openness, so in the interests of Research, he accepted the glass and asked about the much-heralded diversification benefits of a CDO.

Hill seemed determined to oblige.

"The investment banks have combined pools of loans from across the US so as to provide protection from any regional downturn since they are all uncorrelated." He paused and looked around again before continuing.

"You see, this will provide the diversification that will deliver the investor the protection and warrant the investment upgrades that we apply," finished the credit analyst. He took another sip of wine and moved back in his seat to allow the waitress to serve his main course.

An alarm bell went off somewhere in the back of Lester's brain – more niggling than deafening, but suffice to tell him now was the time to really concentrate. He thanked the waitress for his food.

"What do you mean by upgrades?" he asked.

Hill finished unfurling the white napkin across his lap and then placed his elbows either side of his plate and paused. There was a man in a tuxedo in the middle of the room on a precarious-looking ladder. He said a few words and tipped champagne into the top flute so that the waterfall began. The room applauded and both Hill and Lester glanced at him, but went straight back to their conversation.

"Well, the logic of a CDO is the same as the original mortgage bond. In the mortgage bond as you will know, thousands of loans are gathered together and, on the basis that they will not all go wrong at the same time, you create a tower of mortgage loans. The higher up the tower of debt you go, the lower the return but the lower the risk – Triple-As at the very top and Triple-Bs at the bottom. This is a mortgage bond, right?"

Lester nodded to confirm he had followed the explanation, but he released his hands from around his belly in order to move slightly. Hill was almost whispering and Lester was straining to hear. He assumed this meant there was something even more interesting around the corner. He was hungry, but he resisted the temptation to start eating lest he missed something important.

"Well," started Hill, looking around the table before he continued, "in a CDO, you go through the same process, but this time, you gather thousands of mortgage bonds together – usually using the riskier types of mortgage bonds – and use it to build a completely new tower. A CDO is simply this new tower of debt. Now, since the banks have been diligent in their selection process, this new tower of bonds is no longer as risky; it is now a diversified portfolio of assets and allows us to rate it so," continued Hill.

Lester's impersonation of a casual observer continued, but he was finding it increasingly difficult to maintain. He took a sip of wine and instantly remembered why he didn't enjoy it.

"Sorry, Jerry, I know I'm being a bit slow, but why has it become less risky?" asked Lester. He picked up the bottle of wine and topped up Hill's glass once again.

"Well" – Hill coughed to clear his throat – "the argument is that since the Triple-B bonds are collated from all over the US, they're uncorrelated, diversified and less risky than when you invest in a single, stand-alone Triple-B mortgage bond. That's the argument that the banks put forward and that's what drops out of their models."

Hill placed his glass back on the table and then stared blankly ahead – avoiding eye contact altogether. Lester thought he looked like a man that had just made a confession.

Lester picked up his knife and fork, as if he was interested enough in his food to start eating.

"And how many of the Triple-Bs that form the CDO get upgraded, Jerry? I mean just an estimate; I imagine it depends on the underlying bonds and the locations of the properties that they're secured against. But during the process, how many go from Triple-B into the A tranches?" asked Lester.

"Well…absolutely, that's difficult to say because each one is different," started Hill, as he unfolded and then refolded his arms.

Lester waited, and took a sip of water as he leaned back into his seat – pretending that the answer was barely of passing interest to him.

"Well…ballpark, I'd say around 65–70% are re-rated to A tranches and some go to Triple-A," replied Hill. Once again, Hill studiously avoided eye contact as he replied.

Lester's skin tingled as the adrenalin coursed through his veins. Jerry Hill was admitting to him that the banking industry, in collusion with the rating agencies, took the weakest of the mortgage bonds and merrily rebranded them as A tranches on the basis of some spurious diversification argument – they were completely miss-selling something that had already been miss-sold and calling it a CDO.

As Hill refilled the glasses, Lester's own gaze drifted away, as he tried to process the information. His eyes rested on the centrepiece in the middle of the room – the Champagne Tower. It was impossible to miss the analogy. If there was ever a symbol of fragility, which perfectly embodied his emotional state right now, this was it. A tower made up of identical Champagne Coupes precariously placed upon one another – the security of the ones higher up in the structure completely dependent upon the durability of those occupying the lower levels. If the lower levels faltered, the whole tower would topple into oblivion.

These CDOs – the unregulated derivatives that the banks were making billions of dollars out of – would be exactly the same.

He picked up his wine glass as both men stopped talking for the first time in over an hour. They just sat for the next five minutes in complete silence, but every few moments, Lester's eyes were drawn to the fragile structure in the middle of the room.

★

An hour later, and Lambda's CEO found himself practically alone in the Westchester Suite – there was a small group of delegates on the other side of the vast room still talking and a handful of staff completely engaged in the clean-up operation. But other than that, he was on his own. He decided it was quiet enough and looked down at the glass of wine in his hand. He picked it up, drained it and closed his eyes, as the oaky liquid slipped down his throat. He still didn't like the taste, but needed something stronger than water following his conversation with Hill.

Nervously, he got up. He knew he'd slightly over-indulged and made sure he stood slowly. Once he knew he could balance properly, he moved off and crossed the dining room floor straight towards the tower of glass. When he arrived, he paused, looked around and then bent down. He carefully pulled one of the glasses out from towards the bottom. He observed as the tower swayed slightly, but nothing else happened.

He was trying to decide whether he was disappointed or not, as he walked out of the Suite and towards the lifts. He pressed the elevator button and took out his pocket notepad. Even if the tower in the room hadn't collapsed, he still thought the name he'd come up with for the CDO was apt.

He had just written down 'Crap Disguised Otherwise', when he heard one almighty crash. The lift doors opened and he walked in. He put his notepad away, patted his jacket pocket and nodded knowingly to himself.

Chapter Eight

The alarm clock on Andrew Longmire's mobile woke him as planned at 4.30 am on the morning of the AGM. He put the bathrobe back on and crushed his feet into the towelled-slippers. The extra-large pot of coffee that he had arranged through room service duly arrived and he thought about his visit the day before to the small office suite in Knightsbridge. Whilst there, he had done three things; ran through his presentation standing at the lectern provided, adjusted the air conditioning to reduce the temperature as much as possible to accommodate his propensity to perspire on such occasions and made a mental note of where certain pictures were hanging on the walls.

He used the pictures as a series of prompts to move through his presentation. So as he was making the point about 'profits being up by 28%', he would be looking at the portrait of the old gentleman at the back of the room to the left, and when he wanted to remind his audience that 'it was all about the future', he moved his head purposefully towards the Dutch landscape on the right-hand wall.

After pouring his first coffee, Longmire retrieved the ironing board from the wardrobe and used it as a makeshift lectern on which to rest his laptop. He adjusted it to precisely the same height as the stand from yesterday afternoon and positioned it so that he could see himself in the mirror if he turned 90 degrees. He then walked to the other end of the room and propped-up the rectangular-shaped coffee tray against the back of the sofa – this was the old gentleman. The Dutch landscape was already in position and broadly at the correct height courtesy of the plasma-screen TV on the opposite wall.

When he was satisfied that he was back at the venue, he started his stopwatch and ran through the presentation. The first three attempts were OK; the prompts in the room worked well and he managed the presentation in his allotted time – but Longmire wanted perfection. He had another coffee and reviewed his notes and then set-off once again. Much better. He reset the stopwatch and went again, and again and again. Each time he ran through the slides – or a certain part of the presentation that he thought was key – he registered improvements. He did this for the best part of two hours until he was satisfied.

At 6.30 am, he took a couple of questions from his audience; the aggressive private wealth manager was, aptly thought Andrew, the pyramid of three toilet rolls he had stuck on the desk in the corner of the room and the awkward journalist was the hairdryer he hung by its cord from one of the wall-light fittings.

After he was happy with the answers he'd provided to questions he thought likely, Longmire had a shower, cleaned his teeth and had a shave. He then walked back into the main suite to dress. He opened the suit carrier that Sam had prepared for him and removed his best navy-blue suit and favourite tie and cufflinks. That's when he noticed the shirt.

He had not unpacked last night since he knew his shirt was hanging up in the suit carrier and he had built in sufficient time to iron it anyway. But there was no point ironing a BLUE fucking shirt! Andrew momentarily panicked. He couldn't wear anything other than a white shirt to important meetings and his wife damn well knew that! Stupid bitch! He looked at the shirt again and shook his head slightly. Bloody hell, she wasn't stupid she knew exactly what she was doing – she had done it deliberately. He'd deal with her later, but for now he needed to procure a white shirt from somewhere – he glanced at the clock – 7.15 am, he still had time to sort it.

Three hours later, the Chairman, and still the largest shareholder of First Capital, Steve White, was introducing the new CEO to the audience. Longmire walked confidently from his seat at the front of the packed AGM room to the steps that led up to the podium just as he had done the day before. He managed them without incident. He placed his papers on the lectern and as Steve finished his introduction, Longmire located his 'hooks' – old gentleman to the left, Dutch landscape to the right. As he did so, he noticed some members of the audience adding another layer of clothing.

Longmire was wearing a crisp, brand new white shirt. It had a Windsor style collar, double cuffs and a classic fit. It was freshly ironed and Longmire felt fantastic! *Sam would be so pissed off.* After he discovered her treacherous act, Longmire had called the manager of the hotel. Kamil hadn't batted an eyelid.

"This happens all the time," he'd remarked. Longmire assumed he was referring to the tendency for people to forget items of clothing rather than acts of sabotage by their partners. Anyway, Kamil had taken care of it; he had asked for the CEO's measurements, neck size and style preferences. Just over one hour later, Longmire had taken ownership of a new shirt that fitted perfectly.

Longmire thanked the Chairman for his kind words, although he filed away in a particular compartment of his mind that the introduction was a little less generous than it could have been, and proceeded to deliver his maiden speech at the maiden AGM of First Capital. The presentation was a stunning success, and the practice had certainly paid off – Longmire came across as passionate, confident and above all – for the shareholders at least – very knowledgeable about the property debt business. The CEO of First Capital didn't begrudge a penny of the £350 he'd given to Kamil.

Andrew and his fellow directors were then asked to take a seat on the podium in a line facing the audience and so Longmire, Steve White and the CFO – Mick Marshall – took their places and the Q and A started.

A question came from a private investor who was seated at the back of the room? Could Mr Longmire please enlighten him on what he means by *'cutting edge lending techniques'* and apologised to the remainder of the audience for his level of ignorance. The remainder of the audience released a collective sigh of relief – as if it was grateful that somebody else had posed the question that they all wanted to ask.

Longmire listened carefully and thought back to his preparation early in the morning; he knew how he wanted to respond.

"You will understand that I can't go into too much detail on this point since the techniques that we have developed are proprietary to First Capital, have cost us a lot of money to develop and are therefore commercially sensitive," replied Longmire, and he quickly continued with his explanation.

Andrea White was sat in the third row; arms tightly folded around her trying to keep warm, and an ice-cold grimace on her face. She thought Longmire's claims about new lending techniques were 'absolute ballocks' and could tell from her husband's expression that he felt the same. But having a shameless, self-promoter like Longmire take the share price higher suited their needs. They would have been prepared to sell the business to Longmire at 100p per share, but the arrogant arsehole had overpaid by 25% and so they'd sold to him at 125p. Then it got even better – as the price rose, they continued to sell down their holding and yesterday's price of 165p was particularly satisfying. Longmire could do all the self-promoting he wanted as far as she was concerned.

There were a few more technicalities around some of the financial statements that Mick Marshall as the CFO dealt with and the meeting came to a close with teas and coffees being served in the break out area in the adjoining room.

"Bloody impressive CEO I thought Rupert," said one of the fund managers to his colleague, as they were queuing for refreshments. Andrea was right behind them and continued to eavesdrop.

"Yes, and you know what? It might be time to increase our holding in First Capital; the numbers are all heading in the right direction and this guy really does look like he knows what he's doing."

Andrea smiled and looked over to her husband who was now cornered by ecstatic shareholders stood on the other side of the room in front of a large Dutch landscape painting. Normally, such misguided praise for Longmire would be incendiary but she allowed herself a wry smile at the thought of Longmire overpaying for their shares and waited quietly for her coffee. She glanced over at him. The CEO beamed for the camera as the journalist took a photo of him with an elderly couple – shareholders who were clearly delighted with their investment in First Capital. He appeared so relaxed and confident that she couldn't help wondering what it would take to unsettle Andrew Longmire and how he would react if something didn't go his way?

Gloria had been cleaning hotel rooms in London for 17 years and had seen most things. She was used to being on the receiving end of all kinds of mess – a result of travelling executives who just wanted a release from their day-to-day responsibilities. As she entered to clean this particular room, however, she knew there was something wrong immediately. It wasn't particularly dirty – in fact, it was downright clean by most standards. But it wasn't the hygiene that unsettled her. It was the bizarre arrangement of room furniture she found disconcerting.

There was a pyramid of toilet rolls deliberately, almost meticulously, positioned on the corner table. What purpose could that possibly serve? The tea tray propped up on the back of the sofa in portrait style – almost made to look like a painting – just odd but not distressing.

Then came the hairdryer. The window was slightly ajar and the black, upside-down Remington, was swaying in the slight breeze, suspended by its cord from a light fitting. The wall bracket was a small, upright, wooden structure with a cross piece that came out of the wall like a gibbet. She shivered as she closed the window and released the cord to return the hairdryer to the cupboard in the vanity unit.

She then went to empty the wastebasket and picked out the crumpled newspaper on the top. Underneath was something dark-blue. It startled her. Coiled around the cylinder of the plastic bin was a piece of fabric – navy-blue. She unfurled it and held it up. It took a few seconds, but then she realised what it was, or had been. It looked like somebody had hacked it to bits with a machete in a fit of rage. What sort of man would do that to a perfectly good shirt?

Chapter Nine

Sam Longmire and Paula Poorish had just completed their weekly workout session with Angus Ross. The two friends had met through Ross, who was the personal trainer at the gym and spa facility they used just outside Woodbridge. The friends were at the poolside, sipping ice-cold water and toying with the idea of further exercise – but the endorphin rush had worked its magic and both were enjoying their post-workout state of bliss rather too much.

"Well, he'll know for sure now. To be honest, I was expecting a call last night or stupid-o'clock this morning; the moment that he found the wrong shirt was packed. He's probably furious," said Sam. Her voice was a little faint and she'd pulled her knees up to her chest as she spoke.

"For goodness' sake, Sam. You nearly sound remorseful. Just remember he thoroughly deserves it for the way he's treated you," replied her friend.

No more than ten feet away, the steam-room door opened and once the veil of piping-hot steam had dissipated into the vaulted wood and glass of the spa's ceiling, the sculptured figure of Angus Ross appeared. He looked like a man that had dedicated his life to the pursuit of physical perfection. He was just over six feet tall with a tanned, muscle-toned upper body and a serrated six-pack that appeared to be made out of reinforced concrete. His powerful legs and glutes were the legacy of a once stunningly successful professional football career. He still lived in Ipswich, but no longer led the life of a premier league footballer; instead, he worked at the exclusive spa facility in this affluent enclave on the Suffolk coast.

As he sauntered across to the plunge pool, Paula unashamedly stared at his legs, and, when he'd gone past leered at his well-rounded backside crammed into the deliberately small, sleek black trunks.

"Oh my god, Sam, has he got the ultimate action man arse or what?"

Feeling a little ashamed for the second time in as many minutes, Sam agreed that her friend was probably right. Paula continued to talk about Ross' body – in an amazingly high level of detail thought Sam – before her tone changed and she returned to the 'pathetic' behaviour of their husbands. She took a sip of water before continuing.

"There are two things I think we should do, Sam. Firstly, if you are going to be treated like staff, I think you should be paid like staff – learn to become expensive, darling. Secondly, in order that Andrew understands what a demanding schedule you have, we need to engineer a few days away for you where he has no choice but to stay at home and look after everything."

"Well, the first is straightforward," replied Sam. "I'm not exactly a novice when it comes to spending money and I'm prepared to work harder at it in the long-term interests of my marriage!"

Paula smiled and raised her glass of water in agreement, but her attention was drifting. She couldn't help looking over Sam's right shoulder at Ross. He was stood a few feet away under one of those power showers, pretending to prepare for a swim by deliberately splashing water against various parts of his body: his six-pack, upper thighs and those buttocks.

"But the second point will be a little more difficult. Andrew's mum and dad live around the corner and I know they'd be over like a shot to help him out," said Sam, who had now lost the battle for Paula's attention.

When Sam stopped speaking, there was a split-second delay before Paula looked back at her. Her blank expression informed Sam that her friend hadn't heard a word she'd said. Paula put her water down, and asked, "Shall we try the steam room?"

After the moist heat of the Turkish steam room had cleansed them, they headed for the changing rooms – satisfied they'd done enough to justify lunch. Paula may have been ten years Sam's senior, but she had kept herself in great shape, and genetics had been kind. Her naturally slim frame was augmented by the gym work and her body belied her forty-eight years. She had long, auburn hair that most of the time was worn in a ballerina bun and a pretty, if unspectacular, face. Her skin was pale, and she resembled a porcelain statue but without the coldness. Sam could not help but notice the underwear that her friend was putting on after her shower.

Sam thought her own bra and knickers were expensive. They were comfortable before sexy, but still perfectly presentable. Paula's took this to another level. She was pulling on black silk and lace panties and if Sam hadn't known better, she'd have assumed that her friend was meeting her husband in the afternoon for another endorphin rush rather than having lunch with a girlfriend. Paula caught Sam's glance.

"Carine Gilson, darling. It's the best lingerie in the world for my money and I insist on it. It's bloody expensive, but Paul has also been persuaded by the attractions of it! Even he stands to attention when I wear Carine Gilson and it gives me a wonderful excuse to visit her boutique in Paris. It's on the South Bank in Saint-Germain-des Pres – we should go there some time and create your own wardrobe."

Sam's mind frantically searched for an image of the South Bank to replace the one of Paula's sixty-year-old, overweight husband *standing to attention* but to her disappointment, it failed.

Once dressed, the two women left for the pub lunch at The Maybush in nearby Waldringfield.

Chapter Ten

"What about a glass of white wine, Sam? I think we deserve it after that session with our little action man."

Sam didn't need much persuading. She was still waiting nervously for the call from Andrew in which he'd no doubt rip strips off her. They ordered two glasses of a New Zealand Sauvignon Blanc and sat at their favourite table, outside overlooking the water. Sam let her gaze slide out over the wide Deben estuary. From her vantage point, she enjoyed panoramic views. To their left was the Waldringfield Sailing Club; sedate wooden sailing boats tethered to the modest dock, and to the right a flotilla of smaller ones was stretched out across the expanse of water for almost as far as she could see. On a hot September day, after the lunchtime rush, it was the perfect place to spend a relaxed Suffolk afternoon.

As the hustle and bustle of The Maybush's lunchtime crowd ebbed away, a large sailing boat manoeuvred itself, painstakingly, into position. A grizzled old captain appeared – complete with the almost obligatory white beard, cap and pipe. He had a stooped posture and moved as slowly as the boat he skippered. With his rope in hand, he located the dock cleats and slowly secured his beloved *Pandora* to the jetty. Once safely fastened, he guided his equally beloved wife down onto the wooden platform and they held hands as they strolled gently towards the shore. And then, as if on cue, the few clouds that were loitering in the atmosphere surrendered completely to an enormous East Anglian sky.

Sam was still considering her woeful burden when she realised the vastness of the clear blue expanse that now enveloped them. Suddenly, her problem – worrying about a phone call from an ungrateful husband whinging about the colour of a shirt – seemed pitifully small against the immensity of nature. She marvelled at the beauty of the moment – the amphitheatre sky, the location and her own, on the whole, blessed existence. She smiled, relaxed further into her seat and stared at the Bevy of swans in the shallow water. Sometimes she had to pinch herself about her financial situation. She'd grown-up in abject poverty and her one dread in life – actually, it was more like existential terror – was being poor. She had vowed that she would never end up like her parents – constantly arguing about money to the point of divorce and, ultimately oblivion. Marrying Andrew Longmire had been a sure-fire way of avoiding poverty. She hadn't married for money, she reminded herself. She'd married for security.

The two friends agreed that it would be a crime to waste such an afternoon worrying about Sam's school pick-up. A few phone calls later and Paula's housekeeper had received her instructions and Sam was liberated from the usual afternoon onslaught. It was about forty-five minutes later that Sam received the call; from that moment, it all went downhill – fast.

She checked the caller display. *Shit, if I answer this, it'll be a disaster. He'll still be angry and he'll easily work out I'm three parts pissed.* She let it ring into voicemail. Paula excused herself whilst she had an emergency text to deal with which related to meeting up with an 'old friend' in the evening. Sam used the opportunity to listen to Andrew's voicemail. She held the phone to her ear and gazed again at the grace and beauty of the cygnets with their mother gliding effortlessly across the Deben.

"Hi, Sam. The AGM went really well. There were a couple of questions at the end, but by people who know substantially less than me about finance, so it wasn't a problem. Oh, and by the way, I think you packed the wrong shirt by mistake – never mind – easy to do I know. Anyway, I found a replacement and I'll be buying more of the same. It was a perfect fit – so it ended up actually doing me a huge favour. Thank you so much, darling! Don't forget, we have two colleagues staying over tomorrow. So I won't be around much on Saturday. OK, I think that's everything. Bye, darling."

In the twenty-five seconds it took to listen to the voicemail, she'd forgotten all about the swans and the Deben; the beautiful expanse of blue sky might as well have been storm-cloud-grey and the immensity of nature was an irrelevance.

Fucking wanker, thought Sam. She didn't know what to be more annoyed about; the fact that the blue shirt ploy had backfired to such an extent that it did him a 'huge favour'; the fact that his voice was so thick with sarcasm that it was obvious that he wanted her to know that he knew it wasn't a mistake; the fact that he had forgotten (again!) to mention that they would have two guests on

Friday night or the fact that a twenty-five-second voicemail from her husband could completely ruin her whole afternoon.

Paula returned just as Sam finished listening to the voicemail for the third time. She was bubbling with excitement about her meeting later, but her own countenance changed the moment she saw Sam's face. Sam hit play and handed the phone to Paula in disgust. With her other hand, she held up the empty bottle of wine and gesticulated wildly to a waiter.

"Fucking wanker," said Paula, handing the phone back. "I think we need to book a trip to Paris, darling – when do you think we should go?"

"Tomorrow," said Sam and then she threw the remainder of her glass back and gulped, spilling some of the wine in the process. They both laughed, and spent the rest of the afternoon plotting and scheming. Sam thought Paula's suggestion – that they find out the dates that Andrew's parents would be away so that he couldn't rely on them – was a stroke of genius, and Paris was booked on that basis.

On finishing the wine, they shared a taxi to Paula's house that then took Sam and Simon back to their farmhouse. Simon finished his homework and Sam drank coffee and tried her best to hide the effects of the alcohol from her thirteen-year-old son. Both were in bed by 9 pm and fast asleep.

Since Paul Poorish was away on business, Paula was free to meet up with her 'old friend'. She took a taxi to Ipswich and met him at his flat. They had a glass of wine in the kitchen whilst Paula remonstrated with him for teasing her earlier in the day. He was stood in a pair of shorts; perfectly formed thighs below his bulging crotch – that view, and the thoughts that accompanied it, always produced an involuntary response between her legs.

"Come on, Paula, we both know you love being teased."

He started to caress the cheeks of her behind and tormented her with promises about what he was going to do. He gently pushed her forward so that she was bending over the island counter in front of him as he tugged the light cotton dress up and slipped his hands inside the black Carine Gilson panties. She could see her reflection in a glass cabinet opposite and began to moan with pleasure, as he gently played with her and continued to whisper into her ear. He continued to tease her for a few moments before fulfilling his promise.

Paula went home in another taxi precisely one hour after she had arrived and thought about her assignations with her 'old friend'. Sex with Angus Ross was fantastic. Her husband insisted on complete darkness whilst she endured banal, functional intercourse with him. He fumbled around in the dark following his orderly sequence of events that never changed – 'push this, pull that, squeeze here'. Ross was the opposite. She had no idea what he was going to do to her next and, even more exhilarating, she found herself asking him to do things to her that she'd never done with anyone else. It was on a totally different level. He could be gentle, slow and follow her lead or he could dominate and treat her like a submissive tart.

The only element of predictability with Ross was the mood lighting. He always insisted on having sex with the lights on. He always wanted to capture her expression – just as he had done tonight.

Chapter Eleven

"Good morning, Lester, and how are you doing these days?" asked Simon Rankin. The senior investment banker at Silvermans didn't even look at the CEO of Lambda, as he asked the question; he appeared more interested in the text he was reading on his mobile.

Lester sat bouncing his knee against the underside of the desk, and shifted in his seat, as he looked at the men opposite. He'd completed his research – including the all-important trip to the US – and he was convinced that betting against subprime mortgages via bonds and CDOs was the right thing to do. But he was sat in front of the big boys now; Silvermans was the largest and most aggressive investment bank on the planet and he knew they'd consider his ideas controversial, if not risible. They were supposed to be the world's experts on the very things that he wanted to invest against. But as he sat looking at his arrogant, ex-colleague in the bank's office building in Canary Wharf another, more powerful, emotion took over and replaced his apprehensiveness.

It could have been Rankin himself and his eerie resemblance to George Watson – his chief tormentor from boarding school. It could have been the smug expressions of self-importance that adorned the faces of the two men sat either side of Rankin, just like the self-appointed adjudicators that found him guilty all those years ago. It might even be the room layout. But whatever it was, it transported him straight back to the Kangaroo Court in the boarding house he'd faced all those years ago. He was gleefully convicted of being homosexual by a small group of older boys, led by Watson, who had then teased and bullied him mercilessly thereafter all the way through his time at that wretched school.

Lester had been sixteen years old at the time. A long time ago, but such was the humiliation on that fateful evening that the whole episode was etched into his memory. Just like the sweetheart initials diligently carved into the Edwardian brickwork of the Boarding House, that evening had a degree of permanence about it that the passage of time would never remove. The school production was

Beauty and the Beast that year and Lester played Gaston – the arrogant former soldier that wanted Belle's hand in marriage. Towards the end of the fairy tale, during the scene where Belle and the Beast share a romantic dance, and with the whole school watching, Lester and another boy found themselves alone backstage, safely behind the castle so that no one could see them. It was completely spontaneous and God did it feel right. Before either boy knew what was happening, playful pushes and joking had given way to curious touching and fumbling and then they were kissing. Soft and gentle to begin with but the fairy tale, the music, the end-of-year atmosphere got the better of them and it became very passionate very quickly. It was the first time Lester had kissed anyone – and he felt dizzy with happiness.

Then next few minutes had changed everything. The Beast – played, appropriately thought Lester, by the first fifteen's number eight – lost his balance during one of the dance routines and fell into the castle. His six-foot three-inch frame and thirteen stones caused the scenery to collapse. The two boys didn't notice at first and merrily continued with their passionate embrace. It was only when Lester heard the shrieks of laughter – that he knew were completely inconsistent with the dance scene – that he stopped and looked up. He froze as he realised what had happened. The whole school audience, including the headmaster, now had a perfect view. George Watson and his cronies never let him forget that night.

Lester had never wanted to attend the boarding school in the first place. He had won a scholarship to take him there; an ironic reward for academic brilliance that actually took him away from everything he loved: his parents, his siblings and his home. The boarding house could never be described as a home. It was a depressing, grey Edwardian structure that he thought resembled a prison. It may have provided shelter from the elements but it failed to protect him from the cruelty of its inmates.

In his case, and for many of his peers, the school had delivered on its single, obsessive promise to deliver a first-class education. Lester's academic achievements were indeed exceptional and had won him his place at Cambridge, but he had never bought the argument that an elite education was more important than formative years spent in a happy home.

Lester forced himself to look up from the notepad that his eyes had come to rest on and dragged himself back to the present. He wanted to get this over and done with.

"I'm doing very well, thank you, Simon," replied Lester, as he observed the three men opposite.

"Are you sure? I hear that Lambda hasn't had a large payday since 2001 and the Tech bubble – you guys must be getting pretty hungry," replied Rankin – in a manner that conveyed categorically to Lester that he'd made a statement and not asked a question.

"We do OK, Simon, but I'd like to discuss with you an opportunity that you may find interesting," said Lester, as he opened his notepad in front of him declaring the meeting open. His mood wasn't improved by the accuracy of Rankin's comment however; the Consortium was still sending him aggressive emails about his lack of success and warning him off the very strategy he was here to discuss.

"Sure, you take your best shot, Lester," oozed the banker, as he sat back in his chair and fondled the knot of his silk tie.

If only I had a gun.

Lester straightened his own tie – a cheap present from yesteryear that hung loosely around his neck, and thought about the younger Rankin; the one he'd worked with at an investment bank a decade earlier. Lester was employed at the time to use his maths to help build quantitative models to provide the academic ballast to complex financial products. Rankin's job, as a keen young salesman, was to sell them. Rankin, asked Lester to lie about what his maths proved or didn't prove in order to improve sales. Lester refused. Lester's boss backed Rankin and tried to intimidate Lester into doing the 'wrong thing'. Lester refused again, resigned and left the bank the same day. Within three months, he'd established Lambda.

The die was cast. Formally, Lester created Lambda to take advantage of rare and, what the rest of the finance industry would describe as, unpredictable events. Actually, it was set up to prove bankers like Rankin wrong: he hated the culture that was developing inside the banks; a new bullying aggressiveness that placed profit well ahead of everything else – including, in Lester's opinion, the interests of his clients.

Lester finished adjusting his clothing, took a deep breath and began.

"Thank you, Simon. I'd like to buy insurance contracts on mortgage bonds and CDOs that pay-out if the bonds and CDOs themselves fail," said Lester.

Rankin's experience showed. He remained outwardly calm. His only physical response was the slight raising of one of his overgrown thickets that sat above his eyes in lieu of eyebrows. It invited Lester to continue, but the youngest of the three bankers couldn't help himself.

"Dr FitzGerald, you do understand that that is like betting against the US housing market and that the bonds would only fail if millions of Americans do not repay their mortgages. This has never happened before in the history of the US – hardly a likely event."

Here we go, thought Lester.

"Well, if that's the view of Silvermans', you shouldn't have any problem in providing me with very cheap contacts, should you? Because if you're correct, they'll never pay-out and you can keep all my premiums," replied Lester.

Rankin obviously felt the need to take over. "I don't think we'll have a problem providing them, Lester, but we will need to discuss the structure."

Bingo.

"I'm glad you mention that, Simon, because I have given this a lot of thought."

Once again, Rankin motioned for Lester to continue – this time by offering a curt nod of the head.

The CEO of Lambda cleared his throat. "Well, when the bonds fail, you will owe me a lot of money and I'm concerned about the ability of your bank to repay me. I'll need some comfort around this," explained Lester. Although he held the narrow gaze of Rankin as he was speaking, he detected the two men either side of his ex-colleague suddenly stiffen.

Rankin sighed. "Lester, you really are delusional these days, aren't you?" his head gently shaking from side to side, as he almost whispered the words. "You want to bet against something that has never happened before; you want to make that bet with the largest and most profitable bank on planet earth, and you're so fucking arrogant you're worried about *our* creditworthiness. Did I understand you correctly?" Rankin's eyes seemed to narrow even further now.

There was a pause.

"Yes, you did," replied Lester.

"Nothing has changed, has it, Lester? You're still an intellectual snob of the first order who thinks he knows more than the rest of us put together," said the banker, as he stood up.

Lester then watched Rankin and his colleagues march over to the other end of the room and huddle together in conference. Lester couldn't make out what they were saying but there were plenty of raised voices and arm waving. He sat pretending not to listen – rather like an invited guest uncomfortably witnessing a family argument unfold in front of him.

When they returned to Lester's end of the table, Rankin continued.

"OK, we'll agree to a pay-as-you go type arrangement. We'll pay out on an incremental basis; so if the bonds weaken, you will be paid on a monthly basis. However, you will need to pay us monthly premiums and then collateral if the value of the bonds strengthens."

"OK, these are the mortgage bonds and the CDOs that I'd like to bet against," said Lambda's CEO.

Lester handed over a copy of the prospectuses. He and his team had been through them time and time again. They had selected the bonds and CDOs that they thought would be the most susceptible to failure. Although a range of investment banks had issued them, the underlying mortgages all had similar characteristics. They had low starter rates that were due to increase dramatically during 2007, they were negatively amortising (so the principal amount owed was actually higher than the original loan when the higher interest rate kicked-in) and many were self-certified. This last point meant that the mortgage company had not verified the salary information the borrower had entered onto the mortgage form when they took out the loan. They were precisely the type of mortgages and CDOs that Jerry Hill confessed to rating during his recent trip to New York: the same ones that the Lambda team now referred to as *Crap Disguised Otherwise* as per Lester's little notebook entry.

He sat waiting for Rankin to terminate the meeting and announce that they would get back to him once they had had a chance to review in detail the nature of the bonds. The pack that Lester had handed over represented months of research carried out by him and his analysts.

Instead, the bankers simply flicked through a few of the documents and Rankin then confirmed, "These are fine."

"What do you mean?" asked Lester.

"We can sell you $85 million worth of insurance for these bonds and CDOs," declared Rankin.

"Could we make it $150 million?" asked Lester.

"Sure we can, Lester. We can do that," replied Rankin, as he winked at his ex-colleague. He picked up his papers to signal the end of the meeting. The bankers promised to be in touch in the next few days with the paperwork and Lester left the building.

The next two appointments turned out to be very similar; investment bankers that thought Lester was mad for wanting to bet against the US housing market and were every bit as confident as the Silvermans' team. They agreed, without hesitating, to sell Lester the contacts he wanted in the volumes he asked for.

Lester caught the tube back to Knightsbridge dreading the call he would now need to make. He'd have to inform the Consortium that he had just made the specific bet against subprime mortgages that they'd instructed him not to.

Chapter Twelve

Joe McGrath was gasping for air. He hung on in the inside and made sure his arms were interconnected with his opponent's. It wasn't pretty, but 'tying-up your opponent' was one way to catch a breather. Sometimes needs must.

"No holding, Joe, no holding. Step back and box," screamed Allen.

McGrath would have loved to respond to his coach, but he couldn't summon the breath to speak, and anyway, his gum shield hindered fluent conversation. He was into his fourth and final round of sparring with Geoff Finn who was a brutal light-heavy – at least two weight divisions above McGrath – and he was tired.

As was the normal routine at Allen's Gym in Clapham, the boxers were made to do their training first and spar right at the end of the session when they were almost completely spent. Allen swore by this formula reminding his fighters that if they could spar at the end of his training session, just think how fresh they would be on entering the ring for a competitive bout. The session started easily enough with a warm-up of skipping and various exercises. There was then an intense circuit training routine that Allen had perfected over the years to ensure that all the muscles that needed a work out received one. There were various stations dotted around the gym that the boxers moved between as Allen called the end of each forty-five second burst of activity. The boxers would need to sprint to the next station and go again – full pelt – for the same length of time.

Allen would always find the right balance between encouragement and discipline, particularly as the boxers tired towards the end of the fifteen-minute circuit.

"Come on, lads" – he would shout competing with the music, as they entered the last few minutes and were all flagging – "this is about mind over matter. I don't mind and you don't fucking matter!" Allen had said that at least once every time that McGrath had trained at the gym, but it still made him smile and somehow lifted him to find a little bit extra in those last couple of minutes.

Geoff Finn, at twenty-four, was three years younger than McGrath and still competed. McGrath worked very long hours as a property fund manager at a bank called Allied English in the city, trained when he could and had given up competing a long time ago. Finally, Allen shouted 'time' and the boxers stopped and instantly tapped each other's glove out of mutual respect and walked back to their corners.

A few minutes later, Allen was speaking to both boxers. "That's excellent work, you two" – he then turned to McGrath – "I know you found that tough, Joe, and I know you were giving away some weight in there. But Geoff's boxing in Birmingham next week and his opponent is a natural super-middleweight so he will be more your size and, importantly, he shares your hand speed. So that was a really important test for Geoff."

"Yeh, thanks, Joe," continued Finn. "God knows why you don't compete anymore – I'm not sure I know many middle-weights that would live with you."

"Are you coming over to The Crown after?" asked Allen. McGrath enjoyed spending time with his trainer and the other boxers. In fact, he felt a lot more comfortable in their company than around his bank colleagues. He loved being a surveyor and working in real estate, but some of the office politics and characters that he had to endure to do it was far more exhausting than any gym-session.

"I'm sorry, I can't tonight, Allen. I'll see you on Thursday though," he replied.

All McGrath needed tonight was his bed – the office was manic at the moment and he'd started this morning at 6.30 reviewing potential property purchases.

McGrath had a shower and then towelled his curly, collar-length black hair. He decided to get on the scales; tonight he was precisely twelve stones and ten pounds. Not bad – although he registered the fact that it was more than a stone heavier than when he competed. However, since McGrath was exactly six feet tall, very few people would have noticed that he was 'carrying a few pounds'. He still enjoyed the six-pack and the inverted triangle body shape that had accompanied him since his teenage years.

He finished getting dressed and then took the over ground train from Clapham to Richmond and picked up his blackberry to check his emails. He started to think about Geoff's comments about him not competing, but the moment the emails came through, he remembered why he couldn't commit to do so. There had been fifteen of them since he'd been in the gym for less than two hours. It all related to the property acquisition that he and an analyst at the bank had been working on.

Apparently, progress was too slow and his boss wanted to talk to him about it tomorrow morning at 8 am. It would almost certainly be another very long day at the office.

Chapter Thirteen

The conference call with the Consortium had just started and James Turner – who was chairing the call – had finished the introductions.

"As you know, gentlemen, Lester has made various investments for the Fund recently that have raised questions amongst you. Specifically, *Credere* now owns insurance contracts on both subprime mortgage bonds and on CDOs. As Lester's briefing note explained, these insurance contracts pay out to us when, and if, the underlying subprime mortgages begin to fail. The purpose of today's call is for Lester to explain his recent decisions, provide an update on investment performance and we'll finish with a Q and A session."

"Mr Chairman, I'd like to ask a question please?"

It was a slow deliberate voice and sounded as if its owner was fed up with the call already, as it crackled through the speaker box on Lester's desk.

"Of course you can, Ron," replied Turner.

He looked towards Lester, the only other person on the call in the Pont Street office and shrugged.

"Right, Dr FitzGerald, I'd like to make three points."

Lester noted that he'd been given the floor on the pretence of asking a question but was intending to make three statements. He felt his posture stiffen slightly.

"Firstly, we pay you to pick stocks on recognised stock exchanges, not to get distracted by esoteric insurance contracts that are privately held between *Credere* and an investment back that will suffer from poor liquidity or transparency or both. It will be the investment banks that determine what these things are worth. Not the open market place and certainly not you.

"Secondly, I have been around a long time and I have heard numerous commentators, investors, journalists and politicians make apocalyptic predictions about the US economy and housing market and none of them have ever been realised during my investment career.

"Thirdly, if buying these insurance contracts represents such a compelling *buying* opportunity, why is the most successful investment bank on planet earth *selling* them to us?"

Turner looked towards Lambda's CEO for a response. Lester thought the man sat opposite him appeared nervous before the call started; now, after that opening salvo, he was doing breathing exercises and had become even more restless. Lester could understand why.

Turner was the reason why each of the investors on the call had decided to back Lambda in the first place. As the consultant responsible for recommending *Credere*, he probably felt exposed – if it didn't make money, his own reputation would come under scrutiny and his clients would understandably also question him. Presumably, that's why he felt the need to fly in from New York and see Lester in person for the call.

Lester stared at the speaker in front of him. He'd only ever spoken to Ron Dale on the telephone – like most of the members of the Consortium, he'd not met him in person. However, he had a clear mental picture in his mind of a big, brash bully who was used to getting his own way. Lester ordered himself to stay calm and relax. He knew his strategy was the right one; he just needed to clarify a few points.

"Thank you for your two statements and the question, Mr Dale. I'd take issue on the first point. We are a total return fund and not an equity fund *per se* as our marketing material and prospectus make clear. Our contract purposely provides me with the flexibility to move between asset classes and select those that are priced to deliver the highest risk-adjusted returns for my clients. I believe that taking out insurance contracts against some of the most dubious subprime mortgage bonds represent one such opportunity."

Turner was gesturing to Lester; his right hand extended out in front of him levitating just over the table. Lester could see it, but chose to ignore it. He continued.

"To your second point, I would like to stress that our investment strategy does not rely on financial Armageddon – although if you want my honest opinion on that, I think we are heading for it. Our insurance contracts will make a fortune if just a tiny fraction of these mortgage pools fail.

"Finally, I cannot answer for Silvermans and their decision to sell these contracts. However, I suspect that Silvermans are holding only a few of them on their balance sheet and are passing the liabilities through to unsuspecting third parties. These are likely to be yield-hungry German, Japanese or American insurance companies, but at this stage, I can't confirm that."

To further his argument, Lester continued. "I have a list of mortgage bonds that Silvermans and the others are happy to provide insurance for against their inevitable collapse. They have not read the prospectuses – to the best of my knowledge, no one else apart from the lawyers that wrote them has. Do you know how I know they haven't read them?"

As his question was met with a stony silence, Lester decided to answer it himself.

"Because they don't care which ones I bet against. It's as if the investment banks think that all CDOs are the same. The price of insurance is driven by what the rating agency says, not by independent analysis of what's in the prospectus. One Triple-B bond is very different to another and I've cherry-picked the absolute worst ones, and the banks have not batted an eyelid. I thought they would get suspicious and adjust their prices, but it's as if they don't care."

The slow, deliberate delivery of Ron Dale once again came through the loudspeaker.

"They don't care, Dr FitzGerald, since they're happy that the rating agencies have crawled all over these things and have rated them. Why do you think you're better at rating a CDO than S&P or True Score? These guys do it all day every day and know what they're doing."

Turner was making some kind of strange whimpering noise with the back of his throat, as he shook his head listening to the discussion.

Lester thought back to the evening dinner with Jerry Hill in New York and the fountain of champagne Coupes.

"With respect, I strongly disagree with your last statement. Look, if you turn to page 17 of your packs, you will find an example of some bonds that we have insurance against."

Turner managed to flick through the papers on the desk and the grating discord of the eight other callers doing the same thing bounced around the room.

"Whilst you're not talking, could you put your phones on mute please, gentlemen?" managed Turner.

Lester continued.

"Most of the bonds are based on mortgages made in California – particularly San Francisco – where house prices have increased the most and I believe will fall the fastest when the adjustment comes. Second, look at the mortgage lender

– it's The Globe Mortgage Company, possibly the most financially incontinent organisation that was ever conceived. They're making loans to anyone who has a pulse. There is a higher than average 'self-cert' percentage of loans – that is, loans that are more likely to be fraudulent. Some of these borrowers won't even have an income. These bonds all have a high percentage of loans where the borrower's interest payments will rocket in 2007, and the rating agencies are nonetheless assigning investment grade ratings to them.

"In less than two years' time, I'd expect these to default in very large numbers when, for the first time, interest payments fall due. These things are happening and the rating agencies are complicit – do you really think that looks like an industry that *knows what it's doing*?" finished Lester, paraphrasing the earlier comment for effect.

Turner's hand was moving up and down once again and he glared at Lester. He mouthed, "Calm down! Calm down!"

Dale responded in his monotone voice, but there was now a definite edginess that was not there earlier in the conversation.

"Dr FitzGerald, can I ask you what the level of the annual premiums we're currently paying for the insurance that you have bought to protect us all from the catastrophic event that no one else seems to believe will happen?"

"I'm not the only person worried about the subprime mortgage market," snapped Lester. He found himself massaging the back of his neck, as he stared at the speaker in the middle of the table.

"I asked about the size of the premiums, Dr FitzGerald," replied Dale – a hint of smugness had now entered his voice. Lester could almost hear him smile from four thousand miles away.

Turner didn't look like he knew what to do, so actually didn't do anything except look like a rabbit caught in the headlights.

"It's around £50 million. Each year," confirmed Lester. He didn't look at Turner, but just stared at the speaker.

Both men in Pont Street now became aware that the other investors had ignored Turner's earlier request. The collective intake of breath was audible.

"And the current size of the fund is what, precisely, Dr FitzGerald?" Dale seemed to be goading him now; emboldened by the response he'd elicited from his fellow investors on the line.

"At the moment, it's around £450 million." Turner was looking at Lester and drumming the table with his fingernails. Lester wasn't making eye contact.

"So, just to be clear: we're paying out tens of millions of dollars a year, every year, forever until something happens that has never happened before. And you are satisfied that giving away over 10% of our fund to the investment banks each year because you know more about the US housing market than they do is a smart *risk-adjusted investment strategy*?"

There was a long pause.

"That's correct, Mr Dale, yes."

Turner wrapped his knuckles on the desk to force Lester to take note. He gave him his strongest 'what the fuck are you doing?' look.

It was Lester's turn to shrug his shoulders. This arrogant bastard on the other end of the phone wouldn't push him around and he wanted Turner to know it.

A second or so later, there was a loud bang. Just like someone had thrown a heavy book down on a desk near the telephone.

"OK, Dr Fitz-fucking-Gerald. I've also read our contract and I'd like to remind you and the other investors on the call that the end of the lock-up period is next year. If these insurance contracts haven't come good by that point, you should expect a redemption notice from me. I will want my investment back immediately, and in full, at that point, and you can kiss your ass goodbye to any repeat business. James, I'm sorry to have to be so blunt, but I don't see any point in beating around the bush here."

James Turner glared at Lester and then apologised to Ron Dale, making some grovelling comment about how he had sympathy with the investors' position.

Lester looked at Turner and did his best to maintain a calm exterior. But inside, he was anything but. He could feel his body temperature rising and his heart react to the adrenaline surge, as he gulped at a breath. He had completely forgotten about the end of the lock-up period. The consequences of Dale's threat began to sink in. How could he be so bloody stupid? The investors could demand their money back way before he expected his insurance contracts to pay out. How the hell would he be able to pay them?

Lester felt like crawling under the table to hide. Turner looked like he wanted to kick him under it.

Chapter Fourteen

It was a crisp Saturday morning; the kind that jolts people into the first few days of winter's falling temperatures. The cold air revealed McGrath's breath, as he walked eastwards along London Wall towards Liverpool Street train station. The sun was still low in the lapis-blue sky and its powerful rays were obstructed by the impregnable façade of cantilevered concrete that is Tower 42 – the tallest building in the City. McGrath stared at the fuzziness of the structure's outline as the immense energy behind it dispersed to the edges of its hexagonal construction. It was a daily battle; nature's most powerful force struggling to overcome the brutality of London's built environment.

He had thought about buying the old 'Nat West Tower' for his fund. At about £250 million, it would certainly solve his immediate problem of getting cash invested into property and his boss off his back. There were just two problems; it wasn't for sale and it was the most inefficient office building he knew. The cantilevering structure had limited the amount of space to rent out to tenants and with it, the rental income. He knew the property fund that owned it and they were welcome to it.

He arrived at Liverpool Street Station a few minutes later than he would have liked, and found himself in a slow-moving queue. He brushed a shock of thick black hair to one side, as he glanced up at the electronic screen – platform 9 was the Norwich train. That, apparently, would take him to Ipswich where he would need to change and catch another one to Woodbridge – presumably one of those noddy ones with two carriages.

As he glanced back down from the screen, he noticed the rear wheel of an expensive bicycle was now occupying the place in the queue ahead of him. He was sure it hadn't been there when he looked up to locate his platform and he knew he only had a few minutes before he needed to be on his way. He politely tapped the female cyclist on the shoulder.

"Excuse me, I'm very sorry, but the queue starts a few places back that way."

"Very interesting," replied the young woman, as she turned to face him. She was only a little shorter than McGrath; her brown hair cut into a short, smart bob and she had a round face. She wore tight black leggings and a bright blue tracksuit top. "I've been waiting here longer than you and I'm not going to miss my train because you don't know how to queue up."

"Listen, I know you weren't there a few minutes ago. I'm not going to make a big thing out of it, but I'm actually in a bit of a rush. And in case you didn't know, you're bloody rude."

Most London commuters are able to detect incipient arguments from at least a hundred metres; watching fellow commuters argue with one another is much more entertaining than anything else they can do whilst suffering the capital's public transport system. Commuters began to arrange themselves accordingly – subtly trying to position themselves to be able to see and hear the inevitable.

A smartly dressed, serious-looking middle-aged man abruptly developed a problem with his earphones. He decided to stop walking – he was only a few feet away from McGrath – removed the offending articles and studied them diligently and waited. A lady in a long, blue overcoat folded her Sun newspaper in half and positioned it so that a micro-movement of her eyes would give her direct access to the performance. She now looked like a character out of a spy novel rather than an NHS nurse. A couple standing nearby halted their conversation and nudged each other. McGrath's queue moved forwards and the girl with the bike was forced to shuffle along with it but she seemed determined to reply.

"If anyone is rude, it's you. So stop accusing me of something I didn't do and piss off," said the girl, as she ripped the zipper right to the top of her blue tracksuit top and turned away.

Charming, thought McGrath. But he really didn't need a full-blown argument with a woman in the middle of Liverpool Street on a Saturday morning. He realised his wait was nearly over and he'd probably have enough time anyway. The girl got served first and led her bicycle away but glared back at him as she left. He could see her looking at him out of the corner of his eye; he chose to ignore it and looked at his watch. Realising that the diversion was now over, the other passengers returned to the monotony of their commutes.

McGrath got his newspaper and just had enough time to buy his coffee before making his way to the platform and boarding the Norwich train. It left on time and crawled out of the station and headed north towards Stratford. As it gently rocked from side to side, he listened to the clickety-click sound as the wheels of the carriages passed over the joints connecting the rails. The sound and the motion made McGrath drowsy and he put his newspaper down, sipped his coffee and looked out of the window. He was listening for the double click as the first pair of wheels of his coach passed over the joints and then tried to anticipate precisely when the clickety-click would arrive as the rear end wheels of his carriage would be immediately followed by the leading pair on the next.

As the train picked up a little more speed and held it, he found that it was easy to get the timing right and he sat there on the border between sleep and consciousness thinking about his older brother. The train's rhythmic swaying and the clickety-clack relaxed McGrath, as it continued north past Mile End and Bow and row after row of Victorian terraced houses.

Small, Victorian terraced houses had been the start of Michael McGrath's property empire. He was initially a bricklayer and then a general builder but soon bought his first modest terraced house in Virgil Street, Grangetown, Cardiff where their mother still lived. Michael sold it; made a £2,500 profit and a keen, debt-hungry property developer had been born. He repeated the trick several times buying small houses and then flats as his confidence grew.

The last twelve years of rising property values, substantial investment in the Cardiff Bay Area and a large amount of leverage had made Michael an extremely wealthy man. In time, and from what Joe McGrath could tell much to his enjoyment, this had allowed him to spend more time in the South of France than the South of Wales.

Michael was ten years older than his brother and was very much the patriarch of the family. Their dad had parted company with Joe, Michael and Mum when Joe was seven – and for bloody good reason as Joe had discovered some years later.

When the younger sibling won his place at university – the first in their family ever to make it to higher education – Michael funded all of the costs. So Joe McGrath was one of those rare UK graduates who finished University with no debt. He had always promised Michael that when he graduated and found a job, his first priority would be to pay his brother back – a promise he was still trying to keep. He planned to talk to his older brother again this weekend. Joe was on his way to Woodbridge to see him as Michael was in the UK visiting a new business associate of his. A man called Andrew Longmire.

Less than an hour later, McGrath's train pulled gently out of Manningtree and headed for the next stop – Ipswich. He was so taken aback by the views across the Stour Estuary that he put down the newspaper he'd been reading.

He could see various wading birds moving on top of the hard, uneven mud flats or operating in the shallow pools by the bank of the Stour in their relentless search for food. The sun had taken care of most of the overnight frost, but there were stubborn white patches wherever the sun hadn't been able to reach and the remnants of the early morning mist were still drifting across parts of the water. The diversity of the birds amazed him: bright feathers, boring greys and brilliant whites. Most of them were tall, with thin, elongated legs and long beaks – they looked like they'd been custom-built to search for food in such an environment.

He let his gaze drift off towards the stranded boats to the right. The tide was out and had left the anchored boats marooned; scattered across the mud flats like abandoned cars in some endless grey car park. They were every bit as eclectic as the birds he'd been watching. A few of the names were visible 'Aunty Joy's' was one and 'Sweet Safran' another. However, they all appeared to have been abandoned. The boats had fallen on to their sides once the buoyancy of the water had been removed by the receding tide, leaving the mud as their only form of sustenance. Their masts were jutting out completely randomly depending on which way they happened to topple. It made for a forlorn setting, but beautiful nonetheless, and Joe had some distant recollection that this was 'Constable County' and began to understand why the great man had chosen this part of the world to paint his landscapes.

The views appealed to McGrath's innate desire to have a much slower pace of life. He loved London – for now – but he was certain that there'd come a point when his craving to be sat in a little boat catching fish would be stronger than his desire to be sat in an office capturing his next property deal. He was entertaining those calming thoughts when he first became aware of the voices.

He realised that they had been there for a while but that he had been so engrossed it was only now that they became more than background noise. There was a single woman's voice, and male voices – several from what he could work out. The dialogue was intermittent but each time someone spoke, it seemed to escalate to the next level. It got more tense and louder, as if a mild disagreement was travelling headlong towards full-on confrontation. He sat up straight; his own London commuter antennae for detecting arguments piqued. He thought the woman's voice was vaguely familiar but was unsure why. As the voices were

75

raised once again, he could make out the odd word from the men. "Great tits…nice ass…yeah, show us…" This didn't sound like a normal commuter dispute; it was getting serious.

McGrath didn't hesitate; immediately standing up, he then moved towards them. There was a gang of three and they didn't see him at first. There was something about their physiques and the way they held their limbs that hinted at adolescence. Tall enough to be men, but not yet sufficiently filled out to smack of adulthood. This observation chimed with their vulgar, teenage vernacular that continued as he made his way down the carriage. He was within a few feet now.

The woman was sat at a table for four and the position she had assumed shocked McGrath into understanding the seriousness of her situation. Her head was bowed, her knees were brought up as close as possible to her chin and her arms were wrapped tightly around her legs. It was as if she was preparing herself for impending violence. Two of the teenagers had placed themselves opposite her and the third stood menacingly over their victim with his back to McGrath. The woman looked up and managed to shock McGrath for a second time. It wasn't just the fear in her eyes – an expression he'd seen a hundred times before in the ring – it was her face; one he instantly recognised. The blue tracksuit zipped to the top – it was the girl with the bike.

Bloody hell, she's not having a good day! thought McGrath. He tried to smile reassuringly at her, but he could see that she was too petrified for it to make any difference. Then another thought struck him. Based on the evidence at Liverpool Street, this girl was no shrinking violet – if she's in this state, these guys must be pretty intimidating.

McGrath assumed that the presence of another adult would bring an end to the teenagers' threatening behaviour, but they didn't show any indication of letting up. As she was now looking straight at him, he asked the young woman whether she was OK. She didn't have the chance to respond.

"Fuck off, Dickhead," said the largest of the boys who had now turned to face McGrath. "Sit back down and mind your own fucking business." He was pointing back down the carriage to indicate the direction he wanted McGrath to go.

"Come on, guys. Three big lumps like you picking on a young lady – really?"

"I told you to mind your own business and sit back down, you little prick, or do I need to escort you back to your seat?" The leader of the group was warming to his task and seemed intent on proving a point to his mates.

McGrath held up his hands with palms facing his aggressor.

"OK, guys, I don't want any trouble. I'll just sit back down and leave you to it."

The girl scowled at McGrath for the second time in as many hours.

The bully completely misinterpreted McGrath's behaviour as cowardice and grew in confidence that he wouldn't fight back. He didn't say another word but threw a wild punch with all that he had instead. It was precisely what McGrath was expecting.

As McGrath had been feigning capitulation, the youth had hastily repositioned his feet – left ahead of the right to maximise the leverage that he would be able to get into a straight right-hand cross. For someone like McGrath – who had spent hours of his life observing and anticipating what opponents were about to do, the youth might as well have used the train's tannoy system to announce his intention. His body weight shifted and a split second later, McGrath allowed the telegraphed long right hand to fly harmlessly over his stooping right shoulder and he slipped inside to deliver his trademark left hook into the unprotected rib cage of the thug.

Paralysed, with excruciating pain and unable to breathe, the panicked youth collapsed into the nearest seat and took up his own foetal position in order to protect himself. McGrath didn't even need to look at him; he knew when the punch landed into the soft tissue surrounding the ribs. If he were lucky, the youth would have very bad bruising; if he were unlucky, a few of them would be cracked.

The other tormentors now edged nervously past McGrath, picked up their friend and moved further down the carriage. He sat down next to the young woman.

"Are you OK?" he asked.

"Yes, I'm fine, but you were going to let those bastards do what they wanted!" she said. "I don't believe it. You don't know how to queue up and you weren't even going to stop them until one of them attacked you!"

He rolled his eyes. "Calm down. Listen, what's your name?"

"Alice," replied the young woman reluctantly, but she looked directly at him. At the train station, when they were arguing, he hadn't paid much attention to her appearance. She had near-perfect skin; it was like the smooth, unblemished surface that a young teenage girl might enjoy and it was soft and warm. The plethora of complex browns and greens of her large, hazel-coloured eyes were swirling together but the greens predominated in the centre with the browns around the edges. She glanced away quickly, as if she suddenly realised he was taking a little too much interest in her. As she did so, the sun caught her face at a different angle and revealed small, damp patches high on her cheekbones.

"I'm Joe, nice to meet you, Alice. Listen, I was never going to leave you with those thugs. I just knew it would be easier if he thought I wasn't going to do anything that's all. I wouldn't leave anyone in that situation – even if they are rude!" He smiled a broad grin and looked at Alice through his big, brown eyes.

She looked back and managed her own smile that quickly turned into a laugh, as she started to relax. She covered her mouth and McGrath wondered whether it was an instinctive act of insecurity or just good manners. The browns of her eyes seemed to take over and generate a warm glow. The greens were still there; darting around the edges, happy with a supporting role for the moment, and exuding sufficient energy to leave McGrath in no doubt there was a lot more to Alice than an inner warmth.

The shrill and completely inaudible train announcement yanked them both back to reality and her smile vanished as quickly as it had appeared.

"Well, I need to get off here, I'm afraid. So if you'll excuse me?" Alice straightened her clothing and got up to gather her belongings.

"Would you like me to walk with you? I need to get off here and change trains anyway," explained McGrath.

He looked around to make sure that he knew where the thugs were.

"No, I'm fine, I just need to collect my bike from the next carriage and then I'll be on my way."

McGrath quickly gathered his own things and tried to engage her again in conversation on the platform to drag out their time together but Alice seemed to have made her mind up. He checked and saw that the thugs had skulked off in the opposite direction towards a small café away from the exit. His two mates on either side were helping the one in the middle who was still clutching his ribs.

He then watched as Alice wheeled her bike along the platform, the November air still cold enough to condense the water vapour in her breath and produce thick clouds that swirled around her. She headed directly into the powerful sunlight that fashioned a silhouette of her shape, as she sauntered along in her tight, black leggings towards the exit. He cupped his hand to his forehead and squinted into the haze, studying until the very last moment when she reached the barriers, turned left and was gone.

Chapter Fifteen

Paula, as instructed, sat astride Ross and faced him so that he could enjoy her journey towards orgasm play out across her face. The mood lighting meant that she could see herself clearly, as she faced the mirrored wardrobes on the opposite side of the bedroom.

Her reflection aroused her even more and she writhed with pleasure as her body obeyed whatever his powerful thigh movements demanded of it. The lace-trimmed red and black Basque was her particular favourite – she knew it took her to the slutty side of sexy, but that's exactly where Ross wanted her tonight. She noticed that the tight discipline of her bun was now foundering. Errant strands of her long, auburn hair were escaping and sticking to the sides of her moist face and sculpted neck and one of the straps from her Basque had slipped off the shoulder. She could feel the flush of euphoria dispersing across her porcelain skin.

Afterwards, they both lay perfectly still, their chests rising and falling as they recovered from their exertions. Paula lay facing the ceiling as Ross gently massaged the inside of her thigh. Paula felt her groin pulsate again, blood would always rush there whenever he touched the inside of her legs: no matter how soon it was after sex with Ross, she was always felt ready for more.

She needed to be up early the next day to travel to Paris with Sam, and reluctantly got up and walked to the bathroom. Showering to avoid her hair getting wet, she repositioned it back into the pristine bun. She then recovered her various pieces of clothing from numerous locations in the flat and dressed. She popped her head into the bedroom to say goodbye to Ross and placed a brown envelope on the kitchen counter as she left for home.

★

A few minutes later, Ross got up, counted the money out of the envelope and checked the recordings. Satisfied that both were in order, he went online to check his bank balance. As he waited for the PC to load, he found himself looking at the team photo on the wall – 29 May 2000, Wembley Stadium. That was one of his best games for the club; he'd had a blinder, scored one of the goals and Ipswich Town had won promotion to the Premiership. It was, without doubt, the happiest day of his life. He looked at the smiles on those faces, including his own. *No wonder we're all bloody smiling, the bonus from that one game was worth more than five year's work as a poxy personal trainer. No bloody money worries then.*

He looked down at the screen as the depressing numbers came up to show him what he already knew. Like his teammates, he thought the good times would last forever, but the money was soon gone and the debts had taken their place. They seemed to be as enduring as the injury that had finished his career. Owing a lot of money to very dangerous people was still a problem for Ross and he didn't have a great deal of time to do something about it.

Chapter Sixteen

Ronald, as ever, had done what he was told. He'd carefully chosen a vantage point so that she could see the stage clearly, but not many would see, much less notice, her. A number of vast, ornate stone columns that supported the ancient vaulted ceiling concealed her from most of the congregation. Four rows back at the end of the wooden pew furthest away from the wide, central aisle of the church in Richmond upon Thames. Ronald was satisfied – on occasions like these, he knew she valued anonymity.

He also knew they were probably the only adults in the church that weren't officially invited to the Vineyard Primary School nativity play. Instead, Clarissa had used her initiative and the school's website to identify the date and time, and organised that he should drive her there.

He sneaked a glance at her out of the corner of his eye. He greatly admired Clarissa, as did everyone, but Ronald had been with her since she'd lost her dear husband and best friend – God rest his soul – almost thirty years ago. The vast amount of work that she did for her charity was admirable and he valued, and shared, her almost Victorian sense of duty and the accompanying self-restraint in times of adversity. As a former Rifleman with the 4th Fusiliers, these 'stiff-upper-lip' qualities were very important to him. But, on occasions such as these, when Clarissa insisted that they take part in these clandestine manoeuvres, their relationship was tested.

So here he was; sat loyally, but unenthusiastically, in the pew next to her. He was wearing a smart suit that he diligently reserved for his occasional chauffeuring duties and the expression he deployed when asked to take part in a spying mission – raised eyebrows and an icy stare that rivalled the artic temperature of the church. He kept his gloves on and sat with a heavy winter coat wrapped around him; his arms crossed tightly watching his warm breath disperse into the freezing, ecclesiastical air. This was as close to confrontation that the passive, mild mannered ex-Rifleman managed – arms folded, silence and cold stares.

He knew she could see her grandchildren now; her head had jolted forward to improve her view. He continued his peaceful protest by staring at a gravestone halfway up a wall about twenty feet away. It was a slab of flaking sandstone; the once intricate chisel marks of the Mason now almost indistinguishable from its stone background. Time had morphed some of the decorative patterns around the edges into a single, indistinct montage in mildew green. It was like looking at an out-of-focus photograph – he sort of knew what the patterns might be, but couldn't be sure. Even so, he could still read the simple epitaph of Mrs Molly James – who died in 1895 at the age of fifty-six. *A loving wife, mother and grandmother.* Clarissa was also all three of those he thought. He turned his head slightly in order to observe her watching Jemima and Edward and smiled, as he noticed her familiar profile. From this angle, her nose was pronounced – a large facial outcrop – but in portrait, it blended harmoniously with the rest of her diamond-shaped face. In fact, it added rather than detracted from her beauty.

When the twenty-minute performance was over, the children were led away from the stage and towards the large wooden doors on the other side of the transept. Each child beamed, as they spotted a loved one. Ronald observed as she craned her long neck to ensure she experienced every last moment of their presence before they disappeared beyond the church doors.

Finally, they were gone and she returned the service card in front of her. She cleared her throat and snuffled. Ronald relented, as he always did; removed a glove and handed her the tissue he'd readied and then focussed once again on the crumbling spectre of Mrs Molly James. Only after a good five minutes did she ask him to check it was all clear. He did, it was and he guided the tall, almost regal figure of his employer through the churchyard and to the car parked a few streets away. He opened the door for her as the first, heavy snowflakes fell on the pavements.

Ronald thought about the epitaph, as she stepped in, *A loving wife, mother and grandmother.* As they say, two out of three isn't bad.

★

A few minutes later and they were heading back towards central London and Clarissa thought about her *home* – the luxurious, but painfully lonely, flat in

Kensington loomed. It was in a beautiful location, just a few streets away from South Kensington station, and worth an absolute fortune – or so the local agents kept telling her. What did they say? 'Luxury and privacy in the heart of London.' The kitchen was handmade; the furniture antique, and the space light and airy – some of the best restaurants in London were within walking distance. Yet, for all that, she wondered whether it could be defined as a home.

She looked out of the window of the car, as she pondered the question. They were crawling along Cromwell Road and past the Natural History Museum to the left. The weather was deteriorating rapidly now and large, heavy snowflakes were beginning to accrue on the wide icy pavements – silently transforming the streetscape before her eyes; grey pavement slabs becoming pristine white blankets. She turned the heat up as she watched a pathetic homeless man looking for refuge in the grand doorway of an Embassy on the opposite side of the road. The incongruity of it startled her – a vagrant inspecting bins amongst the white columns and stuccoed walls of a multimillion-pound property.

But it had also agitated her: it was a reminder of her own incipient financial doom. She wasn't desperate yet, and God knows it should ever come to that, but the family business and the Charity that her family had supported for generations were becoming short of capital. There would come a point – home or no home – that she'd need to consider selling. Almost forty years she had lived there, nestled in amongst the other beautiful Victorian properties in the road, with the walled rose garden and Lucio's – her favourite restaurant less than one hundred yards away.

But the ignominy of it was what really scared Clarissa. Four generations of her family's wealth wiped out in one – the one that she had been responsible for. The great Matriarch was going to need to devise a plan to secure the funding from somewhere.

Chapter Seventeen

Longmire, congenitally incapable of empathy, couldn't understand why the elderly couple in front of him were taking so much time. The CEO of First Capital had alighted from the first-class carriage of the London train at Manningtree Station; he was on one call and had another one booked in for his car journey home. He was late, the call was important and this inconsiderate couple didn't seem to care that he still had work to do.

Northbound trains arriving at Manningtree do so on Platform Three, which requires passengers to use the underpass to reach the exit and car park. He was now walking down the steps towards the underpass and the limited number of passengers all seemed to conspire to move around him so that whichever way he tried, he couldn't get past the couple in front. They were supporting one another now, as they ascended the steps on the other side that led up to platform one and the exit. She was using the handrail with one hand and her husband supported the other as they climbed – slowly, and only when both feet were safely on a step would they raise a hesitant foot to conquer the next. They occupied most of the width of the stairs in their considerable efforts – leaving only a small gap for those passengers to go around them. Longmire was losing patience.

He finished his call and, spotting what he thought was a gap, dragged his stumpy little body around them, but as he did so, he bumped into somebody or something. It felt like he'd hit a brick wall. Longmire turned, and then swallowed, hard. Comfortably over six feet tall with green flight jacket dripping in badges, denim jeans with cuffed bottoms and Dr Martin boots, the man towered over Longmire. Tattoos of diving swallows on his neck and a few facial piercings completed the look. A natural coward, Longmire apologised profusely, deferentially got back in line and prayed for bowel control. The skinhead slowed, glared and then grunted something in Longmire's direction but on balance, seemed to decide not to inflict physical pain on him. As he walked away, he seemed somehow disappointed with his decision.

Longmire remained diligently in line until the exit and then headed for the sanctuary of his Porsche 911. He unlocked it, climbed in and immediately re-locked the doors – surveying the car park for a green jacket and the hooligan that occupied it. After a few moments, he'd relaxed sufficiently to locate the dial in details, joined his call and headed home.

Thirty-five minutes later, he arrived. Opening the front door, he shouted, "Hi, Sam, I'm here."

There was no answer so he assumed she was out – with that flirt Paula Poorish no doubt. He walked into the study to see if she was there and shouted up the stairs a couple of times – still no answer. He opened the kitchen door and Barney, the family one-year-old black Lab that Andrew despised, raced towards him, frantically wagging his tail in excitement and jumped up to greet him.

"Get off, you horrible mutt," grunted Andrew and tried to push Barney away to protect his clothing as only a non-dog-lover can. He then threw one of the treats that Sam and Simon kept in a jar on the sideboard into the utility room. He slammed the door shut after Barney had chased the slim morsel of food.

Andrew then turned towards the centre island to make a coffee – it was then that he noticed the note.

'Andrew,

I will be in Paris with Paula for a few days – shopping. You will need to look after the house, your son, Barney and any guests that you have invited to stay but not told me about. I should be back next Thursday.

Sam.

"You fucking bitch!" he said slowly to himself. He rang her mobile, which predictably went straight through to voicemail; he was intending to leave a tirade but thought better of it and hung up.

He dialled his mum. No answer. Then he remembered; they were on their annual January break to Lanzagrotty. *Bitch. Like the shirt fiasco, Sam has actually thought this through.*

He called his sister, as he stood in the kitchen re-reading the note: I will be in Paris with Paula for **a few** days – shopping…I **should** be back next Thursday. "Bitch," exclaimed Longmire again, becoming more annoyed by the second. *Today was Friday, so since when did a few mean six? A few means one more* *than a couple – three. And what about the use of the subjunctive? Does* should *mean she might be back on Thursday? Does that mean she will be back Thursday subject to having spent sufficient amounts of my money? Does that mean she'll be back if she can be arsed?* "What a cow!" screamed Longmire, as he closed his eyes and forced the handset to his ear.

"I beg your pardon!"

"Oh shit, sorry Nicky, it's only me, Andrew."

"Andrew, is that you?"

"Yes, sorry about that."

"Are you in the habit of making nuisance phone calls?"

"Don't be bloody stupid, sis. Look, I've got an outright emergency here. My wonderful wife has decided to spend *a few days* in Paris at short notice and left me to look after Simon, the house, the dog and run a fucking business! She *should* be back on Thursday next week – but evidently might not be – and in the meantime, I've got business meetings lined up this afternoon and the early part of next week," protested Longmire, sarcastically emphasising the offending terms that Sam had used.

Nicky rolled her eyes and swooned an exaggerated 'oh no'. Then she simply waited.

After a few moments, Longmire shared his idea. "Hey, Nicky, I've got an idea. You don't work, do you?"

"What do you mean, Andrew?" she asked, a knowing smile now breaking out across her face.

"You know, you're like Sam. You spend all day at home and Nathan goes out to work. It's just that it would make sense for me if I could leave you to look after Simon for a few days."

Nicky removed the phone from her ear, looked at the mouthpiece and mouthed the word 'wanker'. She then placed the phone back to her ear and replied.

"Andrew, I can't today or the early part of next week I'm afraid. Nathan and I are flat out with a catering project for a major client and I *should* really be focussing on that in the next *few* days."

"Oh, come on, sis, don't be so bloody selfish. Look, I'll drive him over as soon as he's finished school tonight and bring some of his electronic games; you won't even know he's there."

Nicky looked at the phone again and this time mouthed '*absolute wanker*'.

"Andrew, I'd love to help, but it's a non-starter I'm afraid. Look, I do need to go, but good luck with it all. I'm sure a man with as many talents as you can supervise one child for a few days without the world crumbling in on you. Oh, and say hi to Sam for me when she gets back," teased Nicky.

Longmire cut her off without responding, threw his mobile on the counter and placed his palms on the surface. God, she made him so angry sometimes. Here he was trying to run a multi-million-pound property debt business and looking for a little support from his nearest and dearest and she was pretending to be too bloody busy to do the right thing. And why exactly? Because she deluded herself that running some tin pot catering company in Suffolk was actually a worthwhile existence. He wondered when she would grow up and understand that making a few sandwiches for companies in Woodbridge didn't qualify as corporate high-flying? It didn't surprise him that she said 'say hi to Sam though' – cut from the same cloth them two – bloody ungrateful, the pair of them. Nicky had also been the recipient of a few thousand quid from him when she started out – he thought that alone merited a bit of loyalty from his sister.

His mobile pinged at him and he snatched it up off the counter.

"Hi, Andrew. Will be with you in one hour. Mick."

Longmire decided that he'd need to worry about Simon and the school pick up and any other arrangements he could think of for his son later – it was time to get on with the meetings and calls. He ignored Barney's cries from behind the utility door and headed for the study.

Unusually, it only took two rings before Henry Humble picked up the phone at the other end. Normally, Longmire's private banker was so unhurried it was either voicemail or a vicious-sounding secretary called Lydia that answered. Longmire thought Humble was the private banking equivalent of a sloth; everything he did was slow – painfully slow. He was also an evolutionary miracle – and wondered sometimes how on earth a fifty-odd-year-old Humble continued to survive in such a high-energy environment like private banking? All his peers were twenty years younger and full of get-up-and-go. But he'd performed well for Longmire over the years, just as he'd done for other clients. He may be deliberate and measured but that allowed him to be diligent and think things through, unlike some of his younger colleagues. He'd survived *because* of his slowness not *despite* it.

After enduring the minimum of social niceties, Longmire launched in.

"Henry, I'd like to borrow a further £1.8 million from you on the same terms as before. And, whilst you're at it, I'd like to place a limit order on a further 500,000 shares of First Capital at a price of 190p."

There was a pause; Longmire imagined his advisor on the other end of the phone moving slowly around his desk and making the notes that he would need to complete the instruction. The CEO of First Capital tapped his fingers on his desk in front of him.

"OK, Andrew. Leave this with me. I'll need to run some collateral limit checks and I'll come back to you as soon as I can," replied Humble.

Longmire could hear the shuffling of paper as Humble set about his task.

"OK. Just let me know what I need to pledge against the loan. The best number today is my mobile, but I am in and out of meetings so you'll need to take your chances. But it will be today, Henry, won't it? It's rather urgent."

There was another pause. Longmire looked at the receiver in his hand. Sometimes he felt like reaching down the line, taking a big key and winding the clockwork mechanism in Humble.

"Of course, Andrew. I'll come back to you as soon as possible."

Longmire didn't respond to the ambiguity in his advisor's reply but rolled his eyes. He then prepared for the meeting with Mick, his CFO. Today's meeting was Longmire's initiative; he thought there was a great opportunity to substantially reduce borrowing costs by accessing short-term loans directly from the capital market rather than relying exclusively on the traditional clearing banks. There were risks attached to this, as Mick Marshall had been predictably quick to point out, but Longmire was sold on the idea. That's why he'd invited Tommy Owen – a long-term investment banking friend – to come over and persuade his sceptical CFO.

When both men had arrived, they all went into the study. The two guests were shown to either end of a ridiculously low and uncomfortable sofa and did as much fidgeting as listening. After setting out the problem, Longmire invited Owen to speak, just as his mobile rang. He glanced at the display and deliberately let it go to voice mail.

"I don't understand why any business in 2006 would rely on the clearing banks. Look, the overnight funding that we can arrange for you, will be 30% cheaper than the rates currently being paid by First Capital. Clearers were fine in the '90s, but we're in a world where capital flows more freely than ever before between well-capitalised financial institutions. Why wouldn't First Capital want to take advantage of that?" replied Owen.

"So it's a win/win – we diversify our sources of finance and at the same time, reduce costs. It sounds like less risk and more profit to me. So Mick, what's the problem?" asked Longmire.

"Well, I'm not sure I said there was a problem, Andrew," spluttered Marshall. He looked up from the slides that Owen had provided a little startled – both men were now staring straight at him.

He cleared his throat. "Well, errr, what about the mismatch in timing between the arrangements we would have with the capital markets and our clients? The funding from the markets is, by definition, very short term, but when we make loans to a developer, it might be for several months or several years," said the CFO.

Owen's response was immediate and detailed, almost as if he was expecting that precise question. "That's the beauty of the markets – they're always open. So as one of your facilities falls due, you simply refinance. And, there are hundreds of capital market participants all eager to make short-term loans so the prospect of the market drying up is non-existent."

Longmire was nodding his approval just as his phone went again. He glanced at the screen.

"Excuse me please, gentlemen, I do need to take this one." He left the room.

"Hi, Andrew, Henry here. I've looked at the numbers and you'll need to pledge…2.1 million shares – at today's price that's…now let me see…"

Longmire could hear Humble's plodding fingers tapping out the maths on a keyboard as he stalked the corridor outside the study.

"It's about £4 million worth of your total shareholding of £5.7 million in First Capital," said Humble.

Longmire ran a hand through his hair and released a long breath. He asked Humble to confirm by email. The CEO's mood was lifting. As far as Longmire was concerned, margin lending (borrowing money against the value of shares he already owned) was the eighth wonder of the world – it allowed him to benefit from the increase in share price that he had created in order to buy more shares and gain access to more capital.

When he returned, Marshall and Owen had given up on the sofa and were standing in the middle of the room reviewing the latter's presentation. The CFO confirmed to Longmire that although there was a theoretical mismatch between when they needed to pay back the capital markets and the timing of receipts from their own loan book, it was just that – theoretical. Provided the capital markets remained a rather small part of their funding, the increase in profits more than offset any risk about liquidity drying up.

Longmire smiled at his CFO and then Owen.

Later that afternoon, Longmire reluctantly squeezed his Porsche into one of the remaining car parking spaces at Simon's school and waited for his son to arrive. He waited and waited, as he sifted through a few messages on his phone. Eventually, his car was the only one left in the car park. He called Simon's mobile number for the third time and regretted allowing his son's call to go into voicemail earlier when he was in his meeting back at the house. Although he'd called, Simon hadn't left a message. He called Sam and got her voice mail.

Chapter Eighteen

He was just about to get out of the car and walk down to reception when his mobile went. It was his son returning his call.

"Hi, Dad. Are you in still in London or back home?"

"Never mind where I am, Simon, where the bloody hell are you?"

"Didn't Mum tell you? I'm at Henry's house. They invited me for a sleepover so Henry's mum picked us up from the Queen's House car park."

At least that explained why he hadn't seen Simon after school – they used the car park at the other end of the campus.

"Bloody hell, Simon. I'm not telepathic you know. Why didn't you call to let me know? I've been hanging around school for over an hour now and I've been worried sick."

"I called you this afternoon, Dad, but you didn't answer; like you never answer when I call. And Mum told me that she'd let you know all about it."

She did this on purpose as well, thought Longmire. *She's probably laughing her face off with that Paula revelling in the fact that I've had a wasted trip and am running around trying to find my son whilst she's three parts pissed in Paris.*

"Never mind about your bloody mother! Now wait there and I'll come and pick you up."

"What now? What about the sleepover?" pleaded Simon.

Longmire paused. He quite liked the idea of going home and spending some time alone. He needed to update D66 after the call with Humble and felt a modest pang of guilt that he had been too busy to take his son's call earlier in the afternoon.

"OK, Simon. I'll be there at 8.30 tomorrow morning. Make sure you're ready."

He finished the call, pulled out of his parking space and headed home. He popped into his favourite wine merchant and got back to the house 20 minutes later. He'd intended to cook something, watch TV and then retire to the study with his bottle of wine to do some work.

When he got home, two things prevented him from doing so: no doubt deliberately, thought Longmire, Sam had not left any food in the fridge. Secondly, he'd forgotten about Barney. The one-year-old Lab had now been shut away on his own in the utility room for five or six hours and had had two accidents that Andrew could see and possibly more that he could smell. Barney had taken a particular shine to Andrew's golf shoes. Half an hour later, he'd binned his shoes, ordered a take-away and cleaned up as best he could in the utility room. He'd call a cleaning firm in over the weekend to do the rest.

Whilst Andrew was sat in the study, flicking through some work waiting for his food, his mobile went. It was Michael McGrath.

"Hi, Michael. How's Cannes?"

"Beautiful as ever. I'm sitting on our boat and have just finished a fantastic meal – I'm now enjoying a glass of wine. How are you?"

Thoroughly pissed off. I've got crappy weather; no food in the house and my wife had buggered-off to Paris, thought Longmire.

"I'm fine, Michael. Just about to enjoy some wine myself actually. What can I do for you?"

"When do you think you can make it out again, Andrew?"

Andrew was tempted to say tomorrow, take Simon with him and leave Sam an equally vague note about the details of their return.

"Well, I'll try before the planned March trip, but it's unlikely I'm afraid."

"OK. Look, there's something that I'd like to discuss with you in the next few weeks. I mentioned Pascal Du Luart to you at the garden party where you met my brother. I got to know him because he moors his boat near ours but he's a very successful businessman in his own right. He's now looking to branch out into high-end residential development and has found a fantastic site just outside Cannes where we can refurbish four large Villas that could be amazing with the right approach. They're just what the ultra-rich are looking for, Andrew, and all no more than 30 minutes from Nice Airport. We've been talking about a joint-venture arrangement and I'll run the development project for him. I think you should invest with us – the numbers that we have been through so far look amazing."

Longmire was nodding slowly. He could recall the conversation with Michael and had warmed to the idea instantly. He was determined to be able to spend more time in the South of France in the next ten years once he had completed his task at First Capital. Being involved in residential development in one of the most beautiful parts of the French Riviera was an appealing way to be able to do so.

"OK, Michael. What sort of capital are we looking at?" asked Longmire. He stood up and shuffled around the room focussing on what MaGrath was telling him.

"Well, ballpark, the refurbishment costs will be in the region of €4m and we'll be in for €3.5m on the purchase of the site, but the end-value of each Villa has got to be north of €3m every day of the week. Pascal has said that he can fund €3m, and he'd want to see the same amount of equity from us with the bank funding the balance."

"OK, and what about the profit-sharing arrangements?"

"Not that far yet; all to be agreed, but I think Pascal is an astute but reasonable businessman Andrew. I'm sure we'll find something that works for all of us."

Longmire was nodding again. His doorbell rang. He told McGrath to email him what he had and that he'd look at dates and get back to him with further questions.

When Longmire had finished his take-way, he began to turn his attention to the exciting opportunity that McGrath had called him about. His partner had sent him the link via the Cote D'zur Sotherbys website and he flicked through the photos and then the location map and identified where the Villas were in relation to Cannes and the Mediterranean Sea. He found himself agreeing with McGrath – they were in a stunning location and whilst some needed almost complete renovation, they would be worth a fortune.

He opened up D66 to update the numbers that he'd agreed with Henry earlier. His First Capital holding was now worth £5.7 million – including the extra 500,000 shares that he had agreed to buy today. This was the highest it had ever been. Additionally, Humble would be transferring a further £1.8 million to his private account in the next few days – once he'd converted it into Euros, he'd have around €2.6 million, more than enough to invest with Michael and Pascal. He went to bed a little less annoyed than he had been for the most part of the day and slept soundly through the night.

He was awake by 6.30 am; he got up, descended the stairs and headed straight for the kitchen to make his first coffee. Barney formed a single-handed welcoming committee. A black furry bundle of energy, big innocent brown eyes, oversized floppy ears and his legs stubbornly incapable of gaining any purchase on the smooth floor tiles. The Lab's tail was wagging so furiously with excitement; it was causing him to slip all over the place. Even Longmire's instinctive dislikes for dogs and the vivid recollection of the extensive clean-up operation from the night before failed to prevent a token smile escaping, as he let the dog outside.

The one-year-old Lab and Longmire had arrived at an uneasy truce until normal family life could be resumed. As Longmire made his drink, he pondered what actually constituted 'normal family life' these days. Sam had always been protective and had never been afraid to criticise him if she felt he was working too hard and neglecting her and Simon. But she'd never done this before, or that stupid stunt with the shirt. He was certain that she'd been more appreciative in the past. He wondered what had changed as he glanced down at the note Sam had left. And there it was – literally in black and white.

I will be in Paris with Paula for a few days – shopping.

That bitch Paula – she was the one that was poisoning his wife's mind. They'd known each other what, a couple of years, and Sam's change in attitude coincided almost completely. The trip to Paris was probably all Paula's idea. He took a sip of strong coffee and began to think through what, if anything, he might be able to do about it.

When it was time to leave to collect Simon, he removed the school contact list from the notice board and scanned it. It was in alphabetical order by surname. Brown, Henry – Dukes Park, Woodbridge. Luckily, Longmire sort of knew the dad – Arthur Brown – he was a drab, unsuccessful local solicitor who Longmire had met at various school and social events. Didn't have much to say for himself and the fact that he had stayed local and had never done the 'London thing' attested to his lack of get-up-and-go. Sam knew the wife, and Andrew was grateful that Collette Brown also appeared on the list, as he was unable to recall her first name. He didn't know that Henry and Simon were particularly close but he didn't have a problem with the friendship, notwithstanding the obvious lack of ambition on the father's part.

★

Arthur Brown, despite having been away on a weeklong business trip, was up and about early. It was one of the few times that he could appreciate the peace and quiet of his home before his three children got up out of bed and did what children were good at – making noise. He savoured his early Saturday-morning coffee alone – after a hectic week as the Managing Partner of a large law firm in East Anglia. It also gave his wife the opportunity for a lie-in and he'd just taken Collette a cup of tea, as he wandered back into his study when he heard a car pull up outside. The driver, annoyingly, gave the accelerator one last blast of the powerful engine immediately ahead of killing it and the study windows rattled their disapproval. Brown glanced out to see a black Porsche 911 parked next to the family Vauxhall Zafira and Andrew Longmire marching towards his front door. It was 8.27 am.

Brown quickened his pace to arrive at the front door before Longmire could register his presence and wake the whole house. He had met Longmire at a few events over the years and thought he was a little full of himself and obsessed with money, although he couldn't claim to know the man particularly well. He also knew his own son, Henry, was an acquaintance of the Longmire's boy, but couldn't remember his name.

"Good morning, Andrew, how are you?" enquired Brown, as he opened the front door just as Longmire was about to knock.

"Errr…very well, thank you, Arthur," replied Longmire, tipping his head to one side and looking questioningly at Brown.

The lawyer led them through to the kitchen, made himself a fresh coffee and did the same for his unexpected guest.

"How's the family?" asked the host over his shoulder, as he busied himself with the coffee-making apparatus. He wondered how long it would take Longmire to get on to the subject of money.

"We've just pulled off some amazing property lending deals at the firm I now run and I've recently bought a yacht in the south of France. Sam and Simon are both well."

At least he's consistent, thought Brown, as he raised his eyebrows safe in the knowledge that Longmire couldn't see the expression. "Oh, we do quite a lot of legal work on property lending in the region," he replied, trying to keep the conversation going.

"We don't do much around here at all. We're more London and the southeast – where the big boys are if you know what I mean?" replied Longmire, as he glanced at his watch.

"Of course, I understand that completely, Andrew." He rolled his eyes before turning around and smiling with the coffees.

The two men sat facing one another at the kitchen table and rapidly ran out of conversation.

Brown blinked first.

"Andrew, it really is lovely to see you, but can I ask if there is a particular reason for the visit this morning?"

Longmire stared at the lawyer as if he were a halfwit.

"My son? Simon? He stayed here last night. I'm here to collect him," replied Longmire all open-palmed and wide-eyed.

Brown cleared his throat and then managed, "Errr, pardon."

Longmire simply raised a quizzical eyebrow.

"I'm sorry, Andrew, there must be some mistake; Simon isn't here. I saw all the children when I came home last night and it was just my lot I'm afraid." Brown pulled the top of his dressing gown closer together.

Longmire's fingers were tapping away on the table – like they were beating out the rhythm of his irritation as the two men stared at one another. Longmire seemed to suddenly notice the noise and stopped, but he continued to glare at his host.

"What do you mean he's not here? I spoke to him last night and he said he was here. We agreed I'd pick him up this morning."

Collette Brown walked into the kitchen and the men turned to face her. She had also heard the engine revving outside and had spotted Longmire walking towards the front door. She had calmly, but quickly, got dressed and chosen this moment to enter the fray after eavesdropping for the last five minutes a few feet away in the hall.

Arthur Brown introduced his wife to Longmire and he noticed that the two exchanged pleasantries, perfunctorily rather than warmly. He then explained the problem to Collette who appeared to listen politely.

"Andrew, why do you think he's here?" asked Collette.

Longmire reluctantly provided the full version of events and even recovered the class contact list from his pocket as evidence that his tale of woe had substance. Rather than continue the conversation, he wanted to call Simon, but he had left his phone in the car; there were now two missed calls on the display.

Collette stuck out her hand and Longmire obliged by giving her the slip of paper. She read the list whilst he picked up his coffee and then put it down again without drinking. He looked at his watch, picked up his cup but failed again to convert and the coffee didn't reach his lips for a second time.

Collette Brown had turned over to the second page of the list. "Turner – Henry Turner. He and Simon are good friends. If you spoke to Simon and he said he was at 'Henry's house', it might be worth checking in with the Turners," suggested Collette matter-of-factly.

"I've never heard of them," replied Longmire, as he waved his hand dismissively.

"Really? He's been at the school over a year – came across from Orwell Park after year eight. He and Simon have been best mates for months and have had loads of sleepovers, I remember talking to Sam about it," she replied, her voice thick with sarcasm.

She returned the piece of paper to Longmire.

He snatched it, looked up at Collette Brown, opened his mouth to say something and then stopped short. He began to look down the list. Taylor, Thorp, Turner – Henry Turner. He glanced across the two columns to the right. "Needham fucking Market! That's miles away. I can't believe the incompetence of these people. Why didn't they talk to me?"

He put his hands on the table and pushed himself up quickly, almost violently. His seat, an old delicate farmhouse chair, flew backwards and crashed into the wall behind him. Without apologising or saying thank you, he stormed out of the house. The Browns could hear him swearing all the way along the hallway until their uninvited guest had slammed the front door after him.

"What a wanker!"

"Collette, come on! He was genuinely worried about his son. You can't be too hard on him."

She was rearranging the furniture following Andrew's little outburst. She stopped and gripped the back of the chair that Longmire had slammed against the wall and looked directly at her husband. "Believe me, Arthur, there is nothing, absolutely nothing, genuine about that man."

Chapter Nineteen

Every year, in mid-March, over 20,000 real estate professionals from all over the world descend on the beautiful French Riviera to attend a real estate conference held in Cannes. Although officially, and grandly, entitled *Le Marché international des professionnels de l'immobilier,* it is simply known to all the delegates as MIPIM and is 'The Event' in the annual calendar for anyone who is anyone in property.

And so, on Tuesday, 14 March 2006 Joe McGrath found himself, for the first time, at the eastern-end of the Boulevard de la Croisette, Cannes. The tourist guide and map that had been left in his flat allowed him to plot his progress along the Croisette to the main conference facilities. Although it looked like a road on the map, McGrath soon realised it was actually a wide waterfront Boulevard festooned with palm trees along a central grass strip. It was lined on one side with bright awnings, under which boutiques, galleries and fancy jewellers enticed wealthy residents and tourists in off the pavements. The apartment blocks in which they lived and the art-deco hotels where they stayed also occupied this side. Sandy beaches and the bright Mediterranean Sea bordered the other.

The pavements were generous, allowing residents, tourists and conference attendees to stroll along its 2 km length with ease on either side. It was just gone 9.00 am, already sixteen degrees – with a promise of further warmth to come – crystalline blue skies and one of those mornings that you feel blessed to be alive.

The boulevard was already energised. Outside the numerous cafés and restaurants, staff were sluicing the pavements clean of the night before. The hosed water on the rapidly warming tarmac accentuated the smell of the Mediterranean, fresh ground coffee and the pastries being served by the waiters. It produced a cocktail of fragrances that were unique to early morning Cannes. Almost like petrichor – the smell released by the first drops of rain after a prolonged dry spell – McGrath found it intoxicating.

He continued his walk along the pavement and noticed a chic, middle-aged, and McGrath assumed, French lady taking her small poodle for a walk. The dog was padding around in the pools of water created by the hosed pavements and the woman was clearly in no rush. She wore immaculate, white shoes with a two-inch heel and an open face. Her bright red toenails were on display at the end of the shoe and picked out the jazzy array of stones that were set across the straps. Her trousers were a light fabric and beige-coloured and she wore a pristine white open-neck blouse with three-quarter length sleeves. In one hand, she held her dog lead, even this looked expensive, and in the other, she carried the almost obligatory Gucci handbag – the distinctive GG insignia at the top successfully displayed for all to see. The beige and white chequered pattern of the bag finished off the lady's ensemble. *Quite an outfit for a dog walk,* thought McGrath, but this was the French Riviera after all. As she brushed by, he was momentarily overpowered by her strong perfume.

He continued west and crossed over the road to walk on the southern edge of the wide promenade adjacent to the beach that fronts the Mediterranean. There were blue metallic chairs randomly interspersed alongside the knee-high concrete plinth-wall that separated the promenade from the beach and most were already occupied. Some early morning conference delegates were sat reading emails or talking on their phones as they looked out over the sea. All were wearing their garish orange straps around their neck – insisted upon by the conference organisers – that supported their MIPIM badges and identified them as delegates.

In absolute contrast, there was an old man in sandals, khaki shorts and a decrepit cardigan that was leaning back in one of the chairs with his feet up on the concrete plinth. His hands were clasped together on his chest with his cap pulled down over his face; he was fast asleep. He looked more like a fixture than a fitting to McGrath who assumed he had been there for hours, if not, days. The contrast between him and the quintessential property spiv sat next to him reminded McGrath of his own quandary: his heart and soul were every bit with the old man, but McGrath's brain was hardwired – for the moment at least – for business and his next property deal.

He continued to walk alongside the south promenade and eventually arrived at the Registration Tent for the conference. It was a large, white structure, with 'Welcome to MIPIM' written on the side and a red carpet that guided the delegates into the marquee. Once he'd registered, and was back outside, he slipped his sunglasses back down and consulted the programme that detailed where all the various stands were and what events were due to take place in the main conference hall – the Palais des Festivals. He scanned the document and noticed that at 12.30 today, Ken Livingstone and Bertrand Delanoë, the Mayor of Paris, were due to share the experiences of *'city management against a background of urban, social, economic and environmental challenges'*. McGrath decided he'd be somewhere else.

He looked up from his brochure and saw the Palais in front of him. This was the main conference hall for MIPIM and the venue for the Cannes Film Festival. It dominated the seafront. McGrath stood in front of the six-storey monument to glass, steel and reinforced concrete; it was so ugly he could barely believe someone had paid an architect to design it.

McGrath walked around the other side of the Palais to take a look at the town's beautiful 'old quarter' or le Suquet that climbed above and behind this part the Croisette. He knew he was here on business, but this was one of the main reasons he wanted to attend MIPIM. He'd been reading about it in the weeks leading up to the trip and he'd built in some time into his schedule to explore this part of town. Apparently, it was originally the fishermen's residential area and the steep cobbled alleys were hundreds of years old. The area became the property of the monks of the nearby Iles de Lérins in the eleventh century, and they built the Château de la Castre that could be seen high up on the hillside. He couldn't imagine what the Cistercian monks looking down from the top of the old town would make of the Palais or, for that matter, a property industry hell-bent on self-indulgence.

It was time for McGrath to make his way over to the yachts and keep his appointment with his brother, Andrew Longmire and Pascal who were on the First Capital yacht. He checked the programme for the location again and made his way to the Jetee Albert Edouard, just to the side of the Palais. A little self-consciously, he showed his pass to the aggressive-looking security guard at the entrance who quickly checked his photo. The guards had been warned that delegates were avoiding paying the €4,000 registration fee and borrowing each other's passes to gain access to the harbour area for meetings. Once the guard had satisfied himself that the photo demonstrated a sufficient resemblance to the face he was looking at, he waved it through. McGrath detected a hint of disappointment on the guard's part.

He walked onto the jetty and was met by a flotilla of pristine yachts festooned with flags and other regalia. Each yacht had a private gangway linking the small hospitality tent on the jetty directly to the rear of the boat. There were smartly dressed crewmembers milling around both on the quayside and on board attending to the guests' every wish.

It didn't take him long to find the logo-emblazoned First Capital yacht moored alongside the other multi-million-pound floating palaces. The boat that Andrew Longmire had hired was right up there with the big boys. Every major investment and clearing bank that was active in property lending was represented, and so were the obligatory lawyers, advisors and brokers, but none had a bigger or more expensive boat than First Capital.

Chapter Twenty

McGrath finally finished his ascent and arrived on the upper deck of the *Alsace*. It was over 100ft long, provided four different meeting areas; could sleep eight and entertain up to 75 guests. It was berthed alongside some of the biggest and best yachts in the harbour – Colliers International was one side and Savills International the other. McGrath didn't want to think of the costs that must have been involved in renting it.

The outlook across the millpond harbour back to the 'old town' was breath-taking, as was the view out towards the Mediterranean. The dark-coloured teak flooring with glazed finish was immaculate. The sweeping deck, adorned with sunbeds and cream sofas on one side led to a large parlour equipped with bar, sliding marble table and floor lighting on the other. There was a wooden table in the centre of the deck that could seat twelve, but which was set for four people.

"Joey!"

Only one person called him Joey. Michael McGrath wasn't a tall man, but what he lacked in height, he more than made up for in get-up-and-go. In fact, as far as McGrath was concerned, his brother was a bundle of infectious kinetic energy who had saved many a staid property meeting collapsing into a state of tedium. Michael greeted his younger brother with a customary bear hug.

"What do you think of Cannes Joey?" he asked, as he leant back on one heel and presented the views with a sweeping arm gesture towards le Suquet.

"Unbelievable. It's beautiful," replied his brother. The fact that Michael had gestured towards the old town allowed McGrath to answer and not feel he was being disingenuous – he did think the old town was beautiful.

Michael laughed; his whole demeanour instantly lifted by the presence of his brother. In contrast to Joe's long, naturally curly hair, Michael's was thick and grew straight out – almost laterally from his head. So his hair was always closely cropped. He was shorter than Joe and there was something incongruous about his cheeky baby face when he stood next to his younger brother. There appeared to be much less than the ten-year age difference between the two men.

Michael McGrath beamed as he introduced Joe to Pascal Du Luart, as Longmire was discussing the breakfast arrangements with one of the waiters off to the side. Du Luart was dressed in an Armani suit and expensive-looking leather shoes that were almost identical in colour to the teak decking.

The two men shook hands and McGrath took an instant liking to him. There was something warm and genuine about this guy, he thought, as Du Luart shared his knowledge of the history of the harbour with him.

At that moment, Longmire came bounding back across the deck and greeted McGrath with a damp handshake and very little eye contact. *He's gone native*, thought McGrath. The CEO of first Capital was wearing navy-coloured espadrilles, no socks, light-cream chinos folded up just above the ankle and a short-sleeved pink polo shirt. He also had a jumper that was hanging over his shoulders at the back and tied in a knot at the front with the sleeves – McGrath's pet hate. He was focussed as ever on moving the meeting along and getting on with the next one. "Well, gentlemen," said Longmire rubbing his hands, "I've just ordered fresh coffee, more orange juice and croissants – does anyone want anything else?" After waiting a nanosecond, he continued. "OK, let's get started then. Pascal, welcome once again to *The Alsace*."

"Thank you, Andrew. I should congratulate you on your choice of yacht – she is *magnifique,* as we would say!" replied Pascal, as he kissed his pinched hand and then threw it open with his outstretched palm facing the sky. "And, as a Frenchman, I must also acknowledge the excellent choice of name, my friend. It's always enjoyable to remind the Germans that they can't have everything that they want in life!"

"You're very welcome, Pascal." Longmire had the Joint Venture Agreement in front of him and picked it up. "Just to refresh our memories gentlemen, I'll summarise where this document is at the moment. After some lengthy negotiations by Pascal, the vendor has finally agreed to sell to us. Well done, Pascal." The Frenchman acknowledged Longmire's praise with a confident nod and smile but didn't interrupt his host.

A few hundred yards away, a helicopter skimmed low over a large yacht, which was manoeuvring in another part of the harbour. It was no doubt depositing some of the wealthier delegates that didn't have the patience for the forty-five-minute taxi ride from Nice Airport. After the noise abated, the four men discussed their agreement in detail. It was then decided that by the end of the week, before MIPIM was over, the four men would visit Pascal's Notary, and sign the contract. Shortly after that, the little consortium would become the very proud owner of its first French property development in the Côte D'Azur.

Longmire and Pascal excused themselves. They had separate meetings, but both started in ten minutes and they needed to leave immediately to get there. They shook hands and the brothers were left on the upper deck alone. They were sat at the long wooden table looking out over the Mediterranean.

Once McGrath was happy no one was around, he turned to his brother. "Michael, you know I haven't got all the money to fund my end of this deal, don't you?"

The older brother went to pour them both a coffee. "You've explained that to me before, Joey. It's fine—"

McGrath cut him off. "It's not fine, Michael. You won't let me pay you back what I owe you already and here you are offering to fund my part of a development."

Michael put the pot down and passed the cup he'd just refilled to McGrath. "OK, Joey. Look, I have a suggestion. Why don't you invest the money you say you owe me—"

"The money I *do* owe you, Michael," he interrupted, as he picked up his cup.

"OK. The money you *do* owe me. That means I need to find less cash to fund my part of the deal. That helps me at the moment, since I can't get my hands on all of it right now. We can sort out the profits afterwards and you can take out what you think should be your share. That way you pay me back, I need to find less cash up front and we're all square. What does that sound like?"

It sounded like exactly what it was to McGrath – Michael being overly generous again. But when it came to share out the profits, he'd be as stubborn as his brother and refuse to take a penny. He'd play Michael at his own game.

"Deal."

"Now then, little brother, did you ever find out who that 'gorgeous' cyclist was you told me about?" His animated baby-face beaming out at McGrath.

"No. And other than a first name, which may or may not be her real one, I've got no idea how to find her."

A few feet below them on the jetty, Pascal was walking away to his meeting with his mobile telephone to his ear.

"Put me through to Mr Dubois. Tell him it's Pascal."

"Hello, Pascal. This is Dubois."

"Strasbourg is the name of the company that will be buying the site. We will all come by to see you later this week to arrange the signing. I want this all done before Longmire returns to the UK."

"Have you met all three men now?"

"Yes."

"What do you think?"

"I think the brothers are fine. I trust them and they're bright. Longmire however, is an imbecile."

Chapter Twenty-One

Russell Square, Central London, seven days ago, 4 am, pitch black, wet and freezing cold. That did not just feel like a long time ago, it felt like a lifetime away from the South of France. Alice, and the group of cyclists she had been riding with for the last week, was about to make her final descent into Cannes after a 1,500 km bicycle ride. It was a glorious 20 degrees, with cobalt blue skies and the companionship of the beautiful French countryside.

There were some very weary bodies amongst the group, but the overwhelming sense of excitement and achievement was palpable as the riders looked across and caught their first glimpse of the arresting blue of the Mediterranean. Alice's eyes began to water and she knew it wasn't simply the rising Côte D'Azur air over-stimulating them. She was thinking of her mother and why she had agreed to do the charity ride.

One of Alice's PR colleagues had told her 'cycling-mad' friend about the inaugural C2C (Cycle to Cannes) cycle ride after she had come across it in the Property Week magazine. The sense of adventure and the beauty of the French countryside had got her attention, but when she found out about the charitable element of the event, she knew she had to do it.

Alice was motivated by the thought of over £100,000 being raised for various charities – the main one being the Sarah Matheson Trust. Alice had personal experience of the fantastic work that the Trust did for unfortunate victims of multiple system atrophy – a neurological disorder with Parkinson Disease-type symptoms. Alice watched in agony as it transformed her mother from a young, active fifty-year-old woman into a shaking, incontinent old lady who shuffled along like an eighty-year-old at the time of her death at just fifty-nine. Alice signed up the moment she found out that the Trust would benefit.

She blinked furiously and rubbed her eyes so that she could focus on the positioning of the other bikes around her. She noticed that Rupert was right in front and eased on the brakes accordingly. He was a thirty-five-year-old architect, and found it difficult to separate his passion for mathematics and everything geometric from the practicalities of bicycle riding. He was resolute that they should adopt the perfect peloton shape with as much precision as one of his engineering drawings. Even more importantly, Peloton etiquette should be respected at all times – no riding too close to the bike in front and definitely no drafting. This last term, Rupert defined as 'riding very closely, and persistently, behind the riders in front to maintain aerodynamically protected in the peloton thus saving energy at the expense of the 'hard-workers'. Alice just thought he was a wanker of the first order and came close to telling him so on a couple of occasions.

In total, there were sixteen other cyclists – all men – and 'home' for the duration of the trip, when they weren't peddling, had been a converted double-decker bus with sleeping-bunks on the top floor. It had been a support vehicle for a Robbie Williams concert-tour, which explained the bar on the lower level.

To maximise publicity, the sponsors had insisted that the riders and their entourage – on their arrival in Cannes – travel the full length of the Croisette and then back again. The group were due to enter the town via le Suquet – the old town on the western edge of Cannes – and travel all the way along the Mediterranean-side of the Croisette, past the Palais until the Casino at the far eastern end. Here they would make a U-turn using the roundabout and head back along the hotel-side of the same boulevard towards the Palais where they were due to finish and be greeted by the crowds, the head of the MIPIM organisation and the Mayor of London no less.

As they rode along the Croisette, the bus driver, as instructed, was blasting the horn to get as much attention as possible for the riders and sponsors. Conference delegates and locals alike stopped what they were doing for a few moments as the cyclists passed and politely clapped generating sufficient interest for other pedestrians further along the route to do the same.

A few hundred yards away, stood outside the Majestic Hotel, Joe McGrath was trying to make a phone call back to the office about a potential property acquisition. He'd been speaking to an agent for over an hour in the underground part of the Palais – a windowless, dark and stale environment – and was sucking in the sea air. He looked up and saw a group of 15–20 cyclists heading along the other side of the Croisette followed by a logo-emblazoned bus that was making a horrific amount of noise.

Catriona's voice brought him back. "Sorry, Catriona, I missed that. Yes, I've just been speaking to CBRE this morning and they're saying we've got a run at this one. You need to speak to their West End team. If you mention my name and that I have spoken to Aaron, they'll send you the files and we can review their numbers. We'll need to be pretty aggressive, but it's West End retail, just off Bond Street so I'm keen that we make a bid."

The cyclists had ridden the length of the Croisette from west to east and had made their U-turn at the Casino and had turned back towards the Palais travelling west. This time, they used the northern side of the road; where it is lined with the hotels and retail units. The pavement here is a little narrower and, accordingly, the pedestrians are much closer. Alice could make out a few faces that she knew dotted along the pavement – they were no more than ten feet away in places. It was turning into a carnival atmosphere as they headed towards the finish. Alice caught a glimpse of two colleagues who were shouting support; she waved, as she rode past.

The lead cyclist was now no more than 20 feet away from Joe McGrath and the people around him started to applaud. The bus driver was now getting completely carried away and more and more people were joining in as the procession continued.

"Joe, where the hell are you? All I can hear are cars beeping at one another – are you sure you're not stood in Piccadilly Circus?" joked Catriona.

"I'm sorry. There's a cycle ride going on and some maniac bus driver is following them constantly sounding his horn." McGrath was now stood with his blackberry pressed against one side of his head and the palm of his hand against the other, straining to hear what was being said to him and looking into the distance.

"Lots of work going on then, Joe," added Catriona sardonically.

He rolled his eyes.

"Look, I'll call you back in a few minutes." He rang off and then headed in the opposite direction from the Palais to find somewhere quieter to make his calls.

As the group progressed along the final strip, approaching the Majestic hotel to the right and the Palais to the left and no more than 500 metres from the finish, Alice glanced over to the nearside pavement. She was stunned. It was an apparition of JOE! She was so shocked she nearly collided with Rupert's rear wheel. She had ridden 1,499.5 km without incurring the wrath of this latex-clad obsessive; to commit a major faux pas now in the last few seconds of the journey would be hugely embarrassing. But she was no longer worried about either the etiquette of peloton riding or Rupert. She only had one, maybe two seconds at most to double-check, but there was no doubt – it was him. He was just finishing a phone call dragging a hand through his unruly hair. She even waved, but it was too late; she'd gone past him and he was out of sight.

Alice crossed the finishing line, dismounted and was just setting off back along the Croisette. She only needed a fleeting glance, but she knew it was him: the hair, the broad shoulders and narrow hips – they were all etched on her memory. Although she had been travelling at speed, she had only been a few feet away and could even make out the square jaw line of his face. If she hurried, he might still be there.

All of the cyclists had now finished and were congratulating one another and they engulfed Alice in the process. The sponsors had arrived, and so were some of Alice's friends, and the President of the MIPIM organisation and Ken Livingstone and all the hangers on. The photographers wanted a team photo. It was hopeless – there was no way she could escape and run back the few hundred metres and expect Joe to still be there. She resigned herself to staying put for the moment. Friends congratulated her and one made the mistake of mentioning the Sarah Matheson Trust. Alice's emotions got the better of her.

That evening, Alice, Rupert and the other heavy-limbed cyclists were enduring their steep, but leisurely climb through the narrow streets of the old town. The organisers had booked a small, family run bistro for their well-deserved celebratory dinner. Alice immediately fell in love with the charm of the place. The group stopped at one of the many vantage points and gazed across at the Croisette below. Alice had little time for the glitz and brashness of the marina area and absolutely loathed the Palais. She looked down at it right now – all lit up in an ugly haze of yellow winking at her through the otherwise beautiful evening dusk like some out-of-place Belisha beacon.

Once rested, the group set-off again along a cobbled alleyway to their restaurant. There was a table-for-two outside occupied by a couple holding hands across it. Alice couldn't imagine a more romantic setting than the one she was looking at. Candles lit the table and a carafe of red wine offset neatly to one side. The old-fashioned menu written in chalk on the blackboard propped up against a low wall with the family cat curled-up next to it. The olive tree a few feet away had small, white fairy lights intertwined with the branches that produced a subtle glow that completed the atmosphere.

That she immediately thought about Joe didn't surprise her. She had spent the last few months doing little else other than regretting her stupidity on that day in November last year when he'd intervened on the train. He had obviously wanted to talk to her and what had she done? She had instantly mistrusted him, questioned his motives and walked away. She had fiercely maintained her independence. "Yippee!" she mocked herself, as she sneaked another look at the couple.

There wasn't a day that went past when she didn't think about him. She could still hear his velvety Welsh accent. "Hi, I'm Joe. Nice to meet you, Alice." She thought he was handsome, of course, but more importantly, now that she had had time to reflect, she knew he was one of those people – like her – that just had to do the right thing. A strong moral compass as her mum would have said. Why else would he have risked his own safety to rescue her when she had been downright rude to him less than two hours earlier. No one had ever done something like that for her before. She winced when she thought of the public dressing down she had given him at Liverpool Street.

The *maître de* interrupted her thoughts. The group was invited into the restaurant and led to their table. Alice was the last to enter and her heart sank as she realised that the only seat vacant was the one opposite Rupert. He'd decided to wear an open-neck, white shirt; she assumed to deliberately display as much of his hairy chest as possible. He did have a jumper, but he did that really wanky thing – it was hanging over his shoulders at the back and tied at the front with the sleeves.

She took a large gulp of wine and comforted herself with the one saving grace she could think of. Up until now, she had had no idea that Joe even worked in property – which presumably he did, otherwise why was he in Cannes during MIPIM week? And, like her, he was probably cloistered in this place for the next few days. He could be in the restaurant next door; she might even bump into him on the walk back down to the marina this evening. It might be a bit 'needle in a haystack' – 20,000 property people and 95% of them men – but it was a start. She knew she was probably kidding herself – serendipity had never played a major part in her life, so why should it suddenly put in an appearance now. But the chance, combined with the white wine, gave her the fortitude to smile politely, as Rupert explained for the third time why he was the best candidate to become the senior partner at his architect firm.

★

At a few minutes past 10.00 am the following morning, Joe McGrath was finishing off a cup of coffee outside a café in the old town. He needed to be back down at the marina in twenty minutes for his taxi to take him to the airport, but he was pleased with the outcome of his MIPIM. He'd been in the bar at the Martinez with some agents and a major investor until three am, but it had been worth it. With that discussion and the analysis that was being done back at the office, it looked like he'd pulled off another cracking property deal for his fund. He was tired, very tired, but life was good although not yet complete.

He took another a sip of the delicious coffee, as he peered out across the old town and thought about the bit that was missing. What would complete the circle and turn 'good' into 'perfect'? He thought about the slower pace of life again. He found it interesting that spending a few days in such a millionaire's playground with thousands of people and hundreds of meetings had led his mind in the opposite direction. One day, he'd leave the property deals and the office politics behind and live somewhere quiet, get married and have children: the simple life.

He drained his coffee, wiped his mouth on the red paper-serviette and was sorting through some Euros to leave for the waiter when a newspaper suddenly came thumping down on his table almost knocking his cup over. The boys that distributed the *MIPIM Daily News* were paid on the number of copies shifted – not on the artistic merit of their delivery. McGrath laughed, as the small paperboy struggled down the cobblestones looking for more opportunities to ditch his wares.

He picked up the newspaper and immediately froze. The missing link, the piece that would transform 'good' into 'perfect' was staring straight back at him. There, on the front page, was a colour photograph of a group of cyclists that were mad enough to cycle from London to Cannes – and some of those guys really did look odd. But in the middle, stood next to the Mayor of London, was Alice Thomas who apparently worked for a London PR Agency called Cornwall. Her tall figure, bob haircut and hazel eyes were just as he remembered them. McGrath suddenly felt wide-awake.

111

Chapter Twenty-Two

Sam Longmire made the final adjustments to her outfit. Navy blue shorts, and matching silk neckerchief tie with a golden fastening in the centre and a simple white blouse. She also wore brand new white plimsolls; the maritime bent to her outfit was deliberate and she hoped would be appreciated. She was stood on the jetty admiring the *Alsace* and looking forward to surprising her husband. She couldn't wait to see the expression on his face.

Much to Paula Poorish's dismay, Sam had regretted the trip to Paris – so much so that she'd actually apologised to Andrew. She'd decided that she just wasn't cut out for the games that some couples apparently play. Paula and her were still good friends, but she didn't want her relationship with Andrew to be like the one that Paula and Paul Poorish endured. She didn't need, actually couldn't stand, the constant battles of one-upmanship that the two of them expended so much energy on. Andrew and Sam had agreed to be more grown up about it all, and from what she could see, her husband was living up to his part of the bargain. In the past few months, he'd found more time for Sam and Simon and, for the first time in their marriage, she actually felt more like a wife than a member of his staff.

So here she was – making her effort. What could be more romantic than spending a little time here together? She thought about that for a moment. The romantic element to Sam and Andrew Longmire's relationship had always been a bit of a weak link if Sam was honest. In fact, if this was going to be a perfectly frank conversation with herself, she'd probably need to admit that she was really talking about sex. His libido seemed to operate on a completely different level to hers and there was no doubt in her mind that this mismatch had caused some of the friction between them. But even here, the last few months had seen marked improvements. She'd been far more open to his advances in the bedroom – and once actually in the kitchen! The fact that she had taken the initiative herself on two occasions was a particular source of pride. She looked up at the *Alsace* and wondered whether she might make the first move this evening; she wondered what sex might be like on a multimillion-pound yacht.

Sam turned and watched the weary bodies shuffling along the quayside; the vast majority wore dark glasses and pale complexions; one middle-aged man looked as hung over as any human being she had ever seen in her life. She assumed she'd been up this morning to catch her flight here before most of them had gone to bed. It was clear that MIPIM was just about over. Many of the boats were being cleaned and the taxi drivers were doing a roaring trade taking delegates back to the airport. The place had that feel about it – the jaded, limp atmosphere that inevitably follows an extravagant party.

Sam walked across the gangplank onto the stern of the boat and spotted a couple of crewmembers off to one side talking – they were enjoying a lunchtime beer and some snacks. *At least not everyone was partying last night,* she thought. Sam walked past them – without bringing attention to herself – and entered the main cabin. There was one pair of blue espadrilles and two pairs of high-heeled shoes neatly placed on the carpet just to the side as she walked in. She removed her plimsolls and gave a second, sideways, glance at the eclectic mix of footwear before moving on. She went on a tour of the boat.

As beautiful as The *Alsace* was, it shared the subdued atmosphere of the quayside – it felt deserted, and although the cleaners had obviously been and gone, it smelled like the boat had experienced a party the night before. The windows were open to flood the cabin with the warm sea air, but the staleness of cigarettes and alcohol was pungent. It was eerily quiet and, despite the shoes she'd seen earlier, she was unsure whether there was anyone else on board. She decided to try the upstairs, but was beginning to think this wasn't a good idea after all. Perhaps calling ahead would have been better? She didn't have a clue where he was; he might not even be on the boat. Perhaps he didn't want to be surprised?

She climbed the stairs to the upper deck and as she turned back on herself, up the last two-three steps, saw her husband.

He was stood facing the Mediterranean with his hands on his hips. Sam would have sneaked up on him and shouted 'surprise!' if it weren't for the rest of the diabolical scene that her brain was frantically trying to process. She stood, rooted to the spot unable to move as the cogs in her head whirred away.

His khaki-coloured chinos were around his ankles, his eyes closed and his chin pointing slightly upwards to the azure-blue sky with an expression of complete ecstasy etched across his face. Besides the tiniest pair of red panties, the girl that was kneeling before him – on a plump white cushion – was completely naked. One of her hands was gently encouraging his testicles whilst the other worked confidently along his large erection, in perfect harmony with her mouth – gliding to and fro, back and forth. Sam stared at her; amazed that such a small girl could make such a large part of her husband's penis vanish – seemingly at will.

The only items of clothing that the second girl was wearing were the bottoms of a skimpy white bikini and a chunky gold necklace. She was sat smoking some sort of rolled-up cigarette and, up until the point she spotted Sam, looked like she didn't know what day it was.

Sam couldn't be sure but both girls looked like they were still teenagers, sylph-like bodies, long legs and small, pert breasts. But there was something about them that smacked of professionalism. Where the hell did a teenager get the confidence to do that to a forty-two-year-old-man for Christ's sake?

The girl in the bikini muttered something in a kind of Slavic language. Sam didn't understand a word, but decided she sounded bored. The girl then dropped her cigarette in an ashtray without bothering to stub it out. On hearing her friend, the other girl stopped what she was doing and wiped her mouth on the back of her hand.

Longmire opened his eyes and glared down at her.

"Bloody hell. Don't stop now, for Christ's sake. I'm nearly there!" There was real anguish, almost panic, in his voice.

But she was already moving away and Longmire seemed to realise that they weren't alone. He turned slightly.

"Fucking hell," he stammered, as he bent down and yanked up his trousers. "Sam, this isn't what it looks like!"

His wife shook her head. Andrew Longmire had come out with some stupid, cringe worthy comments over the years, but this one just about took the biscuit. Well, this was going to be interesting. What was it exactly if it wasn't what it looked like?

"Well, what is it then, Andrew?" she asked, folding her arms.

As soon as his stumpy legs and rapidly withering penis was safely tucked away, somehow Longmire managed to go on the offensive. "Never mind about that. What the fuck are you doing here?"

114

"I thought I'd surprise you, darling," said Sam, raising a single eyebrow – her voice laden with contempt.

Longmire was pulling his T-shirt over his head. The two escorts slipped into their tiny, but immaculate, cover-up dresses and collected their belongings – which, from what Sam could see, consisted of Prada handbags, Calvin Klein sunglasses and a multi-coloured assortment of condoms. They went downstairs and carried their shoes, as they giggled their way across the gangplank to join the throngs of people milling around the jetty.

"Look, let's just calm down a little, shall we?"

"Just fuck off, Andrew!" Sam turned to leave.

"Sam, come on. It's been a hell of a week – I've probably worked 60–70 hours. I just needed a bit of a release. It's a tough market at the moment."

Sam turned back to her husband – her eyes wide open – trying to make sense of the pathetic defence that her idiotic husband had just offered.

"Excuse me? You've had a bit of a busy week so you thought it would be OK to pay two hookers to fuck your brains out?"

"Don't be so bloody crass, Sam," replied Longmire. He actually looked shocked at his wife's language and he paused for a moment. "That's not what I meant at all." Although his voice trailed off at the end, giving Sam the distinct impression that she'd understood completely.

"Listen, Sam, you've got no idea the pressure that I'm under at the moment. I'm trying to provide for you and Simon, sometimes it's tough at the top."

Sam shook her head again.

"Andrew, you're a total wanker. I don't care if you run a bank or the bloody country, it doesn't make it all right for you to screw around!"

With that, Sam turned and left the yacht. She didn't know where she was going to go, but she knew she needed to be on her own.

A few minutes later, Sam Longmire found herself in one of the chairs placed along the promenade. She was looking back across at the shops and hotels along the Crossett in a sort of daze, thinking about what she'd just witnessed. She was angry; of course, who wouldn't be, she thought. Catching your own husband – literally – with his trousers down gave any woman the right to be upset. But there was something about the image of the young girl kneeling before her husband that stabbed away at her indignation. It felt like her mind was trying to remove the raw anger and replace it instead with some rational explanation of what had just happened. She closed her eyes, determined to resist the mind games – the explanation was simple; her husband was a total arsehole full stop.

But as much as she tried, she couldn't prevent her thoughts from returning to the inevitable. A seagull landed on the railing a few feet away and Sam watched it preen. It seemed even the wildlife in this place was self-absorbed about appearances. She then thought about what she really saw when she was stood watching them on the upper deck. It wasn't her husband's unfaithfulness that hit her the hardest. It was the exquisite look of pleasure written across his face – the expression she'd never seen before, the one she'd never been able to induce. That, and the complete lack of inhibition on the girl's part that Sam knew she could also never match. Presumably, the latter begat the former.

Those thoughts whirled around in her head, as she sat and looked at the wealthy shoppers strolling along the Crossett. A middle-aged couple were just leaving a boutique laden with three or four parcels and bags. They kissed before moving further along the pavement. Sam watched them walk away, no doubt discussing their plans for an expensive lunch.

She then turned and looked back over to the marina and the floating palaces. *Actually, just how bad is all this?* she found herself asking. She was as shocked as she was embarrassed that the question, unbidden, had popped into her head, but didn't see any harm in offering an answer. Her husband had paid someone to do something that, no matter how hard she tried, she just couldn't seem to be able to do. Well, not in the way the girl did it – anyway! And it was Sam that still had the financial security that came with being Andrew Longmire's wife. Security – that's all that she'd ever wanted – ever. And she still had it.

She stood up and started walking, wondering where to go for lunch.

Chapter Twenty-Three

It was going to be one of those humid July days in Washington DC. Originally, built on a swamp, the city could be clammy even at 8.45 am. The temperature was already twenty-four degrees Celsius and the humidity a muggy 62%. Nonetheless, and ditching convention, President George W. Bush actually walked the short distance from the White House to the adjacent Treasury Building at 1500 Pennsylvania Avenue. As agreed, he met Chuck J. K. Whiteman II on the steps outside the building.

Before his new boss had arrived, Whiteman had been studying the bronze statue of Alexander Hamilton – the First US Secretary to the Treasury – on the south side of the Treasury Building. On the front of the base of the statue was inscribed:

ALEXANDER HAMILTON

1757–1804

FIRST SECRETARY OF THE TREASURY

SOLDIER, ORATOR, STATESMAN, CHAMPION OF CONSTITUTIONAL UNION,

REPRESENTATIVE GOVERNMENT AND

NATIONAL INTEGRITY

He had read it before. Almost forty years earlier, he had stood right here with his father. Chuck Whiteman Senior had taught history for many years and had been an avid fan of the man and his values. He had spoken to the young Whiteman many times about Hamilton and his achievements. He wondered what his father would have said if he had lived to see this day – his own son about to walk in the footsteps of his hero.

Whiteman was stood imagining how history might record his own contribution to the country he loved.

CHUCK WHITEMAN JR
CHIEF ARCHITECT OF FINANCIAL DERIVATIVES
AND SEVENTY-FORTH SECRETARY TO THE TREASURY

When the President arrived, the two men shook hands warmly and entered the building – grateful for the comfortable temperature of its corridors. They walked through to the north wing and into the ornate Cash Room to meet the guests that had been invited to the ceremony that would see Whiteman appointed to his new role. The ex-CEO of Silvermans Investment Bank, like the vast majority of his fellow citizens, had never set foot in the room.

When he did so, he was awestruck. He thought it looked like an Italian Palazzo. It was of double height; its walls were made from several different coloured marble and the balcony, which ran around the perimeter of the room – midway between the floor and ceiling – had an elegant bronze balustrade. The defining feature of the room however, were the three giant golden chandeliers that hanged from the high ceiling on thick gilded chains. It isn't a room that anyone can attend a meeting in and not feel some sense of history about what's happening.

This was certainly true of Whiteman. As he entered and caught a glimpse of his wife, two children and his mother he felt the sense of history and a rather large lump form in his throat. Other guests included a handful of current and past Bush administration Cabinet officials, a smattering of Silvermans' employees and both Alan Greenspan and Ben Bernanke, the immediate past and current Chairs of the Federal Reserve. Whiteman's eyes met Greenspan's, and he remembered their fireside chat in Jackson Hole the year before. Whiteman knew that the market was with him – for the moment at least, he was right and Professor Rajan was wrong. He smiled: Greenspan didn't reciprocate as President Bush started proceedings.

"Please be seated and thank you for coming. Good morning.

"I'm pleased to be here at the Department of Treasury, to stand in one of its most historic rooms. One hundred years ago, the vaults of the Cash Room were stacked from floor to ceiling with bank notes and coins and bullion – right here in this room. Today, there is no longer any cash in this room, but there's a lot of talent. This historic space reminds us of our responsibility to treat the people's money with respect. And in a few moments, Chief Justice John Roberts will swear in a man that every American can have faith in – Chuck Whiteman."

There was a round of applause from the guests. Whiteman smiled a broad grin and acknowledged the many friendly faces he knew in the room.

"Chuck comes to this position with a lifetime of experience in business and finance. One of the most important tasks facing Chuck is to continue his lifelong commitment to financial deregulation and prevent the Federal Government from burdening our economy with excessive rules that will drive jobs and capital overseas. He's going to be a watchdog to prevent creeping over-regulation and continue his work in derivatives."

Whiteman looked back once again at Greenspan to raise his eyebrows and reinforce the President's comments. The ex-Fed Chairman was looking in the other direction.

Approximately one hour after saying goodbye to his wife and family outside the Cash Room, the new and emboldened Secretary to the Treasury was enjoying the view from his new office. Everywhere he looked, there were landmark buildings that represented the mechanics of government of which he was now a very important part. It reinforced the significance of his new job. Giving up the CEO role at Silvermans had been a wrench, but his successful banking career had allowed him to move beyond wealth. From now on, it was about power and legacy: he'd be making decisions that would directly impact the financial future of all Americans. As he sat looking out of the window, he beamed with the confidence of newly acquired authority.

One of his three mobiles interrupted his thoughts. The ringtone was a distinctive tune and told him that it was the important phone – the other two were used for work and family respectively. He recognised the number on the display, inserted the earphones and slipped the mobile back into his suit pocket so his hands were free.

"Whiteman."

"Chuck, it's Lloyd. I'm just calling to congratulate you on your appointment. I'm sorry I couldn't be there today, but it's fantastic for Silvermans to have an ex-CEO standing shoulder to shoulder with the most powerful man on earth. We've all just been watching your moment on CNBC – how do you feel?"

Lloyd Sinclair – the new CEO of Silvermans – had taken over from where Whiteman had left off and had been handpicked by the former CEO. The two men went back a long way.

"Thank you, Lloyd. I feel pretty good to tell you the truth. How are things at the bank?" Whiteman's six-foot three-inch frame took him to the other side of his office in a few steps where he closed the solid wooden door purposefully; he knew Sinclair hadn't called to congratulate him.

"They're great Chuck, well for the moment at least." There was a slight pause, which Whiteman chose to ignore, and Sinclair continued. "I've been going through the numbers with the CFO, 2006 is probably going to be the best year ever for us."

Anticipating a 'but' on the horizon, Whiteman responded.

"And long may it continue, Lloyd. I have every confidence in your ability to keep producing the numbers."

He was in the middle of his office now, holding his putter with four or five golf balls at his size eleven feet. His baldhead gleamed as a shaft of light flooded the room and he focussed his attention on the shot ahead. He gently tapped one of white balls towards the Auto-Putt returner – a Christmas present from his son. He missed, scowled and moved another ball into position. The sunlight picked out the slightest twitch of the veins that ran along his temples as he readjusted his rimless glasses.

Sinclair cleared his throat. "I guess from listening to you and Mr Bush, we should still be 'Dancing with Wolves'?"

There was another pause. Whiteman gently nodded his head at the euphemism – he'd been expecting it. He missed a second putt and stared at the gift on the other side of the office. Another spasm jerked across the side of his head.

"Listen, Lloyd, I can assure you as long as I'm Treasury Secretary, we're not going to do anything stupid. Sure, at some time, the party's going to ease up, but until then, you need to hold your nerve and make the most of it."

In his office in New York, Sinclair was massaging his short-trimmed beard. "And we're still OK holding these things…you know, on our balance sheet? As house prices adjust downwards, we're coming under pressure from counter-parties to post collateral," he replied – the tension in his voice audible.

Whiteman rolled his eyes, as he moved another ball into position. He remembered why he had nicknamed his successor 'Grow a pair, Sinclair'. He could imagine his replacement at the other end of the line – one eyebrow higher than the other and a wrinkled nose, his usual facial contortion when confusion prevailed.

"Just keep doing what you're doing, Lloyd. I promise you, the moment I see the writing on the wall, I'll let you know and you, and, well; you know the rest."

"Thank you, Chuck. That's been very helpful." Sinclair's facial muscles relaxed on the news and had returned his expression to normal by the time he'd replaced the receiver.

Whiteman steadied himself and tapped again. This time, the putt landed in the returning target and activated the sensor. The ball recoiled and came back to rest alongside the putter in his hand – like an obedient boomerang. He smiled at Sinclair's misplaced concern that the Timberwolf cohort of derivatives might boomerang. He knew it wouldn't; the Timberwolf series of CDOs was his baby, he'd even named it. They had been a licence to print money for Silvermans and if it ever looked like it was in trouble, he was now in a position to do something about it. He relaxed into his next putt.

Chapter Twenty-Four

It was early July and a beautiful day had become a glorious evening in London. At ground level at least, it was a very agreeable twenty-two degrees and the light breeze that coursed around the streets of Knightsbridge brought further respite to those, like Alice and her two colleagues, who had emerged from subterranean London.

Below ground, it was a completely different story. The tube was often insufferable in the summer but the last week or so, temperatures had soared as the European heat wave had inconsiderately decided to embrace the UK. Every few minutes, the PA announcements on the network were superfluously reminding commuters to drink water and to sit down if they felt unwell. The reference to finding a seat was the source of endless caustic comment from commuters who were forced to stand in temperatures that were approaching forty degrees.

So, Alice and her two colleagues were grateful for the air that greeted them, as they emerged from the tube station and spilled out onto Brompton Road. They shuffled along the pavement that was now thick with the throng of pedestrians. Most were heading home, walking deliberately slowly in order to delay the inevitable – the moment that they would have to head below ground and enter the thermal sauna that the Piccadilly Line had become. The three women, all dressed in ball gowns for their evening appointment in the Great Room at the Grosvenor House Hotel on Park Lane, had only travelled two stops – Hyde Park Corner and Knightsbridge after beginning their journey from Green Park.

Alice was in a surprisingly good mood despite the fact that she had had to give up her seat. On one of the very rare occasions that she'd been able to obtain one, a pregnant woman had then stood right in front of her. She hadn't minded – of course. But what she did mind was the expectation – the entitlement almost – of the woman, as she stood in there in righteous indignation. She'd been wearing, rather gloatingly thought Alice, an official TfL 'Baby on Board' badge on the lapel of her blouse and as that bitch Camilla wasn't going to move, she felt it necessary to do so. Then, as only Camilla can, her boss had volunteered maternal guidance to the 'mum to be' and told her how the next few months would 'look like'. That was Camilla's favourite phrase at the moment. '*Alice, what does success look like for you?*' The fact that Camilla was able to make a convincing stab advising on a subject she clearly knew nothing about explained why she was the new managing director of Cornwall PR Agency. In her 55 years, Camilla had never had a child and didn't have a maternal bone in her skeletal frame of a body.

She could, however, talk for England and whilst doing so persuade clients to part with huge amounts of money for the PR advice that she did clearly know an awful lot about. In fact, most of the property organisations that were shortlisted for tonight's awards ceremony at The Grosvenor were Cornwall clients. But first, Camilla, Alice and Rachel were heading for a glass of wine in Beauchamp Place.

The wine bar wasn't busy, which made it even more annoying that the service was slow and the staff unhelpful. The three ladies sat outside and were ignored on several occasions before Camilla took control and practically shouted at a very tall waitress for a bottle of Pinot, three glasses and a jug of water. The tall girl presented them with her best '*you're inconveniencing me*' look before trotting off on her giraffe-like legs in the direction of the bar.

"What award are you presenting, Camilla?" asked Alice, as the three settled into the modest plastic chairs that accompanied the modest plastic table perched on the narrow pavement.

"Young Surveyor of the Year, darling. Let's hope he's a guy and absolutely delish." Giggled her boss.

"You're the worst, Cam. Really, you need to act like a managing director now you know," tormented Rachel.

"When I'm on stage, I will, darling – I promise. But seriously, if it's a man – and let's face it, this is the bloody property industry we're talking about – I'm going to introduce him to Alice. She needs all the help she can get!" Rachel laughed, right on cue. Alice raised her eyebrows at the pair of them.

The waitress arrived still wearing the sour face from a few minutes before and served the wine – tipping it rather than pouring it – carelessly rather than courteously. Cam let it go, but appeared to take obvious delight in telling her that she'd forgotten the water.

That was one of several other annoying facts about Cam, thought Alice. Although she was a skinny bitch – way beyond slim, borderline anorexic actually

– she had no problem attracting men. That was a fact – a depressing one, but a fact nonetheless. And she didn't just attract idiots either; she somehow persuaded the good ones into thinking she was worth the effort. Cam's current squeeze, Robert, was in his early forties, owned his own company and had a body to die for. Alice had no idea what he was doing with her bitch of a boss.

Alice gave Cam an exaggerated, "Thank you" and a glassy stare.

"Oh, come on, Alice. You haven't been on a date in months. A gorgeous, young healthy girl like you – you should be riding some young stud two or three times a day, not that fucking push bike of yours!"

Alice just shook her head with her mouth half open.

Catching her employee's expression, Cam pushed ahead.

"I'm serious. We're human and humans are meant to have sex. If you'd invested half as much time in finding a man as you did on that stupid 4,000-mile bike ride, you'd be fixed up by now."

Bloody hell, here we go again, and it was only 1,500 km.

There was no stopping her boss – she was on one of her rants. She took a quick sip of wine and continued.

"Along with vaginal atrophy, Alice – which is obviously, and directly, related to sexual abstinence – there are a host of other disagreeable illnesses that are caused by not shagging frequently enough. I shan't bore you with the details of the really painful ones, but one of them is looking at me with a face like a slapped arse. So, come on, Alice, drink up and relax for goodness' sake."

Alice grinned, unconvincingly, as the stroppy waitress finally arrived with the water. *Now, she really has got a face like a slapped proverbial*, thought Alice. She hoped that Cam was exaggerating when she mentioned that she looked unhappy – she couldn't stand the thought of looking miserable. Generally, she was fine, but annoyingly, Cam had hit on something. She did take life a little too seriously; she often felt detached in certain social situations and, particularly around men, had serious trust issues. Colleagues had often told her that she needed to lighten up. She'd promised herself that she would do just that – starting tonight. She was determined.

Why Cam was quite so fascinated by her non-existent sex life, she had no idea, but ever since Alice had made the mistake of telling them about 'Joe and the train', Cam and Rachel had felt obliged to save her from herself. They were like two older sisters proffering advice to a younger, naïve sibling. But from what she could tell, both Cam and Rachel were borderline polyandrous. They had both been married and divorced – in Rachel's case at least twice – and neither seemed the least bit perturbed about being in more than one relationship at any single time. Alice was no prude, but the 'ugly sisters' were on a different level! Taking counsel from Cam and Rachel about steady, long-term relationships was like being advised by Enron on business ethics.

Alice was about to steer the conversation around to work, but remembered her promise just in time. This left a pause that was too long for Cam to feel comfortable with, so she took the initiative once more. She emptied her wine glass, and matter-of-factly, said:

"You'd soon have a smile back on your face if you had a boyfriend, Alice. I was with Robert again last night and we didn't get to sleep until 2 am! But I still woke up with a grin from ear-to-ear. In fact, I was thinking about letting him do it again whilst I was cleaning my teeth but remembered I'd promised you two I'd be in early for the pre-meet!"

Oh my God, please shut up.

Rachel was almost rolling on the floor.

"OK. OK. I promise to smile and I promise to make more of an effort in the boyfriend department." Alice grinned a sardonic smile before emptying her glass. "Come on, keep up then, ladies."

Ten minutes later, the Cornwall PR representatives were ready to hit the Grosvenor Hotel.

Chapter Twenty-Five

Their taxi pulled up just before 7 pm as much of the property industry was ambling along Park Lane having cut through one of the many east-west corridors that connect it to the most popular office locations of the West End. Grosvenor Street, Mounts Street, South Street and Curzon Street were particularly well-trodden and provided plenty of scope for the guests to enjoy a pub or wine bar along the way.

Inside The Grosvenor House, the hotel staff and event organisers had been busy. Alice stood, mesmerised, on one of the sweeping staircases that conveyed the diners from the bars and reception areas on the ground floor down into the subterranean Great Room. It was a sight that never failed to impress. She'd read somewhere that, almost incredulously, it was originally an ice-skating rink where, at the tender age of seven, Queen Elizabeth II had learnt to skate. Seeing it in all its splendour this evening, that was hard to imagine.

Tonight it would accommodate 1,200 guests, so Alice looked out over a vast floor area with 120 immaculately and identically presented round tables; their allotted chairs circling them with a degree of geometric precision that even Rupert would have approved of.

She momentarily panicked. *Bloody hell,* she thought, *he better not be here tonight. I can't imagine what that prick would wear to an event like this.* She shook her head, trying to expunge the thought and focussed on the view across the ballroom once again.

The tables were decked out in pristine white tablecloths with obligatory cutlery, glassware and golden three-pronged candelabrum. There were calligraphically designed menus on each table, which stood in between the red and white wine bottles opened and ready to be consumed. Finally, there was a large table number supported by an elegant silver stand so that guests could locate their places. The chairs were fitted with a generous fabric that was secured at the back – where the material gathered – by large decorative bows. For every circle of chairs decorated with yellow bows, there were five blue ones surrounding it and the pattern continued across the vast space – it reminded Alice of a blossoming field of forget-me-nots in early spring.

The three women continued their descent, found their table and introduced themselves to the other guests. Cornwall was a sponsor so Cam had managed to secure a position towards the front where the presentations would be made. The Master of Ceremonies, wearing the distinctive red toastmaster tailcoat, took to the podium to say grace and 'Long live the Queen'. Then, and only then, did he allow his guests to be seated.

Nearly two hours later, Alice had been true to her word and enjoyed the evening indulging in a little too much wine and diligently avoiding the subject of work in the various conversations with the other guests. The alcohol had done its job. Alice was relaxed as Cam was invited to the stage for her big moment.

Cam stood where the Master of Ceremonies had and declared what an honour it was for Cornwall PR to be associated with such a prestigious event and how delighted she was to be able to present this award. She opened the envelope that had been handed to her a few seconds earlier.

"It gives me great pleasure to announce the Young Property Personality of the Year is Joseph McGrath from Allied English."

There was polite applause: there had already been seven awards and fatigue was beginning to set in. Most people wanted to continue their conversations at the bars or head home and a degree of restlessness was evident. Alice quietly sipped her wine. As she swallowed, she rubbed her throat. She was hoarse from the raised voice that had been required to talk to the elderly gentleman sitting next to her.

Cam peered out across the ballroom, shielding her eyes from the powerful stage-lights directed towards the platform by holding her hand up to her brow, and looked for the winner. McGrath's table was located a couple behind Cornwall's and he was now stood up slipping into his jacket that had been hung on the back of his chair. As he made his way to the stage, various people were congratulating him. He had to squeeze between chairs where diners had rearranged the furniture to make themselves more comfortable for the long evening of award presentations. A mischievous grin contorted her face as Cam watched him approach the stage.

Even in a dinner jacket, McGrath appeared athletic. His six-foot frame was slim of waist and broad shouldered and the black cummerbund was pulled taught across a flat stomach – an achievement unimaginable for the vast majority of other male guests. His unruly, collar-length black hair was another feature that set him apart from his, generally, formally coiffed counterparts.

The gap between the chairs of the two tables just before the stage was almost non-existent and McGrath had to ask a rather elderly gentleman to move.

"Excuse me, sir, would you mind whilst I pass by?"

The stuffy old man shuffled reluctantly towards the table to make room and swore under his breath to the young woman sitting next to him.

But Alice wasn't listening. Not any more anyway. It was the accent. The instant she heard the distinctive pronunciation with the happy cadence, her heart raced. The last time she'd heard it was on that train – *'Hi, I'm Joe. Nice to meet you, Alice.'*

She looked up to face him but he had already moved past to get to the stage. All she saw was the back of him, as he walked away and then climbed the few steps onto the platform, but she was still confident it was him. How many property professionals wore their hair that way? Finally, he ambled back across the stage towards Cam allowing Alice to see his face.

The strong jawline and the large, dark-brown eyes framed by his dark locks – it was Joe! She could barely contain herself. An incredulous dazed expression consumed her face. She daren't move for fear that the effort would snap her out of the trance. Her body was entering fight-or-flight mode; her breathing quickened and her heart rate shot up. She was now alert, buzzing and full of energy – a complete contrast to the calm, relaxed mood of just a few moments ago. Suddenly, it didn't feel like she had consumed any alcohol at all.

Cam didn't give McGrath a say in the matter and kissed him on the cheek, as she presented him with his award. She then placed one arm around his waist and the other on his shoulder as the photographer snapped away. Alice noticed how her boss' touch lingered, brushing up against Joe and remaining there a few moments longer than the occasion deemed appropriate – she was practically seducing him in front of the UK property industry for goodness' sake!

'Bitch!' muttered Alice to herself, as she stared up at the stage.

"Pardon?" asked the elderly gentleman sat next to her.

Alice tipped her head to the side and smiled disarmingly. She'd spent the last hour practically shouting at this man and wasn't convinced that he'd heard half of what she'd said. Now, the moment she whispered something she'd rather keep to herself, he'd developed the auditory system of a barn owl.

McGrath was no more than twenty feet away from her now. But the stage lighting prevented him from seeing anyone in the audience. Cam was whispering in his ear as they left the stage together and the Master of Ceremonies moved onto the next award.

Twenty-five minutes later, the ceremony was over and McGrath approached the Cornwall table – just as Cam had requested when they were exiting the stage. He headed straight for the MD of Cornwall PR and received another kiss on the cheek for his troubles, as she greeted him like he was some long-lost friend. McGrath glanced around the other guests as if he was searching for someone.

Alice was in the toilets. She wanted to gather herself, freshen up, reapply a little make-up but most importantly, persuade herself to go and speak to him. She sat in the cubicle as the cackle of conversations continued just the other side of her door. She was finally ready. She got up, one more visit to the mirror for a final inspection and then out into the masses. She stood on one of the large spiral staircases and surveyed all before and below her. She could see the Cornwall PR table and spotted the small group off to one side. Cam was holding court now and Rachel, Joe and a couple of other gentlemen were dutifully attending to her every word.

As she descended the stairs, she thought about Cannes and the missed opportunity. She thought about the train journey and her behaviour at the station and winced. She approached the table, hesitated then swallowed and steeled herself '*you can do this*'. He was now no more than five feet away.

She walked straight up to Cam and McGrath. She smiled and apologised to her boss for the interruption. Then she looked straight at him and said, "Excuse me, I'm sure you don't remember but—"

"Alice Thomas – how lovely to see you again," said McGrath without a moment's hesitation.

He took her hand and gently lifted it up to his lips where he bowed his head to kiss the back of it – all the time looking into her hazel eyes. She detected a hint of expensive cologne, as he encroached into her personal space – his large frame almost incongruous against the gentle, lavender fragrance that swirled around her.

Oh my God, he's even more handsome than I remembered! Trust him, Alice. You can trust him. Did I actually tell him my last name?

Cam, Rachel and the others were suddenly consigned to reluctant onlookers – relegated to the role of passive observers of mutual wonderment taking place before them.

Alice was wearing an off-the-shoulder emerald green dress that hugged her body, as it tapered around her buttocks and upper thighs. The dress stopped about three inches above the knee – in that border region between acceptable business fashion and downright sexy. The length was perfect to display the hard-won muscle definition her sport had afforded her.

She wore a sparkling hazel pendant that nestled slightly above, and in between, her breasts. She still had the smart bob haircut, which, combined with the off-the-shoulder dress, accentuated her long, slim neck. With the help of her heels, Alice's eyes were now able to meet McGrath's on equal terms. She stood virtually six-feet tall in her Christian Louboutin dress shoes.

Alice stole a glance at Cam. She was no longer smiling; her lips were pursed, and the puckered lines drew her mouth into a small ugly hole. *Yep, just like a cat's arse,* thought Alice.

"And how's the cycling going?" asked Joe.

Oh, what a smile. Don't screw this up, Alice, she looked up at him to answer.

Cam looked at Joe and then Alice and then back at Joe. She then shot an enquiring glance towards Rachel, who simply shrugged her shoulders.

Alice could feel herself flushing, but started to laugh about her 'Cycle to Cannes' expedition and her sighting of him on the Croisette when Cam interrupted their little tête-à-tête. She didn't do passive, and appeared underwhelmed that McGrath's interest in her had waned considerably since one of her junior PR associates had come back from the bog.

"Alice, my dear, and how do *you* know Joe?" she asked, ostentatiously twirling one of her over-sized diamond earrings, as she glared at her employee. Her stare – as hard and icy cold as her jewellery – made it clear to Alice that it was less of a question and more of a patronising slight. McGrath gave Cam a sideward glance, as if he'd detected the tone.

"Cam, this is *Joe*; it's *Joe*...from the train!" Alice looked back and smiled again, as she took hold of his arm.

There was a pause. The cogs whirred away, slowly.

"Oh my God, you mean *Joe the Steam*?" goaded Cam in a pathetic Welsh accent. The penny had dropped – Joseph McGrath – Joe.

McGrath snorted and leaned into the CEO of Cornwall, looming over her.

As Cam looked up at him, he had a face like concrete. "I'd stick to PR if I were you, lovely girl," he said in an exaggerated rich accent, but loud enough for others to hear.

Rachel covered her mouth to contain spontaneous giggles, but her shoulders heaved, giving her away.

"Well, I think you'll need to excuse us, ladies. Alice and I have quite some catching up to do." With that, McGrath took Alice's arm and turned away from them, guiding her back up the sweeping staircase. Cam was rooted to the spot, her mouth opening and closing but unable to speak. Alice felt like Cinderella; she had been to the ball, her prince was whisking her away on his arm and she'd left the ugly sisters behind.

They found a bar and she sat on a stool whilst he stood, as they faced one another.

"Phew, for a moment there, I thought you fancied my boss," smiled Alice, as she took a sip of her drink.

He feigned to choke on his and returned the mischievous grin. "I hope you're not disappointed Alice" – putting his hand on her thigh and moving a little closer – "but I prefer women to stick-insects."

She laughed out loud. *No, that's not a disappointment at all, Joe McGrath.* She moved her legs slightly to allow him to move a little closer; they tingled as the surge of anticipation built and she felt the rush of blood pulsating in her groin. As Joe revealed how he'd seen the photo in the *MIPIM Daily News* and then dug around to find out more, Alice's stomach twisted and knotted with nerves. That's how he knew her last name; that's how he knew she worked for Cornwall PR and that's how he knew she'd be here tonight.

Alice Thomas began to have second thoughts about serendipity, as she gazed into those big, brown eyes.

Chapter Twenty-Six

Paula was stood in the kitchen of Ross' flat and shouting across the island counter at him. At the end of another utterly pleasurable assignation, he'd gone and ruined it by asking for more money – again! This was a long way away from the start of their relationship just over a year ago.

She'd fancied the pants off him when they met at the gym and had flirted outrageously to get his attention. Ross was twenty years younger than her, handsome – with a god-like body – and was an ex professional footballer to boot. He'd been open with her from the start; told her he was happy to oblige, but that there had to be a commercial element to the arrangement. In the beginning, that just added to the excitement for Paula.

Yes, she was paying for sex – so what? Men did it all the time, so why couldn't she? Anyway, there were two big advantages to the 'little arrangement' that assuaged her conscience on the rare occasion it veered towards self-reproach. Firstly, it was the best sex she'd ever had in her life. And secondly, she was in complete control for once. He was where she wanted him to be as often as she wanted. For a year, that had given her a sense of power that was every bit as new and gratifying as the sex.

And they were just the pull factors. The push one was just as strong. In ten years of marriage, Paul had never taken her opinions seriously and constantly told her what to do. No wonder she had to reach out and take something else occasionally. It was part deprivation that had led to her relationship with Ross in the first place.

But at this moment, on a cold Monday afternoon, standing in the kitchen of his flat the tackiness of it all struck her. She was having sex sessions with a man practically half her age behind her husband's back and using her husband's money to pay for it! And the man she was paying was stood in front of her demanding more money. What the fuck was she doing? There was nothing exciting about it anymore – it was cheap and dirty.

No, she was cheap and dirty. As she stood there staring at Ross, she could feel his cold, slimy embrace in her panties. Her luxurious Carine Gilson underwear spoilt by a cheap Gigolo. She winced at the place she now found herself in.

"Not again, Angus! I'm not paying you even more fucking money? You're getting nearly £200 an hour from our little arrangement. That's more than most lawyers earn for goodness' sake! If you want more money, I suggest you finish that Information fucking Technology course of yours and get a proper job. The answer's no!"

She made for the door.

"So you're not agreeing to the new terms?"

"Angus, will you listen? It's over. There won't be any new terms – just fuck off. You know, you're such a Dickhead sometimes!"

He used his large, muscular body to block her path and grabbed her arms.

"Before you go, it's only fair that I share something with you, Paula."

Chapter Twenty-Seven

"Let go! You're hurting my arms, you bastard," complained Paula.

"Just sit down, shut the fuck up for once in your life and look at the screen!"

Ross maintained his grip on her upper arms and only released them once he had practically thrown her into the chair in front of the computer. Her incredulous stare, and the fact that she was rubbing her biceps, told Ross she was taken aback by his forcefulness. He didn't care. He was getting fed up with Paula Poorish – *she was as shallow as the rest of them*. And he'd been thinking a lot about 'them' in the past few weeks.

'Angus Ross, the professional footballer', had had no problem attracting 'them'. In fact they'd come flocking and he'd loved it. But he soon discovered that without the label and without the money, 'Angus Ross the nobody in particular' was of zero interest to most of these shallow fucking gold-diggers. That hurt – a lot.

After just about surviving his alcohol-induced self-pity phase after his injury, Ross realised he needed a plan B. Becoming the Personal Trainer at the exclusive Spa and Gym in nearby Melton was actually a logical step. As an ex-professional sportsman, he knew more than most about fitness, exercise and diet and he still had the physique and the looks to boot. He was entrusted with the health and wellbeing of his clients – many of whom were female, wealthy but surprisingly insecure about their own abilities. He would then go to work; building their confidence and, where appropriate, lavishing praise on them week in and week out in the knowledge that many, just like Paula Poorish, were not receiving that kind of attention at home.

By no means all, but enough of his more vulnerable clients would be deluded by his attentiveness – normally those predisposed to flattery – and let him know that there were other areas of their life that he could help with. At that point, once they'd committed, he'd reveal that he was an escort and discovered it rarely spooked them; in fact, it usually had the opposite effect and heightened the interest in their own proposition. Most of his wealthy clients wanted to avoid complexity – they wanted sexual gratification but they absolutely needed to avoid the drama of a relationship that might end badly. Paying an escort who just happened to be your trusted personal trainer was a win/win. Ross was considered to be a one-stop-shop for all things physical – two workouts for the hassle of one. So they'd pay him to train them and then pay him again to screw them.

Making those shallow bitches like Paula pay to have sex with him at least offered Ross a kind of retribution and, frankly, helped service his debts. He'd found it difficult to give up completely the trappings of his former life; although he'd toned it down a bit, the Audi, the holidays and the rent on the flat weren't cheap.

So when the circumstances were right, Ross would take it to the next level. He wouldn't make a habit out of it, but on the couple of occasions, he'd raised the stakes; the financial rewards had been excellent. He'd decided that Paula's moment had arrived.

Paula was sat in the chair fidgeting and her eyes flitted around as she waited for Ross to say or do something – anything. He stood behind her and used the mouse and the keyboard to bring the screen to life. The DVD that he had prepared and was already pre-installed – just in case the conversation turned out as it had done – whirred into life. He stood back in anticipation. He was going to enjoy this.

The audio gave it away before her eyes were able to take-in the visual.

"Harder, Angus, harder!"

It was her voice. They were her screams. Then the image suddenly became clear and Paula's face appeared. Her eyes were glazed, but they were peering directly at the camera as *someone* was entering her from behind and she was leaning over an island counter. It was Ross and it was in his kitchen, she knew that instantly, but you couldn't see his face – it had been deliberately blurred so that he was as unrecognisable as she was identifiable. Ross smiled, as he stood watching his artistic creation.

After two to three seconds, there was an amateurish edit and different footage flashed across the screen. This time, the picture was even clearer and Paula once again appeared to be looking straight at the recorder – just like some porn-film director was there telling her what to do. She was on a bed, this time astride a man – but again, his face was blurred out – as her small breasts reacted to the pelvic movements from below. She was wearing her red and black Basque and one of the shoulder straps had slipped. Strands of hair had escaped the bun, now lopsided and no longer in the central position on top of her head and were hanging loosely around her face. The rivulets of sweat were crawling across her flushed cheeks.

After a few seconds, Paula looked away and screamed for him to stop.

He pressed a button and the screen went blank, as he walked away from the desk – *the stupid bitch didn't have a clue.*

She bowed her head and buried her face in her hands. Ross could hear the laboured breaths behind her fingers, short jerky rasps as if she was struggling for air. He could see her ribs through her T-shirt expanding and contracting, unnaturally, just like an athlete's immediately post workout. Suddenly, she shot up and bolted for the bathroom. He could hear the empty retches from her slight chest through the door.

When she finally emerged from the toilet, Ross was seated, leaning back in a chair and hands behind his head. He smiled an almost a playful grin.

"Why the fuck did you film us, you sick bastard?" demanded Paula. She stared down at him, her white-knuckle fists trembling, as she crushed the toilet paper she'd used to clean her face. He noticed her voice was shaking.

"Be careful, Paula. Remember, you're the one cheating on your husband. I'm going to leave it a few days before I decide what to do, but I guess I have three options." He was watching her closely for a reaction as he went through his list. His ability to obtain the financial rewards he wanted would, in part, depend on what she did next.

"I keep the films here for my own private pleasure;

I sell them to a number of different porn sites for others to enjoy;

Or I send them directly to your husband for him to enjoy."

Paula's reaction to his third option was even more satisfying than Ross dared to hope for and he knew in an instant what he was going to do with his DVD. Her shakes immediately surrendered to the full-blown body tremors that now visibly convulsed through her. He smiled to himself as he thought about her husband's money.

Paula grabbed her bag, but this time, sprinted for the door before he could think about stopping her.

Chapter Twenty-Eight

Lester could imagine the smug banker at the other end of the phone: His feet on the desk on the 22nd floor of the Silvermans' headquarters in Canary Wharf as he looked down – figuratively and literally – on the rest of London. Lester had been left hanging on the line whilst Rankin organised his social diary. He could hear him talking to his secretary about bloody canapés for some client reception at the bank for goodness' sake! God, if only Lester's life was that simple.

He managed a tormented smile. That's exactly what his insurance contracts were supposed to be of course – straightforward. If the housing market weakened, CDOs should fall in price and at the end of each day, there would be a balancing up. If the CDOs fell, his insurance contracts would go up in value and Lambda would receive collateral from the banks. But to Lester's horror, the opaque world of private insurance contracts didn't work that way. Although the housing market in the US was falling apart – everyone could see that now, the bonds and the CDOs held firm.

Apparently, there was no one else buying or selling precisely what Lambda had bet against – so there was no comparable market evidence to suggest what they were worth. So they were worth what Rankin at Silvermans said they were worth and the fate of Lambda and its employees were in his greedy, little paws.

His smile waned and he closed his eyes. He could visualise Rankin and his chief antagonist from school – George Watson. They were both from the same murky gene pond. They took delight in making other people's lives miserable and found ways to inflict as much unhappiness on those around them as possible. It was just another day at the office to Rankin; for Lester, it was about the very survival of Lambda and the livelihood of his employees. He sat and felt the wave of icy panic slowly take hold. His colleagues had all worked so hard to pull the strategy together and now it looked like it was all going to be taken away by the same sort of people that always took things away. He didn't want that to happen; he couldn't allow that to happen.

Ron Dale wasn't helping either. After shouting the odds at Lester on the conference call a few months earlier, he'd followed it up with a few shirty emails and cc'd all of the other investors. As a result, more members of the Consortium were now threatening to withdraw money once the redemption window opened. Lester needed to see some results – soon.

Finally, Rankin pulled himself away from his crab rolls and mini beef Yorkshires.

"Sorry about that, Lester. Now, where were we?" said Rankin. He said it with sufficient indifference, it was obvious to Lester he didn't much care where they had been.

"Simon, this simply can't be true," his body tensing, as he thought about what was at stake. "The bonds and CDOs that I've bet against are the worst ones possible. Our analysts and I handpicked them. The underlying data is getting worse by the day and ever more mortgages are defaulting, and you're trying to tell me that the value of my insurance contracts has actually decreased and that I need to post more collateral!"

A bored sigh came down the line. "Lester, we've discussed this before. The bonds that you shorted do not represent the subprime market generally – they were handpicked, you just confirmed that yourself. You can't expect your specific bets to follow the general market and it's not my fault that your strategy isn't working. Perhaps you identified the wrong characteristics and you're having problems accepting that."

Lester was sat looking out of the window. *No way,* he thought. *I didn't screw this up. We didn't screw this up. We're right.* He knew what the problem was – or rather, he suspected he knew, but had no way of proving it because the bank held all the information.

"And perhaps you're a lying bastard," he seethed, as he watched a pigeon walking along the ridge of a nearby roof; its head bobbing almost violently as it moved.

"And why would I be lying?" asked Rankin. He'd reclined in his chair and was inspecting his fingernails.

"Because, *you're* on the other side of the trade. You hold, at least some, of these contracts on your balance sheet and you can't afford to mark them properly. I knew you guys were stupid, Simon, but I had no idea that you were foolish enough to invest in your own toxic creations."

By the time Lester had finished, Rankin was sat bolt upright in his chair; his eyebrows had been drawn together as the skin knotted angrily across his forehead. Lloyd Sinclair's missives were terse, and almost always rude, and he had one right in front of him on his desk. No one outside the mortgage team was to know that Silvermans had these contracts on their balance sheet. If you leaked, you were fired – immediately with no pay-off. And you did not, under any circumstances, make collateral payments to counterparties without direct confirmation from Lloyd's team.

"Jesus, Lester, now you're being paranoid – I've told you before, we don't carry this exposure. Now get off the fucking phone and get *your* guys to wire *my* guys the money."

There was a click on the line and then nothing. Nothing: just a kind of hollow emptiness that matched the physical sensation Lester felt in his chest. He looked up again and let his gaze drift off through the window to the right and the row of six-storey red brick mansions. The beautiful terracotta brickwork encapsulated the most intricate designs and patterns. After a few moments however, Lester realised it was no use. Today was going to be too bloody awful; even the beauty of Pont Street wouldn't lift his spirits.

"Lester, the analysts are in the conference room. I'm sorry to hurry you, but they have been waiting there for twenty minutes. Troy is already back in with them." His secretary, Susan, had entered his room without him even noticing.

A few minutes later, Lester lumbered his way through the empty office to see his waiting colleagues. They were all in one room at the end of the corridor and he had to pass their abandoned workstations to get there; he swallowed as he took in the strangeness of the scene. Silent TVs with their news tickers still flying across the bottom of the screens, jackets on the backs of chairs and half-written reports on computer screens. The emptiness screamed at him. All those good times that fed the spirit of Lambda and made it what it was. The buzz of people – doing a job that mattered – exchanging ideas, full of energy and zest and now this.

He reached the end of the corridor and opened the door, the friction of the metal on metal causing the hinges to release a tormented creaking sound that gave Lester a start. It was loud enough to break up the few whispered exchanges that were taking place and jolted the room into an eerie silence. His heart sank as he noticed the body language of some of his younger colleagues. They were clutching at belongings, a coat, a purse or a coffee cup; others adjusted items of clothing. Ann was fingering her necklace as she determinedly held her stare out of the window; even as Lester walked right past her. That was the other thing he noticed; very few of them were looking at him as he arrived to speak to them.

"Firstly, I'm very sorry for keeping you waiting. I was on the phone to Silvermans, who I have been trying to speak to for well over a week, so I had to take the call I'm afraid. As you all know, what our analysis suggested would happen to US subprime mortgages is now happening. The developments that we need to see in the underlying mortgage market to make our insurance contracts pay-off are undeniable."

Lester was shifting awkwardly from foot to foot and he knew the nervous quiver in his voice was getting worse; each word seemed to tremble a little more than the last and his shortness of breath was becoming discernible.

"Well, the developments are undeniable to most people, *but* apparently not investment banks who continue to tell me that our insurance contracts are now worth less than when we purchased them.

"Ladies and gentlemen, I also need to apologise to each and every one of you. I know you're all committed financially, mentally and even physically to the success of *Credere*. Letting staff go is the last thing that I wanted to do and believe me, I have delayed this moment and put it off for as long as possible. But unless we do make the changes, I need to talk to you about, the fund will implode and we will lose everything. That's why I have had to agree to let the guys go that are not in this meeting room with us right now."

A stunned silence enveloped the room and Lester reluctantly observed as his colleagues processed the information. Ann seemed more determined than ever to continue her stare out of the window – her eyes began to swim and she blinked furiously to try to clear them. Under the cover of pretending to blow her nose, she dabbed them quickly with a tissue that she retrieved from under her sleeve.

She then stopped looking out of the window and raised her hand.

"Yes, Ann, go ahead," said Lester.

"Where are Sally and the rest of the team? I mean, where physically are they?"

Lester prepared to answer the question. He was stood at the front of the room leaning against a table with his arms settled around his girth and his feet turned inwards. Troy Burrows stood up and joined him.

"Lester, do you mind if I say a few words?" The CEO gestured for his colleague to continue.

"Before we go any further today, I want to tell you a few things that Lester's humility will prevent him from informing you himself." Troy had been with Lester longer than anyone and he was one of the few people that the CEO of Lambda had opened up to about how he felt about all of this. He was effectively Lambda's risk and finance officer – he knew the details of all the positions that Lambda was committed to as well as, and probably better, than Lester.

"Lester has paid each of the unfortunate employees that we have had to let go a sum of money from his own pocket, NOT from Lambda, that is much larger than they are entitled to receive through statutory redundancy payments. He has also made a personal commitment to hire them back the moment the fund recovers sufficiently to be able to do so. To a man and a woman, they have also all been allowed to keep their profit-share arrangements in *Credere*. So when we do make money, they'll get paid out even though they are no longer employees. Lester has also, and once again at his own expense, ensured that all of them have access to the best financial recruitment agency in London to help them find new jobs. I think Lester has done the very best for your colleagues, and believe me ladies and gentlemen, this could have been an awful lot worse.

"And so as painful as this is Ann" – at this point, Troy turned to her – "we have already spoken to Sally and the others today. They're next door in the serviced office accommodation with the recruitment agencies and management consultants."

Ann nodded at Troy and, for the first time that day, looked straight at Lester. She smiled, gave up all pretence of blowing her nose, as she required the use of the tissue once again and mouthed 'Thank You' to Lester.

"Ann, I know you'll want to see Sally, why don't we go there together now and you can talk to her yourself?" asked Lester.

He shuffled along next to Ann to meet his ex-colleagues – all the time wondering whether his weary shoulders would be able to bear the next burden.

Reducing the overheads of the business was going to help. But *Credere* had been required to sell part of its portfolio to pay the insurance premiums and collateral obligations, which, in turn, had substantially reduced the size of the fund. As Troy had reminded Lester, Silvermans had inserted a clever clause in their contracts, which meant that if the size of *Credere* – measured by its net asset value – fell below £300 million, all the insurance contracts with Lambda were null and void – they became worthless. And Silvermans could walk away and not have to pay Lester a penny. *Credere* was now a little over £380 million: at the current rate of losses, Lester had less than a year before his fund would run out of money and they'd all be out of a job. The sense of impotence threatened to overwhelm as he trudged on next to Ann.

Chapter Twenty-Nine

Her mother was already beginning to grate and she'd only arrived two hours earlier. Marina Alfero felt a sudden urge to leave the dining room table and retreat to the refuge of her beautiful kitchen.

She could do that now, of course – seek sanctuary in another room when her mother visited. Thanks to Tina Scales, who had been true to her word and had persuaded the Globe to part with $350,000, they had left Tenderloin behind just over a year ago. Marina and Rodrigo now lived in the up-and-coming Excelsior suburb of San Francisco and the battered and curling linoleum floor covering had become a shiny expanse of white marble-effect tiles stretched out across the kitchen. The ugly cast-iron stove had been transformed into a sleek built-in double oven in mahogany red.

Their kitchen cabinets operated with sublime German efficiency; the drawers producing the expensive pneumatic 'swish' noise as they closed. The Alfero's work surfaces were precision-engineered, black granite counters sat on top of the white cabinets with a line of mahogany to pick out the oven. Generous deep-pile carpets covered the floors beyond the kitchen and face cloths were employed for their intended use – no longer required to plug gaps in bathroom windows.

But for all the beauty of their new home, it just wasn't good enough for her mother, unless, of course, there was an army of children to put in it. It didn't help that Marina's younger sister – who was apparently so fertile that she was able to conceive by just looking at her husband – had upped the stakes again by providing their pushy mother with yet another grandchild. *Sisters*, she thought to herself, as she glimpsed at the photograph of Gabriela and her band of offspring that had been presented as evidence twenty minutes earlier. A sort of arms race of sibling rivalry, she thought; where success was measured by the proliferation of children. But she loved her sister dearly.

Mrs Gomez caught her daughter's glance.

"They have three now, you know," she said nodding towards the picture. "They've done so well. We're so proud of them, aren't we, dear?" She looked at her husband, a broad smile fanning out across her rubbery, circular face.

Marina gently rested her knife and fork against the side of her plate. She used the paper serviette to dab the corner of her mouth and to camouflage the fact that she was nibbling away at her bottom lip.

"Yep, and we're equally proud of these two," replied the father, as he gestured enthusiastically with his hands in front of him.

Marina allowed herself a smile, safe in the knowledge that the barrier she was still holding concealed it from her mother. Her dad, bless him, was always diligent about taking the side of an argument that her mother didn't. It made his life hell, but it never seemed to persuade him otherwise. She sneaked a peep at her mother.

The broad grin was gone and in its place, the scowl; the one that every member of the family knew – and dreaded. The mother glared at her husband, contorting her elastic face as the necessary adjustments took hold – her furrowing brow, the rise in the upper lip and the inverting corners of the mouth.

"Of course we are, dear," she replied, clunking her cutlery down onto the plate. "I'm just saying that they need to decide to get on with it that's all." She turned away from her husband, shaking her head slightly as she did so. She looked at her daughter.

"Listen, Marina, at twenty-eight, I already had my three. Your biological clock is ticking; you just need to get on. A nice house is all well and good, but *this* is the important stuff," she said, as she rapped Gabriella's photo with her index finger. Almost as an afterthought, she asked, "When *are* you going to start a family?"

"Oh Mum, shut up, please!" Marina was shocked at the emotion in her own voice.

Rodrigo and Mr Gomez looked at one another but both decided not to speak.

"Well, I'm only trying to help." Mrs Gomez sat staring at her daughter – arms crossed in front of her.

"Well, you're not helping, so just leave it. I'm not discussing this with you," said the daughter. She'd forgotten just how generous her mum could be with her advice and opinions.

Marina pushed her chair back and left the table, covering her face with the paper serviette again. She entered the kitchen and walked over to the window that looked out over the garden; she stopped there and felt her eyes moisten at the question, the one she asked herself almost daily. *When am I going to start a family?* If only her mum knew the truth. In fact, that was the bit that hurt the most: that she just assumed that prevarication explained the lack of progress. Hadn't she stopped to think that Gabriela's little baby boom might be explained by a combination of factors? It wasn't just about *deciding to get on with it,* as her mum so thoughtlessly put it. The good fortune of potent fertility was a pretty important ingredient.

Marina and Rodrigo had all the kit upstairs to prove that they had made their decision years ago. Safely hidden away whilst her overly inquisitive mum was visiting San Francisco, so that their secret would remain just that. It was in a box – a rather large box – hidden behind clothes and books at the very back of their wardrobe in their bedroom. The sort of place that not even Mrs Gomez would dare to accidently stumble upon.

The box contained a growing body of evidence about how her internal organs prepared themselves each month for the *possibility* of creating a baby. The graphs charting the length of her menstrual cycle, the same plotting her early morning body temperature readings and the recordings of her hormone levels. She even logged the dates and times that Rodrigo and she had had sex around the vital two-day period after ovulation. It was all there – a compendium of evidence that damn well proved they'd made a decision!

And the most heart-breaking point about it all – the part that drained her and Rodrigo the most – was the rollercoaster of emotions. At each new attempt, the pair would miraculously pull each other up to such a level of anticipation that they'd be able to conclude that this time, somehow, it would be different – that there would be another outcome. And then, Marina would discover the despicable truth: both the unfertilised egg and the thickened lining of her uterus flushed-out – rejected – from her body. Nature was supposed to be a mother, and so her *modus operandi* surprisingly cruel, but the chosen means nonetheless, through which she communicated to Marina that she was without child. And then, the next cycle would begin and the emotional rollercoaster would start all over again.

In the past six months, the paraphernalia in the box had expanded to include the equipment required to conduct IVF treatment. The most brutal of which were the hypodermic needles that delivered the hormones that apparently needed 'a little boost'. These were three inches long and Rodrigo, after placing an ice cube on the spot where he would puncture the skin, would have to deliver the serum into the cheeks of her bottom. It hurt like hell. Not one of the more romantic procedures involved in conception was Rodrigo's observation. Marina agreed, but since she was *at the sharp end* suggested that he might want to keep his comments to himself.

As Rodrigo entered the kitchen and closed the door behind him, Marina turned. He looked at his wife – olive skin, the dark, almost Iranian brown eyes and long, black hair. He walked over and put his large arms around her as she began to cry.

"Try not to let it get to you, honey."

"How? How can I do that when she's so bloody insensitive about it all?" sniffed Marina.

She folded herself into the gap that existed just under his shoulder and nuzzled in – the perfect fit; her 5 feet 2 inches snug in his large pectoral muscle hanging off his 6-foot 3-inch frame. She always fitted into that slot – like it was made for her.

"It's the bloody assumption she's making that upsets me more than anything. If she stopped and thought about it for a moment, she might actually work out that there could be something wrong. Why do people like her just assume that because we don't have children, we're not trying?"

"I know, honey. Look, they'll be gone the day after tomorrow. When they are and you're a little less stressed, we can try again. We can go for another round of IVF if you like," replied Rodrigo.

Marina looked at her husband and then gave him another squeeze. Persuading him to go for IVF had been easier than she thought – his desire for children prevailing over his innate caution about finances. But Tina Scales had been right and the mortgage payments were less than the rent they had been paying – the extra cash, along with another credit card, allowed the couple to throw everything they had at the possibility of having children.

They smiled at each other – on a wave of rising anticipation, she kissed her husband; perhaps next time, there really would be a different outcome.

Chapter Thirty

"Knock, knock, hi guys – and how's project NARCISM going?"

Bob Santini looked up from behind his four computer screens, past the three telephones and the two colleagues sat in front of him and glared at the man stood in the doorway. Colin Stewart, the head of risk at Allied English, was stood to attention in his doorway exactly like the soldier he had once been. Santini could envisage how Stewart would have appeared in his grand British military uniform – all shiny boots, fancy epaulettes and brass buttons – it made him want to puke.

"Did someone send you a fucking invite, Stewart?"

"I don't need an invite – I go where I'm needed. That's why I'm here with the 'Masters of the Universe' and our Prop Desk. We need to discuss your subprime mortgage positions and your CDOs," replied Stewart.

Santini seemed to register the sardonic description of his team but let it go.

It was Stewart's job to enforce the Bank's risk rules which, unfortunately for Stewart, had been thoughtlessly entitled Allied English Risk System or (AERS) for short. In the mature and responsible world of investment banking, there's no room for that level of carelessness when it comes to acronyms. AERS was way too easy, and Stewart had been referred to as Mr AERS for years – pronounced, of course, Mr Ass, with the appropriate New York twang.

"OK, Mr Ass what can we do for you?" said Santini, as he dismissed his colleagues with the wave of his hand and reclined in his large leather chair. The colleagues left the room without trying particularly hard to suppress their giggles.

"I see you've trained your protégés to respect authority as much as you do," said Stewart, as he marched into the room and sat down opposite. Santini simply looked across the desk at his old adversary.

Colin Stewart was a 55-year-old ex-British Army Officer who had moved to the US with the bank 20 years earlier. All the way through his adult life, he had been dependent upon one set of rules or another. Rules were good; they brought order and discipline where otherwise chaos would prevail.

From his physical presence alone, it was obvious Stewart was ex-military. His fair hair had been sculptured into a tight one-inch crew cut for the best part of 30 years and had a sense of intransience about it that matched his attitude towards people like Santini. He didn't just stand – he practically stood to attention with his shoulders back and his, still tort, stomach pulled in.

And his ex-military appearance was no accident – as far as he was concerned, it reinforced the hard-won reputation that he had cautiously built up over the years: discipline, rules and order – all essential to protect the bank.

Stewart shot an exaggerated glance up at the display of egotism on Santini's wall and snorted. Mounted on a large wooden plaque, high up on the wall behind his desk was the headgear from a Texas Longhorn Bull. They weren't horns, so much as huge, gnarled tusks and they looked every bit the record-breaking two metres from tip-to-tip that Santini bragged about. They had belonged to '*Killer*', the pretentiously named prize-winning bull from his Longhorn ranch near Austin in Texas and provided a gaudy necktie storage solution for a man like Santini. There were twenty or so silk ties hanging loosely from the horns on display for all to see.

Stewart considered the man opposite him. He could have been Gordon Gekko's son; slicked back collar length hair, which looked like it had been vacuum-packed into place rather that combed, ridiculous Y-shaped braces in royal blue and polka dot pink, matching tie and pink shirt. Everything about him rankled with Stewart and screamed rogue/fraud/shark and on that basis alone, he had him marked as 'high-risk'.

"So how are your insurance contracts against mortgage bonds and CDOs doing?" asked the Brit.

"It's a two-year strategy. I never expected them to pay off until next year."

"You mean they're still losing money."

Santini seemed to swell physically – his self-importance bruised slightly. "What do you want, Stewart? I've got an investment desk to run and I don't have time for idle chat."

"We need to incorporate your little fiefdom into our AERS frame—"

"That sounds painful," interrupted Santini.

"Grow up, Santini; for God's sake, you sound like a schoolboy! We need to build the Prop Desk into our audit routine and September 2007 is the date that's been agreed with James Dickenson. But before then, I'll need the usual risk reports from your team detailing the positions that you hold and a monthly catch up with you to discuss them. We start one month from today with the reports. I'll schedule a meeting in our diaries."

Santini appeared a little dazed, as he listened to Stewart's rapid-fire 'detailing this and scheduling that'. But he remained silent.

"And for what it's worth," added Stewart, "I think your position's crazy."

Santini didn't say anything, but his contemptuous stare was enough to persuade Stewart to justify his statement.

"All I'm saying is that from where I'm sitting, betting against the US housing market doesn't look like a smart idea. Have you heard Bernanke recently – he's adamant that it's all going to blow over and there won't be any widespread impact. If he's right, I don't think the Triple-Bs that you've bet against will suffer and your insurance contracts won't pay-out."

"You're not an investor – what the fuck would you know?"

"You're the one losing the bank's money; I might ask you the same question."

"Stewart, you can have your fucking risk report and we can meet to discuss it if that makes you feel like you're making a contribution. But for the moment, can you get out of my face?"

Stewart, satisfied that he'd made his point, stood up, turned – on the ball of one foot and the heel of the other – by precisely 180° and left the office.

Santini narrowed his eyes as he watched him disappear.

The head of the Prop Desk remained seated and after a few minutes, picked up the one photograph that he had in his office. It was of him, taken about ten years ago, wearing his unchanged business attire holding a white envelope. He wiped the glass clear and studied the elation in his face. He'd never told anyone, but the contents of the envelope was his first ever $1 million bonus paycheque. Many more had followed, but there had been something special about that first one.

He placed it back on his desk and thought about this year's prospects. The bank's Prop Desk – the part of the bank that Santini had fought for and now ran – was set up to invest the bank's own money. It was supposed to be a gigantic profit centre and it needed to be for Santini to make the sort of money that he wanted.

His principal strategy at the moment – and the one Stewart was giving him a hard time about – was holding insurance contracts that paid out if *interest-only negative-amortising adjustable-rate subprime mortgages* went pop.

Santini couldn't resist the deliciously sounding acronym that was produced by changing the terminology slightly to *Negative-amortising Adjustable-Rate Clause Subprime Mortgage* and 'Project NARCSM' had been born.

Although absolutely convinced that his bet against the Triple-B slices of the subprime market would ultimately pay-out, until they did so, he was transferring $115 million per year to an anonymous counter-party. He was happy with his position, but the cost of the insurance was not doing his profits any favours and he knew it would negatively impact his bonus pool.

He needed to change tack. He'd been thinking through the early stages of an idea that would more than off-set his insurance premiums. It was an unbelievably low risk strategy and one that he now decided to act upon.

Chapter Thirty-One

Ann was once again fiddling with her necklace. It was brushing across her lips as she moved her hand backwards and forwards clutching the pendant. She was amongst the small group of analysts that were batting ideas backwards and forwards about the Crap Disguised Otherwise, or CDO, contracts in the small conference room.

Any minute now, she'd be asked for the first time to present a new investment idea to the group. She'd been with Lambda over a year now, but in some ways it felt an awful lot longer. Her lowest point – and she had to concede there were quite a few to choose from – had undoubtedly been the wave of redundancies that Lester had been forced to make. Her best friend Sally had unfortunately been a victim of that horrible day and was still struggling to come to terms with it. Not that Sally hadn't found another job – she had, and a bloody good one – but she'd taken it personally. She swore never to speak to Lester FitzGerald ever again and their friendship had certainly cooled. Sally couldn't understand how Ann could still be working for him.

Ann tried to think of one, any, compensating high points and couldn't. *Perhaps they were still to come?* she asked herself, as Lester started to speak.

"OK, who's next?"

"I guess that's me," winced Ann.

She handed out a five-page deck of slides with the phrase 'Is a CDO a GMO?' on the top cover sheet. Her reference to Genetically Modified Organisms reflected her scientific background. She had graduated with a first in Biology but had soon concluded that that a career in investment sounded far more civilised than a lifetime in Wellington Boots and Barber Jacket.

Steve, one of the senior analysts, joked, "I know these brainstorm sessions are designed to generate new ideas, but 'genetic engineering for hedge funds' really is pushing the boundaries."

Everyone in the room laughed, including Ann. At last, she began to relax a little.

"Well, improving the genetic make-up of some of the investment bankers that we've had to deal with would be an idea that I could fully support!" laughed Lester.

Ann smiled, as she sneaked a look at her boss. He wasn't back to his old self – not by a long way. But he seemed a little better recently. She knew he was still carrying stuff around with him – that arsehole Rankin was being unreasonable about collateral and his own investors weren't much better apparently. She also knew, as the other staff now did, about the £300 million NAV limit on the fund. If it went below that threshold, the fund would be gone. Nonetheless, there was a slight improvement in his physical appearance – he was a little less worn and a little less pale. Even his shock of white hair had recovered some of its old vibrancy.

"OK, I know the title is a little strange and I'm not even sure this is a good idea; in fact, I think I'm missing something because I don't understand some of the prices that I have been given by the banks that I've spoken to. I'll come onto that later," added Ann.

"It's fine, Ann, really. That's what these sessions are for. Just tell us what *you* think about the issues – however whacky the idea sounds. There are plenty of us that can fill in the technicalities," replied Lester.

"OK. Well, perhaps a new way of looking at all of this is to ask ourselves whether a CDO is a genetically modified subprime mortgage bond. In the same way that scientists manipulate the genetic make-up of cells to produce an improved or new organism, so the bankers have tinkered with the original DNA makeup of one tower of debt (the traditional subprime mortgage bond) to create a new, enhanced tower of debt (the CDO). The banks claim that the CDO enjoys significantly higher concentrations of the Triple-A elements relative to the traditional, but inferior, subprime mortgage bond.

"The inference of course is that the banks have harvested the Triple-A DNA from thousands of subprime mortgage bonds to create the CDO – the improved organism. This, in turn, allows the CDO to be 65% (or higher) Triple-A rated. The market's perception is that the difference between a subprime mortgage bond and a CDO is that the latter is an enhanced version of the former."

The team were nodding. Most were now looking at Ann and listening intently, seemingly impressed by her articulate line of argument.

Lester was in full-blown meditative mode; eyes closed, chin up and all-out Buddha-pose with his fingers clasped around his belly.

"But that's not what actually happens as I understand it," continued Ann.

"What does actually happen then?" asked Steve.

What does actually happen, Ann found absurd. In fact, she thought it was plain wrong to the extent that she seriously thought she'd misunderstood and was about to make a fool out of herself in front of colleagues. She took a deep breath.

"It's less a case of inserting enhanced DNA and more a process of transferring the inferior DNA across thousands and thousands of times in order to build up the CDO. Essentially, CDOs are just a new pile of Triple-B rated mortgage bonds that an investment bank, after conspiring with a rating agency, have re-branded as higher quality bonds on the premise that yet another layer of diversification has somehow changed the basic risk profile of the underlying mortgages."

Steve was looking confused. "So, just to be clear, Ann, it's some sort of portfolio diversification argument that creates the increase in the Triple-A content of a CDO not the actual, physical, insertion of large amounts of higher-quality Triple-A bonds."

"Correct, although the banks don't volunteer this obviously, they just keep repeating that a CDO has a 65% (or above) Triple-A bond structure. They have repeated it so frequently and taken the rating agencies with them that the market now just takes it for granted," replied Ann.

Steve looked at Lester, and then shook his head smiling.

"Ahem. Earth calling, Lester."

Lester opened his eyes and looked straight ahead.

"Is that your view also?" asked Steve.

He spoke slowly and was obviously still thinking as he did so.

"Well, I'm no biologist and so I haven't set out the arguments in this way before, but I share Ann's reasoning. The CDO is certainly being mis sold and that's why Lambda owns the insurance contracts that pay out when they fail."

Lester took a couple of moments and looked again at the slides that Ann had given to them. He said nothing but nodded slowly to himself as if another thought was taking hold.

"So the answer to your question, Ann, is no, a CDO is not a GMO?" asked Steve.

"That's correct."

"OK, so what's the SFW?" asked Steve.

There had to be a 'So Fucking What' to every new investment idea that was discussed by the group. Without it, the ideas were just that – ideas – and the weekly meetings would be a talking shop rather than a forum to take an idea and convert it into a strategy from which Lambda could make money.

She finished brushing her hands against the legs of her blue trouser suit and placed them together in front of her to begin. "The SFW is that we bet against the Double and Triple-A tranches of the CDOs rather than just the lower rated Triple B elements that we do at the moment," replied Ann. She pulled away slightly; her face screwed up as if she was waiting for a slap in the face.

There was a few seconds of silence, but the wave of condemnation she feared didn't arrive.

"Hang on, wait a bloody minute, wait a bloody minute…" shouted Lester. His eyes were closed again and his thumb and forefinger were pinching the top of his nose; he raised his other hand to stop anyone else from interrupting his thoughts.

Ann held her breath. The others stared at Lester. No one had ever thought to bet against the Double and Triple-A tranches of anything before. You just didn't do it. It was unchartered territory; the entire global financial community had grown up relying on the security of Triple-A investments. Government bonds were Triple-A for goodness' sake.

"But if the Double and Triple-A tranches of CDOs are really Triple-Bs, we already bet against them. Why would we take the trouble to do more?" asked Steve finally.

"Pricing, it's the bloody pricing!" declared Lester. His eyes were now wide open, as if his Eureka moment had given him a sudden surge of energy.

"Why didn't I bloody see it? You're right, of course, Steve, that we own insurance contracts that pay out if the Triple-B tranches of CDOs fail. But we pay about 2% a year in premiums for the privilege. From Ann's presentation" – he smacked the relevant slide with the back of his hand – "we can see that we could buy insurance for the Triple-A CDO tranches at a mere 0.5 of a percent! And we know that they're really Triple-Bs masquerading as Triple-As."

The room wasn't quite sure how to process this. If Ann was right, the team could effectively insure against the same event happening for a quarter of the cost of the current premiums paid by *Credere*.

"You mean we've been cynical, but not cynical enough?" asked Steve.

"Exactly. Once it becomes obvious to the markets that people can't pay their mortgages, it will stop buying these instruments and start panic selling," said Lester, who now stood up and paced the room excitedly; he seemed unable to stay still. "Ann's GMO analogy is brilliant because it'll be like a massive food-poisoning scare. The banks have sliced and diced the mincemeat so many times no one knows where the poisonous risks are in the financial food chain. They won't be able to differentiate between the lean mince and the full fat stuff. Everything will just be sold off and our insurance policies will pay-off enormously."

The team looked at Lester and then back at the presentation.

"The pay-off is massive because the insurance market is living the same lie as the banks and rating agencies. They're looking at the ratings, taking them at face value and assuming that it will never happen. That's why buying the insurance against the As is so cheap! It's a classic Lambda trade with a 200–1 pay-off profile. Frankly, I'm bloody annoyed that I didn't notice the pricing differential myself, but the idea is brilliant and we have to do this, guys!"

As soon as Lester spoke those last few words, the room fell silent and his colleagues looked at one another nervously.

Lester turned around from the other side of the room and faced them. He paused for a moment, and then placed his hands on his hips as their expressions registered.

"What do you think we should do, Steve?"

Steve looked down at the presentation he was holding and cleared his throat.

"Normally yes, I'd go for it. But these aren't normal times, Lester. We're a few months away from the £300 million limit – if we breach it, I'm sure that arse wipe Rankin will be all over us like a rash and we'll be screwed. Sorry, Ann, I think your idea is great, but the timing's wrong."

Lester nodded slowly. "Troy, what about you?"

"The same. It's a great idea but not now. We'll be coming up against all sorts of covenant limits if we do this. Sorry Ann."

The other analyst in the room also agreed. Three of the senior investment team that had been with Lester for years advising him not to take out further insurance against CDOs.

The room fell silent again. Ann looked at Lester – and noticed the glint in his eye, as he formed his hands into a steeple with the forefingers resting against his lips. The fingers moved slightly brushing against the silver hairs of his beard. He stared back at his colleagues, studying each in turn like he was trying to infiltrate their thoughts. She guessed what he was thinking and a knowing grin stole across her face.

The tension in the room grew and, finally, Troy asked the obvious.

"And…what exactly do you think, Lester?"

He didn't hesitate. His hands dropped to his hips.

"We're doing it. We're right; we all know we're right. The market will move towards us. Ann, we buy insurance against the Triple As."

Ann smiled and thought to herself, *Perhaps this is the compensating high I was waiting for?*

Two days later, Lambda did what no one else in the market had ever done – it bet against the Double-A tranches of CDOs. Lambda was now responsible for paying over even more insurance premiums and the counterparty would never have to pay Lambda a penny unless the Double-As started to fail, and that had never happened before. Meanwhile, the NAV of *Credere* was already down to £355 million – which explained Lester's colleagues' reservation about paying over more premiums. That was only going to speed up the process of the fund literally running out of money.

The banks thought Lester was mad; the man on the other side of the trade thought Christmas had come early and Lester's clients thought he was certifiable: and Ron Dale? He was booking his flights to London in order to share his thoughts in person.

Chapter Thirty-Two

It was the coldest night of the year so far and it was late. It was 11.30 pm as Ross made his way to his Audi at the far end of the car park. This place was so quiet; the crunching of the small stones, as the ice bonds that had formed between them broke, seemed to scream at him in protest. A bright moon gave the scene before him a silvery glow and he looked up at the sky. *No wonder it's cold*, he thought, it was a perfectly clear night; the miracle of the light streaming down to earth from the moon and the stars powerful enough for him to catch a glimpse of the warm air that left his body. He worked his way around the miracle of the constellations. He didn't care for their formal names but he had a familiarity with all of their shapes. He could go through them one by one; they were all here.

The moment made him think about home – or rather his childhood. Sharing a council house with an alcoholic father in Inverclyde, about ten miles west of Glasgow, could hardly be described as home. Homes were where you found happy families, loving siblings and hope not a house with carpet-less floors and vindictiveness throughout.

He recalled the cheap TV set balanced on a stack of old newspapers in the corner of their front room; the four wooden legs supporting the original had become three when his drunken dad had kicked it in a fit of rage. A Saturday night treat for the young Ross was to be on his own so he could watch his favourite programme – Match of the Day. A Saturday evening nightmare – which, unfortunately, was more frequent – was when his dad deliberately came back from the Pub early. Out of sheer malice, and under the threat of violence, Ross would be made to stand with his back to the TV whilst his dad watched the complete programme with the volume on full blast. Just one example, thought Ross, but there were many others.

But the magic of a night sky had always been an escape and represented a choice for Ross. Inhabit the small, bitter world of his father or take advantage of the vast number of opportunities out there. As a boy, he had spent many a cold winter's evening under the skies rather than under the roof of his father's house. He took a deep breath and thought about the opportunity he had been pursuing tonight. A forty-something personal training client had asked him for some extra tuition and he'd obliged earlier in the evening. She hadn't blinked at his suggestion of an evening session, which he took as a positive. He had also stayed behind after they'd finished the 'crunch and core workout' and shared a drink at the bar with her for over an hour.

He'd already established that she was married before tonight's meeting. Now he also knew that she had two teenage children, lived in a large house in Woodbridge and had a husband that she didn't stop complaining about. Apparently, he was hardly ever home – Asia on business too often – and when he was home didn't really appreciate her. She'd made it abundantly clear on at least two occasions earlier that he was away tonight, but Ross had played it cool – no reason to rush. But this looked like it could be fertile ground and he'd decided to step-up the research on the husband. He sounded like he could be loaded; all very promising but some way before we get to the Poorish state of play he thought. Nonetheless, he smiled to himself as he thought about the opportunities that might come his way as a result.

A movement in a bush a few feet away brought him back. He got to the car, unlocked it and popped the boot to put his kit bag away.

"Don't fucking move," whispered the voice from behind. Ross froze. Deathly silence once again. He'd hardly heard *him* – he assumed it was a *he* – but the voice was incredibly soft. He also felt something press firmly against the ridge of his spine. It could be a piece of wood, someone's fingers or it could be a gun. He wasn't about to speculate.

"OK, OK. What do you want?" asked Ross, as he instinctively raised his hands above his head.

"We've got some business to take care of, Mr Ross, but first we're going for a little drive," came a reply, but from a distinctly different voice. This one was loud, tetchy almost angry. "Get in the car and don't think about doing anything stupid or I'll blow your fucking brains out."

That would be a gun then, thought Ross. He did exactly what he was told to do. They got into the car, both men climbed into the back and Ross started the engine. The radio station automatically sprang back into life. "*Oh, I can't wait to see those faces, I'm driving home for Christmas*," came the husky-gravel voice of Chris Rea. Ross wondered what those faces were like behind him.

"Turn that shit off!" demanded the second voice. Ross was angling for a look at them in the rear-view mirror. He could only see one of them and he wore a full-face party mask of a reindeer. *How very seasonal,* he thought, as he turned-off the radio.

"Now then, Mr Ross, I'd like you to drive to your flat and park, as you normally do, in the underground car park. Don't take any diversions; just take your normal route home. Do you understand me?"

Ross drove the fifteen minutes back to the flat, parked in his usual space and killed the engine.

Chapter Thirty-Three

"Now then, Mr Ross. Put this on and lead the way," said the second voice.

It was a Father Christmas mask – red hat, white bobble on the end, half-moon Santa glasses and long white beard. It was as comprehensive as the other men's disguises. The whisperer was an Elf and the abrasive guy was presumably Rudolph, but Ross didn't have a clue about their true appearance. These were the full-face rubbery masks that covered everything and were the choice of bank robbers for that very reason.

"Now don't try anything silly, Mr Ross. This gun will be by your side all the way. Just straight to the lift in the corner, third floor and flat 312. If we see anyone between here and the other side of your front door, we've been out partying and we're just going up for a couple of Christmas drinks. OK?"

This was getting worse by the second. These guys had obviously done their homework. He wondered if they had been inside his flat. Ross slipped on his mask, got out of the car and led the way to the lift. He considered the possible escape routes and glanced at the stairwell to the right. It was ten to fifteen feet away; if he could drop kick the guy with the gun, he might just make it through the fire escape and be able to run. He wasn't as fast as he used to be, but he was pretty sure he could outdo either the Elf or Rudolf.

"Don't think about the fire escape, Mr Ross. I can assure you, I'll blow your kneecaps away before you get close. Just keep walking," threatened the deep voice behind him.

A few seconds later, 'Old George', the caretaker appeared from around the corner.

"Party time is it, Mr Ross," he laughed. Ross was a little surprised, but assumed there weren't too many residents frequently dressed in white training shoes, tracksuit bottoms and a Melton Spa sweatshirt. So much for the disguise. Ross saw an opportunity.

"Yes, we're just heading up for a nightcap. You could join us if you want?" replied Ross.

The reindeer grunted from behind.

"Very kind, Mr Ross, thank you, but I'm afraid I can't keep up these days. Oh, by the way, I'll try and fix those doors tomorrow," he said, as he glanced over his shoulder as he shuffled away. Ross' heart sank further.

They entered the lift and Ross was instructed to stand in front of them, facing the doors; he pressed for level three and waited. The doors moved slowly – laterally – to meet in the middle. As they did so, they bounced across the lift entrance and finally closed with a shuddering thud. The ancient lift system wasn't pretty but the safety mechanism was operating on the car park level – the doors could shudder and make as much noise as they liked, but they needed to close slowly to allow the elderly residents access without getting knocked over.

But on his floor, the safety mechanism had failed a couple of days ago; that's what dear Old George was apologising about. So, although there was a slight pause after the doors opened on level three, they then immediately slammed shut dangerously quickly without warning. In fact, an irate Mrs Walker had already circulated an email to all the residents claiming that several of the 'older' tenants on that floor had been the victims of 'door strikes'. She was already talking about convening a full-blown Tenants' Association Meeting, lawyers and taking the 'filthy rich' Landlord to court. Ross was always amazed at how much time the woman had.

The number three lit up to tell them they had arrived. The lift stopped its ascent. The doors opened, slowly. They bounced and shuddered apart to reveal the flat-numbering system on the opposite wall. Ross hesitated.

"Oi, fuckwitt. This is us, move," said the deep voice behind him, and he prodded Ross with the gun.

This really is a Sliding Doors moment, thought Ross, as he continued to count in his head. He turned towards Rudolph.

"All right, will you just piss off!" And he pushed Rudolph backwards, as he immediately jumped through the gap between the doors.

The man in the reindeer mask was too shocked to respond immediately. It was the first time that Ross had shown anything but complete compliance, and in that split second, the doors slammed together with Ross on the other side.

The two men in the lift franticly pressed the door-open button. Ross knew he only had a few seconds before they'd be out and after him and he raced to the fire escape at the far end of the corridor. Before he could disappear completely, the doors opened and the two men gave chase. They moved quicker than Ross had anticipated and as he reached the car park below, he knew he had no chance to make it all the way through to the far door and took cover behind the wheels of a Range Rover.

The two men entered the car park and immediately stood still. Ross was gasping for air through his open mouth; it was the quietest way he could force the oxygen into his burning lungs. The only thing he could hear was his pulse pounding away in his ear. The men didn't move.

Ross was no more than twenty feet away from them. He steadied himself on his haunches and ventured a look through the windows of the parked Range Rover towards the door he'd just run through. What he saw amazed and frightened him in equal measure. An expensive Mercedes was creeping into the car park. As it gently pulled-up alongside his pursuers, the tyre squeal on the painted concrete surface echoed loudly around him. One of the blacked-out rear passenger windows opened via its electronic mechanism and Rudolph bent down. He spoke to someone in the car, and Ross could hear voices but not well enough to make out what was said. He couldn't see who was inside the car. A few seconds later, the window closed, the engine stopped and there was complete silence once again.

Ping. Ross tensed and cursed his luck. Some idiot had actually sent him a text. The two men moved away from the Mercedes and, slowly, they circled in from different directions towards the noise of the text.

Ping, another text.

For fuck sake, thought Ross. He took his phone out of his pocket to turn it off. He glanced at the screen to kill it.

'No escape!' was on the display.

He switched the phone off and slipped it back into his pocket. He leant across the wheel and took a chance – he wanted to see if he could see their feet, but knew doing so could reveal his own location.

"Don't move, Mr Ross. Don't try and run again and never push me," came the deep voice of Rudolph from behind him. Ross put his hands up above his head for the second time that evening and sighed in despair. As he was led away, he heard the distinctive sound of tyres on painted concrete as the car turned slowly and headed for the exit ramp. Within a few minutes, all three men were in Ross' flat.

Chapter Thirty-Four

"Now then, time to get started I'm afraid, Mr Ross," said Rudolph.

They tied Ross to a swivel office chair in the open-plan kitchen/dining room area. He was strapped around the legs and torso, but his hands were free. He was also gagged.

The whole car incident had really spooked him. Who the hell had been in the car? As they tightened the cords, he really began to understand just how vulnerable he now was.

"OK shit for brains. Just to make sure you understand the seriousness of your situation and the extent to which my client is upset with you, I've just been asked to leave a memento of our visit; one that you'll see every morning to help you remember what a stupid idea looks like. We'll get to the rest of the business in a few moments."

That's when the Elf took out the Stanley knife and strode purposefully across the room towards him.

Ross knew he had one go at this. He took a desperate lunge forward and got some purchase from his trainers on the floor in order to knock the knife out of his assailant's hand, but it was wild and he over-rotated. The wheels of the chair caught on the strip between the linoleum flooring and the carpet, stopped it and toppled the chair forwards directly into the path of the approaching assailant – and the knife. It all happened so quickly, neither could prevent it and both men collided; a grotesque convergence of kinetic energy in the middle of the room.

The result was horrific. The collision had changed the trajectory of the blade and had massively increased the force with which it inserted itself into Ross. The Stanley knife had entered the left side of Ross' neck, and made a fatal incision into the carotid artery.

The blood escaped from Ross' neck with such a degree of ferocity that it splashed against the walls, the furniture and the three men. Ross' flailing, his pathetic attempt to stem the flow with his hands, was futile. Although his hands were free the tie around the torso meant that he couldn't reach his neck no matter how much thrashing around he did.

Ross knew then that the wound would be fatal. Human instinct told him that. The amount of blood he was losing must be inconsistent with life – no need for medical training when it's so obvious. He began to lose consciousness after twenty seconds and he tried to keep still in a pitiful attempt to calm himself – anything to reduce the flow.

But it was relentless. Ross spent the last few moments of consciousness – and his life – looking up at the spotlights in the ceiling. He may have been staring at them but it was the stars of his childhood skies that he saw. The lights flickered, glistened and moved before his eyes and then dimmed and he realised that his own opportunities were now over. In those last moments, he persuaded himself he could see the Plough for one last time and then nothing. He had seen his last night sky – a much greater vastness now consumed the boy from Inverclyde.

Chapter Thirty-Five

Happy Birthday Piglet, and well done on the arrest!

DI Jim Hanson read the greeting in the card from his dad again and rolled his eyes. Hanson was Suffolk born and bred and, like many children, had picked up his nickname at school. Along with his four siblings, he was raised on one of the biggest pig farms in the county but he was the only one of the quintets that discovered he didn't have a passion for pork. After eating several pounds of the stuff every week from the age of three to eighteen, he couldn't stomach spending the rest of his life rearing pigs.

Instead, he chased criminals around the county and left his siblings to expand his father's legacy; they all tended to the pink livestock across large swathes of the Suffolk countryside. Much to the disappointment of his father, Hanson hadn't eaten pork for over twenty years.

So when Hanson had left school and announced his career aspirations to the family, his dad decided that the nickname was still appropriate. It had stuck with him.

The congratulations were for the arrest of the Suffolk Strangler. Steve Wright's DNA had matched that found on the victims and he'd been charged with the murder of five prostitutes in Ipswich. They'd all been killed in the last eight weeks and the investigation had become the largest in the Suffolk Constabulary's history. Hanson had led the team, involving 600 officers from almost every force in the country. He needed the murder of Angus Ross, two days after apprehending Wright, like he needed a pork roast with crackling.

He looked up from his desk and saw Chief Inspector Smith rapidly approaching. He slipped the birthday card into a drawer and flipped open his notebook.

"What's the story with this Ross character?" asked CI Smith.

"Sad end to an unbelievable talent is how I'd describe it, sir," replied Hanson.

CI Smith just frowned at his subordinate.

Hanson, a life-long Ipswich Town fan, felt the urgent need to clarify for his football-illiterate boss.

"Angus Ross was the most talented footballer I ever saw play live, sir. He was a regular in the Town first team at 18 and had every premiership team in the country chasing him. Even Alex Fergusson was chomping at the bit. Then we played those tossers from across the border in Norwich and a big, ugly centre-half managed to break Ross' leg in three places. Doctors said it was a miracle that he could walk – playing again was out of the question."

Hanson consulted his notes. "I've done some early digging and it seems he went off the rails for a couple of years, piled up some debts, and until last night worked as a personal trainer at the Spa in Melton. A cleaner found him this morning with a fatal stab wound to the neck, tied to a chair in his flat. All we know at the moment is that he died sometime between midnight and four o'clock this morning. There was no sign of a break in; in fact, other than him being tied to a chair, there was no sign of a struggle either."

"OK. Sounds to me like your ex-footballer had a more complicated life than that of a personal trainer, Hanson. Keep me informed and make sure I know where you are. You know what the press are like at the moment."

POLICE DO NOT CROSS, written in black on the bright-yellow tape, greeted Hanson as he arrived at the scene twenty minutes later. He met the head of the Crime Scene Investigation Unit, stepped into his white, hazmat suit, placed the distinctive blue bags over his shoes and entered Ross' flat.

Forensics was hard at it. One member was taking photographs of almost everything from as many angles as possible, and two other investigators were dispersing their white powder in various locations to record fingerprints and footwear marks. One of the men was using a powerful torch that fluoresced various bodily fluids: the most obvious of which was the pool of blood around Ross' body. *You don't need scientific equipment to see that,* thought Hanson.

After personally attending the murder scenes of the five young women in recent weeks, there wasn't much that shocked him. But all of them had been strangers. He hadn't recognised any of them in death since he hadn't known them in life. But Hanson felt he knew Ross, and he certainly recognised him; instantly and notwithstanding that he could only see part of his face. He was contorted around the fallen chair and lay awkwardly with his face on the floor but half-turned as if he'd been trying to look up at something. His lips were blue and his complexion beyond ashen; both consistent with death by loss of blood or, exsanguination, if his medical recall was still correct. Hanson looked up at the ceiling, following Ross' eyes, saw nothing except a few spotlights and moved on.

After swapping notes with the SOCO, he then met up with Mills – an ambitious young detective who was in the process of interviewing residents.

Mrs Walker was sat opposite the detective as Hanson came into the room.

"Hello, sir," said Mills. "This is Mrs Walker, a resident in the block and she's been telling me about the victim." Mills invited the resident to repeat what she had just told him for the benefit of his boss.

"Well, I didn't know him very well. None of us did really; he kept himself to himself and never attended the Tenants' Association meetings you know," said the woman. The last point was delivered in an accusatory tone as if his absence evidenced some grave lapse of moral judgment, thought Hanson.

"Anyway, as I said to your colleague, Mr Hanson, he did have quite a few visitors." Mrs Walker immediately raised her palms before continuing. "Not that any of us have the time or inclination to monitor our fellow residents – but it was difficult not to notice at times."

"I understand, Mrs Walker, and do you know anything about them?" asked the DI.

"Well, they were all women, they always appeared in the evening and normally left after about an hour, although sometimes the visits were precisely two hour's long."

DI Hanson managed to keep a straight face as he tried to square the circle between Mrs Walker's alleged apathy towards her neighbours and her detailed knowledge of the victim's guests. He felt he had to ask the obvious.

"But how can you be sure about the times and that the visitors were women, Mrs Walker? You seem to be very precise about it all?"

Mrs Walker flushed and gathered her cardigan around herself.

"Because of the noise. It was obvious when they started and when they finished…if you know what I mean," said replied.

"Mrs Walker?" Hanson asked, raising his eyebrows. Mills squirmed in his seat.

"Mr Hanson," she said, her arms now crossed firmly, "I may be getting on a bit, but I do remember what *it* sounds like you know."

Hanson looked at Mills who was shaking his head.

"Mrs Walker lives next door to the victim, sir, and her bedroom apparently abuts Ross'."

"Ah. OK, I see what you mean, Mrs Walker. Apologies." It was Hanson's turn to squirm.

Mrs Walker shook her head slightly and looked at the DI.

"Did you hear or see anything strange last night?"

"Not a thing, I'm afraid. I had a headache and was in bed by nine pm. I slept right through until 7.30 this morning."

About two hours later and Hanson was at the Spa in Melton. The Manager was pretty cagy – didn't give much away about Ross; didn't really want an inspector talking to his staff or his guests either, but decided he didn't have much choice.

The bar manager, a Mr Yallop, was the complete opposite; in fact, once he got started, Hanson couldn't shut him up.

"What do you think I'm looking for, Mr Yallop?"

"If you want my opinion, an angry husband. Ross had plenty of enemies. He wasn't just a personal trainer; he was sleeping with half his clients. I'd imagine lot of husbands would be delighted that Angus Ross is dead."

Is that jealousy I can detect? thought Hanson.

"How do you know he was sleeping with some of his clients, Mr Yallop?"

"Bloody obvious. Discreet Angus Ross was not," replied the barmen with an ugly smirk. He finished polishing the dimpled pint glass and held it up to the light to check for marks. Once satisfied, he hung it with the rest of his pristine collection above the bar.

"What did you think of Ross?"

"Me? What does it matter what I think?" he asked, as he picked up the next glass and repeated the process.

"You sound aggrieved somehow about his behaviour," replied Hanson. The inspector theatrically produced his notebook and made an entry.

"Sure, I was no fan," nodded Yallop. He put down the towel and the glass, placed his palms on the bar and looked straight at the Inspector. "Ross swanned around here like he owned the place; like he thought he was better than the rest of us. We were never going to be mates. Besides, I'm a Norwich fan, Mr Hanson, and he was a failed Tractor Boy. But I don't take my footballing rivalry to the point of murder. I didn't kill the arrogant shit."

Hanson was just about to correct him about the 'failed Tractor Boy' point, but thought better of it. But he'd keep the Canary in mind. Thinking someone was an arrogant shit was not normally a motive for murder, but in Hanson's book, there was no accounting for Norwich City fans.

He looked beyond Yallop and spotted a couple of women in the other bar area.

"Mind if I ask around a little? Be good to understand what the paying customers thought about our friend Ross," asked Hanson.

"Be my guest," he replied and picked up the towel and another pint pot.

"Excuse me, ladies, I'm sorry to bother you, but my name is DI Hanson." He flipped open his badge and took a seat. "I appreciate that this is all a bit of a shock, but I was hoping to be able to ask a few questions about Angus Ross. I'm just trying to build up a picture of what he was like."

The two women exchanged glances but cleared their bags from the third chair at their small table. Hanson interpreted it as an invite and sat down. He guessed the older lady with the auburn hair in a bun was mid-40s and the taller one with short blond hair a good ten years younger. Both were in full training kit regalia.

"How did you know Ross – was he your trainer?"

"Yes, he looked after both of us," replied the younger woman.

Interesting choice of words, thought Hanson, given Mr Yallop's cynical view of the world.

"Did either of you see him in the last few days?"

This time, the older woman spoke first; Hanson thought a little too quickly perhaps.

"Yes, we both saw him on Monday. He did a session with us here at the gym."

"Did he appear OK? You know, was he acting normally?"

The older woman replied again and confirmed that as far as they could tell, everything was normal. Her friend agreed.

"How long had you known Mr Ross?" asked Hanson. He looked at the older woman.

"About three years, I suppose. He's been my trainer for a little less than that."

Hanson made a note as the other woman replied.

"About eighteen months. I joined the Spa about then and I started his sessions shortly after."

"Did either of you know Mr Ross away from the gym?"

The older woman leaned back in her chair. He noticed the younger one shot her friend a quick glance.

"What do you mean, Mr Hanson?" asked the older woman, as she folded her arms.

"I'm just trying to understand what he did away from work to build a broader picture. Where he lived, did he go out in Ipswich or Woodbridge etc.?"

"No, I'm afraid we don't, Mr Hanson. We just had our training sessions here at the gym and that was it. He was quite a private man actually," replied the older woman.

The younger woman nodded her ascent but didn't look at Hanson.

"I know this is difficult, but do either of you know why anyone would want to murder Mr Ross? Did he have any enemies that you're aware of?" asked Hanson.

"Not at all. Angus Ross was a first-class personal trainer. I can't think of why anyone would want to kill him at all. It doesn't make any sense," interjected the older woman.

"OK. Thank you, ladies. That's been very helpful. Oh, and finally, before I leave, could I have your names? Just in case there's something I've forgotten and I need to come back to you."

"Of course, I'm Paula, Paula Poorish and this is Sam Longmire."

Chapter Thirty-Six

In the end, just two members of the Consortium – James Turner and Ron Dale – came to London for the showdown with Lester. That was Turner's suggestion; with great difficulty, he'd managed to persuade the other members not to attend, arguing that Lester would probably respond better to a small group rather than a large one. Reluctantly, they had agreed, but had given Dale license to represent their views.

Turner and Dale arrived at Lambda's Pont Street office a few minutes early and Susan showed them through to the conference room. They walked past the open-plan area where the analysts were discussing ideas and attracted a few curious glances. Two suits walking through the Pont Street office was not unheard of, but it was sufficiently unusual for one or two staff to take notice; particularly as one of the suits was quite blatant about his own inquisitiveness.

Both the location and the building itself underwhelmed Dale from the start. He wasn't sure what he was expecting: city of London location and a monument to glass and steel? Probably. Instead, the taxi driver had pulled-up outside a Victorian house built from garish red bricks that was punctuated by hideous gargoyles. There were even tacky black window baskets stuffed full of red and white deciduous plants outside balancing on quaint windowsills. The taxi driver had taken them past Buckingham Palace, through the generous leafy streets of Belgravia before decanting them in Pont Street. Dale felt the location belonged in a tourist guide and the building in a museum.

His next disappointment wasn't too far away. The main group of Lambda employees in the open plan meeting area had caused him to do a double take. He thought they looked like a bunch of dropouts; baggy over-sized jumpers, John Lennon glasses, corduroy pants and somebody was actually wearing a bandanna. He'd even seen a female member of staff with no shoes walking around the office in bright pink socks.

The two men entered the conference room, where there was a selection of pastries, fruit, coffees and teas spread out on the table before them. They helped themselves to coffee and Dale was just about to ask Turner what he thought about this bizarre group of people in the other room.

"Good morning, gentlemen," greeted Lester, as he shuffled in to join them.

Dale barely looked up and proffered a tepid smile. He then looked back down to pick up a pastry.

"Lester, great to see you," said Turner, standing up to greet him.

Dale missed a heartbeat, as he realised that the man he'd assumed was a waiter was actually the CEO of Lambda: the guy that James Turner had entrusted to look after his $5million of hard-earned money.

He dropped the pastry, got to his feet and shook hands with the gaunt-looking man stood in front of him. Facial hair, ponytail and scruffy clothes; at least it explained the oddballs next door. Lester FitzGerald was obviously the Patriarch; he looked like the leader of some weird religious cult and the young men and women next door were his home-schooled children. He swallowed as he thought again about his investment in *Credere*.

"Pleased to meet you, Dr FitzGerald," said Dale.

"Call me Lester, please," came the reply.

"Thank you, Lester, and I'm Ron," declared the tall American who was looking down at Lester through his black horn-rimmed glasses. Dale was thickset, and well over six-feel tall, he had short-cropped dark hair and owned a Desperate Dan-sized jawline that was meticulously clean-shaven. He was dressed in a navy-blue suit with a pristine white shirt and red, silk tie; in fact, it was just about regulation investment banking uniform.

They sat down at the table and discussed the weather, the location of Lambda's office and the state of world politics before a few awkward lapses into silence encouraged Turner to take the initiative.

"Lester. Could we begin with investment performance?" All three looked relieved that the small talk was behind them.

"Of course," replied Lester, as he wiped his hands on a paper serviette.

He opened the ring binder he'd brought with him and Dale noticed that it had lost most of its plastic covering revealing the frayed, buff-coloured cardboard beneath. The American shook his head gently and made an indiscreet *tsk* sound at the back of his throat.

Turner jumped into the awkward silence that immediately followed.

"According to your last email, Lester, we're down 17% year-to-date. The US stock market is up 16%. What are the main drivers for this underperformance and what are you doing about it?" continued Turner. He helped himself to another coffee and selected a pain au chocolat from the three-tier cake stand in the middle of the table.

Dale sat quietly. He opened his pristine red folder to reveal a series of post-it notes carefully attached to certain pages within it. The multi-coloured notes started higher up on the page towards the front and appeared lower down as they progressed through the document – a miniature staircase of multi-coloured reminders. Each marker had a number written on it and the colours followed a pattern.

He used both of his large, spade-like hands to delicately place his Mont Blanc pen on the desk above the folder; his thumb and forefinger pinching the top and bottom of the pen and repeatedly sliding it backwards and forwards until he was satisfied with its particular location relative to the file. He gauged the distance attentively, as if it was necessary to satisfy some precise metric before he could formally join the meeting.

Lester observed the ritual, stopped chewing his plastic *Bic* pen and discreetly slid it into the pocket of his tweed jacket. He opened his own file and Dale noticed that the binder ring was broken – one of the clasps didn't close properly and Lester had to carefully rethread the loose-leaf papers back onto the ring one by one. Dale exchanged glances with Turner whilst they waited.

Once he prepared himself, Lester began.

"Well, James, you've known me long enough to appreciate that the short-term doesn't overly concern me. It's the long-term trends and developments that Lambda's investment strategy looks to exploit. I would ask that you judge us on the full investment cycle as agreed at the start of the investment programme. We should look at investment performance in 2008 or 2009 when we have had our full five-year fund life," replied Lester.

"But that's precisely the problem, Dr Fitz – I mean, Lester," stammered Dale, "there will be no five-year investment cycle because you're not respecting what we agreed at the start of our contract."

The American went straight to a red sticker and opened his copy of the Agreement at the relevant page. Turner concentrated on pushing his half-eaten pain au chocolat around on his plate.

"Section 6:4:2 of our agreement states clearly that there will be a lock-up period until 31 May 2007; that's a couple of months away. After that time, the investors will be able to serve a Redemption Notice on the manager and recover their funds within a further three-month period," said Dale. He rested his hands in front of him and clasped his fingers together.

"You need to be aware that the investors have discussed this at length and to a man are minded to do so. You see, Lester, I did warn you about this some time ago and you chose to ignore me. Most people usually regret ignoring Ron Dale." The large American's eyebrows lifted by a fraction, as he looked at Lester and waited for a reaction.

Turner winced; he managed to sneak a half look at Dale and then Lester but seemed to decide to focus on what was left of his breakfast for the moment.

Lester was sat almost motionless. He gently nibbled the inside of his cheek, as if contemplating his options. Finally, he replied.

"*That* would be a very stupid thing to do," he said, allowing the ambiguity to hang at the end of his sentence.

There was silence between the three of them. Turner looked up again and then at the two men in turn. Still silence. Turner blinked first. "What would be very stupid, Lester?" he asked, as he looked at the CEO.

"Serving a Redemption Notice," he replied, returning the eyebrow lift and staring directly at Dale.

The American upped the ante. He continued to look at Lester and slowly tilted his head from side to side in an exaggerated fashion. His right ear virtually touched his right shoulder and then the same on the other side. It sounded like a firecracker going off, as the action popped the bones in his bull-like neck. Finally he spoke.

"So, you wanna tell me why my suggestion is stupid?"

"Delighted, I'm sure," started Lester, as he sat upright. "There are two reasons. Firstly, I'm convinced our insurance contracts will pay-out enormously in the next 12–18 months and you'll be thanking me that I didn't allow you to redeem." He actually smiled at this point.

Dale wanted to come back instantly to address Lester's confusion. *This hippy isn't in a position to 'allow' me to do anything. Didn't he know that? I can do what I damn well want.* He let it go for the moment but needed some sort of conduit to discharge his rising irritation. He resorted to inserting the flexed knuckle of his index finger into his mouth and applying pressure.

"Secondly, if I give money back to investors, it will obviously reduce the size of *Credere*. If this falls below a certain point, the banks can cancel their contracts with Lambda." This second point was delivered as a matter-of-fact, quintessential British understatement.

Turner suddenly turned to face Lester and for the first time in the meeting, forgot all about what was on his plate.

"You mean they become worthless; the contracts are voided if the NAV falls? Jesus Christ Lester! At what fucking level? When does this happen?" he demanded. His gaze bounced between the two men – as if to ask why they weren't more concerned.

Dale didn't move; the index finger was still lodged in his mouth but by now, his eyes were firmly closed.

"I can't answer that precisely, I'm afraid. All the contracts are slightly different so there is no definitive answer, but our best estimate is around £300 million," replied Lester. He shrugged half-heartedly.

"Oh my God, Lester, you don't have a fucking clue what you're doing," said Turner. He stood up and paced the room. "Why did you agree to those clauses? This morning, the NAV was £325 million – I looked it up before we came over. We'll lose everything!" He stopped near the window on the other side of the room; he had his head in his hands, as he faced both men.

Dale had listened in disbelief. This aging hippy; this pathetic excuse of a hedge fund manager whose suit didn't even fit him, was way out of his depth and the banks had completely screwed him. He had thought there was a risk of losing a lot of money with Lambda before the start of this meeting, now he was convinced that the full $5 million would be lost.

He slowly released the finger from his mouth, particles of spittle resting on his lips as he did so. The teeth marks were deep – inflamed indentations around the distorted knuckle. Although he had refrained from speaking during Lester's explanation, it had been at the expense of his immense jaws clamping down ever harder. They had increased the pressure – a kind of automatic reflex as Lester had revealed each new level of incompetence.

"This just gets worse and fucking worse!" said Dale. "And given that you knew all of this; that the insurance premiums and collateral payments were reducing the size of the fund, you and your little band of misfits managed to persuade yourselves that taking out even more insurance was a good idea." He jerked his head aggressively motioning towards the direction of the main analyst room as he spoke.

"That's a classic Lambda trade. We'd be mad not to do it. And yes, my colleagues and me do think it's rather a good investment strategy. I'd also appreciate if you didn't refer to my colleagues in a derogatory way. They're all very bright people, committed to making your investment in *Credere* a success."

"Success, my ass!" shouted Dale, as he thumped the table. The sudden increase in volume and the loud bang made Lester start. Dale was shaking now. He hadn't wanted to lose his cool again with Lester but discovering his investment was now at risk of disappearing altogether was sending him over the edge.

"None of you know what the fuck you're doing. Your latest bet against Double-As is ludicrous. You look like a bunch of addicted gamblers – desperately trying to cover your existing losses rather than acknowledge when you've got it plain wrong. And I find your blatant lack of remorse sickening. Your misguided strategy is now likely to lose your clients all their fucking money and you don't show any regret: no shame, no guilt and no remorse. Don't you feel duty-bound to apologise to us for what you've done?" asked Dale.

Lester stared back at him.

"No, I don't. Everyone in this organisation is doing his or her level best to make this work. All you have done," said Lester, as he waived an index finger across the table, "is whinged and moaned for the past 18 months, and made our life hell with your threatening emails and unpleasant phone calls. Now, if you have nothing constructive to say, I've got a job to do."

Lester managed to close his ring binder and stood up.

"FitzGerald, you're not going anywhere, I want my fucking money back," growled Dale.

Lester stopped what he was doing and met the American's eyes.

"Lester, give us our fucking money back," echoed Turner.

The CEO of Lambda looked at Turner and then back at Dale. Finally, he replied.

"Gentlemen, I have no intention of doing any such thing." And he moved towards the door.

For a big man, Dale moved surprisingly quickly and was in front of Lester blocking his path before the CEO knew what was happening. He towered over Lester and just stood there with his arms folded.

"Excuse me, Mr Dale. This meeting is over," said Lester and moved to the side to get past.

Using his massive hands, Dale grabbed Lester by the lapels of his tweed jacket and pulled him towards him, practically lifting him off the floor in the process.

"Listen to me, you asshole. You think the last 18 months was ugly? I haven't even started. Now I'm gonna serve my redemption notice and I expect my money back in short order. Do you understand me?" He released Lester by virtually throwing him across the room.

Lester stumbled but just about managed to stay on his feet, as he crashed into the table and chairs. He straightened the lapels of his jacket and discovered that one had been ripped.

"Ron, come on. We need to calm down and discuss this," pleaded Turner from the safety of the other side of the room.

"Fuck off, James. You know what? This is partly your fault. You're the fucking idiot that picked this dumb shit to look after my money. Why the hell did you trust *him*?" Dale waived a dismissive hand in Lester's direction, but was no longer looking directly at him.

Lester had picked up a glass of orange juice and looked at it for a couple of seconds. He then threw its entire contents over Dale.

Turner put a hand up to cover his gaping mouth – his wide-open eyes scanning the remnants of a formal business meeting.

One side of Dale's face and suit was covered. He felt the warm, sticky liquid trickling down his neck and he stood motionless, not quite able to believe what had just happened. He cautiously looked down, not really wanting to, but feeling the need to survey the damage to his suit. It had been a present to himself a year ago to celebrate an investment that turned out better than expected. It had cost him $4,000, and now it was probably worthless. Just like his investment in this stupid fund: was there anything this fucking idiot didn't ruin? He felt the adrenaline takeover – pulsating through his body like some violent electric current and he flew at Lester; any hint of self-control now completely gone. Lester seemed to freeze, as Dale knocked the chair out of the way and pinned him up against a wall by securing one of his massive hands around his neck. He applied sufficient pressure to make it difficult for Lester to breathe. Dale tightened his grip even further, leaned in so that his face was almost touching Lester's.

"Jesus Christ, Ron. Will you calm down…let's discuss this," stammered Turner.

Dale ignored him.

"Listen to me, FitzGerald. I'm gonna get my money back and you're going to help me. Do you understand what I'm saying?" He eased his grip slightly to allow Lester to talk.

"Is that a threat, Mr Dale?" gasped Lester.

"You bet your sweet ass that's a threat," replied the American. He then pushed Lester backwards so that the back of his head hit the wall.

Lester baulked at the pain and finally Turner came over and pulled at Dale's arm to lead him away. But the American wasn't going anywhere and he just stood with his eyes transfixed on Lester and tightened his grip again. Dale's vision clouded and he sensed his strength increasing as his rage built. It was a raw kind of power; the kind he hadn't felt in years, and which only seemed to come to him in a fit of rage. He'd tried the Mr nice-guy approach. Reasoning with this arrogant little shit clearly wasn't going to work. It wasn't his preferred choice, but if he needed to resort to violence, he'd oblige. He tightened his grip and Lester's face was starting to turn crimson.

"Now then, you fucking hippy, when are you gonna give me my money back?"

Just then, the door of the office flew open as Troy Burrows and Ann barged through. They'd heard the commotion and were concerned about what was going on.

"Get off him, you idiot," shouted Troy, as he realised what was happening. He tried to help Turner free Lester's neck, but Dale just ignored them and continued to throttle Lambda's CEO against the wall.

Ann found herself in the middle of the room. She spun around looking for something that might help. Dale, Troy and Turner all had their backs to her as they struggled with each other – the tall American in the middle. Then she just ran at him and when she was close enough, kicked him as hard as she could between the legs.

Dale released some sort of high-pitched primal shriek – completely unlike the low, guttural vocal sounds he normally produced. He dropped like a cow that had been shot by the metal bolt to the brain when slaughtered. He rolled around holding his groin as the sense of severe nausea built. It felt like his abdomen was on fire.

Lester slumped down the wall holding his neck and gulping as much air as he could.

Turner and Troy turned to face Ann as one. She was stood covering her mouth as she watched Dale curled up in a ball on the floor. She ran out of the office – scurrying away in her pink socks – down the corridor like a naughty child running from an admonishing parent.

It took several minutes for Turner to get Dale into a chair; even longer to get him to speak and when he did, it was gibberish. The only words that were audible to Turner were 'I'll fucking kill him'.

Troy had taken Lester to his office and, although he was shaken, he was clearly recovering and there were no signs of lasting damage. Lester asked him to make sure the two men left Pont Street immediately.

Five minutes later, Turner cantilevered Dale into a waiting taxi.

Chapter Thirty-Seven

DI Hanson was back at the murder scene with Detective Mills. They were here to gain access to Angus Ross' computer files and anything else they thought they needed to do. It was spooky being back at the flat where it all happened; in fact, they were standing just a few feet away from where Angus Ross had died. The cloying odour of disinfectant hung in the stale air of the flat.

Hanson was looking at the large, framed photos on the wall. He managed a smile as he instantly recognised the team, time and place. No doubt about it – 29 May 2000. Ipswich 4 Barnsley 2 at Wembley to gain promotion from the old First Division to the Premiership. He could name every single player in that photo. There was Ross, kneeling down in the front row, medal around his neck and Town scarf in his hand. He even knew where he had sat inside the stadium to watch the game. Bloody big bloke in the seat immediately in front meant he missed half of it, but it was still a fantastic day!

He looked across to where this young man's life had ended just a few days before. How much can your fortunes change in a few short years? He was on top of the world that sunny day in May 2000; less than two years after that his career was over and now he was dead.

Mills apparently had less interest in Ipswich Town memorabilia and got to work immediately on the PC. They had already been through Ross' mobile and seen the text sent at 12.13 that said 'No Escape' from a pre-paid mobile telephone. Hanson was pretty sure a search through Ross' PC and his emails would uncover something that would help with the enquiries.

The desk was reasonably tidy, and mostly because there wasn't much on it. He noticed there were no photos of family or friends or any of the clutter that populated his own desk at home. A few square, yellow Post-it Notes lined one side of the screen; a reminder to do things that would now never be done. As they started to move around the PC, it became obvious that Ross had been very organised about filing – at least electronically. The directories were in date order and the emails generally filed under various headings so it was easy to find information. They decided to open up a few of the files first and then move onto the emails.

The screen went blank and then a video loaded up and played.

"Bloody Hell," said Mills. "Looks like this Ross bloke enjoyed his porn, sir."

"OK, Detective. Calm down," replied Hanson.

Each file that they loaded up under the heading 'Spa related work' was a video. Each one was filmed either in a kitchen or bedroom, it was always the same man (but his face was blacked out) but each time, it was a different woman. Hanson knew instantly it was Ross. His left forearm was decorated with a large black and grey Celtic cross surrounded by grey-shaded thistle flowers. He'd remembered that from Ross' playing days and you could see it in the photo on the wall he'd just been looking at. After a few minutes, he recognised the rooms. The kitchen was obviously the one just a few feet away and the bedroom scenes he soon determined were also recorded in the flat.

Then bingo. He recognised one of the women. It was the taller of the two women he'd been speaking to at the Spa last week. He checked his notebook.

"Paula Poorish," said Hanson, slowly, and in a *well-well-well-type* delivery.

"Pardon," replied Mills.

"That woman there, her name's Paula Poorish," said Hanson, as he pointed to the screen. "I interviewed her and one of her friends at the Spa last week. Ross was her personal trainer, but she claimed she'd never seen him outside of the gym."

"Fuck me, sir. You mean Paul Poorish's wife?" asked Mills.

"Who's Paul Poorish?" asked Hanson, as he continued to scribble notes.

"With respect, sir, don't you read the newspapers? He's the prospective Conservative MP for South Suffolk. He's a retired businessman – made his money in scaffolding or something – and he's now the red-hot favourite to win the by-election. Being tipped as a potential leader of the Tory party at some point."

"Not any point soon if this gets out, he's not," replied Hanson, tapping his pen against his chin. "Do a search for me on that name."

Within a few minutes, the two men had determined that the internet browser was full of research on Mr Poorish. There were photos of him with various politicians, including one with his wife and John Major. Yep, it was definitely Paula Poorish that had appeared on screen a few minutes earlier.

They found other similar videos but didn't recognise any of the other women. He then checked the emails.

Chief Inspector Smith's hunch had been right – Ross' life was far more complicated than that of a personal trainer. They found the escort correspondence, emails from overly aggressive debt collectors and the hard copy discs of the videos in one of the drawers. They also found a note from Ross to Paul Poorish.

Hanson's mobile went and he walked outside for a few minutes to answer it. He was now satisfied that he'd found a clear motive for murder. The problem was he'd discovered more than one.

As Hanson left, the conscientious Mills felt compelled to continue working; he loaded up more videos, sat back and watched.

Chapter Thirty-Eight

"So far, sir, there are at least three suspects."

"The first is Paul Poorish. He's an aspiring politician—"

"Hanson, I bloody-well-know who Paul Poorish is. I do read the newspapers you know."

Hanson's boss rattled the copy of the *Daily Telegraph* that was on his desk to verify his claim. CI Smith was a career Metropolitan Police Officer; that was until he'd been, unjustly, banished to the backwaters of the Suffolk countryside as penance for some minor indiscretion. He thought East Anglia was as flat as it was boring – unless one had a penchant for pig shit, farmers or carrots – which he didn't. He was proud to be a member of the 'Metropolitan elite' since it defined him on at least two levels.

Firstly, the Met was the pre-eminent police force in the country – obviously. And, secondly, he didn't mind the pejorative nature of its political meaning either. Quite the contrary, he was delighted to be well educated and cultured and if that differentiated him from Suffolk's Yeomen, well, all the better.

"What's Poorish got to do with any of this?" asked Smith, as he took a sip of his four o'clock tea. He held his vintage teacup and saucer like a nineteenth-century British aristocrat – cup in one hand and saucer in the other and sat up in his chair as straight as a die.

Hanson was slumped in the cheap plastic seat in front of Smith's desk. "Well, we've found a ransom note from Ross to Poorish and we have a video clearly showing Mr Poorish's wife being *extremely* unfaithful with Mr Ross. I suspect they were either having an affair or Mrs Poorish was an escorting client of Ross. We don't know whether the ransom note was ever sent – it certainly wasn't emailed from his account."

"These are the sex-tapes that half the department is talking about I assume. I thought you said matey-boy was a personal trainer?" asked Smith, as he swapped the cup and saucer with a delicate piece of Battenberg cake and a white china plate – the latter hovering below his chin to catch any errant crumbs from falling onto his uniform.

Hanson's lips pressed together and he inhaled a long breath before he continued.

"He was. But he was also an escort – we found the correspondence with the agency. I've already spoken to them and they confirmed that they had worked with Ross, although he used a different name. There are a few other sex-tapes in his flat that show him with other women – his face is always blocked out – but I know it's him because of the tattoo on his forearm. I suspect these women were clients that booked an 'in-call' but had no idea they were being filmed. We also believe that Ross may have been sleeping with some of his personal training clients, although I'm yet to verify this."

Smith finished the first slice of cake and wiped his mouth with a napkin.

"Bloody hell, Hanson, your footballing hero has turned out to be a bit of a tart."

Hanson rolled his eyes. "Yes, sir, I'm afraid he got himself caught up in all sorts."

"Ross was also in a lot of debt, sir, which brings us to suspect number two. From what we can see, he owed a local villain – Frank Stones – over £270,000."

It was the Chief Inspector's turn to roll his eyes. "Not Stones! Bloody hell. I might actually have some sympathy for your man – tart or no tart – if he's caught up with that reprobate. We were briefed on Stones a couple of times in the Met." Smith's gaze drifted off to the other side of the room, as if he yearned to be somewhere else.

"And from the email trail, Stones' company was losing patience to put it mildly. He was months late with his payments and all sorts of threats were flying around. Ross needed money; it certainly provided him with a motive to blackmail Poorish."

"How much was the ransom note for?" asked CI Smith.

Hanson fumbled with his notepad and then winced, "£500,000, sir."

"Greedy bastards these footballers, aren't they?" CI Smith's tone was as smug as it was caustic and made it clear he wasn't expecting a reply. Hanson gave a curt nod of the head.

"So we don't know at this stage, sir. Did Stones get to Ross before he was able to blackmail Poorish or did Poorish decide he wasn't going to play ball?"

"You said there was a third suspect, inspector," said Smith, who was now reclining in his large leather chair with his hands behind his head.

"That's more generic I'm afraid, sir. Clearly, there could be angry husbands or boyfriends out there if anyone of them had found out that their nearest and dearest was either having an affair with Ross or was a client of his. We can't rule out that someone just over-reacted."

"Crikey, how many tapes are there?"

There was a pause.

"Hanson?"

"Thirty, so far, sir," he replied, coughing into his hand as he did so.

"Bloody hell! Are there any females in Suffolk your boy wasn't shagging, Hanson?"

"Sir, he's not my boy and I think you'll find the population of Suffolk is over 700,000. So I don't know how you did your maths—"

"You might like to remember where you are, Detective Inspector," said Smith. His eyes had narrowed and he'd leaned forward in his chair with his hands together on the desk in front of him.

"Sorry, sir."

Slowly, Smith shook his head from side to side, as he eyed his subordinate.

"That's the trouble with you farmers," he said, "you're so pissed off with being knee-deep in pig shit, that you've lost all sense of humour. For what it's worth, I think the first two are far more likely, and my money's on Stones. He's an evil bastard. Poorish is so slimy he'd probably try to garner more votes by playing the sympathy card over his wife's infidelity. I doubt he's got the balls for a punch-up let alone murder. Just keep me posted, inspector." He lifted the Royal Doulton teacup and saucer once again and nodded to the door.

The meeting was over.

Hanson took his leave and Smith watched him close the door before returning to the theatre section of the *Daily Telegraph* and his second slice of Battenberg.

Chapter Thirty-Nine

Ann and Troy Burrows – the Chief Financial Officer for Lambda – were sat with Lester in his office. The TV, positioned high on one of his internal walls, was switched on but the volume was turned down to be barely audible. It was nothing more than a background noise and none of them were remotely interested in what was being said anyway. The three were in a full-blown crisis-mode. There were empty coffee cups, discarded sandwich wrappers and empty crisp packets all around the room. Apart from the odd comfort break, the inside of Lester's office was all any of them had seen for over three hours.

Since Dale and Turner's visit in December, the same thing was happening – the mortgage market had been weakening but the banks continued to deny any fall in the price of mortgage bonds or the CDOs. As a result, *Credere* continued to be contractually liable to pay insurance premiums and the fund reduced in size accordingly.

It had now got to the point where Lester received an email on an hourly basis providing the NAV of the fund in real-time. The last one that hit his inbox, half an hour ago, had a spot value of £310 million. Two days before, it had been £315 million. The rate of decline was increasing, partly as a result of the additional premiums they were paying to bet against the Triple-A tranches of CDOs. Troy wasn't above reminding Lester on occasion that he'd disagreed with that decision, but not today. The present was all about two things: how on earth *Credere* was going to be able to pay the next set of premiums, and, what to do about that letter.

Ron Dale had been true to his word. Once he'd recovered from his surgery – Ann's drop kick had caused a testicular torsion – he organised the Consortium into formerly serving a redemption notice. They wanted their money back. An over-aggressive, and probably overpaid, New York attorney had sent both an electronic version and a hard copy just to make sure that Lester understood the magnitude of the situation, and, Lester assumed, to justify his fees. The hard copy was on the desk in front of them – brief, curt, factual and certainly impolite. It reminded Lambda's CEO of the relevant sections of the Limited Partnership Agreement and confirmed that Lambda had three months to return the monies to the investors named at the bottom. If Lester wanted to discuss the situation, he should contact the attorney – his investors no longer wanted to speak to him.

Lester knew that if they paid out the monies in accordance with the notice, it would unquestionably be the end of *Credere* and almost certainly the end of Lambda; it would also mean unemployment for the entire team. They couldn't possibly pay the premiums that were due and give some of the investors their money back.

"OK, why don't we deal with the premiums first? If we don't pay those, the banks can cry foul and tear up our agreements, so let's forget Ron Dale and the awkward squad for a moment," said Troy. Lester thought it was a good suggestion – they'd need to come up with a solution for the letter, but the premiums needed their immediate attention.

Signalling his agreement, Lester moved the letter off the desk and turned to Ann.

"OK, Ann, what can we sell to fund the premiums?"

She was working hard; they all were, but she seemed to be particularly dedicated to help try to save the business. This was her first job after graduating and her baptism of fire was beginning to show. She'd certainly lost weight herself – although who was he to express an opinion about that. She was stooped more than sat and her eyes were dull and heavy. He recalled the first day that Ann and Sally had joined the team, two young, energetic graduates. He'd had to fire Sally when he made half the team redundant and he knew Ann had found that difficult. He couldn't help thinking that it might have been better for Ann's sake if she had also gone. She would have found another job easy enough and it would have been a lot less stressful than being here.

She wiped her hands on a serviette, as she finished her apple and turned to the screen. "Well, we've sold most of the liquid stuff in the past so this is getting trickier. But my suggestion is that we unwind these positions here." She was using a pencil to highlight a short list of securities on Lester's computer screen.

"Will that generate sufficient funds – would we need to sell all of them?" asked Troy.

Lester knew where his CFO was coming from. The portfolio was becoming less balanced as sales had been made to generate premiums. The securities that had been sold were done so on the basis that they were liquid – so could be turned into cash quickly – but without much thought to the integrity of the remaining portfolio.

"I think so yes, but we'll obviously get less for them than this valuation on the screen. The market knows that we're effectively forced sellers so they screw us on price. Every time we sell now, we'll be taking an extra hit as the NAV will fall by more than the cash we generate. It will be a double-hit on performance if you like," sighed Alice.

Lester and Troy looked at one another.

"What's our best estimate of NAV post the premium payment?" asked Lester.

"Well, it is just that, an estimate, but around £304 million," replied Ann in a weary, monotone voice which Lester couldn't remember hearing before. She didn't quite meet his eyes.

Lester rested an elbow on the table and placed his chin in the palm of his hand and looked to the ceiling for inspiration. As he did so, the TV caught his attention and the spectacle that flashed across the screen held it. There were brand new houses with '*foreclosure*' signs stuck in the middle of their pristine green lawns; distressed-looking people ferrying belongings out of the properties in flimsy brown cardboard boxes; a family stood in a driveway looking back at a charming house with a veranda wrapped around it and crying. The ticker tape at the top of the screen stated '*The Globe is bankrupt*'.

"Shit, sorry, Ann. What's this?" He grabbed the remote and fumbled around trying to increase the volume.

The images continued and the newsreaders comments were overlaid.

"Today, The Globe Mortgage Company, the largest subprime mortgage lender in the US, has declared itself bankrupt and filed for Chapter 11. It has reported that it will cut more than half of its workforce with immediate effect."

"Jesus, Lester. That's the Globe – most of the bonds and CDOs that we bet against were stuffed full of mortgages from those guys," said Troy. He stood up and edged closer to the screen. Ann and Lester remained seated but their eyes were now locked onto the news report.

"We understand that the company simply ran out of money. Apparently, the rate of defaults within its mortgages has risen to unprecedentedly high levels. The company's finances have been overwhelmed."

"Bloody hell. I knew they were having difficulties, but this is unreal. They had 20% of the market in certain locations. If they've gone pop, this is a game-changer. There's no way the banks can ignore this," said Lester.

The newsreader introduced the Chief Economist from some investment bank – apparently, an industry expert who would know what had happened.

"Well, as you say, Cathy, this is unprecedented. Nobody could ever have expected this rate of failure. This is something that has simply never happened before," he replied.

Lester stood up, trance-like and turned the sound back down – he'd heard enough, more than enough.

He then turned to his colleagues. "It's happening, guys. This is it!"

"Ann, can you brief the others" – he nodded in the direction of the open plan area – "and have them closely monitor the ABX index in the next hour? If subprime mortgages tank, we'll see it there first."

"Troy, can you ask one of the team to call the banks and ask them what our positions will look like following this news? This is Armageddon for subprime bonds so our CDO positions have to go up."

As Troy and Ann left the room to give the team the good news, Lester pulled out the redemption letter and read it with a new sense of purpose. There was something that Ann had said a few moments before that didn't chime – he couldn't put his finger on it, but something wasn't right. He re-read the section of the letter that outlined the key parts of the LPA.

A few moments later, Troy and Ann came back into his office.

"They're on it, Lester. They'll give us an update in a few minutes – needless to say, they're a lot happier than they were ten minutes ago," said Ann. Her eyes were wide, rounded – and she was fidgeting – as if impatient to get on and do.

Lester smiled. "OK. Let's spend a few minutes on the agreement and the awkward squad. Ann, what did you say earlier about the double hit on the NAV if we sell these securities?" Lester was pointing back to his computer screen.

She explained once again, and Lester closed his eyes to concentrate on exactly what she was saying.

"As we sell these less liquid assets, we're effectively forced sellers. I understand that we have to do it, but from a future performance perspective, it's madness. The investment returns for the investors that remain in the fund are clearly compromised."

"That's it! That's it! Troy, can you pass me the agreement please?"

Lester knew he'd seen it written down somewhere and he reviewed his decrepit ring binder. It contained the 200 odd page document that was the agreement with the investors.

"What section of the LPA does the letter refer to, Ann?"

Ann picked the letter up off the desk and told him. He flicked through the sections furiously. He couldn't find what he needed and the broken clasp was releasing the pages making his job more difficult.

"Damn, I know it's here somewhere, I've seen it written down." He continued his search through the document.

"What. What have you seen written down, Lester?" asked Troy.

"*Compromise*, I know the agreement prevents us from doing something that would 'compromise the remaining investors'. We're not allowed to do it for the reason Ann has highlighted – it makes sense. I know it's here but I can't bloody well find it!" By now, the document was in three or four different chunks and Lester swore, as he struggled to find what he knew was there.

"May I?" asked Ann, as she helped herself to the keyboard and mouse on Lester's desk. He moved out of the way and looked at Troy – a questioning eyebrow raised as he did so.

She looked at them and grinned. "The electronic version of the LPA is filed under LEGALS on the A-Drive." She commandeered the chair and sat at Lester's desk – shoulders back, chest thrust out and started tapping away proficiently.

Troy and Lester, two self-confessed computer Luddites, smiled at one another with the same, 'why didn't I think of that' expression on their faces.

Less than a minute later, Ann had opened the *Word* document. She used the word-search facility to locate occurrences of *compromise*.

Bingo! It appeared in several clauses, but the one that Lester had remembered was the one that would save them.

Twenty minutes later, Ann read out the draft of the reply that they had composed for the New York attorney.

Dear Mr Lewis,
2 June 2007

Request for Redemption Payments under Section 7:5:3 of the LPA with Credere

Thank you for your letter and email dated 31 May 2007.
Section 7.5:6 of the Agreement states that
'The Fund Manager will be able to defer Redemptions in the following circumstances:

- *Where there is no tradable market in the underlying securities held by the Manager;*
- *Where there is a market but the prices achievable will substantially compromise the interests of the remaining investors.'*

It is my considered opinion that the above circumstances currently and accurately describe the market conditions for both subprime mortgage bonds and CDOs. Consequently, I will not be complying with my clients' redemption request.
I trust you will inform my clients of this decision accordingly.
Yours sincerely,

Lester FitzGerald

"Great, I'll send it out later today. Email it to the lawyers and tell them I need their view in the next hour. Let's assume that deals with the Consortium for the moment," said Lester.

Buoyed by the progress they had made in the last thirty minutes, the three of them then bounced their way through to the open plan area. This was the first good piece of news the team had had in months, so he knew his colleagues would be excited. As he walked in, Lester was shocked by what he found. Silence, and a collection of faces as long and as miserable as the Agreement they had just been reviewing.

"What's going on?" asked Troy.

"That news on The Globe came out over half an hour ago," said Steve, as he glanced at his watch. He then looked back at his Bloomberg terminal. "Since then, the ABX index hasn't gone down. It's actually up! This is madness!"

"Has anyone spoken to the banks?" asked Lester. He couldn't hide the anger from his voice. This was getting ridiculous.

"Yes, I have," replied another analyst sat on the opposite side of the room. He was pinching his skin at the throat and Lester noticed his gaze flitting around the room, as he peered through his granny glasses.

"I spoke to a colleague of Rankin's at Silvermans. She said not to hold our breath, that these markets aren't necessarily correlated and reminded me of the extreme complex nature of the products we bought."

Troy threw his arms up in the air and turned around in frustration.

"That's total crap!" said Lester.

"I know. I know, I told her the same," said the analyst, as he ducked slightly and held his palms up in self-defence. "She said she'd review the positions again tomorrow morning and then she hung up. She had another appointment apparently."

Lester wanted to explode. His own experience of dealing with Rankin and his colleagues was the same. They were rude and evasive and if they didn't want to continue the conversation, they'd end it. He couldn't have a go at one of his colleagues because the banks were behaving unreasonably.

He walked to the front of the room, with the white board on the wall behind him and turned to face his colleagues, all of whom were now watching him. He could feel his body tensing and tugged at the back of his shirt as he felt the perspiration trickling down his skin. He leaned against the front desk to steady himself; he was sucking in as much air as he could but he began to feel light-headed.

The last time he stood precisely where he was now and spoke to colleagues was when he announced that they had to make half of the team redundant. He thought about the people that he'd lost and tried to imagine what they were all doing. Hopefully, they all had jobs and weren't feeling as stressed as him. He blinked and wiped his brow.

Then he thought about the news report. Today, the largest subprime lender in the US had blown-up; it had run out of money because the rate of mortgage defaults was so high. It should have been the catalyst that forced the murky world of mortgage derivatives to its senses but so far, it hadn't changed a thing. Instead it brought home to Lester the crushing reality of Lambda's own precarious financial position and why the company had arrived at this point. He'd driven Lambda into the ground by pursuing the strategy that he'd insisted upon. His company was no better than *The Globe*, and was also about to run out of money. They could probably defer redemptions, but instead the last few weeks of liquidity would be sucked-up by premiums and collateral payments. So what was the difference? It just delayed the inevitable: a pathetic end to a business that he had ruined through his obsession to beat the banks.

The air seemed to thin even more and Lester began to feel dizzy. He looked around the room and realised that everyone was still looking at him – waiting for a response. Then the desks and the colleagues and the computer screens started to move – slowly at first – but then, they began to flash by him like he was speeding down a tunnel and everything was racing towards him as it narrowed. Then suddenly, it all stopped and everything went black.

An hour later, Lester was promising the doctor that he'd listen to his body and his friends and take it easy. Susan had insisted on calling the ambulance and the paramedics had arrived a few minutes after Lester regained consciousness. He'd fainted and started to fall along the length of the desk he'd been leaning against and Troy had managed to break most of his fall. But he still had a bump on the side of the head, which he now held an ice pack against.

He assured Susan that he'd take the rest of the day off and go home, but he wanted to do one thing before he left. Ann had received confirmation from the lawyers and he reviewed the letter one last time. He knew he should send it. But a Rubicon would now be crossed; there would be no turning back; the Consortium had already sent the redemption letter – they'd now go to war to get their money back.

He put the ice pack down and directed his mouse towards the send button on his computer screen. It hovered there whilst he imagined an incandescent Ron Dale receiving it and wondered what the aggressive American's next move would be. He was reminded of Dale's answer to his question.

"*You bet your sweet ass that's a threat,*" the American had replied. Lester felt the back of his head and found the bump that was still there from his head being pushed against the wall. He was getting quite a collection of bumps and bruises.

He clicked on the send button and left the office.

Chapter Forty

"Well, *I* don't think *you* should go, Sam. She's a fucking tart who deserves everything she gets. She was unfaithful for fuck's sake! I don't think you should go anywhere near her," announced Andrew Longmire. He was sat on a stool in the kitchen reading some papers for a conference call later that day.

Sam looked pointedly at her husband. She'd forgiven, but certainly hadn't forgotten the scene on the back of the *Alsace* in Cannes.

"That's rich, Andrew."

It seemed to be enough to remind him of his own transgression and he looked up quickly from his work.

"That's different. I was under a lot of pressure and it was one, weak isolated moment. Paula Poorish was having sex with a man half her age and using her husband's money to pay for it," replied Longmire.

"Oh, I see. It's the source of funding that makes the difference, is it? Only a banker could come up with that one, Andrew. You used your own money to pay for sex, so that's OK then," replied Sam. She looked at her husband and an embarrassed half-smile stole across her face.

"Sam, this isn't about me. It's about that tart."

"Stop calling her that. You haven't got an empathetic bone in your body, have you? She made a mistake, but she's not a criminal and she's certainly not a bloody murderer."

"Well, we'll see what the police investigation says about that, shall we? Anyway, why have you got so much sympathy for her; is there something you're not telling me?" Longmire was finger tapping the kitchen surface.

"What's that supposed to mean?" asked Sam. She delved into her handbag to find her car keys and avoid eye contact.

"You don't put in an appearance in these tapes, do you, darling?" asked Longmire, as he looked at his wife and grinned.

Sam looked back at him. This was her husband at his diabolical worse. He asked a question with that stupid bloody grin on his face; the one he put there to 'prove' he was only teasing – but which allowed him to gauge a reaction.

"Andrew, you're such a dickhead sometimes, do you know that? Is that what you really think of me?"

"Come on, Sam," he replied, intensifying the smirk right on cue, "you know I'm only joking."

"Mm."

Sam left to keep the promise she'd made to Paula the night before.

With his wife out of the way, Longmire returned to First Capital's interim results for the year ending December 2006 and the rest of his paperwork. Profits were up for a third straight year and the share price had moved on again accordingly. It was 255p on the screen on his laptop. There was also a memo, which Longmire had written, introducing the team to the new Chairman of First Capital. Steve White had finally decided to step down. The replacement was a bit of an old duffer, but much more pliable. Longmire grinned, as he attended to his paperwork.

Sam was finally let through the police cordon that prevented the braying journalists, and anyone else without permission, from entering the half-mile-long driveway to the Poorish residence. Flashbulbs exploded and she could hear the shrieks from reporters, as they tried to ask her questions even through the firmly closed windows of her car. Having successfully negotiated the press gauntlet, she drove up the drive and parked just outside the house.

She didn't know what to expect. She had thought her friend was holding up well, but then she'd got the call last night. Apparently, Paula had been struggling for over a week, since the last time the two had met, but had imploded the moment she saw yesterday's Daily Mail – and who could blame her?

As she stood there looking at the large oak-wooden door, she was suddenly struck by the building's silence. She recalled the welcoming sounds that normally emanated from within it; Simon playing in the house with Paula's pets trundling through this grand entrance at will. There was always noise and energy oozing through the Suffolk-Pink walls of the farmhouse – the perfect home, or so it seemed to her then.

But today, the house seemed uninhabited, almost abandoned. She could hear the gentle flow of water cascading over the water feature in the front garden and the dull, monotonous hum of the A12 – nearly a mile away – both sounds revealing themselves for the first time. The heavy door creaked on its hinges and swung slowly, as if it had now become reluctant to reveal its contents.

Sam breathed a sigh of relief, as she realised it was the housekeeper who stood behind it. The last person she wanted to see was Paul Poorish. She led her through towards the kitchen. The cold flagstone floors and the low ceilings, supported by the russet-coloured oak beams, provided an overpowering sense of confinement. Most of the curtains on the small, casement windows were drawn. She wondered if this is how her friend felt – hemmed-in, confined, almost imprisoned in her own home rather than face the outside world. Whenever Sam had walked through the house in the past, cosy, warm, lived-in were all adjectives that would jump out at her, but not today.

She entered the kitchen and looked at Paula, stooped over the end of the breakfast table cradling a glass of water. She was staggered at how much her friend had changed – so much so that Sam wasn't sure she'd have recognised her out of context. There was no beautifully presented ballerina bun sitting on top of her head and no immaculate skin-tight black leggings to show off her amazing figure. Instead, limp, unwashed strands of hair hung down past her shoulders and across her face like dirty string. Her eyes were puffy and her face slightly bloated – presumably through crying. But her clothes were the biggest surprise.

The baggy tracksuit bottoms and over-sized sweatshirt swamped her slight frame. It reminded her of something that she couldn't quite place and it was difficult for her to imagine Paula's pristine Carine-Gilson-best underneath such an outfit. If Sam had been asked to describe her friend in one word, she would have used crushed. Then she had it, and the hairs on the back of Sam's neck stood up, as she realised her friend's attire reminded her of a prison-issue grey tracksuit.

And if the salacious press coverage in yesterday's newspapers had anything to do with it, this was where Paula or Paul or both of them was heading. There had been outrage in the town about Ross' murder and the pressure on the police to make an arrest was growing relentlessly. Thousands of heartbroken fans had lined the streets in and around Portman Road at the funeral procession for Ross. Then came the leak and the public suddenly knew about the sex-tapes and the involvement of a rich politician's wife. It was all a splendid gift for the newspaper editors who'd decided to play-up to the public's sympathies and peg Ross as the victim in all of this: who cared about the truth – that didn't sell newspapers. Sam could remember the gist of what was reported in the tabloids the day before:

"Poor, under-privileged Scottish kid who turned Ipswich Town FC into a force to be reckoned with once again but heart-breaking injury curtailed stunning career. A bored, rich politician's wife then seduces the vulnerable genius. The perverted wife commits their moments of passion to tape but her husband discovers the evidence. We understand the husband, the once prospective conservative candidate for Suffolk South, Paul Poorish, is helping the police with their enquiries."

Sam went over, pulled her friend up on her feet and gave her a bear hug. She couldn't help but detect the slight odour that hung around her loose-fitting clothes.

"Paula, come on. Let's get you some fresh water and a cup of coffee," said Sam, as she surreptitiously smelt the glass. She could make out the slightest hint of something – *Vodka?* She poured the remnants down the sink and flicked on the kettle.

Paula collapsed back into her chair, and looked up at her friend.

"Oh, Sam. This is torture. I can't go anywhere or do anything. Everyone hates me."

"The police aren't stupid, Paula. They'll find out who did this to Ross and arrest them. Those bastards outside will then move onto something else and they'll leave you alone," reassured Sam, as she nodded in the direction of the window.

"But it's the bloody tapes, Sam. Everyone thinks it was me that made the recordings and that I'm the guilty party in all of this. All the papers seem to think Ross is an angel. He's not; he was bloody horrible to me and used me like a piece of dirt!"

Sam had known about the tapes the day after Ross' murder. Paula had told her about the affair, the money, the tapes and Ross' threat to blackmail Paul.

"Has Paul seen the tapes?" asked Sam, as she finished making the drinks.

Paula went for the 'water' that was no longer in front of her as if she needed it in order to continue. Sam handed her the coffee and sat down opposite.

"That's another thing, Sam. I honestly don't know. Paul's never been the best at communication and it's not exactly an easy conversation to have with your husband, is it? *Excuse me, darling, but have you actually seen the tapes of me shagging the man who was trying to blackmail you? Oh, and by the way, could you pass the salt and pepper?"*

The friends caught the expression on each other's face and both managed an incongruous laugh.

"Where is Paul?" asked Sam.

"I assume he's in the drawing room; been mooching around there for days. He's devastated; for the moment at least, his political career is in ruins. The Party has already told him that unless someone else is successfully convicted for the murder, it would be political suicide for them to nominate Paul. There's no smoke without fire and all that. As far as they're concerned without a conviction, people will think I did it, he did it or we both did it."

Acknowledging the possibility that one of them could go to prison was too much. She crumpled and Sam came around to comfort her. The friends held one another – each looking over the other's shoulder – Paula sitting and Sam kneeling.

"Do you think he did it, Paula?"

Sam felt her friend tense-up and her grip tighten – like Simon used to when he was young and Sam had asked him to tell her the truth. There was a long pause and then her friend spoke in fragments.

"Of course not, Sam. Anyway, we were together. We were here all evening that night," replied Paula. Sam continued the embrace, and kept looking over her shoulder; grateful she couldn't see her friend's face.

"Sam, how did I get here? I'm going to lose my home, my husband and everything else. How could I be so bloody stupid?" sobbed Paula, as she buried her head into her friend's shoulder.

Sam looked across the vast kitchen, as she cuddled and rocked Paula. Her hand gently massaged the back of Paula's head as she considered that question for the umpteenth time – yes, *how could you be so bloody stupid?*

Her friend had insanely, in Sam's opinion, risked her financial security. Yes, she knew Paul was a little controlling, and that he was not the most attentive, or the most exciting, but which husband was? And if there was anything more sinister going on – like Paul was having affairs or was violent towards his wife – she was certain that Paula would have spoken about it. She never did.

Her own husband was often a wanker of the first order – the little question and answer session this morning borne testimony to that fact. But to have an affair would risk everything. The home and financial security that she had worked so hard to obtain; that she had spent her young life craving for and much of her adult life worrying that she'd end up losing. She wasn't prepared to jeopardise that for anything.

But although this was Sam's default position, a sort of permanent mental state when it came to all things financial, she admitted there was a part of her that thought otherwise. She closed her eyes and hugged Paula again. Not out of sympathy this time. A much stronger sense had taken hold and Sam could feel her eyes start to glaze. Deep in the recesses of her mind – probably where the truth is to be found, thought Sam – it was respect that she experienced – respect and admiration. Paula had actually done something about being unhappy. Sam knew she never would. As she hugged her friend for a few moments, it was that feeling that grew.

A few seconds later, she opened her eyes and the view shocked her back to the present with a jolt. She wiped her eyes frantically.

Paul Poorish was glaring at her from the entrance to the kitchen. A cold, narrow stare that made the hairs on the back of her neck stand up once again. He smiled; an ugly twist to his mouth, and then turned and walked away.

Chapter Forty-One

Lester sat bolt upright in bed, with a hand placed across his chest as he struggled for breath. The perspiration that had made his bedclothes hot and wet had now turned them icy cold – they were clinging to his skin like a wet shirt on a wintry day. He shivered, as he glanced at the bedside clock – 3.48 am.

He'd woken because of the recurring nightmare that wouldn't leave him alone. It had started, as it often did, back at school and the Kangaroo court, but the venue was devoid of logic in time or space. The self-appointed judges were now random selections of old school bullies and his present-day antagonists. Simon Rankin was there wearing Lester's old school blazer – granite grey with a bottle-green rope braid trim around the lapels, pockets and two inches above the end of the cuff. Watson (one of his childhood demons) was sat to one side of the Silvermans employee but he appeared a combination of his former self and James Turner.

When Lester looked up to the long, wooden bench where the eclectic group were sat, the room was definitely the old boarding house that held so many unhappy memories for him. The wall behind the bench was divided by the wooden dado rail about one third of the way up; drab semolina wallpaper above and some putrid shade of green – that doesn't exist in nature – below. He'd never forget that combination – he doubted anyone would. But every time he looked around the rest of the room, the venue morphed into a modern, open-plan office; he could see distant relatives dressed in smart office attire and high-rise buildings dominated the view when he looked out of the window. Canary Wharf or New York beckoned – but he wasn't sure which.

The piece of paper on the desk in front of him was the letter he'd sent back to the New York lawyer a few days before. The dream, he now realised, was the depiction of a court scene where the verdict on the validity of Lester's refusal to pay out his investors' redemptions was imminent. The sense of doom was too great each time that Ron Dale, dressed as the *Beast* from the school production, used one of his enormous hands to raise the gavel to furnish the court with his decision and Lester would wake-up – soaking wet and struggling for breath.

He'd had enough. It may have been before 4 am, but the thought of lying on cold, damp sheets was less appealing than getting up at silly o'clock. He showered, dressed and headed for the office. There were always the Asian markets. He'd see what was happening out there before London opened.

The two figures dressed in black slipped on their balaclavas and entered Lambda's offices from the Pont Street entrance. It was 3.55 am. As she expected, the security code was the same and she effortlessly disarmed it. It was her accomplice, however, that was the professional. He was well-paid for his unique set of skills – breaking and entering but with a particular penchant for the burglary of high-end financial institutions. He had spent the last three years helping financial institutions steal secrets from one another. In 2007, global financial espionage was doing brisk business.

Whilst she had dealt with the security code, he had unpicked the lock in a matter of seconds and they moved steadily through the Lambda office suite. She led him through the narrow corridors, past reception and the analyst room and further along until they arrived outside the office that they were here to access. Dr FitzGerald was the name on the door that became highlighted as the torchlight came to rest on it. He passed the light to his companion who illuminated his work and he dealt with the lock – once again within a few seconds, the door swung open.

He took back the torch and gestured to the woman as if to say – *over to you.* He then leaned against a wall and helped himself from the inverted water dispenser nearby. He drained the water into a cup whilst he shone the torch for his colleague. The sound of air bubbles replacing the water in the plastic barrel gave her a start.

She retrieved the security codes from behind the frame of the Vitruvian Man artwork to the right of the desk, closed her eyes and took a calming breath before she logged on. She searched Lester's email account, his hard drive and the main server and then, after a couple of clumsy attempts, inserted the data stick into the side of the machine. She paused, tugged at the base of her balaclava and took another deep breath.

Lester put his key in the Yale lock and opened the heavy wooden front door to the Victorian building. She was far too focussed to hear him enter; she had saved the first document and was on the hunt for the second. But the professional's instincts were well honed for detecting any change in background noise. He knew in an instant that they had company. He put down his water and quietly retrieved the small wooden truncheon that always accompanied him whilst he worked.

He whispered into her ear and she frantically flicked between screens looking for the last document that she needed.

Lester flipped the light switch in the hallway and wondered why the alarm wasn't on. He'd have to give the security firm a call. They should inspect the office around midnight and turn the alarm on themselves if it wasn't activated already. He walked along the corridor towards his office. Before he got there, he stopped as he noticed the door was slightly ajar, not closed and locked as he had left it. There was a dim glow emanating from inside – not powerful enough to be the ceiling lights, but perhaps his computer screen? He stood and listened for a few seconds – nothing.

He crept the next three feet slowly and put his arm out to open the door just as the water dispenser next to him decided to refill. He jumped back and into it and had to hold onto to the plastic barrel to prevent him and the equipment falling over.

Then he pushed on the door, walked in and found someone sitting at his desk dressed in black and wearing a balaclava. The shock had barely registered when the blow hit him from behind.

"What the hell are you doing?" she demanded. The professional casually replaced the truncheon inside his jacket pocket, just like the office employees that normally stood in the room might slide a pen into a suit-jacket at the end of a meeting. Lester was prostrate, face down, with his head practically touching her feet.

"You didn't say anything about violence! We're supposed to take the files and leave, you stupid bastard."

He moved towards her and then stopped – like he was suppressing his initial instinct. "Shut up, you stupid bitch, and save the information. He'll be fine in a few minutes – nothing a few Nurofen won't sort."

She clumsily finished her task and took the data stick. She looked down at Lester and shook her head.

"Come on. We're leaving," her accomplice informed her. She followed him through the office without saying another word. They took the office-cleaning uniforms out of their rucksacks – complete with security passes – changed, and placed the black clothing into their bags. They let themselves out and walked onto Pont Street. Anyone that saw them now wouldn't give them a second glance. He checked his watch – perfect, at 04.15 am, the city was stirring; the sight of uniformed cleaners slowly moving across central London on their way to work on early morning busses, on foot or on the tube marked the start of another perfectly normal day. He deliberately slowed his pace and tersely told her to do the same – it's a well-known fact, he informed her, that people walk faster when they're leaving work than when they're arriving. He needed people to think they were doing the latter.

Chapter Forty-Two

It was a beautiful May afternoon in paradise. Lloyd Sinclair, the CEO of Silvermans Investment Bank, could hear the waves of the Atlantic Ocean breaking on the shore no more than a hundred metres from where he was sat – in the garden of his weekend pad in the Hamptons. It was a walled enclave and what went on inside, stayed there. Sinclair loved the place; ninety minutes from his very public life in the hustle and bustle of New York, the people and the media attention to the closed perimeter of walls and fences at his private mansion. He loved the contrast.

Today was particularly private. He was hosting his annual 'thank you party' to some of his most loyal lieutenants. The rules were simple: only the largest fee earners at the bank were invited and you had to be male – although you couldn't move for girls, the moment you stepped inside the grounds of Sinclair's property. The parties were legendary, and Simon Rankin had been trying to get an invite for years. It was only his CDO sale commissions in the last twelve months that had finally won him his rite of passage.

Sinclair stood up and surveyed the scene before him. The centrepiece was his heart-shaped swimming pool, around which most of the guests were mingling. The infinity pool, with an L. and an S. boldly monogrammed on the bottom, looked out over a sunken garden where sun loungers were positioned amongst the cone-shaped miniature fir trees and ornamental art. The late spring sun was powerful, its beams reflecting off the shimmering water, as it slipped gently towards the lip before disappearing over the edge. The well-stocked bar to the right was staffed by scantily clad waitresses, their crisp white skirts picking out the white in the mosaic tiles of the pool. To the left, a breakout area with more loungers, potted olive trees, and comfy sofas set out on the expensive travertine shell paving stones.

He could see Rankin taking full advantage of the female company that Sinclair's team had organised. Every taste was accounted for; if men wanted some chat time with beautiful women, that was fine; if they wanted a little more, that was also fine – the girls were being sufficiently well paid to be suitably broad-minded. They had been organised via an agency by Sinclair's (male) personal assistant. The CEO wouldn't even see the invoice; the one that would be marked-up as 'research and marketing' would be signed-off by someone else. Rankin was talking to a beautiful girl who looked young enough to be his daughter. She was sat on the end of a sun-lounger with her feet planted on the floor and her long, tanned legs wide apart, confidently taking up the space in front of her.

Sinclair walked over to the bar, ordered a refill of his coca cola and sat talking to a few colleagues. Most were also pacing themselves and cradling soft drinks, water or light beers – the men were all veterans of Sinclair's parties and knew there was a long way to go. They shared a few jokes and stories about earlier events and then Sinclair's mobile vibrated in his pocket. He pulled it out and could see it was Chuck Whiteman – an unexpected and unsolicited call from the Treasury Secretary's private phone – and that could mean only one topic of conversation. He took the call and excused himself.

"Good afternoon, Chuck, how are you?" he asked, as he made his way inside his home. But it seemed Whiteman had no time for pleasantries.

"Listen carefully, Lloyd. I wanted to come and see you in person, but there's no time. So we'll have to take the chance on the phone. I'm sure you've seen the mess that The Globe has got itself in. Well, I've just had access to the underwriting files at that shop and my team have been speaking with some of the executives there and I have to tell you, I'm worried," said Whiteman.

Sinclair was now hurrying to his study – this sounded like they needed privacy. 'Worried': had Chuck Whiteman, his former boss, the ex-CEO of Silvermans and now the top finance official in the US Government actually used that word? He'd known Chuck Whiteman for twenty-two years: he'd been with him the day he told colleagues that he had cancer and needed to take time out from the office; he'd seen him with his back to the wall in a room full of irate shareholders. He'd seen him angry; he'd seen him bitter; he'd seen him sad. But he'd never once heard him admit he was worried – about anything. Sinclair opened the door to his office and shut it firmly behind him.

Whiteman continued.

"Look, I won't bore you with the details, Lloyd, but the Globe, and the other mortgage companies that my team and I have had access to have been fraudulent.

Some of the loans that these guys made were outrageous; I mean they're not just bad loans, they're corrupt." Whiteman paused to clear his throat.

"Lloyd, you need to stop dancing with the wolves – immediately."

Sinclair had been stood leaning against the door, but as soon as he heard the instruction, his heart cratered, like a lead weight was dragging it downwards. His knees almost buckled and he practically threw himself into his high-backed leather chair behind his desk.

"Chuck, what the fuck are you talking about? You know damn well we've got billions of those CDOs on our balance sheet. And we continue to churn out new ones even today that haven't been sold."

He fumbled around in the desk drawer, pulled out the cigarettes he was looking for and lit one. He took a long draw and waited for the nicotine hit. He rarely smoked, but when he did succumb, it was mainly when he was in his private study and the pressure was on; Whiteman's news was like the twisting of a valve that released torrents of the stuff. Silvermans had sold CDOs to their clients, but they also held them on their balance sheet to demonstrate an alignment of interest and, because up until now at least, they'd made the company a fortune. In the last twelve months, owning the CDOs had boosted profits by 20%. Sinclair took another drag.

"For Christ sake, Lloyd, don't be so fucking naïve! You've got time and you probably won't get the best prices but start moving the stuff off to insurance companies, clients or hedge funds – whoever is stupid enough to sit on that side of the trade. But you have to do it – now.

"If my hunch is correct, these things are gonna collapse because the underlying loans are so rotten and there'll be one hell of a hiccup in the financial markets sometime very soon. I want to make sure that the banks, and particularly, Silvermans are nowhere near it. If the banks were associated with all this stuff, we'd get vilified by the press – you know they hate us."

Shortly afterwards, Whiteman excused himself in order to attend another meeting. Sinclair clicked his mobile to finish the call, fumbled around lighting another cigarette and scanned the spreadsheet he'd opened whilst talking to his ex-boss. The Timberwolf cohort of CDOs were all there lined up in chronological order on the bank's balance sheet; Timberwolf 1 through to 4. Many of them had been sold to clients, but the bank also had exposure to them, and on Sinclair's numbers about $25 billion worth. They were rated Triple-A securities and supposed to be safe – but if Whiteman was right, they were all about to collapse in value.

He ran a hand across his beard and focussed. He was under no illusion that all Whiteman was interested in was protecting his legacy. He'd practically invented derivatives; the last thing he'd want was the banks, and particularly his previous employer, being associated with a car crash regarding CDOs. But whatever Whiteman's motivation was, Sinclair knew that he needed to change the bank's positions. He closed the spreadsheet down, stubbed out the cigarette and went to find the man he had in mind for the job.

Rankin wasn't where he'd left him and, because the girl with the long legs wasn't there either, he had a hunch where he might find them.

Rankin was stretched out naked on the bed in one of the five guest rooms. He was lying on his back with his hands behind his head gazing up at the ceiling; white recessed square panels with decorative golden trimming and a light in the centre of each one. Alternate panels were frescoed with half-naked murals of men, woman, boys and girls or bizarre androgynous combinations thereof. He twitched his nose and sniffed in the remaining fragments of the white powder that was responsible for his blissful state before he exhaled a long, satisfied breath.

Rankin looked across at the girl lying naked beside him. She was already facing him, propping herself up on an elbow. The credit card, rolled-up twenty-dollar bill and a small plastic bag were on the bed between them and he could still see the faint remnants of white lines across her pert breasts. He smiled, as he thought about the rest of the powder that was now working its way around the inside of their bodies.

As he looked at her, he wondered why on earth she was doing this for a living. She had a perfect body, an angelic face and the longest legs he'd ever seen. She could certainly be a successful model. Perhaps she enjoyed what she did? She was certainly very good at it. Anyway, he was feeling ecstatic; his heart was pounding and he had so much energy that he could go ten rounds with Mike Tyson. Instead, he thought he'd go another couple of rounds right here right now. If she felt anything like he did, this was going to be even more passionate than before!

As if reading his mind, she smiled and placed a confident hand between his legs and began to massage him expertly. She seemed to know exactly what it was he wanted before he even knew himself. He lay back and had just closed his eyes to allow the other senses to take over when the rapping at the door began. It wasn't a polite, curious knock; to determine if anyone was in the room, it was an aggressive thumping that demanded immediate attention. He could hear the door handle being tried and, finally, his boss' voice on the other side.

"Simon, we need to talk. Open this fucking door right now!"

The girl gave a half-hearted shrug, as she removed her hand and glided away to the en suite. Rankin got up, hopped around clumsily, as he struggled into his shorts. His feet were sticking to the lining material on the inside and he lost his balance a couple of times – he swore, as he stumbled around the room.

The door rapped again.

"OK, OK. I'm coming, give me a second," shouted Rankin. He threw a cover over the paraphernalia on the bed and opened the door.

"Jesus, Lloyd, what the hell's going on?" he asked.

Before Rankin could move, Sinclair had walked over to the en suite and knocked on that door also.

"Excuse me, miss. I need five minutes with my colleague I'm afraid."

Five seconds later, and just as Sinclair was preparing to knock the door down, the girl sauntered past them as if they were a polite queue waiting to use the toilet. No hint of awkwardness on her part, no sign of self-consciousness. Just long, steady strides taking her to the other side of the room and the exit.

"Lloyd, what is it? What couldn't wait?" asked Rankin. He had his hands on his hips now and gave his boss a stare – one that was severe enough to indicate irritation, but not harsh enough to overlook the bank's corporate hierarchy.

Sinclair turned and closed the door firmly. "We need to off-load the bank's CDO positions," he replied, meeting Rankin's eyes.

That was probably the only thing the CEO of Silvermans could have said at that moment that would have got his attention. Up until that point, Rankin had assumed he'd be back having fun within a few minutes, but this sounded serious – very serious. He'd spent the last two years carefully building up a CDO exposure at Sinclair's behest, made billions for the bank in the process and now the guy was telling him to undo it all.

"What are you talking about, Lloyd?" asked Rankin, as he rubbed his eyes and blinked furiously – he needed to concentrate.

"I want all our CDO and subprime positions moved off balance sheet. Either sell them to clients or buy insurance against their collapse but do it right now."

Rankin now stared at his boss. "Lloyd, I don't think we should do that – some of our counterparties are on the verge of going pop. If we can just hold our nerve for a few more—"

Sinclair took a step closer.

"Simon, don't question me. Just get on with it!"

"But Lloyd, this is mad, the counterparties are going to roll over any day, I know that for a fact! We'll clear up. Can't we do this next month rather than now?"

Rankin had effectively staked his reputation on the success of CDOs – unwinding his positions was going to be agonisingly embarrassing.

Sinclair leaned in even further – he was almost nose-to-nose with his subordinate.

"Simon, you have a choice. You start selling down now, or you move out of the fucking way and I get someone in who will start selling." Rankin's dilated pupils looked back at his boss.

"OK, OK, I get it." He raised his hands in capitulation.

"When do you want me to start?"

Sinclair looked at his watch. "You've got an hour."

"What!" replied Rankin.

"There's a car outside waiting for you, Simon. Get dressed, get in it and get to the office. Start work on this as soon as you get there."

Rankin didn't have a choice, his head tipped back on his neck as he looked at the ceiling once again.

"OK. I'm on my way," he replied. He set about gathering his belongings. Sinclair watched him for a few seconds, as if he was processing another thought.

"Make sure you give me a written update of progress by close of business today – whatever time you finish."

And then, almost as an afterthought, Sinclair added, "Oh, and Simon, I'll send the girl to the hotel – she'll be waiting for you when you finish tonight. Remember, expensive habits require a good job and a happy boss."

Ten minutes later, Rankin climbed into the black limousine and let the soft leather seats and headrest do their job. He closed his eyes and eased into the lumbar back support as the driver set off. He thought about the CEO's dictum. Effectively, the bank would need to go from poacher to gamekeeper so when the music stopped, the bank wouldn't be exposed to a collapsing CDO market. In fact, Silvermans would now be motivated to see CDO prices fall, even though their clients were continuing to own the CDOs and anticipated that prices would continue rising.

As the limousine began the final part of the journey across Manhattan to the Broad Street office of Silverman, Rankin began to come to terms with the new instruction. It would be a busy couple of weeks, but he'd get it done. How bad can it be? In fact, how bad was any of it, he'd start the process in the next few hours and then hurry back to his hotel.

His mobile phone pinged a message to him as he thought about what would be waiting for him at the hotel. He glanced down at the display.

SIMON, IT'S LESTER FITZGERALD HERE. I CANNOT GET THROUGH TO YOU ON YOUR LANDLINES. CAN YOU PLEASE CALL ME AS A MATTER OF URGENCY!

Rankin closed the message and snorted, as he threw the phone onto his jacket next to him. He needed to talk to that arrogant arsehole like he needed a hole in the head. His London office had been passing on the messages all week. Lester FitzGerald could bloody well wait.

Chapter Forty-Three

Lester had been dreading this call, but he needed to confront James Turner. His nightmares had gotten worse since the assault in Pont Street and, tellingly thought Lester, James Turner and Ron Dale had gone from bit parts to being front and centre of the teasing and bullying that played out as he tried to sleep at night. The Consortium had now joined forces with Rankin and the other bankers and they were all jumbled together in the kangaroo court – like a kaleidoscope of evil – all determined to make him and *Credere* fail. Ron Dale had been there last night sat at the wooden bench laughing and joking with two figures dressed in black wearing balaclavas.

The more Lester thought about that morning, the more certain he became that the break-in was something to do with the Consortium. *Who else wanted him to change his mind?*

Hi dialled. He was tapping an index finger on his desk as he waited for the connection. After two and a half rings, a softly spoken woman confirmed it was James Turner's office.

"Good. I'd like to speak to him," said Lester.

"May I ask who's calling," enquired the receptionist, after an understandable hesitation.

"My name is Lester FitzGerald."

There was a pause and then. "Oh…I'll see if he's available. Please hold."

Lester was left waiting for a few moments, which did nothing to lighten his mood. His extended forefinger kept tapping away at the desk more quickly and more furiously with every moment that passed. Finally, Turner was on the line.

"This better be bloody good, Lester. I thought our attorney's letter was quite clear – if you want to speak to us, you go through him. I assume you're calling to apologise for sending that crass letter?"

"And why would I do that, James?" said Lester.

"Because you've finally seen sense?"

"And why would I be in a position to do that; because you arranged for someone to knock some sense into me? Is that what you mean?"

"Excuse me?"

"Don't feign innocence with me, James. Who did you pay to do it, some thug that you know or did that bully Ron Dale organise it?" snapped Lester, he could feel his whole body tense now.

"Lester, what the hell are you talking about?"

"You expect me to believe that you had nothing to do with this after all the threats that you and Dale have made?"

"Lester, back-up a minute. Do you want to tell me what the hell is going on?"

"The break in, James! A couple of thugs broke into my office, pinched information off my system and smacked me around the back of the head. So you'll have to excuse me, but the only threats I've received have come from you and the Consortium. So, did you have anything to do with it?" Lester stood up from his seat, as he asked the question.

"Jesus. Of course I didn't, Lester. Are you OK?"

"Why do you care if I'm OK or not? You think I'll crumble because you guys organise for someone to physically assault me? You think that will make me change my mind, sell my positions and give you your bloody money back?" He walked around in a tight circle looking at the floor as he spoke.

"Lester, I had nothing to do with it; none of us did. That's not our style, but you'll be hearing from our lawyers in the next few days." There was a brief pause. "We're suing you, Lester – we'll get our money back, even if we have to go to court."

Lester didn't give two hoots about them suing him. This was all going to be over in a matter of hours or days at the most; not months, which is what it would take a legal process to decide. *Credere's* NAV had fallen to £302.5 million. A movement of less than half of 1% would no doubt result in a gloating phone call from Simon Rankin telling him the contracts were voided. And a movement of less than half of 1% was nothing given the market gyrations that were now taking place.

But if James and the Consortium didn't break into his office and assault him, who the hell was it and what did they want? After the call, he fell back into his chair and pondered the question further.

Chapter Forty-Four

In mid-June 2007, two Bear Stern funds in the US that held CDOs collapsed. The investors were notified that they had not just lost some, or even a large part of their capital; Bear Sterns had to inform their clients that the investment was now worthless. Pension funds and insurance companies, and, of course, their individual policyholders began to pay the price.

Lester had called all his counterparties every day, sometimes twice a day, for a week. The person he most needed to speak to was Rankin, but he'd been told he was on a trip to New York – but why that meant he couldn't speak to Lester, he had no idea. There was no one, it seemed, he could speak to that could help. With the demise of The Globe and now the Bear Stern funds, *Credere's* contracts should be increasing in value rapidly.

Those he didn't want to hear from, of course, seemed to have no problem contacting him. Just as James Turner had promised, the lawyers confirmed that Lester's own clients were now in the process of suing him. He was barely surviving. Every day, the markets buffeted *Credere's* assets around the £300 million NAV threshold – some days, it was just above and others it was marginally below. They could still lose everything, and knew the mood in the office was delicate. But he clung wearily to the old adage that 'no news is good news': until Silvermans actually contacted him to highlight the limit was breached, he could still hope.

Then on the afternoon of Thursday, 21 June 2007, Lester received the call he'd been dreading.

His office line rang and he pressed the hands-free button on the phone. "Good morning, Lester FitzGerald." Ann was in the office with him and stood up and pointed to the door questioningly. There was a nervous pause on the other end of the line and Lester waved for her to stay.

"FitzGerald, it's Simon Rankin here from Silvermans. I've been reviewing your position with us and…well…I'd like to discuss something important."

Ann and Lester looked at each other in horror and then simultaneously at the real-time feed on the screen. The NAV was south of £300 million. Lester held his head in his hands. This was it. This was the call.

The more the conversation progressed, the more Rankin's telephone manner appeared odd; matter-of-fact authoritative was the sense that the banker undoubtedly wanted to convey, but it wasn't working. Something was stopping him.

Lester's mind was racing. Rankin didn't do conciliatory – ever. He recalled all the conversations that he'd had with this reptile in the past two years; from the first negotiation on the 22nd floor of the Canary Wharf tower to the aggressive demands for collateral payments ever since. Rankin had always been haughty; made sure that Lester felt the full extent of his contempt. But today, something was different.

"Simon, I've been trying to reach you for over a week to discuss this – where have you been?"

Ann was furiously rearranging her necklace, running it back and forth, and she sat back as far from the loudspeaker as she could. She'd had to speak to Rankin in the past about making payments to Silvermans. She made a face at the phone – rather like the one a teenager might make on being told by an unreasonable parent that they can't stay out all night.

"Well, unfortunately we had a simultaneous power outage and a system failure but we've managed to sort that out. Everything has been resolved," came the response.

Lester believed that no more than he believed in the symmetry of financial data.

"A global investment bank that doesn't have computer backup for these things. It takes you out for a week? Come on, Simon."

Ann glanced at the loudspeaker and then immediately turned away again. She continued to fumble with the comfort blanket hanging around her neck.

"Listen, FitzGerald, I've been working my nuts off for two weeks to sort this shit out and I've barely slept. So I suggest you shut the fuck up and listen."

Ann opened her eyes and sat upright; she was now perched on the edge of her seat. Lester looked at her with raised eyebrows and a quizzical gaze. If Rankin was about to deliver the final, fatal blow to Lambda, why did he sound so upset? And why was he taking so long? Rankin was the kind of banker that went straight for the jugular – no messing.

"Now, do you want to hear what I've got to say about these positions or are you going to whinge all day long?"

"OK, Simon. Why don't you outline what you have in mind," replied Lester. He glanced at Ann. She didn't meet his eyes and sat with her hands clasped under her chin – as if she was praying. She leaned into the speaker in anticipation.

Rankin cleared his throat. "As you will be aware, we have witnessed a rapid deterioration in the subprime mortgage market in the very recent past. The collapse of The Globe and Bear…"

The hairs on the back of Lester's neck began to rise, as he realised what had changed. Rankin was reading from a prepared script – it was blatant. The tone had changed, the word order and cadence flowed – not at all how Rankin normally bludgeoned his way through sentences. Lester dared to hope. If he was reading from a pre-agreed text, the lawyers had crawled all over it and that meant Silvermans were taking this seriously. If they were taking this seriously, perhaps, finally they would change their positions. Lester held his breath.

"…and so, we can confirm that we are now able to begin moving the pricing of your insurance contracts to reflect the current market conditions. In accordance with those contracts, we will immediately transfer funds to *Credere*," concluded Rankin. The banker almost spat out the last word as if his body was undergoing a reflex moment and trying to expel something repulsive from his mouth.

Ann stared at Lester, witnessing the other transaction taking place – the one that was moving in the opposite direction. It was the one that was just as quiet as the bank transfer and in a sense just as ethereal, but it was equally significant. The resentment and anger that had been stored up within Lester was shifting – away from Lester and moving towards Rankin.

"I think you mean, Simon, that your bank has now managed to secure a net short position so you're happy to mark my contracts accurately for once because it's now in your best interest to do so," said Lester.

Ann smiled at the speaker.

"Jesus, don't push your fucking luck, FitzGerald," exploded Rankin. "I suggest you get your guys to call our guys and we'll arrange for the transfers. OK, don't call me; I don't need to speak to you. If something happens, I'll call you."

"Blimy, Simon, it's good to hear that you're being so magnanimous about all of this."

216

"Fuck off," replied Rankin and then the electronic click, as he hung up.

The transfer of funds between financial institutions is ubiquitous. It happens 24/7 and is often conducted without either party being aware it is even taking place – a painless, unemotional event. But this was going to be different – this was a transfer from Simon Rankin to Lester FitzGerald – it would be both painful and emotional. And it wasn't just the money that would be moving from one party to the other. There would be a transfer of power from Rankin to Lester; it was a transfer of success from Silvermans – the global investment bank – to a pesky little hedge fund that Rankin had promised to crush, and it was a transfer of professional kudos from one financier to another.

"Oh my God, Lester. That's it – we've done it. They're going to transfer the funds!" said Ann, as she looked across at her boss.

Lester could barely hear her voice; it seemed distant, as if she was in another room. His overwhelming sensation was of floating, like he was leaving behind his own body and becoming an observer of his actions. Physically, he knew he was still in his seat in his office, but as he turned to look out across Pont Street, mentally and spiritually, he was with the birds soaring across the Victorian rooftops totally unburdened.

For almost two years, Silvermans had bullied, lied and schemed him. During that time, Lambda had been paying the bank premiums and collateral that it could not afford. The possibility, and more recently the probability, of his company going under had affected his health – it had even changed his appearance; he had been forced to make half his team redundant to save money. His own investors would no longer speak to him other than via a lawyer.

He held his gaze out over the skyline and each breath he took seemed to release more of the poisonous burden that had weighed on him for months. He was feeling more elated by the second. The whole call had lasted less than eight minutes, but it seemed to have removed two years of misery. Only now that the weight had been lifted did he realise just how all-consuming it had become. When he looked down at his empty hands, he realised he was shaking. The tears welled up behind his eyes with such rapidity that he was barely aware it was happening before the pressure broke through the film surrounding them and allowed the crystalline liquid to escape onto his cheeks.

He turned in his seat to face Ann. She embraced him and she also sobbed. After all this time, he'd won. He'd beaten the bullies and the bankers. It was the first time that Lester FitzGerald had cried since boarding school.

Chapter Forty-Five

Bob Santini smiled at the photo on his desk – the one of him with the white envelope in his hand – and thought about his bonus pool. The Globe had gone, the mortgage market had continued to haemorrhage and finally, the Bear Sterns funds had collapsed. At first, the movement was glacial, but now that the tectonic plates of the global financial system had shifted, they had done so decisively, irreversibly, and more importantly, in his favour. Project NARCISM was now Allied English's biggest success – ever.

On his last estimate, the insurance contracts that he had in place against the demise of mortgage bonds and CDOs would add a cool $950 million of profit to the Prop Desk – and he'd be keeping a part of that thanks to the agreement he had with the bank. James Dickenson had already called to personally congratulate him on the success. Santini suspected that the CEO needed the Prop Desk profit – he'd heard things were going less well in fixed income at the moment. He returned the photo and strutted out of his office.

Colin Stewart's risk management team were located on the first floor of the same building; appropriately, some fourteen floors beneath the heady heights of his own office and practically in the cellar. In all his time in the bank, Santini had never ventured down to the 'basement'. He had no reason to. Everyone there worked for Stewart, and anyone with half a brain wouldn't do that for more than five minutes. But today he would make an exception – he decided to grace them with his presence.

When he'd made the descent into the murky depths of the lower floors, Santini found Stewart sat at a bank of desks in the open plan office with several colleagues. They seemed to be sharing a joke about something. *Perfect*, thought Santini.

"So, Stewart, you still know more than me about investing?" he asked – making sure that his voice carried and as many people as possible could hear him.

He'd arrived unannounced and stood opposite his adversary. He wore a pristine blue shirt with white collar and cuffs. His top button was undone and his tie was loosened appropriately. He'd left his jacket behind in his office and had both hands in his dark blue trouser pockets. His long, slicked back hair glistened under the high-specification ceiling light panel that he was stood under.

Most of the staff stopped what they were doing and stared. By no means, all of them had even met Santini, but not many men answered to the description that accompanied his reputation – and fewer would have the balls to be here and chasten Colin Stewart – so they all knew who it was goading their boss. Stewart vs Santini was the Allied English equivalent of Ali vs Foreman. The storied guardian of the bank's risk positions going head-to-head with the bank's biggest risk taker who had the self-conceit to call his strategy Project NARCISM. An ex-military man who was the rule maker and enforcer against the biggest rule breaker in the bank. It promised to be a fascinating encounter and neither man was expected to back down.

"Excuse me?" replied Stewart, as he looked up from his desk his chest swelled slightly.

"Excuse you? And why should we do that, Stewart? What have you done? Well actually, let's consider that for a moment," said Santini, as he strolled causally along the bank of desks. "Anyone else interested to know why your head of risk wants to be excused?" He was rising to his task and he stopped and faced his audience.

"Just hang on a minute, Santini. I don't need to be excused from anything," said Stewart, as he stood up. But the momentum was all with the head of the Prop Desk now.

Santini raised his voice. "Mr Stewart here considers himself to be an investor." He was facing Stewart over the bank of desks; feet planted wide, hands still in his pockets. "He advised me a few months ago that my insurance contracts against the subprime market would never pay out and that I was being reckless."

Santini started to strut along the desks again and looked out over his audience.

"So your enlightened head of risk here thought it would be prudent to incorporate me into his AERS. Now I told him we weren't nearly close enough for that, but he wouldn't listen." Santini stopped talking and smiled.

Those confident that Stewart couldn't see them smothered laughs. The others looked on, stony-faced. Stewart had his vast military chest puffed out and his hands on his hips, as he glared at the man opposite. His face was reddening by the second.

"So we had to write risk report after risk report for him and I had to listen to him whilst he told me Ben Bernanke knew more about investing than I did.

"But, you know what, ladies and gentlemen, it doesn't matter now, and do you know why it doesn't matter?" He was grinning, removed his hands from his pockets and rubbed them together in parody of a TV villain to indicate that he knew something they didn't.

"Because the Prop Desk has just made $950 million profit and counting."

"So Stewart" – Santini looked to face him now and pointed a long delicate finger – "why don't you take the $950 million profit, put it in your risk model and shove it up your AERS?"

The audience turned to Stewart; curiosity the overwhelming expression on the wall of faces now staring at the head of risk.

He didn't make a move for a moment. He just stood at ease – hands were now behind his back and his feet placed slightly apart. A few colleagues exchanged glances wondering if it was their man that was going to back down.

He then cleared his throat. "Santini, I'm still the head of risk and if I want to ask for a risk report from you, I'll damn well get one. And until you've sold ALL your positions related to subprime, I still consider you a danger to yourself and, more importantly, the bank."

He marched around to the other side of the desks, his colleagues and Santini watching his every step.

"And next time you want a meeting with me or my team, I suggest you make an appointment. Now then, you've had your little rant so you wait here for a second. I want to show you something."

He walked past Santini as if to retrieve something from a nearby office, but then stopped immediately behind his victim. Santini smirked at his audience and performed an arrogant 'so-what' shrug; palms facing up to the ceiling and his head cocked to one-side.

In an instant, Stewart reached around Santini's neck with his right arm and held him in a vice-like chokehold. Santini's trachea immediately compressed; he could feel the rings of cartilage caving in on themselves as the pressure built. It was agony and he began to fight for each breath. There were gasps from the audience. Santini began to panic, as he realised that he was suffocating. His eyes were now wide open and he tapped in furious submission against the massive forearms of the man he'd just been humiliating. A few seconds later, just as other team members plucked up the courage to intervene, Stewart released the hold and the head of the Prop Desk collapsed onto the floor at his feet. He was clutching his throat, sucking in as much oxygen as he could and all but crying.

"And one more thing," said Stewart, as he stood directly over the cowering Santini, "you ever talk to me like that again, and I'll insert that ridiculous tie rack of yours so far up your ass you'll be able to pick your nose with the fucking thing."

Stewart apologised to the ladies present for his language and use of violence and then calmly walked out of the office.

Santini was slumped on the floor – his hair no longer the smooth, glossy surface of a few moments ago but a chaotic morass of out-of-place greasy strands. He held his throat as Stewart's staff went back to work around him. It was like he didn't exist.

Chapter Forty-Six

Rodrigo snatched up one of the letters from the kitchen table; his eyes narrowed as they locked onto the Mortgage Company emblazoned logo at the top and a bitter smile stole across his face. The cruel irony of their situation registered with him for the 100th time since they'd received the first communication. How quickly the sweetest dream can become a worst nightmare.

"Jesus Christ, Marina, where the fuck does $1,300 per month come from? They can't just make it up. Are you sure this is the right document?" shouted Rodrigo.

Rodrigo had been doing a lot of shouting recently, and he hated himself for the vicious circle he'd allowed to envelop him. The more he thought about it, the more he snapped at his wife, the more he snapped at his wife, the angrier he became with himself and the system that had brought them to this point.

He looked down at Marina and felt a sudden pang of guilt well up inside. It was her eyes that was the biggest change. They had been the first of many things that attracted him when they met; they were somehow different to other Mexican girls – Marina looked Middle Eastern, Iranian almost. They were dark and mysterious, but it was the energy they imbued that he found almost hypnotic – like two pristine black pearls reflecting a powerful light. But when he looked at them now, their darkness resembled pools of despair – two listless ponds incapable of sustaining life.

And that was the other struggle Marina faced at the moment: that she herself was incapable of sustaining life. They were still on the rollercoaster of emotions of IVF cycles, and they were still failing. But in the last few months, even that had had to stop. They were now too stressed to continue and the heavily revised monthly budget certainly wouldn't stretch to the costs.

"Yes, it's the right one, honey," replied Marina. Rodrigo could tell she was fighting to hold onto her bottom lip.

Marina scanned the first document again and read it out.

'...your reduced interest payment period has expired and as per your mortgage contract, we are increasing the rate to a level which is consistent with this product. Your monthly payments will be $1,380 per month from the 1st July 2007'.

"So our repayments were around 500 bucks a month and these assholes now want over thirteen hundred? How the fuck can that happen?" he asked the question of himself, and looked out of the window as he thought about the unfairness of it.

He continued, "I remember that mortgage lady saying that there will be a *modest* increase in our monthlies once this teaser rate was finished. She never told us it would almost triple! What a bitch."

"I'm sorry, honey," replied Marina. Her bottom lip finally broke away now and tears arrived for the third time since she had attempted to eat breakfast. "It's all my fault."

Rodrigo immediately went to his wife. "Marina, it's not your fault, honey. It's the system. That bitch mortgage lady got us to sign something that she didn't explain properly and that asshole that ran the company – well, that's why he's all over the newspapers. We didn't stand a chance against those crooked assholes."

It was a few minutes whilst Marina just sat and nestled into her husband's shoulder – she found her little pocket of comfort and stayed there.

As he was holding her slight frame with one arm, Rodrigo used the other to find the article. He knew he shouldn't read it again; it often worsened his mood, but he couldn't feel much worse than he did already, so what the heck? The San Francisco Examiner had given it the cryptic title *'Of Mice and Men'* which didn't mean much to Rodrigo. It was an investigative piece about the fraudulent nature of something called subprime mortgages and saved its most severe criticism for The Globe Mortgage Company. The Globe no longer existed – it had run out of money and another mortgage company – called Pinewood – had bought it for $1 following the company's collapse earlier in the year. Pinewood now processed the Alfero's mortgage.

The article went on to demonise the corrupt brokers that had been mis-selling the Globe's mortgage products – particularly something called an *interest-only negative-amortising adjustable-rate subprime mortgage* – the Globe's most profitable mortgage product and apparently, you didn't get much more subprime than that. 'A truly evil product' lamented the journalist.

Marina and Rodrigo had never heard of it, but when they checked their documentation, they were horrified to discover that that's exactly what Tina Scales had sold them. And, according to the article, the bitch could have expected a commission of up to $20,000 for doing so! Apparently, the Globe only owned the mortgages for a short time before selling them off which meant the Globe assumed none of the risks. That's why, so the article stated, 'the Globe was giving million-dollar mortgages to waitresses'.

The couple sat for a few moments – Rodrigo consoling his wife and reading, Marina trying to hold it together. He glanced at the address on one of the bank's letters:

578 Laurel Pines, Excelsior, San Francisco, 56472

He remembered seeing the address of their new home written down for the first time on the day they moved in. Marina had written it on a postcard to send to relatives and doubly underlined it as if to emphasise their joy about moving in to their own home. Now when he looked at those few words written down, it was torture. The very thing that was supposed to bring so much joy to their life had become the source of unbearable stress. It was also going to destroy their dream of becoming parents – the mortgage payments would now swallow all their cash. There'd certainly be none left over for their IVF treatment.

"What about refinancing, honey, can we do that?" asked Marina.

"I'm sorry, I didn't get the chance to talk to the appraiser," he replied, a little too slowly he realised.

Marina turned to her husband and yanked his arm playfully. "Honey, come on. What did they say?" She put her head back into her pocket and whispered, "I can deal with it; we just need it all out in the open so that we can decide what to do."

Rodrigo closed his eyes and said to his wife, "Two-hundred and forty thousand."

He sensed his wife wince and then increase the pressure on his arm, as she did the same maths as he had done. Rodrigo refreshed his memory by scanning the article again – it made unpleasant reading but at least it explained how the scam worked.

Marina and Rodrigo had been started-off on a 'teaser' interest rate for two years that was way below the market interest rate. The deferred interest that they should have been paying during the first two years was simply added to the outstanding principal of the loan – no one had ever explained that to them. Then, the interest rate was adjusted (substantially upwards) on the second anniversary. So, thanks to Tina Scales and the Globe Mortgage Company, the Alferos now owed more money than they had originally borrowed, were paying an interest rate on the loan that was never declared to them and they were enduring all of this for the privilege of living in a house that was now worth $110,000 less than they had paid for it.

The article claimed there were millions of people like the Alferos in America – all of them duped into signing something they didn't understand. Apparently, it was a 'ticking time bomb' that one day would explode and force millions of people to lose their homes. Rodrigo refolded the newspaper and sighed, rocking Marina gently as he did so. He'd almost given up hope.

Chapter Forty-Seven

It was 32 degrees and the humidity was just about as high as Paul Poorish had ever experienced in his life. Just walking the few metres from the air-conditioned beach-hut to the outside breakfast area in the morning was taxing enough to leave his shorts and T-shirt drenched. It didn't matter; he could spend the rest of the day relaxing by the pool if that's what he wanted to do.

As Poorish settled himself at a table and looked out across the swimming pool and the beach beyond, he thought to himself that he'd be doing a lot more relaxing in the next few years. He looked up at the palm trees swaying in the warm gentle breeze, then closed his eyes and filled his lungs with the pure air. He'd spent a little bit of time in Thailand, but he'd never been to Phuket – he loved it.

"Excuse me, sir, coffee?"

"Yes please, just leave the pot," replied Poorish, as he turned his wife's cup over. Poorish guessed the waiter was late teens or early twenties. He was wearing his pristine white uniform and sandals and not the cream chinos and blue shirt from the night before. He had served them at the 'Sea View' restaurant and here he was back in the morning putting in another shift in another immaculate uniform. Poorish spent a moment reflecting on his own work ethic, as he helped himself to coffee.

He'd been a relatively young man when he started Rosebridge Scaffolding, nearly thirty-five-years ago. He'd often worked through the night in the early days to ensure quotes were completed and the back-office operated properly and then appear on site the next morning for a day on the tools with the rest of the team. Rosebridge had become the 'go to' firm for commercial scaffolding projects anywhere in East Anglia. It had taken a long time, but he was rightly proud of what he'd achieved. Which is why, since they'd hit a few cash flow problems, he wasn't about to throw it all away because of a few banks that wanted to call-in their loans.

He took another sip of his coffee and checked his watch; 08.30, she'd just be finishing off her morning swim he thought and scanned the sea front. He could see her now, using the palms of her hands to push the water away from her eyes and cheeks, as she stood chest-high in the sea. He folded the dressing gown that he had brought for her and put it on the back of the chair where he knew she would sit. He looked over again, as she walked slowly out of the Andaman Sea towards the shore; each step revealing a little more of her beautiful body, as the beach-incline lowered the water level. How many women in their mid-late forties could get away with wearing a bikini? There weren't many, and even fewer that looked like Paula. Frau Schmidt, on the other hand, looked like a sack of spuds in her all-in-one black swimsuit. She was waddling besides his graceful wife as they reached the shore; now the waves just lapping at their ankles. They had met the German couple a few days earlier and although Olga was younger than Paula, she looked ten years older.

"Hello, darling." Paula bent down and gave her husband a peck on the cheek. "Did you sleep OK?"

"Yes, thank you. How was the swim?" asked Paul Poorish, as he deliberately caught the man sat behind Paula ogling his wife.

"Beautiful. You should join us one morning," she replied, as she put on the dressing gown.

"We're running out of time for that I'm afraid," he replied, as he pulled out the chair and allowed her to sit down.

Her shoulders slumped, as she looked at her husband. "I know. I wish we could stay here; it's absolutely wonderful. Thank you again, darling, for the best holiday of my life.," and she raised her orange juice. He did the same, the glasses chinked and the couple stopped and appreciated just how lucky they both were for a few moments.

Paul Poorish knew his wife had been ecstatic about the trip. Even before they left for Thailand, she wouldn't stop talking about it, and whilst she had been here, she was even more animated about 'his wonderful idea'. It wasn't the fact that it was Thailand – she knew her husband had a few friends and a little bit of business here, and that was fine. It was simply the fact that he had invested the time and the money for them to be together and away from Suffolk. But once the police had arrested Stones for the Ross murder, the press had left them alone and Poorish thought they should move on and so here they were.

It was a sign she said to him last night. A sign that there was hope that they could find reconciliation after all that they had been through in the past twelve months. She had apologised to him again for her error of judgement and he had expressed regret for his lack of empathy. Last night, they had held hands over dinner and cuddled on the way back to their beach hut. He had no doubt that tonight Paula's objective was to consummate their reconciliation and he had zero problem with that.

★

So, at 8pm that evening, the couple took their seats in their favourite restaurant. Poorish had ensured that they got the table for two closest to the shore and a little separated from the main restaurant. It was a more private experience, and you could hear the waves lapping up on the beach just a few feet away. Perfect for the romantic meal that he had planned. He'd tipped the headwaiter – heavily – explaining that tonight was a very special occasion.

He wore a new pair of chinos, new blue shirt and brown leather sandals. She was wearing a hugging white dress that accentuated her athletic figure and her long, auburn hair was in a bun. And it was the perfect evening thought Poorish; the wine was excellent, the food delicious and, most importantly, the company even better. The couple talked for hours without interruption.

Afterwards, they took their shoes off and strolled along the beach. Poorish took his wife's hand and squeezed it; she responded in kind and as she cuddled into him, he returned the expression of affection. Poorish smiled, knowing that they looked just like any other couple on holiday heading back to their accommodation. They stood looking out over the moonlit sea and it was only then that he admitted to himself he was actually feeling nervous. He dragged the moment out for as long as he could – until Paula finally persuaded him to follow her.

When they got through the front door, it was the husband that took the initiative; it was important that he was in control tonight. He pulled his wife towards him and kissed her for the first time in over a year. It wasn't a nervous, slowly, slowly kiss, but a full-on, urgent passionate encounter that left Paula in no doubt about the direction of travel.

"Wait here, darling," she whispered into his ear. "I'll be back in a moment."

In the bathroom, Paula slipped into her favourite. The Carine Gilson lace-trimmed red and black Basque with matching panties. She reapplied a little lip-gloss and surveyed the finished product in the mirror with her hands on her hips and a satisfied expression on her face. Then a smile broke out and she fist-pumped before taking a couple of moments to gather herself.

When she reappeared, Poorish had also changed and was in his bathrobe standing behind a chair in front of the vanity unit. He couldn't help but smile; she looked absolutely stunning and her feigned nervousness – the biting of the bottom lip and the blinking of her eyes – a nice touch, he thought. But her selection of lingerie was an unexpected bonus. This was going to be a very special night. He invited her to sit in order that he could massage her neck and shoulders. It was her turn to smile. His feather-like neck and shoulder massage was his only concession to the pretence of foreplay. Early on in their relationship, it was always the prelude to sex, but there had been precious little of that recently. She readily accepted his invite and sat down.

"I'm sorry, darling," he began. He'd practiced the opening lines of this apology many times. He wanted it to be perfect. He wanted his wife to be completely relaxed; she had to be relaxed. "I know I've been a swine, but I promise the future will be different."

She started to say something but he quickly placed his hand over her mouth to prevent her. It was a gentle touch and he continued to apply it to her throat and then her neck as he started his routine. His hands explored her body as he stood behind her and stared at her expression in the vanity unit mirror. He knew she liked to be watched; it obviously excited her that there was an audience. The height of the chair relative to the mirror framed her body perfectly – everything from her midriff upwards was captured – just like a framed picture.

She moved an arm in response so that she could reciprocate the teasing, but he stopped her.

"Don't move, darling," he whispered, "I need you to completely relax and enjoy this. I want to make it up to you."

He then reached into the pocket of his bathrobe and extracted the two pieces of chord that he had put there earlier.

He whispered to her again, "Don't move, and just relax." His touch was as light as a feather – just the way she liked it – as he caressed her neck and upper body.

He wasn't sure if she was enjoying it, but she was certainly submitting to his requests – out of sympathy, probably, but at least she was playing along, he'd happily give her that. Her body was now almost limp.

He tied the chords around her legs and then her upper body. She looked at him in the mirror, as he finished tying the knots. A kind of quizzical expression fleetingly moved across her face; the restraints were a new addition to the routine, but it seemed anything went tonight. She submitted and closed her eyes.

He continued to apply his fingernails deftly to her skin. Kneeling, he gently moved his hands from her toes, to her feet, legs and body as he continued to monitor her expression. He liked the fact that she had left her hair in the bun. That part was important too.

He released a couple of strands from the nest on top of her head and pulled them into place. He studied his handiwork in the mirror in much the same way a hairdresser might upon completion of a flawless cut. The strands were dangling down the sides of her cheeks and one was pulled diagonally across her face: picture perfect. Finally, to complete the image that had become etched on his memory – the one that had wormed its way into his cerebral cortex and stubbornly remained there – he gently removed one of the straps from her shoulder.

He bent down and kissed her on the cheek. "Why don't you open your eyes, darling?"

Obediently, she did so and gave a dutiful smile whilst her eyes made the necessary adjustments to the light. Poorish then moved to one side so that all Paula could see was the reflection of her herself, framed by the mirror in front of her. Her countenance changed in an instant. It went from an expression of total submission to one of absolute panic in under a second.

He knew then that the penny had finally dropped.

She opened her mouth to scream but it was too late, the gag had come down in an instant and before any sound had left her body.

Chapter Forty-Eight

Poorish roughly tied the knot at the back of her head and stepped away to consider her reflection. His cold eyes stared at his wife.

She frantically wriggled to release herself but the Hitch-Knots he had used held firm and she couldn't move. He watched the grip of panic takeover her face as her cheeks flushed.

"It's no use, Paula, you're not going anywhere."

"I must admit, I thought you'd get it a little earlier than you did, especially when you put on this little number." He was in her face now; flecks of spittle colliding with her face as he spoke. He yanked on the fallen strap to reinforce what it was he was talking about.

"In fact, that's what pushed me over the edge, darling. Take a good look, Paula, because that's what I've been looking at every day for the past year."

He stood behind her again and forced her head straight ahead so that she looked directly into the mirror.

"The last thing I see before I go to sleep and the first thing I see when I wake up is what you're looking at right now: you, with your hair hanging down from your bun, wearing that slut's uniform whilst being fucked by another man. Every day, Paula! Do you know how that made me feel?"

She was crying, her pale skin had been replaced by a glowing hue and her perspiration glistened under the yellow lighting around the vanity unit.

"For goodness' sake, Paula, it's too late for the tears. You should have thought about that before you made me look like a fool and ended any hope I had of becoming an MP. You didn't actually think I'd forgiven you, did you?

"You were unfaithful with a loser like Ross and he sends me a fucking tape of it! Then the idiot had the stupidity to ask me to give him money. He cried as well, you know, when it finally dawned on him his pathetic little life was over."

She was sobbing uncontrollably now, but her muffled sounds weren't audible above the air-conditioning units working to cool the hut.

Poorish removed the Stanley knife from his bathrobe. He held it up in the mirror so that Paula could see. He then did what he should have done months ago.

★

Ten minutes later, Paul Poorish left the beach hut without even a glance at his wife's limp body slumped in the chair. He walked through the grounds of the hotel until he found the side entrance he'd located earlier in the holiday and met the two men waiting for him.

They got into a car and drove away. The larger of the two men passed him a small holdall. The contents of which represented his new life. A new identity; a new passport and the backup papers necessary to reside in Thailand for as long as he wished. The appropriate authorities had been 'dealt with' and the bank accounts were also registered to his alias.

He'd disappear into the heaving mass of people that was Bangkok – fourteen million inhabitants. He could live there like a king for as long as he wanted and no one would ever find him.

Chapter Forty-Nine

Sam was sat reading the East Anglian Daily Times at the breakfast table in the kitchen. Barney was nagging her: sat at her feet, looking up and employing his big brown eyes to create an infant-like expression that normally provoked a response: A walk, or more food if he was really lucky. But the newspaper's headline had Sam's full attention.

'Rosebridge Scaffolding declared bankrupt – leaving hundreds unemployed and angry creditors.'

Police are trying to contact Paul Poorish, the Chairman of Rosebridge Scaffolding, regarding the collapse of his business. It has been declared bankrupt and owes millions of pounds to local suppliers and customers, who in good faith paid for part of their projects in advance.

It is understood that Mr and Mrs Poorish are in Thailand together on holiday. Earlier in the year, it was revealed that Mrs Poorish had been having an affair with Angus Ross – the ex-Ipswich Town football star – who was later found dead in his flat. The couple had been helping the police with their enquiries concerning the murder but were later removed from the investigation and Fred Stones – another local businessman – is still being held without bail for the crime.

No one was available for comment, but sources close to the company claim that up to £3 million is missing from the company accounts.

Sam's jaw dropped as she continued to read the article. Paula had given her no indication when they'd said goodbye to one another ten days before. The police had dropped her and Paul from their enquiries, and the husband seemed to have started the forgiveness phase and organised the holiday as a gesture of reconciliation.

"Oh my God," she muttered slowly.

Just as she did so, Andrew Longmire barged into the room in search of a much-needed coffee. His conference call was going badly and what he really needed was a break for a couple of hours, but he wasn't going to get it.

"What's wrong with you?" he barked, as he smashed the filter holder of the De'Longhi coffee machine against the bin to empty its spent contents. Barney immediately retreated under the kitchen table and lay down.

Sam hadn't realised that she had spoken out loud and was reluctant to share the information with her husband. She'd been listening to his tantrums through closed doors for the past hour and he wasn't known as a particular fan of the Poorish's at the best of times; God knows what he'd make of this. Reluctantly, she slid the newspaper along the table – he could read it for himself – and moved around to make a fuss of the dog in the full knowledge it would irritate her husband.

She, and the newspaper article, succeeded. Within a few moments, Longmire had a full head of steam.

"Absolute bastards. I told you these people were trouble the moment you got caught up with them, didn't I? Can you imagine how sick they have to be to deceive their customers and shit on their employees like this? I hope they get caught and brought back here to face the music," declared Longmire with righteous indignation.

"Oh, come on, Andrew. It's a newspaper article; I bet half of its speculation. You haven't got a clue whether it's true," replied Sam. Barney skulked away – his soulful brown eyes looking up at the alleged grownups in the room – and retreated to the safety of his basket. Sam continued.

"Anyway, what's wrong with you? All I can hear is shouting and banging coming from the study. Who the hell's on the phone?"

He stepped away to focus on his cup of coffee – as if to increase his personal space. He didn't respond.

"Come on, Andrew" – persisted Sam – "you came back from London with a face like a slapped arse on Wednesday and you're still Mr grumpy nuts. What's going on?"

At least that got a reaction, even if it was Longmire at his caustic worst. He banged his cup down next to the coffee machine.

"What's going on? What's going on? Well, since you ask, darling, let me enlighten you as to what's going on in the real world, shall I? You know, the parallel universe that that exists outside that bubble of comfort that you and that stupid bitch Paula inhabit."

OK, he's definitely having a bad day.

"Once upon a time, and I'll try and keep this very simple for you."

Thank you so much, darling.

"Once upon a time, there was a very profitable bank called Northern Rock and now there isn't – it's fucked. The wankers that managed it ran out of money and it's now propped up by a man called Darling; that's right, dear, Alistair Darling is the Chancellor of our magnificent Exchequer. The housing market is collapsing around us and the stock market is shitting bricks whilst giving our shares a pasting at the same time. And everyone except me seems to think that First Capital is somehow involved in subprime lending.

"Apart from those little trivialities sweetie, life's a dream."

Longmire didn't give his wife a chance to respond, went back into his study and slammed the door shut behind him. He re-joined the call with Mick Marshall and Hugo Smith – First Capital's auditor. They were both trying to persuade Longmire that some of the credit markets post Northern Rock were freezing up and it was beginning to impact First Capital's ability to access funds. Longmire had a very different opinion.

Chapter Fifty

"This better be good, Hanson, I'm on my way to the New Wolsey. Oscar Wilde's *The Picture of Dorian Grey* is playing – saw it in the West End a few years ago. Bloody fantastic. Can't imagine it'll be half as good here by the way," said CI Smith. He hadn't even looked at the Inspector who had been shown in by his secretary.

"Apologies, sir, I wouldn't want to prevent you from going to the *theatre*. Would it be more convenient if I came back later?" asked Hanson.

The Chief Inspector looked up, searching for evidence of mockery in Hanson's face that would corroborate the tone of insubordination in his voice. Satisfied he couldn't find any, he jerked on his jacket.

"You can talk whilst I finish getting ready detective – and make it quick," said CI Smith.

"I've just taken a call from the Met, sir. They were informed this morning by the Thai authorities about a crime which I think is relevant to the Ross murder case."

Smith stopped in his tracks. He knew all about the Poorish's 'alleged' holiday in Thailand and the collapse of their business. If the Met had got a call, this was going to be serious. He also knew that Hanson, unlike him, believed that Paul Poorish had been involved in the Ross death and not Fred Stones who was still in police custody.

"OK, Hanson, what is it?"

"Paula Poorish has been murdered Sir and Paul Poorish is missing, but is a suspect in the Thai authorities' murder investigation."

Smith collapsed back into his chair and closed his eyes. "Bloody hell."

"Go on," he continued after a couple of seconds, but the pained expression on his face left Hanson in no doubt his boss was reluctant to hear the rest of the story.

Hanson sat down opposite Smith and consulted his notebook.

"She was found by the cleaners in the Poorish's beach hut on the morning of the 12 December. There was no sign of Poorish and from what they told me, his belongings are still in the room. His passport was still there and his clothes hanging up in the wardrobe. They didn't find any cash and the room was untidy rather than ransacked.

"So we could be looking at a break in and Poorish has been abducted and the poor wife got it?" asked CI Smith, but his tone was hopeful rather than confident.

"Possible, but unlikely in my opinion, sir."

"Let me guess, Hanson, you think Poorish killed his own wife?"

"Yes, sir."

Smith sat back in his chair and crossed his arms.

"And why doesn't that surprise me, Hanson? OK, humour me, why are you so confident?" he asked.

"The way she was murdered, sir. These are the photos of the murder scene that have been sent over from the Thai force." Hanson slid the printouts of the photos over the desk to his boss, sat back and waited.

Smith slipped on his half-moon reading glasses and scanned the first photo. It was a side shot of the victim slumped in a chair. She was wearing black and red sexy lingerie with black stockings and suspenders. She had been bound and gagged and her body was ashen white since it had been drained of blood. The wound in her neck was also clearly visible.

The CI massaged one of the veins in his temple as he stared at the photo. He gently shook his head.

"I can't believe it," he muttered.

He went to the next photo that had been taken from the front of the victim. Her head was slumped down to one side and the only thing holding her body up were the chords around her legs and torso. Once again, he shook his head as he recalled the photos from the Ross murder scene.

The next photo was of the murder weapon – a Stanley Knife covered in blood. "I can't believe it," he said once again.

He finally looked up. "OK, Hanson, you win. Whoever killed Paula Poorish, either killed Ross or knew precisely how it was done. Since Stones is in a prison cell in Suffolk, he couldn't have killed Paula Poorish in Thailand. Paul fucking Poorish must have killed both of them."

"That was my conclusion also, sir," answered Hanson.

CI Smith picked up his phone and spoke to his secretary. "Ann, please send my apologies, something important has come up and I won't be attending the theatre. Can you bring in some tea and cake, please?"

Chapter Fifty-One

"Simon, how wonderful to hear your voice again. You owe Lambda a few more hundred million dollars. How do you expect to pay us?"

"Fuck you, Lester."

"Now, now Simon, I thought you were the bank that cared? Please excuse my directness, but do you think Silvermans are worth the money – I hear you have been having a little barren spell yourself recently."

Just as late 2007, in early 2008 the global financial system faced meltdown. Northern Rock continued to teeter on the brink of collapse, various investment banks – including Silvermans – were beginning to announce unprecedentedly large profit warnings and the subprime mortgage market in the US was now in free-fall.

Things had turned so sour that the trust was being sucked out of the system completely; the market was now suspicious about everything and everyone. The rating agencies were also caving in and had finally begun downgrading. Attention had now turned to the supposedly high-quality tranches of the CDOs that only *Credere* had bet against. Investments that were proclaimed Triple-A a few weeks before were now Double-B or worse. The market was not just confused; it had lost faith.

So the Triple-A tranches of the CDOs that were the subject of Ann's presentation, collapsed: totally. The financial market was trying to understand how something that had been rated Triple-A – alleging the same level of security as a US Government bond – could become worthless.

The mincemeat had been sliced and diced into so many products by the banks that nobody knew where the risks were any more – and no one believed anyone who claimed they did know. As far as the credit markets were concerned, the whole food chain was contaminated.

"OK. I can understand your position, Simon. I'd also be a little anxious about explaining this one to Lloyd Sinclair. I assume I'm not the only one. If you've been stupid enough to repeat the trick with others, I bet you'll break the bank."

"Well, unusually for you Lester, you're right about one thing – it will break *the* bank. But it won't be *this* bank. I know you'd be delighted if it was us that were standing behind your insurance contracts, on the Triple-A's but we're not. It's time for you to call your nearest and dearest I'm afraid. The bank that bet against you was Allied English."

Lester FitzGerald froze.

Chapter Fifty-Two

James Dickenson was at the Century Club in the same elegant, but sparse, room that he had shared with Bob Santini three years earlier. He had vivid recollections of that meeting – Santini, wearing his trademark gaudy braces and upsetting the waiters with his complete disregard for the Club rules. Dickenson braved a half smile. Santini, as he'd since found out, didn't do rules. But it had taken the CEO of Allied English a little too long to work that out.

Up until ten days ago, Dickenson was running one of the most profitable companies in the UK. But that had all changed and, thanks to Santini, Allied English was in dire financial straits for the first time in its history. Overall, Dickenson still had that look of shock; the reverberations of the biggest surprise of his life still playing out across his face. The heavy eyelids and the black, puffy sacks under his eyes were an instant giveaway; he looked like he had hardly slept in the last few days. Even the expensive, made-to-measure suit couldn't conceal the sagging posture of the one-time resplendent deportment of the CEO of Allied English.

As Lester sat opposite his friend, he stared at the floor, as if he couldn't quite bring himself to look at Dickenson in his present state. When he spoke, he did so in quiet, muffled tones.

"James, I am so sorry. I had no idea—"

Dickenson raised one of his large, manicured hands and interrupted.

"All this time, Lester. All this time, since you told me about *Credere's* bet against the Triple-A CDO tranches, I've been trying to work out who was betting against you – who was the idiot on the other side of the trade. And now, I know. It was us – Allied bloody English!" Dickenson's vacant eyes peered out over St Stephen's Churchyard.

Lester squirmed in his seat.

"You do know that I had no idea who the counterparty was, don't you? I just assumed it was Silvermans or that they'd passed the trade onto an insurance company. I never, for one moment, suspected it was Allied," murmured Lester as he finally looked up at his friend.

Dickenson released a long, slow sigh, but held his gaze out of the window. "You know what, Lester? Neither did I. I had no idea what Santini and our Prop Desk was doing until it was too late. When we asked the questions, they just kept coming back with their Triple-A ratings and promises that it would all be fine. But they'd bet the bloody bank on the assumption that the high-quality parts of a CDO would never fail."

Dickenson's view was now of the small garden that still held very personal memories for him. Even though it was over a quarter of a century ago, he could still recall the look of bitter disappointment on his father's face as he told him of his decision to pursue a banking career at the expense of the family business. He looked at the small, wooden bench in the far corner. He'd never noticed before, but today it looked isolated, marooned; out there on its own in some way. The small garden and the various shrubs and plants that were thriving, and clearly well attended, were located away from the stranded piece of furniture.

Up until a week ago, if anyone had asked him about his decision, he'd have laughed at any suggestion of regrets about choosing banking. It had given him everything: wealth, a sense of achievement and respect from within and beyond the financial community. But now, he was less sure. In the past few days, the knives had come out as quickly and as viciously as the financial markets had collapsed; colleagues, editors and even politicians had turned on him. He was being ostracised by people that a few weeks before would have pleaded to have five minutes of his time. He was beginning to feel isolated himself.

His thoughts triggered the recollection of his mother's reaction to his decision. At first, he'd been angered and shocked by her response. What sort of mother disowns a son because she disagrees with his career-choice for goodness' sake? But over the years, he'd begun to sympathise. He assumed it was the arrival of Edward and Jemima. His own children, understandably, had given him a different perspective – a parent's outlook. He could now appreciate how she must have felt – how hurtful it must have been to his mother for him to turn her down. Her own son – her only son – choosing to work for a faceless bank and refusing to take on the family empire and follow in his father's footsteps.

"What do you think, will or could…I mean, just how bad is it, James?" asked Lester, fumbling for words.

The CEO of Allied English turned back towards his friend. He noticed that Lester had leaned into the table to get closer and his hands floundered around in front of him: fingers locked tightly together, then hands flat on the table, then he gently rubbed the inside of a palm with a thumb – all the time staring at Dickenson through thoughtful, compassionate eyes.

Dickenson avoided the question. He shook his head gently from side to side, as he watched his friend.

"Lester, it's OK, really. I don't blame you for any of this. In fact, you did exactly what you said you were going to do." Dickenson had also leaned forward and placed a hand on Lester's arm.

The irony of that statement wasn't lost on either man: Lester had, indeed done what he'd set out to achieve. The friends sat there quietly for a few moments but there was little trace of awkwardness – just a comfortable silence between them. They hadn't run out of things to say to one another – they could have spoken for hours. It wasn't the stubborn silence endured by acquaintances when each insists the other makes the first move – neither thought the other had erred. It was a solemn stillness of two old friends calmly reflecting on the cruel twist of fate that had brought them to this point.

James Dickenson had decided to back Lester as a kind of insurance policy against a collapse in the subprime mortgage market. But in doing so, one of *Credere's* biggest trades was to bet on the collapse of the CDO A-tranches – the purportedly safe pieces. Unbeknown to Lester or Dickenson, that counterparty turned out to be Bob Santini and the Prop Desk at Allied English. Dickenson's insurance policy had, unwittingly, bet against his own bank, won massively and just about destroyed the whole company in the process.

Bob Santini was already gone. His necktie furniture had been ignominiously removed from the wall of his former office and was on the back of a lorry with the rest of his belongings travelling south to Texas. Santini himself was flying first class with American Airlines from Newark to Austen. It seemed blowing up a 200-year-old bank hadn't dampened his appetite for executive travel. He'd been sacked the moment Dickenson became aware of what he had done and no one, apparently, was interested in his claim against Stewart for physical assault.

Indeed, as the news broke and Allied English staff became aware of what he'd been up to, a few of them told Santini they'd like to finish the job.

And what he'd been up to was breath-taking. Between October and December 2006, as Lester FitzGerald was looking to *buy* more insurance against the Triple-A tranches of CDOs, Santini was looking to *sell* it. He desperately needed the insurance premiums to create the income to cover premiums he was paying out and that were blowing a whole in his bonus aspirations and causing Stewart to ask so many questions.

So, Santini had gone out to the market and sold insurance contracts on roughly $20 billion of Triple-A CDO tranches. These were the ones that Ann had argued were definitely not genetically modified and therefore were not Triple A. Even they turned out to be Crap Disguised Otherwise.

The mortgage bonds became worthless as the rate of mortgage failure increased. And up until very recently, the rating agencies had regarded them as Triple-A so they were held on the Allied English balance sheet as risk free with no contingency capital held against them. The losses were enormous. As at January 2008, it was likely to be in the region of £13 billion: a brash New York bond trader, with a penchant for braces and exotic ties, had inflicted the largest trading loss in UK corporate history.

Chapter Fifty-Three

Monday, 18 February 2008 was a miserable morning. The grey clouds were heavy with moisture and hung over the City of London's square mile like a blanket of doom, discharging their droplets of cold water on a workforce wretched from the news the night before. The commuters scurried along the dank pavements to seek refuge from the inclement weather in their warm, dry offices.

Mick Marshall – the CFO of First Capital was one of them. He had reached his identikit, hermetically sealed office block and disappeared inside grateful to leave the elements behind. But the financial tempest that had reared its ugly head once more was waiting for him and everyone else that entered the building. Newspapers set out in the reception areas, a plethora of TV screens tuned to 24-hour news channels, computer screens blinking their stream of market data and the internet on each and every PC – the ubiquitous medium of twenty-first-century technology pumping a never-ending flow of information about Alistair Darling's announcement.

The Chancellor of the Exchequer had declared, on behalf of the British Government, the nationalisation of Northern Rock. Journalists were describing it as the banking equivalent of a Tsunami and that the tidal wave of destruction would now crush any weak link in the banking chain. A lack of trust seeped through the financial community as banks nervously waited for the next victim to be revealed.

In a career that spanned twenty years, Marshall had never quite seen anything like the last few months. As he prepared the 2007 full-year financial results for the company, he became more concerned as time passed. In the end, he'd felt the need to prepare two versions of the truth.

The first, and more generous portrayal of the company's performance, produced a large profit and was clearly going to be more palatable to the CEO. But that version scared Marshall. The second one he knew his boss wouldn't like, but if he were a betting man – which he wasn't – he'd put money on

Longmire accepting the reality after a couple of hours' argument. He'd eventually understand the arguments that Marshall had prepared. But ever since Longmire had taken over at First Capital, profits had only ever gone in one direction. How would he react to a fall?

In the boardroom, half an hour later, he found out.

"But that's the fucking point. We're not Northern Rock! They were a shower of shit and we're not. We need to get the message out there that we've got a different business model. Anyway, yesterday's decision has nothing to do with our 2007 results. You're both overreacting. They'll sell the bloody bank for a profit in a few months when all this blows over, you mark my words," proclaimed Longmire.

Marshall didn't believe that for a moment, but it was his boss' opening gambit. He was going to push quite hard for the status quo and the higher number – it was part of the game – and Marshall understood that.

"But, Andrew, we're coming under pressure at both ends. The banks are too scared to roll over our short-term debt as the three-month loans become due, so we're digging into cash reserves or paying ever-higher rates of interest to attract new capital. And our own clients are beginning to defer payments for the first time – they're struggling to pay what they owe us. We're caught in the middle," argued Marshall.

Hugo Smith – the company's external auditor – was the only other person in the meeting and chose to make his first contribution. He cleared his throat and started.

"Andrew, if I may?" asked Hugo.

Longmire moved in his seat and released a long, audible sigh.

"This is why both Mick and I believe it would be prudent to reinstate our previous assumptions about bad loans. As a management team, I think it is now reasonable for you to expect a certain percentage of these loans to go bad."

Longmire looked at Marshall and raised his eyebrows.

Marshall nodded his agreement.

Smith continued – interpreting the silence as a sign to do so.

"I can remember when we agreed to the FRS adjustment in the first place, gentlemen. We also agreed that we would review it over time. That time has come; we should take at least some provisions for bad loans and substantially reduce the profit of £5.1 million accordingly."

Smith finished. Marshall sneaked a glance at his boss out of the corner of his eye, as Longmire undid the top button of his shirt and loosened his tie. There was a sheen of moistness across his upper lip and forehead. *Shit, that's not a good sign.*

"Well, thank you, gentlemen. Thank you for the lecture on how NOT to run a business."

Marshall braced himself. *Here we go.*

"Hugo. Not-a-fucking-chance." Longmire's forefinger jabbed aggressively at the auditor on each of the five syllables in his riposte.

"We're not reinstating anything." He got up from his seat and held the report that Marshall had spent weeks preparing. "These assumptions were total bollocks then and they're total bollocks now. We still can't predict which loans will go bad and any guesses we make will be just that – guesses. It will mislead our shareholders and we're not going there."

He held the report in one hand and slapped it dismissively with the back of his other hand, as he continued.

"And frankly, Hugo, this is why I pay you what I pay you. You must be the most expensive fucking auditor in the country so I expect a little more loyalty."

Smith looked crestfallen. Agreeing with a man like Longmire had been the easy part. He'd not envisaged just how tough the hard part might be until now.

Marshall took a deep breath.

"Andrew, as your CFO, I'd ask you to stop and think about this. I'm a lot closer to the front line than you are and I'm not quite sure you appreciate—"

"No, Mick. You don't appreciate!" shouted Longmire.

The CEO marched over and looked down at his colleague. His bulbous eyes were almost out on stalks and produced a cold, hard stare that Marshall had never witnessed before. He suddenly felt like he was being X-rayed by some callous, calculating machine.

"You don't appreciate how hard I've worked in the last five years to turn this sleepy, unprofitable heap of shit around; you don't appreciate that we have increased profits year-on-year for the last five years and you certainly don't appreciate how lucky you are to be part of all of this. We're not going to change our P&L because of some stupid fucking journalists. The market will settle down in a few weeks."

"I'm not sure that it will, Andrew. This is serious. Our clients really are struggling and we're finding it increasingly difficult to fund ourselves. I'm not being too dramatic when I say the business is in the early stages of running out of cash. Unless something changes—"

Longmire cut him off for the second time. *Another first,* thought Marshall.

"Don't be so fucking ridiculous, Mick. We're not running out of cash. We'll be booking a profit for 2007, and a big fucking profit at that."

It was Marshall's turn to look crestfallen. For the first time in fifteen years of working together, he couldn't meet Longmire's eyes.

Longmire finished the meeting by unilaterally declaring that the provisional profit statement that PR would send to the press would remain at £5.1 million for 2007. He thanked Marshall and Smith for their 'enormous' contributions with a deliberately insincere grin before leaving the room.

Smith then made his excuses in order to keep another appointment.

Alone in the Boardroom, Marshall looked down at the two columns of numbers on the crisp, white First Capital-headed notepaper – two versions of the truth staring at him, vying for his attention and jostling with each other on the page. As an accountant, he could defend either, they both followed the accounting rules that he had applied throughout his career and neither was a lie. They just adopted different assumptions about uncertain events. *This happened all the time, didn't it?*

But half an hour later, he was still there, vacillating backwards and forwards between the two sets of figures. Avarice, a happy boss and a large annual bonus pointing him in one direction: ethics, certain unemployment and fear of the unknown the other. He looked up from the papers and caught his reflection in the window. The sombre greyness of the sky outside was sufficient to produce his silhouette but not enough for him to see the detail of his face. He was grateful; the silhouette was enough. The slumped shoulders and a sagging posture – a pathetic hologram of a complicit yes-man.

If Longmire wanted the higher number, Marshall knew that's what he'd get. That thought depressed him. The one that sickened him was that the CFO knew he wouldn't do anything to stop it.

Chapter Fifty-Four

The Alferos were sat in the plush waiting room of the Pinewood offices. Marina looked around the room; leather chairs, expensive artwork and a tropical fish tank along one of the walls all smacked of money and sophistication. She found it all a little intimidating. The couple were waiting for their meeting with a 'Mortgage Modification Officer' – they weren't familiar with the term, but apparently, it was somebody who might be able to help them keep their home. That the person was extremely busy, and all of the appointments were running forty minutes late was stressing Marina even more. Each time the double doors buzzed open – allowing staff to march the next customer through to the interview rooms – Marina's head jerked upwards suddenly as if it was remotely operated by the electronic mechanism.

She tried to focus on something else. The bright-coloured poster nearby – an advertisement for Pinewood Mortgages – grabbed her attention. The title read 'Important Variables' and in the centre was a picture of a house, encircled by $ signs. Pointing away from the circle were a series of arrows that highlighted the variables; Loan-to-value-ratio, Debt-to-income-ratio, Collateral details…the list seemed to go on. She took a couple of deep breaths as the familiar feeling took hold, the one where things confront her that she finds confusing and that she doesn't understand.

Mortgages, money, loan documents – they all seemed to use terminology that made no sense to her. In fact, she sometimes felt *they* invented words so that they were deliberately confusing. The poster hadn't helped – if anything, the summersaults in her stomach were becoming more frantic.

As Marina rubbed her stomach, the little girl sat next to her decided to introduce herself.

"Hello, I'm Elsa. What's your name?"

"Hello, Elsa, my name's Marina," she replied, grateful for the interruption.

Marina and Elsa's mum shared glances; the former's smile sufficient to reassure the mother that Elsa's decision to strike-up a conversation was not an intrusion.

The little girl had been drawing in a pad and wanted to share the results of her picture. In the foreground, to one side, were the family members. Elsa had drawn her mum, dad, brother, herself (all holding hands) and Nelson – the Golden Retriever puppy. They all stood together in the garden of a house that occupied the centre of the page. It was a square house – two-dimensional – with a triangle roof, four windows and a door in the centre. There was a pencil-thin line of smoke billowing out from the chimney and a winding path leading up to the entrance.

It was a six-year-old's perception of happy family life and the home was at the centre of it. Marina looked at the mum, who was now talking to Elsa's younger brother. She assumed that the mother, and presumably everyone else in this waiting room, was here to fight for the right to keep their home. She intended to do the same.

Marina suggested that a large yellow sun in the top left-hand corner would finish it off, as the two continued to discuss the picture. It would have been an easy mistake for someone to think it was mother and daughter having the conversation. Rodrigo stared at his wife with the little girl and smiled.

The doors buzzed open again and Marina looked up obediently. It was finally their turn and they were instructed to follow a young man towards the interview room, within which, Mrs L. Crabshaw was waiting. As they entered, Marina was surprised that the lady didn't stand up or greet them. Instead, she extended a long thin arm to indicate that they should sit, as she continued to look down at the paper in front of her.

Marina looked at the light-boned woman perched on her seat in front of them. She dressed like a schoolmistress; ankle-length pleated skirt, cream-coloured blouse, no make-up and a pair of black horn-rimmed reading glasses. Her nose was thin, hooked and reminded Marina of the angry eagle positioned in the centre of the *Bandera de México.* Her face was hard and her complexion ashen bordering on anaemic. In fact, the only colour to her otherwise cold, almost alabaster countenance was a large, brown wart smack in the middle of her chin with a few errant whiskers growing out of it. She looked as stern as she did miserable, and when Marina noticed the wedding band on the third finger of her left hand, she instantly felt a sense of sympathy for the man who had put it there.

"Good morning, Mr and Mrs Alfero. My name is Mrs Crabshaw and I will be dealing with your request that we grant you a mortgage modification. Can you start by informing me how your financial circumstances have changed since you signed the mortgage contract?"

At this point, Mrs Crabshaw made eye contact with the young couple as she removed her glasses and let them fall around her neck on the silver chain. Marina noticed that the woman's eyes moved in a quick, jerky fashion – as if she was weighing up her next move.

"Well, I'm not actually sure that they have, but—"

"Very good" – interrupted Mrs Crabshaw – "we can confirm, therefore, that there have been no changes to your financial circumstances whatsoever, Mrs Alfero," as she replaced her glasses, picked up her pen and ostentatiously ticked a box on the piece of paper before her.

Marina and Rodrigo exchanged glances.

"But, Mrs Crabshaw," interjected Marina, "I didn't mean nothing has changed."

The Pinewood employee pushed the glasses to the top of her head and glared across the desk.

"You confirmed a moment ago that there had been no change in your financial circumstances, Mrs Alfero. You just said it." She took the initiative once again.

"Are you still a *dancer,* Mrs Alfero?" Marina assumed Mrs Crabshaw had placed the emphasis on the noun to convey her disapproval.

"No, ma'am. I'm now waiting tables at a downtown family restaurant."

"And your income now, relative to when you were *dancing* at the time you signed the mortgage contract, Mrs Alfero. Would you acknowledge that this is higher?"

Rodrigo sat silently in his chair. He crossed his arms and his face tightened, as he followed the conversation.

"You know it is, Mrs Crabshaw, because I wrote it in my letter." Marina recalled the time she had invested in writing the two-pager; it had taken her seven attempts to get it right. She'd sent it in a month earlier along with the hideously complicated Pinewood questionnaire that had also taken Marina hours to complete.

"Ah, the letter, yes. How could I forget?" replied the Pinewood employee. She held up a sheet of paper covered in schoolmistress-red ink.

"Mrs Alfero, with all due respect, I found it very difficult to follow. So I will ask you once again, has your income increased or decreased?"

The muscles in Rodrigo's jaw tightened slightly, but once again, he didn't speak.

"It's gone up by around $300 a month compared to when we bought the house," she replied.

"Thank you, Mrs Alfero. You see my problem? You have signed a mortgage contract. Your personal circumstances have not deteriorated – they have improved. So, could you explain to me why we should change the terms of our contract for you?"

Crabshaw's stare was now focussed on Marina who felt completely overwhelmed. She hesitated and averted her gaze towards the floor; somehow, the mortgage employee was actually making her feel guilty, like she was being accused of a financial crime.

Rodrigo leaned forward in his chair.

"Listen to me, you stupid bitch!"

"Rodrigo!" exclaimed Marina.

"Mr Alfero, there really is no need to insult me. I'm trying to help you," replied Crabshaw.

"Bullshit, lady. You're more interested in making us look stupid. You want to know what's changed? I'll tell you what's fucking changed."

Marina recoiled as far as she could into her seat, stared at the ceiling and asked for help.

Mrs Crabshaw met Rodrigo's stare, employed an arrogant smirk and nodded with him in sardonic agreement. It was almost as though she was goading him.

"We got a letter from your company in May last year saying that our monthly mortgage payment had almost trebled! Why don't you understand that that's a change in financial fucking circumstances?"

"Mr Alfero, I should like to remind you that you're in a professional environment. Whilst I appreciate that this may be a new experience for both of you" – at this point, she paused and conspicuously looked down her long nose at Mariana's legs and then at Marina, before continuing – "it certainly isn't for me. If you continue, I will be forced to terminate the interview."

Marina shifted in her seat and tugged hard at her skirt.

The Pinewood employee continued.

"The mortgage contract that you signed had a teaser rate to help with your initial payments. It was made clear to you when you signed that after two years the rate would increase. This is not a change in your financial circumstances and I think it is deceitful for you to pretend that it is."

"But no one ever explained that the increase would be that large and we can't afford the payments anyway. Why can't *you* see that?" asked Rodrigo.

"Mr Alfero, shall I tell you what I see? I see a couple that have more money now than they did two years ago. I see a couple that signed a legally binding contract with a mortgage company that made it clear at the time that after two years, the monthly payments would increase. I see a couple that, having enjoyed the subsidised, lower rate, now want to renege on their financial commitments at my company's expense."

"But we can't afford the payments," replied Rodrigo.

"Could we please—" attempted Marina.

"Did you lie on the application form?" asked Crabshaw, ignoring Marina's attempt to calm the situation.

"What?"

"Did you lie on the application form, Mr Alfero?" repeated Crabshaw.

"No, we did not," replied Rodrigo glancing at his wife, unsure of where this was heading. Marina was dumbstruck; she sat gaping at the two of them in disbelief.

"Then, in my opinion, you can afford the mortgage since otherwise you would not have signed the contract."

"Jesus Christ, lady – are you for fucking real? We're here trying to sort this out and all you want to do is insult us," replied Rodrigo.

Mrs Crabshaw pushed on.

"Mr Alfero, you're a *delinquent* and *you're* asking *me*, unfairly, to release you from financial commitments that you freely entered into. I would like—"

But this time, Mrs Crabshaw didn't get any further.

"What did you just say?"

"Pardon."

"Delinquent? Did you just call me a fucking delinquent?"

Marina shuddered.

Mrs Crabshaw smiled, before adding.

"Yes, I did, and if you read section 4:2:8 of your mortgage document, Mr Alfero, the term is defined as 'someone who fails to accomplish that which is required by the contractual agreement'. You're in breach; that's what a delinquent is."

"Marina, I'm out of here before I do something I really regret. I'll see you in reception. Mrs Crabshaw, I hope I never have to see you again, but if I do, please do the world a favour and burn that fucking thing off the side of your face before we meet!" He slammed the door, as he left.

For the first time during the meeting, Mrs Crabshaw's smirk disappeared completely and she brought one of her hands up to her chin. Marina's countenance hadn't changed – her mouth was still half open, as she wrestled with the temptation to laugh and the very real need to cry.

"Mrs Alfero," began the mortgage officer, as she slowly recovered, "it's God's will that at some point in all our lives, we need to experience difficulty. It is how we deal with it that's important and I don't see anything here that a little hard work and discipline will not fix." She signalled the end of the meeting by closing the folder and putting away her belongings.

Marina stood up and pulled the sides of her skirt downwards as hard as she could. She said goodbye to Mrs Crabshaw and went to leave the room.

"Mrs Alfero, I think it is only fair that I warn you that if the mortgage payments continue to deteriorate, I will have no choice but to recommend to my employer that we begin foreclosure proceedings." Mrs Crabshaw was still seated, her scaly fingers with the black-painted fingernails clasped together in front of her.

Marina saw Elsa in reception on the way out. The little girl waved and held her family picture up to show Marina that she'd added the sun to the left corner. Marina returned the smile and then walked away quickly before Elsa could notice the tears.

Chapter Fifty-Five

Alice kissed her husband for the third time that morning and congratulated him again.

"Thank you," replied McGrath, laughing as he wiped the ice cream away from his cheek that he knew his wife had deliberately left behind. She grinned her mischievous grin; the one that he'd fallen in love with that night he'd won his award at the Grosvenor. He almost felt like a teenager soaking up the warm spring sunshine sat on Richmond Green; Mr Wimpy in one hand and a wet wipe in the other cleaning his cheek. *Almost* felt like a teenager that was, because a few inches away, sleeping soundly in her carrycot was their three-month-old daughter. Megan was neither planned nor unplanned. She was simply the blessed product of two people so confident and happy in their relationship that neither worried about the possibility of Alice falling pregnant. When it happened, neither was surprised but both were overjoyed.

McGrath didn't need anyone to remind him he was a lucky man, that he'd found the missing piece of the jigsaw required to make his life whole. Ever since the evening at the Grosvenor, his private life had been perfect. He and Alice had talked for hours that night and met the following weekend for something that resembled a date. Alice cycled over to McGrath's, the house where they now lived, and insisted that the bike was parked inside lest someone took a fancy to it whilst they went out. He had never known anyone park a bike in a house before, but didn't mind one bit. The two enjoyed a walk down to the river for lunch and another marathon 'getting to know you' session. Alice moved in within months of that night, they'd been married in 2007 and her expensive bike was still parked in the hallway.

The source of his wife's pride – McGrath's appointment to head up Allied English Properties (AEP) at the tender age of just thirty-one – was evidence that his working life was also on a high. He would become one of the youngest departmental heads at the bank and he couldn't wait to get started. He would run his own team, gain experience in a broader range of properties, cover residential and commercial as well as international real estate. It was a fantastic career move for him and well paid. Not immediately, but in time, it would allow him and Alice to one day slow down, enjoy that small fishing boat that they discovered they both yearned for and live away from the hustle and bustle of London.

Alice finished her ice cream and glanced at her watch. "Come on, we'd better go before Megan's next feed," she said.

McGrath's mobile went and Alice waved at him to take the call, as she took charge of the carrycot. They walked towards home – along one of the myriad of narrow, ancient paths that criss-cross Richmond Green – with Joe a few paces behind, his phone pressed to the side of his head.

"Joe? It's Andrew Longmire here." McGrath was struggling to hear. The line wasn't perfect, and a 747 was in its final descent with Heathrow just a few miles to the west.

"Hi, Andrew, how are you?"

"Fucking worried, that's how I am, Joe."

Given the tone of his voice, McGrath would have gone for agitated or at least irritated before worried, but he kept his counsel.

Instead, he asked, "Why, what's up?"

"Do *you* know where Michael is?" he asked curtly. McGrath thought his tone had already notched-up a scale to angry and he didn't like the emphasis he placed on *you*.

"Andrew, what's going on?" he asked.

Alice turned and looked at her husband; she'd heard the intonation change and the higher tone. She slowed her walk and drifted off the path onto the grass amongst the early spring daffodils. She carefully placed the carrycot on the grass and busied herself with Megan. The baby was beginning to stir and Alice looked up to the aeroplane and scowled.

"Well, I was hoping *you'd* be able to tell me that, Joe."

"I assume he's in Cannes, Andrew, but I haven't spoken to him for, well, a couple of weeks now."

"He's not in Cannes. Well, he's not in his villa anyway. We've been there and it's empty. It also looks like it's been ransacked. I can't get him on his mobile and he won't reply to my emails. Joe, your fucking brother's disappeared."

McGrath thought back to the last few times he'd tried to speak to Michael, and a shot of guilt flushed through him. He'd called his brother a few times in the last month or so, and had left voice messages. It was a little strange that Michael hadn't returned his call, and he hadn't been overly concerned. But the truth was that he'd been so wrapped up in his own world, the bank and his promotion that he hadn't tried overly hard.

"Let me make some calls, Andrew. I can try some of his Cardiff-based guys that look after his UK business but *I* haven't heard from him," replied McGrath. He caught Alice's questioning glance and gave her a shrug of the shoulders: he really didn't have a clue what to make of this. But despite the glorious April sun, he felt a slight chill steal slowly down his spine, as he ran the possibilities through in his head.

"Has he ever done this before?" asked Andrew, who was at least beginning to sound a little more conciliatory.

"Never – well, not to my knowledge." McGrath continued to walk along the footpath.

"Bollocks! This is really important, Joe. You need to know the whole story."

McGrath swallowed and pushed the phone harder against his ear.

Andrew cleared his throat. "We know the villa is empty because Pascal went around there all guns blazing. For some reason, Michael has withdrawn £150,000 from the Strasbourg account and Pascal can't pay the contractors. So the building work has come to an abrupt halt and our French friend is talking legal action and police as the next steps. He's put two and two together and made five – he's accusing Michael of doing a runner with the money."

"Don't be fucking stupid – you know my brother wouldn't do that." It was Joe's turn to become angry. He stopped abruptly in the middle of the narrow footpath, unwittingly blocking a jogging mum with a buggy who seemed to have appeared from nowhere. She was dressed in go-fast Lycra bottoms, baseball cap, dark shades and her buggy had the oversized wheels; the type that marked her out as someone that wouldn't let motherhood get in the way of a training schedule.

"Arsehole!" she shrieked, as she swerved onto the grass to avoid him. She lost her footing as she did so and stumbled for a few paces and then fell flat on her face – the buggy careered towards Alice and Megan. Alice jumped into the way of it at the last moment, just preventing it from colliding with the carrycot.

The mum stood up and dusted herself down – her Lycra was ripped and a graze rapidly appeared on her pale white knee now poking through one of the legs. Her sunglasses were a few feet away on the footpath. She looked straight at Alice.

"I assume you're waiting for that arsehole?" she asked, pointing behind her.

"Excuse me?" replied Alice. She was rubbing the side of her shin where it had taken the brunt of the impact from the buggy, as she looked at the woman through incredulous eyes.

"It's his bloody fault. He stopped in the middle of the path; I had no choice. Look, he's ruined my bloody tights. Oi, get off the bloody phone, will you?" shouted the mum, as she retrieved her eyewear.

McGrath was oblivious; closed eyes – completely focussed on what Longmire was telling him.

"Calm down, Joe. I'm not saying that he stole the money but you and I will have to deal with an irate, excitable French businessman who thinks that we've all shafted him and he's livid. We need to clear this up. If we don't, we can kiss goodbye to our fucking money in France. Call me the minute you hear anything." There was a click and the phone went dead.

McGrath stared blankly at the phone and then saw his wife and another woman a few feet away looking daggers at one another.

"Are you for bloody real?" asked Alice, as she looked the mum up and down. "You nearly push that poxy buggy into my baby and all you're worried about are your stupid tracksuit bottoms?"

"Listen, dear, they're Fabletics compression-fit running tights not tracksuit bottoms. And these *were* a pair of Oakley Half Jacket by-the-bloody-way," said the mum, as she threw the shattered sunglasses back down on the ground. "And I wasn't anywhere near your baby until numb-nuts here forced me off the path. You want someone to blame lady, here's your man." She turned to McGrath who was frantically trying to catch up with events.

"He didn't *force* you to do anything, you silly woman. I saw the whole thing; you weren't looking where you were going, you lost your footing and let go of the buggy. Take some bloody ownership!"

McGrath felt like he was watching one of those aggressive rallies at Wimbledon. His head moved from side to side – flitting between Alice and this Lycra-clad jogger; each woman trying to up the ante with each new volley of assault. And both were getting angrier as a rebuke would come back just as quickly as they'd served the last one. McGrath hurried the last few steps to reach them.

"OK, OK. Ladies, I'm sorry, but can we calm down please?"

The mum turned to Alice, a jutting chin and a sneer of a smile on full display. "You see, I told you he should apologise." She then turned on McGrath. "And you want keep off that bloody phone and have a bit more appreciation for the others around you. Lots of people use this Green you know." She wagged a finger in McGrath's direction.

Megan was awake now and Alice bent down to pick her up. She scowled at the mum and clearly wanted to go again, but comforted her daughter instead.

The mum yanked her buggy into position and set-off, limping as she did so noticed McGrath, down one of the footpaths that led to the remains of Richmond Palace and the River Thames beyond.

"Crikey, Alice, what was all that about? Are you OK?" he asked.

"Ownership, Joe. Bloody ownership! She wasn't looking where she was going and wanted to blame somebody else. So she lashes out at the nearest person she can find. She nearly ran over Megan with that ridiculous contraption for goodness' sake. And you know what? She didn't even check on her own child – not once."

McGrath put his arm around Alice and Megan and they stood quietly for a few seconds. He kissed his wife's forehead.

He then picked up the carrycot and they walked along the path once again.

After a few steps, Alice asked who was on the phone and whether everything was all right.

"That was Longmire, he can't get hold of Michael and £150,000 has gone missing from the bank account for the development in Cannes I told you about. Apparently, our friend Pascal is shouting foul play and threatening legal action."

"That's ridiculous! He thinks your brother stole the money?"

"Unfortunately, yes."

Alice tugged on her husband's arm, as they walked to try to comfort him. All Joe could think of was '*ownership, bloody ownership*'. He couldn't believe it for one moment, but if he'd taken the money, Michael would need to take responsibility for it.

Chapter Fifty-Six

As he drove west over the Second Severn Crossing, a light drizzle welcomed McGrath into the Principality; it brought a wry smile to his face. He loved Wales and his hometown, but he didn't miss the weather. As he drove further and night closed in, the rain worsened until it was sheeting down. It was becoming downright dangerous now and was enough to darken his mood, which in turn was enough to remind him of the call he'd had with his new boss that morning. With the wipers on full blast and moving from side to side like some hysterical metronome, he strained to see the road ahead. He cursed Dave Arnold and the headache that was forming right between his eyes.

Arnold ran the Global Restructuring Unit at Allied English Bank. The GRU, as it was called, was there to 'support the bank's small business clients that were having commercial difficulties'. Whatever it might be, the GRU offered advice and support to the client. If, however, the restructure didn't work for whatever reason, the assets would need to be sold and this is where Allied English Properties and McGrath came in. He and his team would be responsible for stabilising the assets and then selling them in the open market.

When he'd told Arnold in the morning that he had a family issue to deal with in Cardiff, his new boss had shown zero sympathy. "What, you need a day out of the office before you've actually had a day in it?" he'd asked derisively. The upshot was that he'd given McGrath twenty-four hours; after that, he was expected back in the 'bloody office'. That was the reason he was driving now in the dark and the rain and not tomorrow morning, as was his original plan.

As he arrived in Cardiff, the rain eased and he drove through streets he knew well. Although the familiarity calmed him and his annoyance waned, a sense of nervousness replaced it. He didn't know quite what to expect and his mum hadn't expanded on, '*I've got your brother here and he's in a hell of a mess*'. What made a multi-millionaire property developer – normally living in the south of France – turn up on his mother's doorstep in Grangetown *in a hell of a mess?*

He tried to recall the last time that the three of them had been in Virgil Street together and actually spent a night under that Victorian slate pitched roof of number 12. He couldn't pin it down precisely but it probably would have been around the time he finished university. He could still see his mum in his graduation photo on the steps of the college and her looking up at him from her five feet nothingness. She was all frizzy hair and her best outfit, but she had an odd expression on her face – somewhere between absolute pride and obvious amusement that her macho son was wearing a kind of 'silk dress'.

Ten minutes later and he had finally arrived. Mrs McGrath opened the door and stood before him in the narrow hallway of number 12 – all wrinkles and red cheeks with a shock of tight corkscrew white hair that grew laterally out from her scalp. The frizzy ends just about met both sides of the doorway that framed her. McGrath walked in and closed the door behind him. Mrs McGrath reached up, wrapped her arms around her youngest son and buried the side of her face into his chest. She began to cry. Gentle whimpers to begin with, but the sobbing grew louder and Joe could feel her chest heaving as she cried. Mother and son spent the next few minutes in their embrace stood in the hallway. It was eerily quiet and the only audible sounds were Mrs McGrath's intermittent gasps for air. McGrath began to comfort her and repeated, "It'll be OK, Mum," as he rubbed the back of her head, flattening the curls as he did so.

Mrs McGrath then led her son along the hallway towards the back of the house. She held his hand and he followed – the width of the hallway insisting that they proceed in single file. He noticed the photographs on the wall, as they made progress – that photo of the graduation, the photos of Michael at the boxing gym and, next to them, Joe at the same gym a few years later.

The kitchen looked much the same as Joe remembered. He noticed the bottle of gin on the table and the single tumbler.

"Where is he?" asked the son.

"Upstairs, in *his* room," replied the mother, lifting her eyes to the ceiling.

McGrath couldn't be too precise about the dates, but he knew for sure that it hadn't been *his* room for the best part of twenty-five years, but this wasn't the time for pedantry.

"Should I go up?"

"I'd leave it for tonight, Joe. He's probably asleep."

"Have you told him that I was coming?"

She didn't speak; just nodded as she refilled her glass.

"Not happy about it then?" The intonation and raised eyebrows turning it into a question.

Mrs McGrath slowly replaced the bottle on the table and met her son's eyes – a sheen now covering her own.

"I don't know whether he's happy or not, Joe. He doesn't speak. He's not said two words to me or anyone else since he turned up on my doorstep a few days ago," she replied and went for the tissue she always kept in her cardigan sleeve.

"Has he seen a doctor?"

Mrs McGrath hesitated and then seemed to choose her words very carefully. "Two. I managed to get old Doctor Thomas around and he asked for a second opinion. They're both coming back tomorrow to talk to us. They don't think this is the best place for him at the moment, Joe. They think he needs" – at this point, she hesitated and looked down at the table – "professional help." She almost spat out the last two words, as if they left a sour taste in her mouth. The admission, that one of her own had some kind of mental problem, seemed a little too much and she covered her mouth as the tears came once again.

Her son got up, walked around the table and put his arms around her. "It'll be all right, Mum. I promise," he whispered.

She grabbed his hand and crooked her neck so that his arm formed a comfort pillow against her cheek. They remained like that for a few moments as she gently cried and savoured her son's physical presence. She then dried her eyes, apologised for being 'silly' and returned the tissue to the inside of her sleeve.

The following morning, as consciousness pricked and jabbed at his senses, McGrath knew he wasn't at home in his comfortable bed with Alice. His neck was stiff where the cushions hadn't been able to fend off the arm of the sofa for the entire night and his back ached from the sagging foam supports. His eyelids slowly unfastened themselves and his eyes began to adjust to the surroundings. The dim orange hue from the lamp still shone and the drab Artex ceiling continued to hang over him like a crimped fog.

He plucked up the courage to turn his neck slowly – certain in the knowledge that the action would inflict pain as the muscles unlocked themselves from the clutches of the sofa arm – and his eyes focussed on the centre of the room. He went from half asleep to wide-awake in a heartbeat.

"Jesus Christ, Michael! You scared the shit out of me!"

Michael McGrath was sat in an armchair. His legs were crossed, his elbows were on the armrests and his hands made a steeple in front of his face with his forefingers gently nestled against his lips. His round face was expressionless and he simply stared straight ahead at nothing in particular. McGrath sat up and studied his brother. He was dressed, casually, but not untidily and his dark hair was a little longer than normal. Physically, it was like looking at Michael McGrath – for the most part, he appeared his normal self; weight, height, size; even his clothes. At some superficial level, someone might think there was nothing strange.

But McGrath wasn't someone: it was his only sibling sat there in front of him. He sensed immediately that the charade of his physical appearance belied some awful abnormality that had actually occurred within. Something deeper inside Michael, where it really mattered, had been fundamentally altered.

Nervously, McGrath moved closer, kneeled down and placed a hand on his brother's knee, as he stared into Michael's eyes. He saw nothing but emptiness; like two hollowed passages that led into some deep, cavernous space behind them. There would be no '*Hey, Joey*' and the obligatory bear hug today. Thoughts scrambled through McGrath's mind – *How? Why? When?* – all questions that popped into his head, as he tried to comprehend how someone as full of energy and life as Michael could have become so vacant. He had sat still for longer in the last few minutes than McGrath could ever remember in his life. The happy, animated face that could lift the mood of any room had morphed into some blank, expressionless mask; it was an eerie sensation.

As agreed at 9.30 am, the doctors came back to the house. They were stood in the front room and Michael was still sat in the same position in the armchair.

"Mr McGrath, your brother is suffering from stress. He is in a particularly acute state of catatonic stupor that has been caused by this stress. This is going to take some time to resolve and during this period of treatment, I would ask that Michael not be exposed to anything that will cause him further trauma. I understand from Mrs McGrath that your brother was a property developer?"

The use of the past tense grated. "Yes, he *is*, that's right," replied McGrath.

"Well, it would be counter-productive if he was exposed to any of the problems that are no doubt occurring in such industries at the moment. Your brother simply can't deal with any problems at the moment."

"How long will the treatments last?" asked McGrath.

The doctor looked down at Michael and paused for a second.

"That's too early to say, I'm afraid. There must have been some acute trauma either physical or psychological that has led to the catatonic episode. Treatment will normally consist of our psychiatric medications and psychotherapy. We will start immediately and we'll let you know of progress. This could last days, weeks, months and I'm afraid on occasion, years, Mr McGrath."

Joe's mum squeezed her son's arm as the doctor provided his explanation. When the doctor had first mentioned 'Catatonia', she had thought it had some reference to a war-torn Balkan country and had taken immediate offence. But she was slowly beginning to come to terms with what was at stake.

The doctors got their wish and mother and son agreed to the suggested treatment. They would return later that day to take Michael McGrath away. Mrs McGrath showed the doctors to the front door and McGrath tried to come to terms with the fact that the 'men in white coats' would be visiting number 12 Virgil Street.

He found himself standing in the front room with a hand placed on Michael's shoulder, as the older brother remained seated in the chair motionless beside him. He was looking through the sash window. The outlook onto the narrow pavements, the concrete lamppost in the foreground, the row of identical terraced houses on the other side of the road, and his brother's ethereal presence next to him transported him back twenty-odd years.

His recollection of that day was still vivid despite the passage of time, and he gripped Michael's shoulder, as the images took hold. His dad had given him a thorough beating and he was sobbing; stood on his own pretty much where he was standing now. Joe was seven years old at the time. He could see his dad, mum and Michael just outside on the pavement. Mum and Dad arguing and then Dad exploding into a fit of rage that made Joe cry again. He punched his mum and Michael immediately threw himself at Dad to protect her. It was a typical fearless act by his big brother – the first of many that Joe had witnessed over the years. His older brother wasn't afraid of anything.

Two minutes later, Mum and Michael had walked back into the front room. He never set eyes on his dad again and from that point on, Michael stepped up and looked after both him and his mum – he was the patriarch. It was only years later that Joe had finally persuaded Michael to tell him the truth.

He blinked furiously to keep the tears at bay as he turned to his brother. He found himself looking down at a man that he'd spent his entire life looking up to. Joe's eyes began to swim, as he knelt down.

"I promise you, Michael. We'll beat this. Whatever it takes, whatever it costs. You looked after us, now it's our turn," he said.

For the first time in their lives, Michael McGrath needed Joe McGrath more than the other way around.

Chapter Fifty-Seven

A little later that morning, McGrath drove the two miles into the centre of Cardiff to meet up with 'Giant George Getaki' – Michael McGrath's right-hand man when it came to his property development business. He was sat in the corner of the café drinking coffee and wasn't difficult for McGrath to spot. Getaki was a tall guy – always had been – but age had unkindly assumed that a sizable middle-age spread would now complement his hitherto lanky frame. He was wearing a skin-tight Cardiff City football top, that had obviously been purchased way before age had made its harsh contribution. As Getaki stood, he offered McGrath his right hand whilst simultaneously tugging the top down with his left. McGrath smiled inwardly, as the giant of a man attempted to protect his modesty.

"Alan, can we have some more coffee please?" asked Getaki and he motioned for Joe to take a seat. "And can I have double egg on toast please? Joe, you hungry?"

McGrath declined the offer of food, and sat down opposite Getaki.

"When did you arrive?"

"About ten last night; pretty straightforward trip actually, so I can't complain. Listen, George, I've seen my brother and he's in a hell of a mess. He's not even speaking. He can't function – I'm not even sure he knows what day it is never mind that he ever owned a real estate business."

Getaki shook his head.

"Shit. I'm really sorry, Joe. I haven't seen him for over a month. He flew back from Cannes for a quick visit and then went back. After that, it was murder even trying to get hold of him."

Alan brought the coffee. Getaki hijacked the sugar bowl and stirred most of its contents into his fresh coffee before continuing. McGrath reassessed whether it was just the ravages of time that had transformed Getaki's body.

The big man continued. "Each time I did speak to him, he seemed to know less and less detail about what we were doing. Things that he used to know off the top of his head, all of a sudden, he just didn't know. I tried to tell him he needed to come back as the creditors were getting ever more aggressive and demanding payments left, right and centre. The banks have been the worse – bunch of bastards if you ask me."

Getaki then looked up and covered his mouth.

"I'm sorry, Joe. Except present company of course."

McGrath gave him a warm smile. "No worries, George, I won't pretend to be proud of being a banker at the moment." Getaki had known that Michael's younger brother had ended up in banking – in London somewhere – but that was about it.

McGrath picked up his coffee and took a mouthful; it removed his smile and he presumed part of his oesophagus. He instinctively went for the sugar and then immediately changed his mind.

"What were the banks jumping up and down about anyway?" asked McGrath.

"I brought these with me. You can keep them; doesn't look like I'll be needing them again anytime soon."

Getaki handed Joe a plastic wallet that contained the details of Virgil Estates' recent developments.

McGrath scanned the documents: a hotel development in north Cardiff, a completed office development on the outskirts of Cardiff Bay and a retail park near Bridgend.

Alan came back with the eggs on toast; the undercooked yoke and egg white quivered and glistened together in one viscous slimy mix, as the plate banged down onto the plastic table. McGrath was happy he'd abstained.

McGrath looked back at the documents and then asked, "Are you sure there's no equity in any of these?"

"I'm sorry, Joe. I've looked at the numbers every day for weeks now. It's hopeless. Your brother was a great developer but the banks have screwed him over this time. We were only a few weeks away from opening the hotel; we had a string of good bookings – both on rooms and functions – but we ran out of cash a few days before we were due to open. The bank demanded their valuer undertake a new open market value and suddenly, we were in breach of two banking covenants. We lost control; they kept demanding payments for this and a penalty for that. It continued until they bled Michael dry."

Getaki picked up his knife and fork and smacked his lips, as he prepared to devour his double ectoplasm on toast. He looked straight at McGrath.

"There was nothing wrong with the hotel, Joe – or the other two schemes by the way. If the bank hadn't behaved like complete bastards, I'm pretty sure your brother would have kept his business and his sanity."

McGrath could feel his heckles rising. "Do you know which bank he used?"

Getaki put down his knife and fork and wiped his mouth with the paper serviette. He retrieved a couple of the papers from the table.

"Well, your brother dealt with the banks, Joe, but let's see, it was The Global Restructuring Division or something," said George, as he sifted through the pages.

As he did so, McGrath closed his eyes and silently shook his head from side to side.

"Ah, here it is. The GRU at Allied English," replied George, "fuck knows why they all have such poncy names." He picked up the HP bottle, added to the existing mound of brown sauce on his plate and went back to his breakfast.

McGrath was in a trance, staring out of the window. After a few moments, Getaki seemed to notice that McGrath was lost in thought.

"Joe, you OK?" he asked.

No reply.

"Joe? What's wrong?"

McGrath blinked and then turned to face Getaki. "Sorry, what? Yes. Sorry George, I'm fine. It's just been a rough twenty-four hours," he replied in a halting voice.

Getaki glanced at his watch and moved the empty plate to one side. "Look, apologies, but I promised the wife I'd pick her up from work. Please give my best to your Ma. Tell her I'll call around later in the week. He stood, gave his defiant Bluebirds' strip another tug and shook hands with McGrath once again.

"George, one more question before you go. Michael had an interest in a development in France. I'm not sure how much money he made on it, but—"

Getaki raised his hand. "Sorry, Joe. Your brother had already thought of that. About three weeks ago, he transferred £150,000 from a French account. He said it was his share of the profit. That was the final chunk of the money that Michael threw at those bastards at the bank before they told him they were pulling the plug anyway. Bloody shame he threw that it into the pot; could have been a nice nest egg for him."

Joe winced, as he watched Getaki leave the café. It may have been a final desperate act, by a very desperate man, but Pascal wasn't lying; his brother had stolen the money. But as he looked down at the bank's letter headed paper, he also began to understand what role Dave 'bloody' Arnold and his own employer may have played in all of this. He felt a quiver in the pit of his stomach and a sudden craving for fresh air.

Chapter Fifty-Eight

Andrew Longmire was in a good mood. He was wearing a brand-new suit, a crisp white shirt – the style that Kamil introduced him to all that time ago – and a Hermès silk tie. Alone in the lift, he preened himself in the mirror as it ascended to the 14th floor of the City Headquarters of First Capital. The lift slowed after the 13th and then came to a gentle stop as the doors opened to the sound of a bell and then the swish of the mirrored doors. He reassured himself one more time that the Windsor knot was perfectly positioned and then stepped out and headed for the Boardroom where his fellow Directors would be waiting for him. He was looking forward to the meeting; the main business was the formality of approving his recommendation that the final results for 2007 should be £5.1 million – another record-year for the company's profits. This would then lead to a conversation about the level of his personal bonus with the Chairman of the Board – and then, almost certainly, another record would be broken.

That was just as well he thought, as he tugged his cuffed sleeves; he needed the money. Somehow, last year's million had been spent and the salary, as ever, was already spoken for with the mortgages and servicing the loans he had from Henry Humble at the private bank. He needed the annual bonuses to keep rolling in.

As Longmire strutted along the corridor, he recalled the meeting he'd had with Mick Marshall and Hugo Smith a couple of months earlier in the same room. It was bloody hard work but they had, eventually, relented and seen it his way, but only after the follow up emails and calls. That reminded him, Mick Marshall had still not returned his voice messages. It was strange that he was still sulking – he'd normally come around by now.

Part way down the corridor, Longmire glanced across to the bank of secretaries' desks and smiled. None of them met his eye – all far too busy frantically checking their screens. He registered that as unusual but continued the long walk towards the end of the corridor. He began to sense that something wasn't quite right; he couldn't put his finger on what it was, but he felt his mood change slightly.

A few steps later and he realised what it was. Where was everybody? Whenever a Board Meeting was about to start, at least a few of the other fourteen directors would be milling around outside; last minute phone calls, rearranging travel plans with the assistants he'd just passed or small groups swapping notes about the agenda. But the floor was deserted except for him and the secretaries that were too busy for social pleasantries.

He glanced back and caught them staring at him. They pretended otherwise – immediately returning to their computers. He walked the last few steps and arrived at the large, heavy, wooden doors. He paused briefly, realising he was slightly out of breath. He then slowly opened the entrance to the boardroom.

He was met with an eerie silence as he walked in and, for a moment, assumed the room was empty. He then did a double take, as he realised that it wasn't; there were three people sat next to one another at one end of the vast oval-shaped table. The Boardroom was large and double-height; it made the three of them seem like a long way away, but they were instantly recognisable.

Steve White – the ex-Chairman of First Capital was sat in the middle. On one side was his sulking CFO – Mick Marshall and on the other, Steve's wife – Andrea White. The Whites were looking straight at him – Steve smiling and Andrea sneering – but Marshall didn't look up from the papers on the desk in front of him.

"Good morning, Andrew – glad you could find the time to join us," said White, ostentatiously lifting his left arm allowing him to read his wristwatch.

Longmire declined the opportunity to apologise. He was only seven minutes late.

"What's going on, Steve? What are you doing here?" asked Longmire. He settled his squat frame gingerly into one of the high-backed leather chairs that surrounded the table – there was plenty of choice. Normally, every place was taken and the lack of bodies in such a large space began to feel unsettling. He wasn't panicking, but this was clearly not going to be the meeting he'd anticipated.

"It's just the four of us today, I'm afraid, Andrew. Let me bring you up to speed." White's voice rumbled around the expansive Boardroom as Longmire shifted in his chair.

"I asked Mick to be here, since he's crunched some numbers for me."

Longmire noticed that Marshall held his focus on the papers and didn't look up. Had he done so, he would have seen Longmire remove the white handkerchief from his breast pocket and feign to blow his nose.

"You see, for some time now, I've been puzzled by the company's ability to continuously post profit after profit despite deteriorating economic and financial circumstances. Notwithstanding the fact that many of our peers are reporting a fall in profits or outright losses, First Capital keeps churning out record-breaking results," said White.

"What can I say, it's now a well-run business?" retorted Longmire with a sardonic smirk plastered across his face. He returned the handkerchief to his pocket.

"I think we'd all prefer it if you didn't say anything for the next few minutes," said Andrea White; she spoke like a flinty schoolmistress and locked eyes with Longmire. They stared at one another with mutual contempt.

Steve White cleared his throat and continued.

"The Chairman has decided to step down, Andrew, and the Board has invited me back to be the Chairman on an interim basis until we can find a replacement."

Longmire never had much time for Steve White's replacement, but at least he didn't interfere. He knew White coming back was not good news; for a start, his own bonus discussion just got a whole lot more challenging. He looked out of the window as a silent, distant plane coming into land at City Airport caught his eye.

Without giving Longmire the opportunity to overthink it, White continued.

"As Chairman, I'm not going to accept your recommendation for the 2007 results, Andrew. On the numbers I have seen, I think the £5.1 million profit is delusional. In fact, it's borderline fraudulent. I've asked Mick to review the financial statements with me and I have agreed a trading loss for 2007 of −£3.5 million. Given the large discrepancy with the interim results that Mick acknowledged he signed off on as recently as March, he has tendered his resignation. I am still considering whether to accept it – although I have to say, he has my sympathy. From the email trail I have seen, there is no doubt that he, and many others, were coerced into producing the original number."

Bloody hell. Resigned, what do you mean? And a loss of −£3.5 million…That would kill the share price. Longmire's head was spinning; he was desperately trying to retain a calm exterior, but inside his guts were all over the place. What the hell would that mean for his bonus?

"You should also beware, Andrew, that I have agreed the £3.5 million loss with the managing partner of our external auditors and every other member of this Board. They're not here because they don't need to be. They have already agreed to the revised results and approved the communication that I am about to send out to the market via our PR agency," continued White.

The CEO's attempt to retain the calm exterior didn't last very long.

"What fucking communication? What the hell are you talking about, Steve? I haven't approved any press release," replied Longmire.

Andrea White coughed and leaned forward in her seat, a slight upturn in the corners of her mouth discernible.

"Given the contents, I hardly think it appropriate that you do approve it. But I want you to read it, Andrew, because Mick and the previous Chairman are not the only ones who will tendering their resignation around here," said White.

"Take your time. I've instructed the PR agency to release it in" – he lifted his left arm again – this time for dramatic effect – "five minutes."

He glided a piece of A4 paper across the polished surface of the table. It hovered, silently, and came to rest in front of Longmire. The CEO slipped a forefinger between his neck and stiff white collar and yanked – hard. He looked at White and then picked up the communication and started reading.

STARTS

London Stock Exchange Announcement – First Capital
Final Financial Results 2007

Results

First Capital today announces its final financial results for the year 2007.

It is senior management's judgment that the interim results, published on the 30 March 2008, materially overstated the company's profitability. The revised, and final results, which the Board has approved, are a financial loss of £3.5 million.

There are two explanations for the discrepancy between the preliminary and final results.

One is the on-going deterioration in financial markets with opinions continuing to change on a weekly basis. The second is the difference in opinion between the Board and the CEO regarding the carrying value of balances.

Dividend Policy

In light of the market pressures and the company's poor cash position, the Board has decided not to declare a dividend.

Management Change

Due to the dramatic discrepancy in the Company's financial position between the interim results issued in March and the final results today, we can also confirm that the CEO (Andrew Longmire) has resigned with immediate effect. We are also undertaking an internal investigation into 'accounting irregularities'.

Sir Andrew Smith has also left the company, and Steve White – the previous Chairman, and original founder of the business – will take over as interim CEO and Chairman until a successor can be appointed.

London, 15 June 2008

ENDS

Longmire finished reading, screwed up the statement into a tight ball and threw it back at White. It ricocheted off a coffee cup and landed in front of Marshall and his pile of papers. Longmire got up and stood behind the high-backed chair, his clammy hands trying to find purchase on the smooth leather upholstery.

"This is bollocks," he said. "There's nothing wrong with the £5.1 million. It's a fucking conspiracy that's all this is. The markets will settle down in a couple of weeks and we'll be back to making money."

He was grateful he had something to hang onto – his knuckles turned white, as he grasped onto the seat. By contrast, his large round face was now a strong red, inclining to purple.

For the first time since Longmire entered the room, Marshall looked up from his papers and met Longmire's eyes. He then stood up, slowly and without blinking, held the stare of his former boss.

"Andrew, for goodness' sake, will you give it up – you increased profits because you took on more risk. That's it. There never were any new lending techniques; there never were any moments of financial genius Andrew – you just used more leverage than anyone else, and—"

"Now listen to me you—" Longmire tried to interject; his globular, brown eyes seemed to protrude out in front of him even further than usual.

"No! You fucking well listen to me for once." Marshall pounded the table with a first and glared at Longmire.

"The short-term funding through the capital markets was fine as long as it remained a small part of what we did. But you kept increasing it; you wouldn't bloody listen. So in the end, we share a business model with Northern Rock. Congratulations!"

Longmire went to interrupt again, but Marshall wouldn't be denied. He kept ploughing ahead.

"Your unreasonable insistence that we continue to assume we have no bad loans. No bad loans! Our clients are dropping like flies and you want to ignore it to protect the P&L.

"And now the credit crunch has found you out and you don't like it. You're behaving like a spoilt child, Andrew!"

The Whites glanced at each other, conveying information via a series of facial expressions and lip twitches that had evolved into their own marital language – rather like two flag semaphore experts, husband and wife conversing without speaking.

Longmire stared at Marshall as one of the powerful down lights picked out his glistening forehead.

"You ungrateful bastard!" he was almost whispering. "You owe everything you have to me. CFOs like you are two a penny. Where's your fucking loyalty?" demanded Longmire.

"Loyalty is something you earn, Andrew. You can't buy it." Marshall almost spat out the last sentence and then sat back down.

White let the statement hang there for a moment before continuing. "I'm not sure there is too much else to say, Andrew, except invite you to sign your resignation letter," he said, reaching into a folder and extracting another piece of paper.

"What if I don't resign, Steve? As far as I'm concerned, I've done nothing wrong except turn a losing company around and make it profitable." At this point, he scowled at Andrea.

White immediately stopped what he was doing and looked up at Longmire.

"If you don't sign, Andrew, you will never work in the city again – I'll make sure of that. It would take the FCA five minutes to conclude that you were manipulating financial statements if these emails were to find their way to their offices." He tapped the pile of papers that were in front of Marshall with his pen. "You'd not only be banned from being a company director, you'd be lucky not to go to prison."

White then pointed an accusatory finger at Longmire and slowed his cadence for effect. "And, given that *you* have almost certainly ruined the company that Andrea and I spent twenty years building, I suggest you don't try me on this one."

In contrast to the booming tones of the earlier part of the meeting, the Chairman's voice was now rich with emotion. Andrea White's death stare nearly forced Longmire to step backwards; it felt like her eyes were boring into the back of his skull. He knew this woman didn't like him, but he sensed hatred now that was so much more powerful than he'd ever experienced before.

There was a brief pause as Longmire considered his options and looked away from Andrea White. Then, almost in slow-motion, a playful grin began to unfurl as a moment of enlightenment dawned on him – it was as if he'd suddenly worked out some ridiculously complex puzzle and was about to delight in his own genius. He released his grip on the chair and then leaned confidently on the top of it with his elbows.

"I'm not as stupid as you look, Steve. If you release that statement, you'll cripple the share price – and destroy your own wealth in the process. You're bluffing," said Longmire. He actually smiled at the three of them, raising his eyebrows as he did so.

For a moment, no one said a word. Marshall shook his head slowly and then closed his eyes, rolling the lids with a thumb and forefinger. White made a steeple out of his fingers and his head cocked slightly to one side in thought. Andrea White continued to stare at her arch-enemy but she gently nodded her head and, very slowly, her expression softened. A Mona Lisa smile formed across her lips – as if she knew something that he didn't.

Longmire – somehow – was oblivious to the body language. So much so, that he actually interpreted the pause that accompanied the silence as capitulation and grew in confidence that he'd called White's bluff.

"Andrew, we don't own any shares in First Capital. After I resigned and no longer held an executive position, I was free to trade like anyone else. Andrea and I sold out over 2006 and 2007 – I think we averaged 285p per share, didn't we, darling," asked White, as he glanced at his wife, "with the final little flurry in December last year."

Andrea White's knowing smile now broadened out evenly across her face.

"That's right, dear," replied his wife – not once letting her eyes move away from Longmire. The smile transformed into a full on smirk, as she held her stare.

Longmire found himself relying on the back of the chair once again for support. His knees buckled and almost gave way as a sudden coldness struck at his inner core; he'd been the fool buying at 285p while the White's had been selling – the final humiliation. He'd actually been complicit in his own financial destruction.

"So, you see, I won't be destroying my wealth by releasing that statement, but I will release these papers to the FCA if you don't sign the resignation letter."

Longmire was still smiling, but it was one of intolerable anguish as he finally accepted his fate.

It was a bloodbath. By lunchtime, the shares had been suspended twice by the London stock exchange and there was no liquidity – at any price. Anyone left holding shares was stuck with them. The last number on the screen that blinked in front of Longmire was 2.5 p per share. He'd missed five calls from an irate Henry Humble at his private bank. He had no idea that Humble had the energy to sound so angry. But his bank had been caught out by the rapidity of the fall and was also stuck with worthless stock.

During the most traumatic morning of his entire life, Longmire had gone from the CEO of a profitable company to the ex-CEO of a company that had lost over 90% of its stock market value. He'd lost his job and his wealth. He was now worth just under £145,000: a few days before, D66 had insisted it had been several million pounds.

He dragged himself along the pavements towards Liverpool Street, joining the legions of worker-ants busy with their daily toil. He set off for Woodbridge to tell Sam the happy news.

Chapter Fifty-Nine

McGrath was in his office waiting for Dan to arrive for their biweekly. The meeting was a chance to discuss the assets that would be transferred from the bank's Recovery Unit into Allied English Properties. McGrath's team then implemented new business plans and sold them on to the highest bidder.

He'd been doing it for a couple of months now, and had discovered in pretty short order what the real raison d'être of this part of the bank was. The chat with George Getaki in Cardiff had alerted him to the possibility, but he wanted to make sure. Meanwhile, his brother was still in the same catatonic stupor and the people that put him there were now his colleagues. He had to walk past them every day; dressed in their pristine suits speaking in their annoying Estuary-English accents. He shared the coffee machine with them, as he listened to their banter: chitchat that included mocking clients who broke down when they were told that the bank would be foreclosing. They gave almost worship status to people like Dave Arnold who made the decisions to do so.

Most of them, McGrath felt he had to assume, were almost certainly complicit in what was going on and therefore criminals. Well-dressed and well-spoken criminals, but that's what they were. The realisation of where exactly he worked didn't foster job satisfaction. But he wanted to stay-put for the time being; it would only be a matter of time before what he was waiting for would turn up.

Dan tapped on the door and entered the office.

"Good morning, Joe. I have the latest batch of assets coming across," he announced through his lazy, nasal drawl.

McGrath studied the twenty-something-year-old from Slough who'd perched himself on the seat opposite. Apparently, he'd joined the bank as a trainee and gone to night school and, like McGrath, was a chartered surveyor. Perhaps the length of his tenure, relative to his age, explained why he'd become indoctrinated so completely into the culture – immune, perhaps even oblivious, to what he actually did on a day-to-day basis. McGrath was still trying to work him out, but assumed Dan didn't know any different – he just did what he'd always done and not thought too much about it. Like a goldfish, he simply didn't know the difference between right and wrong – amoral rather than immoral.

Dan cleared his throat and began.

"The client was a hotel developer, and much else besides from what I understand. He was only a few weeks away from opening and ran out of cash just before being able to complete. Dave Arnold and the 'body snatchers' instructed their usual Valuer and made sure the results put the developer in breach of a couple of his banking covenants. It then got flipped into the GRU."

McGrath watched, as Dan delivered the summary in his usual casual manner; expressionless face and monologue tone. The 'body snatchers' was a term of reverence often banded around the office. The fact that Dan employed it without batting an eye in a formal meeting with his boss revealed the kind of culture that Arnold and his cronies had successfully cultivated. But the reference to the hotel was unusual; it got his attention.

"Where's the property located?" asked McGrath.

"North Cardiff."

Check.

McGrath blinked at his screen and slowly pulled a hand through his hair. He paused momentarily.

"Sorry, Dan, I just need to send this guy a reply, but carry on. I am listening." McGrath continued to tap away gently at his keyboard but was depressing random keys.

"Sure. It's actually a bloody good scheme," said Dan, as he read his notes. "Developer had done his homework and there's a strong market in that part of Cardiff for a mid-priced hotel but with good links into the city centre. Sort of place that'll be heaving when Wales play at the Millennium – short taxi ride in and out of town and massive discount on the city-centre names on Queen Street. I might stay there myself next time I go and watch the rugby; I assume the rates will be cheap enough now!" He snorted loudly and displayed a wide, annoying grin after making the last comment.

"What's the history with it?" asked McGrath. He looked up from his screen and caught the twinkle of mischief in Dan's eyes.

"From entering the GRU usual story, I'm afraid. Arnold insisted that the developer increase his personal guarantees in return for further support."

Check.

"The developer did just that, but five weeks later, Arnold and his guys decided they didn't believe the revised business plan anyway and refused to forward any cash."

Check.

McGrath's tapping on his keyboard was becoming heavier and heavier.

"Without the cash, the value continued to fall and then further breaches, obviously. The company's now gone and the asset needs to be transferred to AEP. Down to us to sell it now. There are another couple of schemes from the same developer we also need to get rid of."

Check.

As Dan finished, he pushed the file towards his boss like he was discarding a free evening newspaper. He leant back and slipped his hands in his trouser pockets, as he stretched his legs in front of him. He actually looked like he might yawn.

"But they're good schemes – there should be a decent profit for us in all of this. I'll visit the assets, get the business plans sorted and give you my view on pricing ASAP."

McGrath was the new boy, but even he knew that when the assets had passed through from the Recovery Unit, it represented the end of what was likely to have been a brutal odyssey at the hands of Dave Arnold. His own brother's mental state was evidence of that, but Dan looked like he'd just been discussing the weekend weather.

McGrath sat silently. He dry washed his hands and then used his right thumb to massage firmly across the ridge of his knuckles of his left. He felt the trauma of last night's gym session and considered what damage a left hook would cause to Dan's smug expression. He managed to control himself. He didn't blame Dan; he was just a pawn in Dave Arnold's elaborate charade.

Dan left the office a few minutes later and started to prepare the business plans for his boss.

McGrath had known that at some point the file would come across his desk. So he'd been patient. When Dan had gone and with the door closed, he opened his desk drawer and retrieved the file that Getaki had given him. It was the same one he'd just been discussing, but represented Virgil Estates' version of events.

He spent the afternoon in his office reading every note and every email in the bank's file. He was stunned. The level of collusion between the Valuer and the bank and the gratuitous fees were blatant. But what pushed McGrath over the edge was the bank's demand that his brother pour more money into the project when they patently had no intention of providing further support. They were just using his brother to create higher revenues to increase their own bonus packages, then steal the property and recover what they could. McGrath could clearly see this by crosschecking the dates on formal letters sent to his brother and the bank's internal memos from the file Dan had left him.

McGrath sat staring at one of the letters on Virgil Estates headed paper. He'd called his mum last night and there was no improvement. Michael was still stuck in his own little world, unable to communicate with anyone and as far as they could see, oblivious to what was going on around him. He recalled the doctors' analysis – *"There must have been some acute trauma that has led to the catatonic episode."*

McGrath looked at the bank's file and shook his head slowly. Being screwed for extra fees; being required to pour the last drop of your personal wealth into a company that you had spent twenty years building and then watching the bank take it down anyway: that all sounded acutely traumatic to McGrath. They were the real cause of all this. They'd robbed his brother of his wealth and taken away his sanity – all within a few short months.

He took copies of everything that was in the bank's version of Virgil Estates and several other files besides. Then, he began to develop the germ of an idea that was going to get his brother's money back: every last penny of it.

Chapter Sixty

Andrew Longmire and Joe McGrath occupied one of the meeting rooms on the executive floor of the Allied English head office in the City. They were both sat in padded leather chairs around a rectangular-shaped wooden table. The gilt-framed portraits of former CEOs of the bank adorned three walls – the fourth was a floor-to-ceiling window with views down on to Moorgate. The plush carpets and Villeroy & Boch tableware added to the sense of grandeur that the interior designer had aspired to. There was even a bowl of luxury Sprüngli truffles on the tray where the coffee pot had been placed – although neither man had much of an appetite.

Shunning the state-of-the-art telephone conference equipment, Longmire's private mobile telephone was on loudspeaker in the middle of the pristine table for the pre-arranged call with Pascal. There was an incongruity between the blackberry's cheap, tinny sound and the opulence of the room it ricocheted around.

"Joe, I'm very sorry to hear about your brother. You must keep me informed of how he progresses," said Pascal.

"Thank you, Pascal. I will," replied McGrath.

He couldn't detect a hint of sincerity in Pascal's voice. The Frenchman was still raw with anger and his tone belied his suspicion that Longmire and McGrath knew more than they were letting on. All that they kept repeating was that Michael McGrath was very ill and that they were still trying to locate the money. The fact that the funds had ended up, in a roundabout way, at his own bank was not something McGrath, or Longmire, felt the need to share with their French development partner.

"Nonetheless, what has happened has caused me much embarrassment and almost ruined our project, gentlemen. As sad as all this is, we should not pretend otherwise. I cannot persuade the construction team to go back on site until we pay them hard cash," continued Pascal.

"Hard cash is something that Joe and I don't have, Pascal," interjected Longmire. The former CEO of First Capital was already down to rolled up shirtsleeves and a warm glow across his face had settled in for the afternoon. He leaned forward into the table, as he spoke into the phone.

McGrath stole a glance at the man sat next to him. He understood it didn't do to be too sentimental about a man like Longmire, but nonetheless couldn't help but feel a tinge of sympathy. According to the Financial Times, he'd 'blown apart First Capital by a combination of an egregious use of leverage and incompetence'. There was even a suspicion of fraud. McGrath was well aware of all of this.

But Longmire had arrived early for the meeting – at McGrath's request – to discuss an idea he had. They had also ended up talking about their private lives and it turned out that Sam, Longmire's wife, was on the verge of leaving him and taking their son with her. She, by all accounts, was pretty screwed up herself; a close friend had apparently been murdered and 'Sam wasn't coping.' McGrath was trying to understand why Longmire should think anyone would be able to cope with that, when Longmire continued. He told McGrath – and this is what clearly hurt the most given the look of tormented anguish on his face – that he was in dire financial straits. Whether he was laying it on thick for his benefit, McGrath wasn't sure, but he had all the outgoings of his previous lifestyle and none of the income. Andrew Longmire desperately needed money from somewhere.

The mobile's tacky speaker was mutilating Pascal's normally silky French tones, but it couldn't prevent him from making his next point unambiguously.

"OK, gentlemen, then I will need to inject further funds and, as a result, we will need a new arrangement. The money that went missing was £150,000, but it has cost us much more than that due to the delays. And every day means we're selling into a weaker and weaker market. I'm no longer confident in our original profit forecast.

"So the first €1.5 million profit will come to me. After that, we share the balance out between us."

McGrath watched Longmire. He flicked a forefinger across an eyebrow before he pummelled the keys on his calculator with his chubby index finger. The proposal was so one-sided McGrath could do the maths in his head. Even the original, and probably over optimistic, profit estimate was around €2 million;

with the delays and deteriorating market, Pascal's solution effectively gifted the Frenchman all of what was now left.

"Why €1.5 million, Pascal?" asked Longmire. He had finished his calculations and was stood up; the palms of his hands spread out on the highly polished surface before him. He eyed his blackberry with suspicion.

"Because I said so, Andrew. Believe me, if you don't accept this offer, I will go to the authorities," came the distorted reply.

"OK, Pascal, none of us want that," said McGrath before Longmire had the chance to reply. "Give us a couple of minutes to discuss it. I'm going to put you on mute."

Longmire walked over to the full-length window and looked down on the streets below. McGrath muted the phone and watched, as the remnants of sweaty handprints on the table-surface slowly evaporated. He sighed faintly to himself, as they disappeared altogether.

"Listen, Andrew, this is over, it's gone. What value is left in those assets will vanish into the Côte D'Azur air or into Pascal's pockets – but either way, we won't see any of it."

Longmire turned back.

"Is that fucking thing on mute?"

McGrath double-checked and nodded confirmation.

"OK. This French bastard is going to screw us. I know when I need to cut my losses, Joe, but this other idea you talked about – we need it to work and work quickly. As you said, Michael's got us into this mess and you need to get us out of it."

"Agreed, Andrew. But remember. Not a penny more, not a penny less. Are we agreed on that also?"

"Yes, of course we are, Joe."

Chapter Sixty-One

As Whiteman stared at the painting, and loosened his tie, the absurdity of all this suddenly struck him. Here they were; him, the Secretary to the Treasury, and six CEOs from America's most powerful investment banks sat in the boardroom of the Fed Reserve Building, New York – the most secure and physically imposing building he'd ever been in. It looked and felt like it had taken the six years to build that he'd been informed about on one of his first visits. The giant blocks of Indiana limestone and Ohio sandstone used in the construction formed walls that were so thick they seemed impenetrable. Even in the painting on the wall, the building looked imposing; like a fortress of money – solid and permanent – to encourage the trust that the whole system relied upon: for Whiteman's money, the architect and the thousands of men involved in its construction had succeeded.

Irony had placed him and the CEOs in this building on this day to discuss this particular topic: deliberating the crumbling wreck of the global financial system in this enduring monument to trust and stability. He sighed to himself quietly – the architects of the building had clearly done a much better job than he and the architects of the financial system.

Normally on a weekend, the property is vacant save for the Federal Reserve Police Force that guard it 24/7 and a few nerdy economists who have nothing better to do other than practice their arithmetic: but this was no ordinary Saturday. On 13 September 2008, it had become a battleground, where Whiteman was trying to save one of the oldest and most prestigious banks in US history from bankruptcy and he had precious little time left to do it in.

He swallowed as he considered the hand he was about to play and how the CEOs would respond.

"I'll make my case one more time, gentlemen," said Whiteman. His glance around the room flitted between the CEOs.

"Without one of you, or a consortium of some sort, stepping up to the plate, this company will collapse. If that happens financial markets will panic, the money owed by Lehmans will never be repaid, increasing the prospect of even further banking failures. Who knows which one…" he thought about adding '*of you*' but decided against it. "Who knows which one will be next." But Whiteman tried his hardest to flash a cold smile across the table.

He knew each of them personally. He knew the names of the wives and in many cases the children and in one case, he was a godfather. He'd mentored many of these men before him, as they climbed the same treacherous career ladder of investment banking that he had once done. They'd been hugely grateful when he'd been at Silvermans and battled with Washington to ensure that derivatives remained unregulated and allowed all of them to make huge amounts of money as a result. Now all he wanted was someone, anyone, to work with him so that Lehman Brothers could find their way out of this mess. Without it, the company would collapse – undermining even further the little trust that was left within the system.

One of the bankers brought him back.

"Listen, Chuck, without the Fed stepping in and playing a major role here, we're not gonna touch this. Lehman is a real estate hedge fund disguised as an investment bank. It's got too much exposure to the markets. If its liabilities are half this amount, I couldn't in all conscience ask my shareholders to support a purchase at whatever price. I don't think you'd be any different if you were in our shoes."

Other than the odd muffled cough of accord, most of the men remained silent. Some were looking at each other and nodding their heads. It was obvious how they, and all their advisors, felt.

Whiteman sat back in his chair and considered this. The room fell silent, save for the antique grandfather clock in the corner of the room marking time. It reminded Whiteman of the urgency of the situation and he looked down at the information pack in front of him. Lehman Brothers' biggest problem by a long way was the huge portfolio of hopelessly overvalued CDOs that they still owned. The bank had been more active than most in creating them and now that the toxicity of the underlying mortgages was revealing itself, the CDOs were falling in value and were probably near worthless.

If the company's CDOs were marked correctly, everyone around the table knew its debts were way higher than their assets. It was bankrupt; it was just that

Whiteman didn't want to admit it. He shifted in his seat to try to get comfortable but failed and he did the maths in his head. What was the value of the gold in those vaults a few floors below? Eighty feet below ground level, in the cool subterranean corridors, the gold was carefully stored in different compartments; each chamber had a padlock, two combination locks and needed at least two guards to access it. There wasn't a precise – or even an official – valuation, but one estimate he recalled put it at around $380 billion, and that, apparently, was 25% of the world's official gold reserves: it held more of the stuff than Fort Knox.

Lehman's debts were now in excess of $600 billion. He shuddered slightly; one single investment bank had managed to accrue liabilities of almost half of all the world's gold reserves. And it had happened on his watch and to a large extent was due to the derivatives that Whiteman himself had championed.

He looked up at the clock again, and he noted that they'd been in the room for three and a half hours.

"Gentlemen, I suggest we reconvene here tomorrow morning at 8 am. I'll email you later this evening with various options that the Federal Government may be able to consider to help form a potential solution," said Whiteman. The bankers shuffled out, one-by-one, each man looking like a busy executive that had had his precious weekend stolen from him.

They met again the next morning and Whiteman spent another three hours trying to arrange a package to save the bank. Despite the 'sweeteners' from the Government, no one budged. At 1 pm on Sunday, 14 September, Whiteman gave up and flew back to Washington.

In the early hours of Monday, 15 September, Lehman Brothers filed for bankruptcy. Like Bear Sterns – which had failed in March – an institution that had survived two world wars and the 1930s depression was gone – forever. It had been the fourth-largest US investment bank and employed 25,000 people worldwide. When the New York stock exchange opened later that morning, its reaction to the largest bankruptcy in US history was brutal; it fell by 4.5% – the largest one-day decline since the 9/11 attacks. The market now assumed that more banking failures were unavoidable.

★

On the morning of the 16 September, just two hours before Whiteman was due to present proposals to President Bush to prevent further collapse within the system, the crisis took on yet another dimension. There was a knock at his closed office door. This was highly unusual – the whole department knew not to disturb the boss when he was preparing to see the President.

"Excuse me, Mr Whiteman. I wouldn't disturb you if this wasn't urgent, sir," said the Government mandarin, as he shuffled into the room. He moved slowly, as if he was unsure what to do or say next.

Whiteman was stooped over the morass of papers on his desk. He'd removed his glasses whilst he was working and the stretched-out hand was still flat against the top of his mottled head as he glanced up towards the man who'd interrupted him. His shirt was beyond wrinkled; it was dishevelled and complemented the general chaotic appearance of his surroundings. Screwed up pieces of paper, discarded coffee cups, a banana skin and post it notes were strewn across the normal pristine polished oak surface of his desk.

He straightened his spine and placed a hand on his lower back as he did so. The aching reminded him just how long he'd been sat there.

"What the fuck is it now?" he grunted. He could feel his pulse increasing and the fluttery feeling begin to stir in the pit of his stomach. After the last forty-eight hours, his nerves were nearly shot and he had a very bad feeling about the timing of this interruption.

The mandarin hesitated, like he was unsure whether to sit down or stand. He decided on the latter, but eyed one of the two exits in Whiteman's office.

"I haven't got all day!" demanded Whiteman. He threw his pen down onto the wreckage of his desk and looked up at the clock on the wall behind the advisor.

The man stood in front of him, swallowed and then stumbled through the next few sentences.

"It's the United States Insurance Group, sir…We've just had a call…em, from their CFO. They owe" – at this point, he checked his notepad and Whiteman noticed his hand shaking, as he flipped through the pages – "they owe $90 billion to holders of insurance contracts against the recent falls in CDO prices. I'm sorry, sir…they've just informed me that they don't have the money." The man pulled his head downwards – like a turtle retreating into its shell.

Silence. There was no verbal response from the Chief Secretary to the Treasury. He just gazed back at his advisor with a complete lack of focus; his eyes widened and his complexion blanched. It was as if he'd just been told the world had stopped spinning.

USIG was several orders of magnitude larger than Lehman Brothers and another, but more important, hub in the centre of the world's financial system. If it failed, aeroplanes wouldn't be able to fly and most insurance policies would be null and void – the *financial* world would, indeed, stop spinning. That was bad enough. But there was another, very particular, reason why Whiteman had developed an inability to speak.

If USIG went, it would take its trading partners with it. They included various types of organisations, but they were mostly investment banks that had used the insurance company to cover their own CDO positions. It was the investment banking community that was owed the majority of the $90 billion and without payment, further bank failures were inevitable. It would be like a house of cards – each failure setting off another: and it would take his legacy with it.

He began to think about the braying journalists and an eerie sensation crept up his spine. A realisation – one that he knew he should have arrived at much sooner – hit him hard in the base of the skull. He rubbed the back of his neck and rolled his shoulders. The fact that banks like Silvermans had reversed their CDO positions by buying insurance against their collapse didn't mean that the liabilities were removed from the system: it just meant that they had been passed on to someone else – in this case USIG. It was like a gigantic game of financial pass the parcel, and when the music stopped, it was USIG that was left holding it. The problem was that the package wasn't some gift-wrapped present; it was a toxic bundle of liabilities of epic proportions. In fact, it was so large that USIG didn't have the funds to settle it. The investment banks that thought they'd moved their liabilities on to USIG would now have to bear their share of the burden. Banks like Silvermans were now exposed to the collapse in CDO prices.

Images of what-might-be flashed through his mind. The questions, the accusations and insinuations about his role in all of this: he dreaded it. He wondered about the Timberwolf cohort of CDOs and how exposed Silvermans would be now. Although it was three years earlier, he could still hear Rajan's warning at Jackson Hole – the one that now turned out to be prescient. *Derivatives could eventually destroy their own firms – or even the entire financial system.* Whiteman closed his eyes and massaged his eyelids with the palm of his hands.

"Sir?"

Whiteman had almost forgotten somebody else was in the room. Finally, he managed to speak – his monotone voice faltering throughout his question.

"Are there any banks…which are…em…particularly exposed to the…$90 billion?" he asked. He rubbed the back of his neck again; the pressure was building once more.

The advisor instantly looked down at his papers as if avoiding eye contact had suddenly become paramount.

"Yes, sir, I'm afraid there is. There's one bank in particular."

Two hours later, Whiteman was sat in the Oval Office with the President of the United States to persuade him to authorise the biggest bailout the country had ever seen. The payment, he informed the President, was essential to save the country from imminent financial catastrophe. He was silent on the impact it would have on one investment bank in particular.

Chapter Sixty-Two

Lester FitzGerald was slumped in a chair surrounded by an assortment of cardboard packing boxes, odd pieces of office furniture and an eclectic bunch of memories. He was in the open plan area in Pont Street – where, in the last five years, he'd experienced many of the highs and lows of running *Credere*. The analysts, like all of the Lambda employees, had long gone and so was Lester's appetite for running a hedge fund business.

As he sat, almost tasting the disinfectants and other potions the landlord's cleaners had used, he thought about those experiences. Some had been sweet – although not as cloying as the chemicals he breathed in – but too many had been bitter. It was now obvious he'd won the intellectual arguments against the banks. Of that there was no doubt. He had the money in his account and, generally, eight hours of uninterrupted sleep a night to prove it. There were no demons in the small hours sitting in judgement about him any longer.

But as the last few months had passed, and news flow continued about mortgage defaults, foreclosures and the millions of people losing their homes, Lester began to understand for the first time the human cost of the industrial-scale game of Monopoly in which he had taken part. He'd been so obsessed with beating the likes of Rankin, his colleagues and their over-complicated mathematical formulae that he hadn't thought about whether his investments would impact anyone else.

Sitting in Pont Street, in a property that was once a home, the irony of the whole situation struck him even harder. Lester had taken the time to appreciate the history of the building; he'd obtained a copy of the original title deeds. Constructed in 1880, it provided a family home to the Thornes. Dr Arthur Thorne, his wife, three children and several staff had lived there for over thirty years. They had only moved out when Dr Thorne died. One hundred and twenty odd years later, a company – Lester's company – had occupied it as an office for just five years: a house built to provide a home for one family was then put to commercial use, so that Lambda could play its part in taking away millions of homes from others.

And what about the banks? He may have beaten them, but they certainly weren't the losers in all of this. The US government had just made an example out of Lehman Brothers, but apart from that – nothing. In fact, no sooner had the banks started to whinge than the regulators and politicians were rolling out the 'too big to fail' argument right across the US and the UK. So the taxpayer was bailing out the banks – another irony not wasted on Lester. He wanted to throw up at the thought of the financial gangsters being bailed out by the very people they'd cheated.

This realisation brought Lester to the conclusion that he would close down the fund. He certainly had no appetite to work on behalf of the Consortium any longer. He picked up his laptop and re-read the last note that he would send to his ungrateful investors.

All,

Making money out of investment banks' hubris is fine with me. Making money out of ordinary peoples' misfortunes is not. I'm ashamed to admit that our investment strategy has, in part at least, made money from the latter. I was so obsessed with beating the banks and winning the intellectual argument, that I was blinded to the wider implications of what we were doing.

When I started this fund, it was almost a game. It was, as difficult as it is for me now to admit, supposed to be fun. The banks were delusional about the risks that they were taking because their financial models were flawed. Everyone knows that now – they have been exposed as incompetent, conceited and, in most cases, corrupt.

But now, we discover that these financial institutions haven't lost at all. Bernanke and Whiteman have just announced a bailout programme that will see the vast majority of banks survive and most bankers keep their jobs. I think they knew; they knew that the government would save them. Perhaps they weren't as stupid as I thought they were after all – just a lot more devious than anyone could have imagined.

That's why I have decided to close the fund. Something has died inside me as I have realised whom the real losers are in all of this and that Credere, unwittingly, played a role in their tragedy.

As you are all aware, I have returned the majority of the profits to you already. To date, you have collectively received $2.1 billion, or a return in excess of 430%. The final accounts are now complete and I will be sending you a balancing cheque. The total profit to the fund will be marginally higher.

However, a small surcharge has been deducted from all of your accounts that I will use to right some of the wrongs that Credere has inadvertently inflicted on others. In the circumstances, I am sure you'd agree it is the least we can do.

Gentlemen, I wish I could say it's been a pleasure.

Good-bye.

Lester.

As far as Lester was concerned, the investors in the Consortium were entitled to a special place in hell. They had all received cheques from *Credere* (representing the vast majority of their returns). They had quadrupled their original investment at a time when the global stock markets had all but collapsed. But to a man, they had not been in touch. Not even a thank you. Not even James Turner.

The other payments had also been made – and these had come out of his pocket. He'd looked after the staff that he'd let go when he closed the fund and hadn't skimped. He'd provided a pay-off, which, on top of their profit-related bonuses, ensured many of them, would never have to work again anyway.

He'd also been true to his word and tracked down the ten employees that he had to let go when *Credere* had nearly ran out of money. He had, as promised, paid them their share of the profits from the fund and some were in the highly unusual position of becoming millionaires via a payment from, not their current employer, but a previous one that had sacked them just over two years before. All of them except one had contacted him to say thank you.

Lester put down his laptop and retrieved the furrowed copy of the San Francisco Examiner from his satchel. Most of the bonds that Lester had bet against were based on subprime mortgages in California, so he made a point of keeping up to speed with developments in the Golden State – and The Examiner was his favourite way of doing so. The article that had struck a chord with Lester described the unfolding catastrophe 'as the largest forced movement of people since the 1930s rural migrations that John Steinbeck had written about'. And of course, that was Lester's problem; he felt more mouse than man as he considered the suffering he'd inflicted on innocent people.

He packed his satchel and took one more look around the office before leaving. As he walked away from Pont Street, he felt like he was leaving the scene of a crime.

Chapter Sixty-Three

Unfortunately, for James Dickenson, the timing of his attempt to raise fresh capital for Allied English couldn't have been worse. In October 2008, when the company was hoping to secure its funding, there were a series of events that made that task virtually impossible.

Firstly, on 8 October, the Federal Reserve, the Bank of England and the European Central Bank all cut half a point off their key interest rates in the first unscheduled rate move since 9/11. That they did so was further evidence to the markets of how just how panic-stricken the authorities had become. On 13 October, the British Government announced it was part nationalising the Royal Bank of Scotland, HBOS and Lloyds TSB. It did so in order to save them all from total collapse. And finally, on the 15 October, as if passing judgement on the previous two events, the FTSE 100 suffered its fifth biggest drop in history; it fell over 7% in one day! Confidence was shot.

Allied English's share price was down 73% in three months, but, almost unbelievably, the bank had a more pressing problem – it was rapidly running out of money.

Alasdair Darling, the UK Chancellor of the Exchequer, had had a torrid couple of weeks. But on the 16 October 2008, Lord Groves, the Chairman of the Board of Allied English added to his troubles. He called him on a point of emergency. Darling, who had been told two hours earlier that the London Stock Exchange had suspended Allied's shares, decided he should take the call.

"Alasdair, I'll keep this simple. We're running out of money," declared Lord Groves.

"Good morning to you too, Henry," replied Darling. The silver-haired Scot settled back into his green leather-backed chair as far as he could. He could sense straight away that the normally unflappable Lord Groves was nervous. This was likely to be more trouble.

"Apologies, Alasdair, I'm sorry to have to be so direct, but we really haven't much time I'm afraid," said Groves.

"How can Allied English be running out of money?" asked the Chancellor. He held the phone in-between his cheek and shoulder, as he reached into his red despatch box to retrieve some papers.

"Quite simple, and probably the same reason you were forced to nationalise the other three. We're contractually bound to pay out billions regarding our US subprime business and we can't access the credit markets. Our attempt to raise money is like pushing tar up a hill and our share price has collapsed."

"How long can you last? I mean when will you need the money?" asked Darling, his absurdly coloured eyebrows now contracting fiercely across his forehead.

"We're talking two to three hours and that's it."

"Fucking hell! Is there anything else you want to tell me?" asked the Chancellor, the crudity of his response jarring against the refined Scottish brogue.

"No. I think that's enough for one day, Alasdair – don't you?"

And so, late on 16 October 2008, the UK Government agreed to the funding request from Allied English. The UK taxpayer bailed out James Dickenson's bank, became the largest shareholder and forced the resignation of both Dickenson and Lord Groves.

As Lord Groves was having his little tête-à-tête with No 11 Downing Street, Dickenson left the bank – not contractually, but mentally, physically and emotionally, he was gone. He knew his formal dismissal or his staged resignation was now just a formality and no more than hours away and that he'd never walk through those grand, revolving glass doors again. So, that was it – the end of a thirty-year banking career. He purposefully strode towards the junction of Moorgate and Great Swan Alley just a hundred feet or so away.

There he stopped and looked up at the elaborate crest of the Worshipful Company of Clothworkers on the side of 20 Moorgate and the inscription below "My trust is in God alone." He had worked in the office building around the corner from the junction for twelve years and had never once felt any compulsion to concern himself with the crest. That was, up until a few months ago. From then on, as the financial crisis hit, deepened and finally paralysed his bank, he found himself drawn ever more towards it. It was as if it held some magical power over him; some heady hypnotic pull that, disconcertingly, seemed to be getting stronger as his own position at the bank got weaker.

Dickenson studied the majestic design for a few moments: two griffins guarding either side of a black shield with an ermine fur chevron between two large, silver hooks. The hooks were called habicks. His mother's interest in heraldry and knowledge concerning the Worshipful Company in particular had embedded this piece of information in his memory many years ago. Finally, a Ram – echoing the source of the raw material, and ultimately the company's wealth – was stood above the shield.

He recalled the hugely significant role that the company had played in his younger life. The same coat of arms that he was looking at now had sat atop the wrought iron gates to the family estate in Oxfordshire and it had appeared on the side of the new building at his old boarding school – a philanthropic donation from his mother some forty years ago. Various ancestors on his mother's side had been intricately linked with the management and his maternal Great Grandfather had actually been Master – a position once held by Samuel Pepys no less.

The family money was now securely invested in property and Dickenson Estates was one of the largest private property companies in the UK, but the foundations for the family wealth were firmly laid by the textile industry in the 19th and 20th Centuries: a fact that had been pressed upon the young James Dickenson relentlessly. Indeed, Dickenson Estates had made substantial donations to the organisation in the past.

It made him think about his decision all those years ago not to run the family business and how it might have turned out differently. He couldn't help thinking that Dickenson Estates would be a less aggressive place to work than Allied English and he actually started to regret that fateful decision to go into banking. The admission hit him like a bolt out of the blue. Up until then, he'd had a few vague 'what-if' moments about running Dickenson Estates, but nothing sufficiently strong for him to concede regret about his illustrious banking career.

He turned away. He needed some thinking time to clear his head and understand the significance of his own confession. He thought he'd broken free from the family, its history and traditions many years ago, but now he wasn't so sure. On a deep subconscious level, he asked himself whether he'd ever really wanted to break free? Nothing seemed as certain as it once did about his career and his feeling towards his family.

He wrapped his long, winter coat around him and turned left into Moorgate towards the Bank of England. It was overcast now and large threatening grey clouds loomed in the slither of skyline that remained visible between the tall buildings on either side of the road. He strolled along the streets thinking about his long list of 'what might have beens'.

There was a newspaper vendor under the pink and yellow limestone supports of the No 1 poultry building next to one of the entrances to Bank tube station. The headlines appeared on a poster attached to the side of the man's mobile kiosk. 'DICKENSON TO GO!' written in large capital black letters stared at him, as he approached. Bricks and a few old-fashioned weights held down the vendor's wares, as the wind whipped through the concourse area around the limestone supports.

He bought a newspaper and the elderly vendor offered a toothless smile of appreciation; his rolled-up cigarette glued to his bottom lip.

"Fank you, Guvnor," said the man, as he passed Dickenson his change – the cigarette bouncing up and down violently, as he spoke but the end still firmly moulded to the man's mouth.

Dickenson read the article and the clouds overhead seemed to darken even further – reflecting the creeping gloom of his mood. It almost felt like dusk at one o'clock in the afternoon. Written by the editor of the newspaper and a man he knew well, it was vicious, merciless and full of half-truths, and read as a personal polemic against Dickenson. He looked up from the newspaper as the first spears of jabbing rain thumped down onto the pavement. It wasn't a gentle patter, but an aggressive pounding of spite and malice every bit as vindictive as the article he was reading.

Strangely, his first thought was for his mother. All of a sudden, what she thought about all of this was important to him. It was uncanny how everything kept coming back to her these days.

★

The next morning, in her flat in Kensington, Lady Clarissa Dickenson was at her desk in the study by 8 am. She glanced at the photo that Ronald had managed to snap for her one sports day – Edward and Jemima, her grandchildren resplendent in their shorts and T-shirts on a happy June day a couple of years ago.

This was routine – up early in the study and reading. Usually, she was pouring over various reports and accounts from Dickenson Estates and fretting about her impending financial doom. Thank goodness, it was a private company; she couldn't countenance her financial embarrassments being splashed all over the front pages of newspapers. Unfortunately, it appeared, her son didn't enjoy that privilege.

So today she was stooped over the cheap newsprint of the hurtful articles spread before; her spine arched like the tensioned wood of a musical bow. The headlines were varied but all too predictable; 'Taxpayers forced to bail out arrogant banker', was one and 'Dickenson gets the chop!' another. The headlines may have been different, but the underlying message was the same. They described how her son's greed had caused the downfall of a 200-hundred-year-old institution; that the bank was now 90% owned by the UK Government, and that it was all James Dickenson's fault. In fact, her son should be barred from holding office in a public company ever again.

The knives had first come out in January when Allied English had announced the first big trading loss, but today was gruesome. It was as if the journalists had selective memory; all the good that her son had done for the bank was wiped clean and all that was left was an intense focus on the current crisis. Their twisting of the facts and headline-grabbing assertions sapped her energy even more and she slumped further at her desk as she wondered whether her son would be able to cope with all of this. He was used to success and things going his way – everything he touched at Allied English seemed to turn to gold, up until now. But it hadn't always been like that and she recalled how as a boy he became vulnerable the moment things moved against him. He'd needed her support then and she couldn't help but wonder about now.

She dwelled on her son's vulnerabilities for a few moments, as she retrieved the leather-bound compendium from the top drawer of her desk. She'd been working on the chronicle of her son's meteoric banking career for more than two years now; the awards, the interviews with the Financial Times, the logging of every corporate merger and acquisition and the photographs. Her particular favourite was the one with the Prime Minister at the reopening of the Allied English offices in the City. It hadn't taken too much effort, she'd got some help from a journalist friend – but even she thought it looked rather impressive.

She matter-of-factly slipped the latest article into the plastic wallet to update the compendium. She straightened her back and pushed up the sleeves of her dressing gown beyond her elbows. Once that was done, Lady Dickenson picked up the telephone and then paused.

Should she call? Was the timing right? She replaced the receiver.

Twenty minutes later, she tried again and this time her nerve held. It *was* the right time to sort this out once and for all.

Chapter Sixty-Four

"Hi, James, it's Lester here. How are you bearing up?"

"Good morning, Lester. I assume you've seen the press? Looks like I've gone from hero to zero as they say."

"Yes. Bloody savages," replied his friend.

They continued to discuss recent market developments, before Lester got to the real reason of the call.

"Listen, James, this is a long story and one that I'll share with you in full when we meet, but have you ever heard of an odious little man called Simon Rankin?"

"Bloody hell, that's good timing, Lester. I hadn't until, well, about a week ago I think. He called me to make an appointment; he's at Silvermans and said that he'd like to discuss something with me that I'd find helpful given my current circumstances. I'm in the city tomorrow, so I've agreed to meet him at the Century Club. It seems my diary is pretty empty at the moment."

There was a pause on the line, and then. "James, do you mind if we have a pre-meeting and that I and an ex-colleague join you at the Club?"

The next day, Dickenson was sat at his favourite table sipping a spicy tomato juice in the familiar surroundings of the Century Club bar. He was talking to the headwaiter – Harry – who, thankfully, was as discreet as the uniform he was wearing. Dickenson knew that the man stood in front of him was completely aware of the bank's troubles, but he was tactfully leading the conversation in directions that would require no mention of it. Harry was dressed in the timeless uniform that the Club had introduced the day its doors opened in 1867: a golden-yellow tie, crisp white shirt, pleated trousers and the all-in-one black waistcoat apron. Two overlapping, golden Cs were embroidered onto his lapel.

As further patrons arrived, Harry politely excused himself and Dickenson was left to ponder the other eternal features of the Club. The Queen Ann furniture, the royal crest carpeted floors and the rules that supported the ambience had always remained constant. It was an oasis of stability in an otherwise complicated and constantly changing world. He decided that that's what it was that he liked about the Club the most. His world had got far too complex and he'd certainly had enough change for one lifetime.

Another, identically dressed waiter approached his table to inform him that Rankin had arrived. He thanked him and very specifically asked that the guest should be kept in the hallway and that Dickenson would collect him himself in a moment. Dickenson got out his mobile and sent a text.

A few moments later, Dickenson and Rankin climbed the L-shaped staircase to the private dining rooms on the first floor. As they settled into their seats, Dickenson considered whether Rankin was nervous or just a fidget. His eyes constantly shifted beneath his caterpillar-sized eyebrows and he crossed and uncrossed his legs three times in the time it took for the two Englishmen to discuss the weather.

The room was one of Dickenson's favourites. Large enough to accommodate another five people at least, the two men sat at one end of the immaculate wooden table. A drinks trolley was nearby and the antique wooden room separator – the one that was an oil painting depicting the seasons of the year on each of its four panels – was at the other end of the room.

Simon glanced around and cleared his throat.

"Listen, James. I'm really sorry to have to do this to you, but Silvermans have been making all sorts of cutbacks. The arse-wipe that was my boss decided that they can operate without me, so I'm out of a job and I'm broke, or I will be if I keep paying the school fees, the maintenance for my first two wives and the mortgages." He combed his fingers through his black hair before bringing his hands together and clasping them in front of him. He paused, briefly, before clearing his throat and continuing.

"I know that you invested personally in *Credere* and that you profited from the collapse of Allied English." He stared directly at Dickenson as he spoke, almost threatening him to deny what he was saying. "In fact, you didn't just profit from it; your decision to back your old mate, Lester FitzGerald, caused the collapse of a two-hundred-year bank and resulted in the British taxpayer picking up the tab.

"I can only imagine what these wankers would make of that." He held up his copy of the Daily Mail for effect.

"They'll crucify you. It wasn't your incompetence that broke the bank – you robbed the bloody place!"

Dickenson looked down at the table and shook his head.

"How did you find out?" he managed, as he slowly looked up to meet Rankin's eyes once more.

Dickenson immediately detected Rankin's rigid posture soften, as if the man opposite was relieved that his response had been the right one. He even had a glint in his eye and gave Dickenson a kind of knowing, half shrug.

"Sorry, James, I can't reveal my sources." He continued, "Look, I appreciate this is a bit of a shock, but my offer is not an unreasonable one."

"And what exactly is your offer, Mr Rankin?" asked the ex-CEO of Allied English.

"Two million quid. I give you the document, you never hear from me again." Rankin offered a playful grin this time.

Lester had told him Rankin was an unpleasant individual and it was proving to be pretty accurate assessment, thought Dickenson, as he looked across the table. But blackmail? He wondered just how much financial difficulty Rankin was in or whether, like many of his peers, he was just being greedy.

"And what happens if I don't agree to your blackmail?" he asked.

"Harsh description, James, very harsh. But the answer's simple. The information will get into the wrong hands. I'll go to every newspaper in the country – starting with these boys," replied Rankin, as he tapped his newspaper again.

"It'll cost you your legacy and probably your liberty."

Dickenson raised an eyebrow. *Bloody hell, this guy really is poison*, he thought. He then placed both his hands on the table in front of him and leaned in.

"Before you do that, Mr Rankin, I think it's only fair that I inform you that I know precisely how you obtained the information."

Rankin immediately lost his smile.

"Bullshit, you just don't want me to go to the press because it'll blow your fucking legacy apart. Now listen to me. Two million quid and I'm gone. You won't hear from me again. You must have made ten times that with that lucky bastard FitzGerald." He'd resorted to looking around the room again – his glance seemed to flitter all over the place.

Dickenson pressed on.

"You paid a professional to break into Dr FitzGerald's office in Pont Street. You took the information whilst you were looking for the positions that *Credere* held. You needed those to be able to destroy Dr FitzGerald. You needed to know how close his fund was to running out of cash so that—"

Rankin cut him short.

"Yes, and I would have destroyed the bastard if my stupid fucking boss hadn't bottled it," he replied, slapping the table in front of him with the palm of his hand.

"Once I had that information, I knew that he was days away from Armageddon. So I was going to let him squirm and then deliver the message. Anyway, James, yes, I did steal the information and no, I don't give a fuck that you know. Who's going to believe you ahead of me these days?" He stared across the table with hard, flinty eyes.

There was a short pause.

"Thank you, Simon. That's been very helpful," said Lester, as he and Sally walked around from behind the four-season screen at the end of the room. "Sally, did you get all that?"

"Oh yes, Lester, every word," said Sally, holding up the small tape recorder that was still whirring away.

Rankin looked at his former employee.

"You stupid bitch. What do you think you're doing?"

"Shut up, Simon. God only knows why I was so bloody stupid to listen to you in the first place. But I'll testify, Simon – I don't care what it means for me personally."

Rankin didn't have much of a choice. Go to the papers with a coup and end up with a criminal conviction and no hope of another job in banking or get up and walk away from the Century Club. He cut a sorry figure, as he skulked out of the entrance and into the city.

After Rankin had left, Lester took Dickenson to one side.

"James, I appreciate today has been tough, but that's the last we'll hear from Rankin; don't worry. But I have one more favour to ask. I need you to meet someone who has wanted to speak to you for some considerable time."

Dickenson pulled his long face into a longer one – he'd had enough for one day. Blackmail, bloody blackmail! He knew some of the people he'd worked with over the years were aggressive, money-grabbing maniacs, but blackmail. These were the sorts of people that he'd shared a career with: now the chips were down; they were showing their true colours.

"Please, I promise this won't take long," lied Lester. He directed Dickenson to another small room. He knocked and opened the door for his friend and gestured for him to enter and immediately stood back and hurried away.

James Dickenson watched him leaving and then stepped inside.

Sally had called Ann and confessed about the break-in the day that she'd received her *Credere* bonus. She had been feeling terrible about the whole thing anyway, but Lester's integrity – paying her a bonus that he was under no contractual obligation to do had shocked her into action. She'd been working for Silvermans since she's been laid off by Lambda and was persuaded by Rankin to get the information he needed. She knew it was wrong, but she had been angry about losing her job and in a moment of weakness had agreed to it. But Lester's selfless act had brought into focus the stark contrast in cultures between Lambda and Silvermans. So she'd told Ann everything even if it meant she could end up in trouble with the police.

Ann had sat and listened to her former friend with a cold expression. Thirty minutes later, when they parted, it was for the last time.

Chapter Sixty-Five

For a moment, it didn't register. But as his mother unfurled her long legs and stood up to greet him the familiar, awkward frame and the misbehaving limbs were unmistakable. The thin nose, defined chin and high cheekbones completed the diamond-shaped face – the master template from which all Dickenson features were forged. In some ways, it was like looking at his reflection.

He then moved forward to greet Clarissa Dickenson for the first time in twenty-five years on legs that had unkindly chosen precisely now to disobey his instructions. He almost stumbled, as they met in the centre of the room and held one another.

"Mother, why now? Why are you here?" managed Dickenson, looking over her shoulder as they embraced. Paradoxically, it was when he couldn't see her that her physical decline struck him. He didn't notice it at first, but now that he was holding her, it was obvious.

The person that had disowned him all those years ago was a robust fifty-five-year-old woman. The person he was holding now was a delicate old lady; she'd lost weight and yes, she was tall relative to most women, but shorter nonetheless. He thought about the passage of time and its obvious physical cost and couldn't help wonder whether an equally harsh mental and emotional price had also been paid.

After a few seconds, she released her fragile grip so that she could look at him. "To apologise: I'm here to apologise, James. Why now? Well, that's much more complicated, but I'd offer stubbornness if you pushed me." She tried a smile, but seemed to change her mind halfway through.

"James, I can't do this any longer. I know now that I shouldn't have pressured you into taking that job. You were far too young. You were right; you should have stayed in banking and then, if you wanted to, come across later. It sounds pathetic now, but at the time, I was devastated and I thought you were being ungrateful.

"So I ranted and stewed for a few years, but recently I have come to realise it was all my fault and I wanted, well actually, needed to tell you."

They sat down in unison and crossed their legs. Left over right and the right foot pulled in almost underneath the chair. Manoeuvring long limbs without damaging furniture was an art well practiced by mother and son alike.

As he listened to his mother, he became aware of the other change that seemed to have taken place. It wasn't just the physical transformation, she seemed different emotionally. As far as her son's eidetic memory was concerned, Clarissa Dickenson had always been a severe individual with a reputation for making sanctimonious judgements. It would take a very generous friend indeed that could describe her as a naturally sympathetic person.

He couldn't recollect hearing his mother apologise before for anything – ever. Not even a grudging expression of regret about a minor faux pas. Yet here, she was apologising.

The pugnacious fifty-five-year-old woman had become a vulnerable eighty-year-old lady. He actually began to feel guilty about the decisions he'd made. He was even feeling embarrassed about the fact that his elderly mother had contacted him and not the other way around. Wasn't it him that should be trying to make amends?

Chapter Sixty-Six

Jim Hanlon, the state attorney appointed on behalf of the Alferos, was seated alongside his clients in courtroom number one of the Superior Court of California, San Francisco. His best suit, clean shirt and new tie all conspired, superficially at least, to portray the image of a confident legal executive: appearances could be deceptive.

He closed his eyes and massaged his face, his fingers squeezing the black velvety cushions that had formed above his cheekbones. He let his hands fall to his knees and he blinked heavily, almost hearing the skin yield as the eyelids closed and reopened – like degraded rubber being stretched and released. He leaned back in his seat and took a couple of moments to think about the case and the reason for his exhaustion.

When Marina and Rodrigo Alfero first came to see him, he was delighted. Their case against Pinewood – their mortgage provider – was very strong, exceptionally so in fact. The Home Affordable Modification Program, or HAMP as it was colloquially known, had been introduced in March 2009 by the Obama administration. It was a godsend for the Alferos – 'it could have been written for you', he remembered telling his clients. As he explained, the legislation meant that mortgage companies, like Pinewood, were obliged to offer loan modifications to people, like the Alferos, where certain criteria were met. A modified loan meant an extended payback period or a lower interest rate, or a blend of the two but the intention of the legislation was clear – it was there to help people hold on to their homes and not let greedy mortgage companies steal it from them.

It soon became clear, however, that there were two problems for Hanlon and the Alferos. The first was that the criteria were open to interpretation – a 'matter of opinion' and not a 'matter of fact': that's why a judge was here to help them decide. The second problem was staring at Hanlon right now across the jam-packed courtroom from the witness stand: Mrs L Crabshaw – the key witness for the Pinewood defence. She was arrogant as well as smart; traits that normally led to a witness performing exceptionally poorly or exceptionally well on the stand. Unfortunately, for Hanlon, Crabshaw appeared to fall into the latter category and seemed to be able to soak-up pressure like a sea sponge absorbed water.

A TV reporter coughed and Hanlon's view drifted upwards to the press gallery; a small seating area perched high up above the courtroom with rod-shaped pine balustrades. That was the best place for the press as far as Hanlon was concerned – behind bars. He'd been an attorney in San Francisco for over twenty-five years but hadn't been involved in anything quite like this. A US-wide mortgage company against two Mexican immigrants – the local and national press were dubbing it the 'David and Goliath of the mortgage crisis' and the media interest around the case was insane. When the circus of reporters and film crews arrived, that's when Hanlon's sleepless nights and the nausea had really kicked in.

Hanlon was doing his best for the Alferos, but Pinewood was a large and powerful organisation, and in a way, they were desperate. If they lost the case, it would open up the floodgates to others – right across the country. As far as they were concerned, it was a war – and one they couldn't afford to lose. And because 'Goliath' knew the Alfero's case was so strong, they had put a legal team to work that made Hanlon's practice look like a bunch of amateurs – and he knew it. As his attention turned to his next encounter with Crabshaw, Judge Bell called the courtroom to order and asked Hanlon to begin the afternoon session. He adjusted his tie and walked past the opposing legal team – eight qualified attorneys all doing their best to fix him with intimidating stares. He approached the witness stand and looked up.

"So, Mrs Crabshaw, I understand that you and your company didn't consider that the near threefold increase in the mortgage repayments represented a 'change in financial circumstances'. Could I ask why?" he asked.

Crabshaw looked down her nose at Hanlon, taking full advantage of her elevated status on the raised platform of the witness stand: her eyes were probably a full metre above his. Even Hanlon – old hand that he was – felt uneasy when the tall woman did that stare thing. Her cold eyes never seemed to leave his as they followed him – tracking him around the courtroom like *she* was the one probing *him* rather than the other way around. When she was ready, she spoke.

"It's all there in the contract that they signed. It's a straightforward mortgage document, anyone who read it would have known that the increase would occur and when. So, by definition, nothing changed; events just unfolded as the contract anticipated. Why do *you* think that something had changed, Mr Hanlon?" said Crabshaw. She gave him one of her head tilts and the intonation at the end of the sentence made clear to everyone in the courtroom she was asking a question.

Hanlon took a deep breath and started counting. *God, this woman was a bitch!*

There was a ripple of laughter from up above. The members of the press and the public who queued determinedly every morning to gain entry to the prison-cell gallery found the duel between Hanlon and Crabshaw fascinating.

"Thank you, Mrs Crabshaw, but Mr Hanlon is asking the questions," interjected Judge Bell. He then directed his glare towards the individuals that misunderstood the purpose of his courtroom and the noise abated as quickly as it had begun. Judge Rufus Bell, or 'Redneck Rufus' as he was known when the he wasn't within earshot, was a man of few words and fewer pleasantries. He was able to command his courtroom through a series of nods, glares, stares and a myriad of other facial tics and expressions, and spoke only when absolutely necessary. Hanlon had seen him in action many times before. On one occasion, he recalled how a single arching eyebrow had paralysed a prosecuting attorney into submission. But it was his penchant for plain talking, his short temper, and the slow, deliberate Georgia drawl that earned him his nickname.

Hanlon looked at the judge and received a curt nod of ascent in return. He could continue.

"Thank you, your honour."

When he'd heard Redneck Rufus would be residing, Hanlon's emotions had been mixed. The man's judgements were peppered with examples of 'the small guy' triumphing over 'the large corporates', – that was clearly positive for the Alferos. However, the septuagenarian had spent his formative years in the Deep South. It would have been impossible, in Hanlon's view, to grow up amongst the poor white farming communities in Georgia in the 1940s and '50s without some of their innate prejudices and biases taking hold. Hanlon, and a few others who bothered to do their research, also knew that Judge Rufus Bell's decisions had an element of racial discrimination to them.

Hanlon cleared his throat and moved on.

"Do you think your mortgage documents are straightforward, Mrs Crabshaw?"

"Of course."

Like, that's so obvious; you don't need to ask the question, you retard.

Wishing he'd posed the question differently, Hanlon walked back to his desk and picked up a thick document.

"Mrs Crabshaw, this is the mortgage contract that the Alferos signed. Forgive me, but could you highlight to the court the wording that sets out the near threefold increase that my clients are now being asked to pay?"

The mortgage employee had a copy of the same document in front of her. She released her grip from the sides of the witness stand and unfurled her long fingers. Hanlon watched, as she deployed them; deftly dividing the lengthy document – allowing her to move effortlessly between various sections without rummaging through pages.

"Appendix two, clause 5:4:2," she said, matter-of-factly. "It clearly states that this type of mortgage product has a variable rate of interest and that it will increase on the second anniversary of the mortgage. It's there in black and white," she confirmed before looking over the top of her glasses and downwards towards the attorney.

"I'm not sure what could be *more* straightforward, Mr Hanlon," she finished.

As a precaution, Judge Bell scowled up at the gallery. Nobody laughed on this occasion.

"Forgive me, Mrs Crabshaw, could you tell me which page you're on?" asked Hanlon, as he deliberately fumbled through the document in order to exaggerate its length.

"Well, I'm not sure that's relevant," she replied and looked down at the number just above one of her fingernails. "Page 56, second paragraph," she said, archly.

"Thank you. So let me make sure I've understood this correctly. The vital information that my clients needed to rely upon was on page 56, in an appendix to the contract. The wording, although stating that the payments are variable and will increase on the second anniversary, do not provide any hint that they will treble—"

"Objection, your honour. The payments did not treble. Factually incorrect," shouted one of the eight Pinewood attorneys.

Hanlon raised his hand to Judge Bell and apologised immediately. "I'm so sorry, please forgive me. Increased by a multiple of 2.8." Hanlon threw a sardonic smile in the general direction of the army of attorneys sat opposite and waited for Crabshaw to respond.

"I'd make two points, Mr Hanlon. One, assuming your clients can actually read, they should have availed themselves of the helpful information in the appendices detailing what it was they were signing up to. That's what it's there for."

Jesus, you really are a bitch!

"Secondly, all of this was explained to the Alferos at the original meeting with the Globe before taking out the mortgage." The second point was accompanied by the wave of a dismissive hand.

Hanlon knew that was a lie. A large financial moneymaking machine had taken advantage of two naïve people – preying on their aspiration to better themselves and buy a home. They had sold them a mortgage because it drove the company's short-term profits, not because it was a suitable product for the Alferos.

"Mrs Crabshaw. I can confirm my clients' ability to read – thank you for your concern," said Hanlon, as he gave the witness a small nod of his head.

A few smothered chuckles from the gallery evidenced that the audience was still enjoying the rivalry, but on this occasion, it wasn't enough to incur the wrath of Judge Bell.

"Your second statement is, however, baseless. We have asked for the file notes from that meeting and all of the supporting documentation. There is no evidence that either a verbal or written explanation that you claim occurred took place at all."

"I thought you said they could read?" asked Crabshaw, as she threw a brief, but indignant, look across the floor to the Alferos.

"Excuse me?" Hanlon couldn't keep the surprise out of his voice. *Could this woman actually be more disrespectful?*

"If you'd like me to talk louder, Mr Hanlon, I'll happily oblige."

That answered that then.

Hanlon scrutinised Redneck Rufus from the corner of his eye. The judge's hand was covering his face and he almost looked pensive. Almost. But Hanlon could see that the corner of his mouth was turned upwards and his cheekbones were pronounced. He was actually smiling at Crabshaw – almost imperceptibly

– but that's what he was doing behind the strategically placed hand. Hanlon swallowed.

Crabshaw continued.

"Anyway, both their signatures are on that document. So they knew precisely what was going to happen and when and make no mistake about it," finished Crabshaw.

The gallery wavered on the brink of laughter again and Judge Bell seemed to sense as much.

"Mr Hanlon, I think you may have reached an impasse with this witness. I think she is saying that the Alferos were informed and you are saying they were not. I have understood the point you have been trying to make." The judge's southern accent seemed to emphasise the last few words and the tone was curt, bordering on aggressive.

'Trying to make'…not sure I like the idea of that. Hanlon considered pushing back and then noticed the expression that accompanied the judge's tone.

"Thank you. I have no further questions at this point." Hanlon sat back down.

The judge turned to the witness. "Mrs Crabshaw. That's been very helpful. You can step down please." It was the difference between night and day. The tone was almost unrecognisable from a moment ago: bubbly, lyrical and charming, as he spoke to the witness.

"You're very welcome, your honour." Smiled Crabshaw, who was now a visage of radiated smugness. She virtually skipped away from the witness stand, staring across at Hanlon as she did so.

A few minutes later, the attorneys were asked to sum up. Judge Bell then called the session to a close and thanked the participants. He would make his decision in two days' time when he expected to see everyone back in his courtroom.

Hanlon remained seated – flattening out the puffiness under his eyes once more as he considered the Alferos' chances.

Chapter Sixty-Seven

The court attendant announced Judge Frank Bell's arrival and everyone duly rose and, abruptly, stopped talking. After acknowledging the observance of courtroom etiquette, the judge sat down and spoke with the clerks sat at either side of him.

The room became eerily quiet as the judge prepared to address the courtroom. He wasn't known for wasting time in announcing his decisions.

"Firstly, I'd like to take this opportunity to thank all of the parties for the information that I have had to consider during the course of this trial. My findings and decision are as follows."

Marina sat with her legs crossed in her ankle-length blue dress and flat, sensible shoes. She squeezed her husband's arm, as she leaned into her comfort pocket and closed her eyes for a few seconds. She knew the next few moments would be life-changing for them. Without the IVF, it seemed that having the child they desperately wanted would be all but impossible, and without the mortgage modification, they'd be lucky to hang on to the house let alone fund fertility treatment. She thought Hanlon had done a good job, but had no idea if he'd done enough to persuade the judge.

Marina noticed Mrs Crabshaw – sat erect with her arms folded – staring right at her. *She still looks like a miserable old school mistress*, she thought.

"I find that Pinewood's claims that their mortgage product was easy to understand and that it set out clearly the implications of the low 'teaser rate' are less than credible."

There were a few intakes of breath around the room; Crabshaw didn't blink; Marina squeezed Rodrigo even more tightly.

"There is a limited amount of supporting documentation that was provided to the Alferos and even less evidence that the terms of the loan were clearly explained to them. Although the increased payments have proven to be beyond the reach of the Alferos, no one could have known that at the time the contract was signed.

"Finally, and crucially in this case, I have to comment on the contract that bound the parties together. Although I have seen clearer and more straightforward contracts than the one that has been the subject of this court case, it is not as misleading as the plaintiffs claim. It does set out, sufficiently clearly in my opinion that the interest charges were due to rise. A contract is, after all, a contract.

"I am therefore ordering that Pinewood are under no obligation to provide the Alferos with a mortgage modification."

Marina closed her eyes and buried her head in Rodrigo's chest. He just looked blankly ahead and hugged his wife, as her shoulders began to heave and the first of the tears arrived. He glanced across at the other side of the room.

Mrs Crabshaw remained seated; her chin high and shoulders back, as she met Rodrigo's eyes. Her satisfied smile broadened, as she registered that it was her he was looking at. The team around Crabshaw had all stood up; they were high-fiving one another and generally milling around – excitement rapidly taking over from the initial relief. The courtroom buzzed as it digested the impact of Judge Bell's decision. But Mrs Crabshaw didn't move. She sat silently; watching the Alferos as if all that mattered to her was their reaction – as if the real victory was witnessing their pain. She seemed indifferent to the celebrations that were going on around her.

She tapped her fingers against her chin – highlighting the ugly wart in the centre as if to remind Rodrigo it was still there. She looked at him and, in an obvious mocking fashion, pulled her face into a look of dejection.

Rodrigo stared back, motionless at first. He then whispered something to his wife and made sure that Marina's sister took over comforting her. He stood up and swallowed, deeply, as if he'd just made a decision. He then walked to the other side of the courtroom. Marina saw what was happening and tried to break away from her sister.

"Let go, Gabriela, he'll do something stupid. Please, Gabby!"

Her sister looked at Marina.

"What do you mean? Who, for goodness' sake? What are you talking about?"

But it was too late; Rodrigo was already there – three feet or so away from a smirking Mrs Crabshaw. Marina had seen that expression on the woman's face before when she'd provoked Rodrigo into a reaction at the Pinewood offices.

That day, he'd completely lost the plot. *Oh, please God, don't let him do anything stupid – not here, not now.*

Rodrigo halted immediately in front of Mrs Crabshaw; his large frame towering over her, as he stood perfectly still, like he was considering what to do next. Marina could see Crabshaw was still smiling, almost goading him.

Rodrigo then bent down, never taking his eyes off the Pinewood employee, and picked up a pen that had fallen to the floor. He then calmly handed it to her.

"I think this belongs to you. Oh, and congratulations, Mrs Crabshaw," he whispered. "You must be very proud of yourself."

Without giving Mrs Crabshaw the chance to respond, Rodrigo turned and walked back to his wife. Marina's heart was almost in her mouth, as she stood and hugged her husband. She peered around him and caught Crabshaw glaring at them. The woman had won the case – her company would probably reward her financially for all her efforts – but her expression didn't suggest happiness at all. Yes, she was smiling, but she'd twisted her mouth into a bitter grin as she'd watched Rodrigo retreat. As Marina stared back at her, she finally understood what it was: it was a look of disappointment. She'd wanted Rodrigo to do something stupid right here in the courtroom in front of everyone because for her, this was personal.

Marina's moment of satisfaction was fleeting, however, as the realisation of what had happened took hold. Goliath, as he normally did in the world of finance, had won – and without a miracle, it was impossible to see how she and Rodrigo could even think about lodging an appeal. They'd almost certainly lose the house now and as for children – well, she couldn't bring herself to even go there.

As Hanlon was leaving court alone, a short man carrying a decrepit leather satchel approached him.

"Excuse me, Mr Hanlon. I was unfortunate enough to have just witnessed the injustice that took place in there." The man pointed back to the courtroom.

"Tell me about it," replied Hanlon out of the corner of his mouth. The lawyer kept walking.

"Mr Hanlon, I'd like to introduce myself and discuss an unconditional offer of financial support to fund the Alfero's appeal."

Hanlon stopped and looked at the man – he now had his full attention.

Chapter Sixty-Eight

Lady Clarissa Dickenson couldn't resist reading the article one more time before carefully placing it into the file where she had already created the appropriate space. She had decided to place it at the end as a last chapter or an epilogue, perhaps; a fitting end to a long journey. James had seen the compendium and, understandably, had become very emotional. What was it he said? 'It's a wonderful thing for a mother to have done – invested so many years of your own life following my career in so much detail.' She'd promised to hand over the completed compendium today.

She read:

Financial Times 16 September 2009

In an emotional statement, Lady Dickenson has confirmed that her only son, James Dickenson, will become the CEO of Dickenson Estates. If follows a long running feud between Lady Dickenson and James, who chose a banking career ahead of the family business in 1980 that caused mother and son to be estranged for almost thirty years.

Lady Dickenson was the only child of Lord George Dickenson and famously retained her maiden name when she married in 1932. James Dickenson, and his two children, is the only surviving member of the Dickenson family.

He was sacked as the CEO of Allied English in October 2008 after the 200-hundred-year-old bank required a Government bailout following record trading losses associated with the subprime mortgage crisis in the US.

James Dickenson will succeed Arthur Grant who has decided to take early retirement after running the family business for over a decade.

This newspaper is also aware that an undisclosed (but substantial) donation has been made to the Worshipful Company of Clothmakers. The Worshipful Company supported the textile industry, which is how the Dickenson family created its fortune in the nineteenth century.

The source of the donation has not been declared, but it is believed to stem from the profits from James Dickenson's long banking career before leaving Allied English in 2008. The Dickenson family and the Worshipful Company of Clothmakers were unavailable for any further comment.

She slid the article into the last page of the leather-bound book and folded the plastic cover over neatly, sealing it into position. She thought that the reference to her 'making an emotional statement' was particularly touching – she'd tried her best.

Lady Dickenson closed the book and completed the simple greeting card on the front:

Dearest James,

Welcome home, and congratulations on your new appointment!
All my love.

Mother.

Twenty minutes later, she met Jemima and Edward for the first time.

Ronald and Clarissa were sat at the table in Lady Dickenson's kitchen two days after the family had been reunited.

"Well, you must be rather pleased with yourself, Clarissa Dickenson," said Ronald in a curt, sardonic tone.

He nodded to the black and white kitchen counter that ran along one side of the room. On the mottled marble work surface was an oversized bouquet of roses from James, standing in a huge glass vase – the thick, velvety petals were a deep red and the scent had been perceptible the moment he'd entered the flat. Next to the vase stood two gilt-framed photographs; Edward and Jemima – two innocent and handsome teenagers looked out across the room at them.

"What could you possibly mean?" she asked – more than a tinge of sarcasm evident in her question.

She reached for the teapot and poured them both a cup.

Ronald deepened his tone.

"I know what you did, Clarissa. I just don't know how you could; I don't know how he fell for it and I have no idea how you can be so bloody blasé about it. He's your son for goodness' sake."

He noticed his voice was shaking.

She didn't reply for a few moments. She finished pouring and then stared at him – with eyebrows slightly raised and a nonchalant head tilt. She looked curious rather than angry – as if he'd surprised her in some way.

In the quiet pause that she'd manufactured, he could hear his own nervous breath. It had quickened the moment he'd confronted her. He inhaled to calm himself but it hitched slightly in his throat and produced an uneven gasp that was even more audible. He covered his mouth and coughed. When he arrived at the flat a few moments ago, he knew he'd say something – he'd have to, he just didn't know how to broach it. But such a display of genuine love and affection from James and his children for the benefit of someone who could be so cynical and calculating, just seemed so vulgar to him. It had tipped him over the edge the moment he sat down.

Finally, she said, "Be very careful, Ronald. Now, in your own time, tell me what it is that you think I have done?" He noted the patronising tone.

"Why, after all this time, have you made it up with James?" he asked, leaning back in his chair and folding his arms.

"He's my son and I love him dearly," she replied, placing her hands to her chest in parody of some on-stage damsel.

Ronald didn't speak. His expression was pained as he stared past her and out into the cold grey clouds beyond the window; their sullen appearance reflecting his own mood.

His distress would have been obvious to a stranger, but for someone that had known him for thirty years, it was palpable – the noisy breathing, the tightness in his expression and a stubborn refusal to make eye contact.

She crashed her cup down into the saucer.

"Oh, for goodness' sake, Ronald. I'm eighty-one years old, do the bloody maths! I actually have a relationship with my grandchildren before it's too late, the Worshipful Company is saved and we have a competent CEO running the business. The family legacy will now continue and, thanks to me, my son has a job. So what's the bloody problem?"

"What's the problem?" he slowly repeated. "You're a liar, Clarissa Dickenson, that's the bloody problem." He still refused to look at her and stared away gently shaking his head.

"Ronald. I told you to be very—"

But he didn't allow her to finish.

He turned to look at her, but slowly, as if he had to force himself to deal with the confrontation. He wore a mixed expression – one of anger and the subconscious effort to conceal it that forged itself into an awkward teeth-baring sneer.

"You lied to your own son, Clarissa." He could hardly believe he was saying those words to Lady Dickenson. He'd never spoken to her like that – ever. But that was before he'd worked it all out and overheard her telephone conversation in the kitchen whilst re-hanging a picture in the hallway. It had only been last week, but it had been eating away at him ever since. She'd been on the phone to her best friend – Maeve – telling her how she'd secured funds from her ungrateful son and now had access to her grandchildren. That he'd also fallen for the compendium – hook, line and sinker. But it was the detached, matter-of-fact tone that had really shocked him – as if she was talking about some minor business transaction rather than making up with her only son: a son that had been estranged for the best part of three decades.

His breath was uneven, and caused him to speak in short sentences but he continued nonetheless.

"You don't want anything to do with him – you just wanted access to his children and his money. The Worshipful Company needed a vast cash injection, as did Dickenson Estates. You didn't swallow your pride and contact him for love and forgiveness, you took advantage of him and his good nature. You made a simple commercial decision. You needed money and he had plenty of it."

He stood up to leave, heaving himself up from the table.

"Ronald, don't be so bloody righteous and sit down." Clarissa Dickenson didn't suffer the same agonies over confrontation and her expression was a straightforward snarl, as she pointed to the seat where Ronald had been sat.

He took it, not quite sure that this was really happening. He'd worked with Clarissa all this time, but they'd never had a conversation like this.

She continued. "The day James chose banking over running my family's business was the day he stopped being my son. That's not changed. His father and I gave him everything and the little shit threw it back in our faces. He got lucky and made a few million that the business and the Worshipful Company could do with at the moment. So he's paying us back with a bit of interest, but it's nothing more than he owes us."

Ronald did stand up this time.

"I'm sorry, Clarissa. I'm not taking you anywhere, not today, not ever. Do what you like." He turned and made his way to the door.

"You leave, Ronald, and that's it. James isn't the only man around here who's expendable."

He paused, briefly. But he didn't turn back; he left the car keys on the kitchen counter next to the photographs and walked out of the flat. As he made his way to the nearest tube station, he thought about Edward and Jemima and wished them good luck in their new relationship with their grandmother – they were probably going to need it.

Before he reached High Street Kensington, Clarissa had already booked a taxi to take her to where she wanted to go.

Chapter Sixty-Nine

Chuck Whiteman stood up and raised his right hand.

As he did so, the press gauntlet went into overdrive and the electronic whizz of the cameras almost drowned out the few words that were spoken as he was sworn in. The former Secretary to the Treasury sat back down and took a sip from the glass of water on the green baize cloth that was taut across the large table in front of him. He noticed his hand was shaking – not violently, but enough to corroborate the quivering, twitchy feeling that was already building in the pit of his stomach. He immediately clasped his hands together on top of the baize and glared at the committee members.

So appalled by the idea of appearing at the investigation, Whiteman had rejected the committee's initial request to attend and then ignored their subsequent demand. He was only here because the committee subpoenaed him to be so and his lawyers verified he didn't have a choice. The Permanent Subcommittee on investigations was a government committee set up to consider, amongst other things, financial fraud in the US. The implication was obvious and that angered him. What happened during the financial crisis was unfortunate – but nothing more, and it certainly hadn't involved fraud. This was a conspiracy led by misguided politicians that felt they needed to be seen to be doing something and supported by the media who needed to sell newspapers and keep their ratings high. The protestors – the idiots holding pink placards with SHAME written in large black capital letters – were silent but stood just a few feet away to the side.

Stirring up public disaffection with someone of his calibre, who had done so much during his career to help his fellow citizens, apparently made for good entertainment. That's why so many TV cameras were here too; directing their lens at him – trying to spot a chink in the armour of a successful banker. The Committee's investigations were broadcast live right across the US and the rating levels suggested – much to Whiteman's irritation – that the average American had a keen interest in finding out what role he'd played in the unfolding of the subprime mortgage crisis.

One of the journalists caught his eye – the one from the Washington Post that made a habit of wearing outrageously loud ties. He was sat with the rest of them – on the floor in between his green-covered desk and the imposing arc-shaped wooden bench that the Chairman and the rest of the committee occupied. Today, he looked like he was caught in some 1960s' time warp; a psychedelic-coloured flared tie hanging casually around his neck, like he was reporting on a Mammas and Pappas pop concert. He'd written an article joking that summoning Whiteman was the only way to get him back to the capital.

But on one level, the article was right – he hadn't set foot in the city since Barak Obama had decided he wanted someone else to be the Financial Secretary to the Treasury. Whiteman thought back to that steaming hot day in May 2006, his first day in charge of Government finances – the statue of Alexander Hamilton and the ornate cash room where he was officially appointed with his family looking on. It had been a proud day, and took place just a few hundred metres from where he was sitting right now. The journalists and film crews were different then of course – polite, attentive and respectful. He winced at the thought of family and friends watching this witch-hunt on live TV and he reminded himself to focus.

Although it wasn't an official courtroom, and he wasn't officially on trial, the room, the manner in which it was set out and the behaviour of the people in it, smacked of culpability; somebody was guilty of something. Whiteman looked up again at the wood-panelled walls of the room, then the Chairman and his colleagues occupying the raised arc of wooden benches in front of him. Perhaps Mr Labin didn't wear the black robes of authority, but it was apparent he was every bit as powerful as a Supreme Court judge and this was his domain. The booming voice of the Chairman brought him back and the stenographer's rapid tapping reminded Whiteman that he and his legacy were absolutely on trial on this miserable Monday in DC.

"Mr Whiteman, thank you for your attendance. We'll continue with the questioning of Mr Sinclair before we come you."

Whiteman nodded wanly. He sensed that his ex-colleague – *grow a pair, Sinclair* – would struggle in such an environment. He'd find out in the next few minutes. An inquisitive hush descended the room as the questioning entered a new, edgy phase.

"Mr Sinclair, at the time you sold the 'Timberwolf 4' CDO to your pension fund clients, one of your team sent an email to a colleague. It's in your pack and dated 7 July 2007. Take a look," offered Mr Labin.

The attorney sat next to him located the email from the five-inch-thick white ring binder in front of Sinclair.

Labin cleared his throat and then read the email out aloud.

"Boy, that Timberwolf 4 was one shitty deal."

Jesus Christ – what idiot wrote that? thought Whiteman. His skin tingled at the mention of Timberwolf. He folded his arms.

"Mr Sinclair, what do you think about selling CDOs to pension funds that your own people think are crap? Does that bother you?" He looked down at Sinclair from his position of authority over the top of his half-moon reading glasses.

Whiteman squirmed in his seat. The chairs that he and his ex-colleagues were made to sit in were obviously designed to be as uncomfortable as possible and their position – in front of, but lower than the Senators – reinforced the aura of a courtroom that the media played on, the public demanded and the government facilitated.

"I think some of this can be taken out of context. And I think that's very unfortunate to have on email," stumbled Sinclair. He then tried to recover. "What I mean—"

But the packed committee room erupted in laughter at the response and Labin was on him in a flash. Whiteman glared at the laughing journalists.

"Unfortunate to have on email? Unfortunate? What does that mean; that it's perfectly OK as long as you don't put it in writing?" asked Labin. He'd removed his glasses and raised an eyebrow in a mocking fashion. More laughter.

Whiteman looked up at the bench. There was the faintest movement in his jaw line as he slowly grinded his teeth and studied the Chairman.

"No, that's not what I meant. I think it's unfortunate in any form," replied Sinclair. He nibbled on the inside of his bottom lip.

"So did your guys think Timberwolf 4 was crap or not?" pressed Labin. It looked like the ex-prosecutor was enjoying this.

"We don't think anything is crap that we sell to our clients," replied Sinclair.

The Chairman tried a different tack.

"Is there not a conflict, Mr Sinclair, when you sell a CDO to somebody and then you bet on its demise at the same time and you don't disclose that to the person that you're selling it to?" he asked.

A door slammed in another part of the large room and an agitated clerk remonstrated with the person who happened to be standing closest to it. Somebody was guilty of something.

Sinclair hesitated. "In the context of market-making, that is not a conflict," he stuttered, as his eyebrows set off in different directions. He actually looked baffled by the question – as if putting himself in his client's position had never entered his mind before. The close-up shots captured by the TV cameras portrayed his expression perfectly for the millions of viewers watching this remotely – it was almost an admission of guilt – a banker seemingly confused that ethics should make a claim on his time.

Again, the audience and the journalists in the packed room sniggered and seemed to spur the Chairman on to probe further.

Whiteman's gaze flitted around from place to place and he tugged at his shirt collar. He eyed the press and others in the room; his eyebrows lowered and pinched together as he considered their hypocrisy. Every single one of them had benefitted – just like every American – from the last two decades of economic stability that people like Whiteman and Sinclair had helped deliver. They didn't complain when they were able to secure new, cheaper mortgages that allowed them buy ever-bigger houses. They didn't complain when their investment plans went up and up and up. Now things had gone wrong they all wanted a scapegoat – someone else to blame: all of them cowards that didn't want to face the truth. It was their fault not his. Bankers didn't force pension funds to buy CDOs and they certainly didn't force anyone to take out mortgages.

"But, Mr Sinclair, do you think that pension funds would buy CDOs from you if you had said, 'Mr client, although we're going to sell you this CDO, we want you to know that we're going to buy insurance that will make us a profit if it collapses. We just want you to know that, Mr Client. Is that OK with you?' How many CDOs do you think Silvermans would have sold if that had been your guys' sales pitch?"

Once again, Sinclair looked utterly bewildered that a banker should consider having such a conversation.

"The clients are buying an exposure. We're giving them the risk that they want. They don't care and nor should they care what our views are. They wanted exposure to the housing market and that's what they got. The unfortunate thing is that the housing market went south very quickly," he replied.

Chairman Labin shook his head.

Whiteman's pulse quickened now and he began to hear the thump against his eardrum – synced with the rhythm of his heart. He stared at Labin as he massaged the side of his face. This ex-prosecutor was extraordinarily well briefed and, evidently, hated investment bankers. And worse, he was obviously hell bent on playing up to the TV cameras in the room; Labin and the other Senators were more interested in making the bankers look like criminals than take the time to understand the complexities of the financial world that Whiteman and Sinclair occupied.

"OK. Let's make this even clearer for you," said Labin.

Sinclair's posture sagged and Whiteman heard a lengthy exhale from his one-time colleague.

"One year after the 'shitty deal' email was sent, your clients had lost almost all of their money by investing in the CDO that you sold to them. Silvermans however, were several hundreds of millions of dollars to the good because your guys had bought insurance to bet against Timberwolf 4. What do you expect your clients to think about this?"

Whiteman thought back to the phone call when Sinclair was at the Hamptons. *Stop dancing with wolves, stop dancing with wolves.* It was like someone had inserted an amplifier alongside his eardrum now; thud, thud, thud. He used a handkerchief to clear the veneer of moisture gathering across his forehead. This was as close as he wanted Labin, or anyone else, to get to Timberwolf.

Audiences across the country were in raptures – people were missing work to continue to watch Mr Labin tie the bankers in knots. Some were shouting at the screen as their emotions ran away with them, incredulous that a bank could benefit financially, as their clients lost money. The people in the committee room were holding on to every word now. Even Whiteman conceded to himself that the straight-talking Senator had a gift for cutting through the complex world of financial jargon that he and his colleagues used. Labin was just saying that the banks sold 'stuff' to clients that they knew was crap and then benefitted financially when the same 'stuff' collapsed. You didn't need a PhD in finance to understand that.

"As I said earlier, Mr Chairman, what is unfortunate is that the client received what they wanted from us but the housing market collapsed quicker than most people expected."

"Mr Sinclair, can I ask you how much money you made on your insurance contracts against CDOs?"

Whiteman winced and then took a sip of water – his throat felt like sandpaper.

"You can, sir, but I wouldn't tell you," Sinclair replied in his monotone voice.

"Why not?"

"Legal privilege: I'm not obliged to answer specific questions about our profits on particular types of deal other than what is already in the public domain," he replied, as he scanned the Silverman lawyer's face.

"So you wouldn't argue with my estimate from your financial results for 2009 that put this at several billion dollars?"

Once again, Sinclair swapped glances with the attorney before confirming he wouldn't argue with it.

"Mr Whiteman, sorry that you've had to wait, but I wonder whether you can help me with the timeline here?"

Whiteman returned his handkerchief to his pocket, clasped his hands together once again and leaned into the microphone. "Yes, I'll do my best, Mr Chairman."

"On the 15 September 2008, Lehman Brothers collapsed without a government bailout. They were gone – history."

Whiteman nodded wisely, trying to radiate the aura and confidence of a man that had once been the Secretary to the Treasury. He readjusted his glasses with a thumb and forefinger and recalled the meeting with the six CEOs on that weekend almost two years earlier in the Federal Reserve building in New York.

"Can you share with us the thought process behind your decision to let them fail?"

"Theirs was a hopeless case I'm afraid, sir." Whiteman then spent five minutes posturing through the usual technical jargon as to why Lehman had held on to too many of its subprime mortgages and got caught out when the market turned. He discussed the last ditch meeting he'd held with the banks in the Fed Building and how he had worked tirelessly to try save them. Unfortunately, as sad as that was, it hadn't been enough.

Labin removed his glasses and looked at Whiteman from his vantage point above, as if he was considering which question to ask next. Whiteman glared back and noticed the subtle, knowing smile that had crept across the Chairman's face and then the gleam in his eyes.

"On 16 September 2008, the next day, the US Federal Government, on your recommendation, provided the first component of a government bailout to a company called USIG.

"Why didn't you treat USIG in the same way and let them fail? What had changed in 24 hours, Mr Whiteman?"

Sinclair instantly gulped a glass of water and closed his eyes as he drank; as if thwarting *see* and *speak* would help prevent *hear*.

Whiteman's body tensed and, almost subconsciously, it slid backwards until it was pressed firmly against the upright support of the leather chair; like an animal instinctively withdrawing from a source of danger. Then he was motionless, except for the small muscle twitching on the side of his head. Whiteman eyed Labin and then each of the other senators – an arc of spitefulness on the half-moon-shaped wooden bench opposite him. He felt the muscles in the nape of his neck contract, as he recalled the last time he had become the hunted. The cold wintry afternoon, the small clearing in the Teton Mountain range and the pack of Timberwolves – also forming a semi-circle around him, another arc of danger moving in for the kill.

Sinclair finished his water; his shoulders drooped even further, as he sat staring blankly at the papers in front of him. There was heightened interest from those watching – on the screens and in the room. They had all heard of USIG and knew that it was at the centre of the financial crisis but few understood why. They had a sense that Labin was about to enlighten them.

"Well, firstly, Mr Chairman, I'd like to make clear that it wasn't just my decision," faltered Whiteman. The audience in the room leaned in almost as one, as if it had detected the sudden hesitancy in the banker's voice and were trying to get closer. The room fell silent except for the shuffling of feet as the audience vied with each other for the best view of Chuck Whiteman. Everyone was staring at him now; transfixed.

The ex-Secretary to the Treasury swallowed again and then continued – deliberately and cautiously.

"But the decision *we* made was that if USIG had failed, the implications for the US and the global economy would have been catastrophic: planes would not have been able to fly, nothing would have moved anywhere. We were looking at Armageddon in that scenario, sir."

"And that's the only reason for the difference in treatment?"

Whiteman's elbows were planted as wide apart as possible on the table in front of him and his body was sat erect as he met Labin's eyes; that Chairman's smile a little less subtle now than a few moments before.

"Yes, sir, that's correct."

"OK, Mr Whiteman. Do you recall the size of the bailout that USIG received that you and your colleagues approved?"

"In total, I can't remember," he lied. His legs were tightening now, like the muscles were preparing themselves to sprint. He massaged his chin once more – the thump, thump, thump in his head continuing.

"Let me remind you – USIG received $180 billion from US taxpayers."

"That number sounds about right, sir," he managed. *Bastard,* he thought, as he held the Chairman's eyes.

"On 17 September – the very next day after USIG had received their money – do you recall what USIG did with the first $20 billion of it?" asked Labin.

Whiteman could hear the electronic whizz of the cameras as the photographers readied themselves to capture his response in an otherwise silent room. It felt like people were holding their breath in anticipation. The millions watching on live TV screens in public spaces were willing for Whiteman to respond. They had no idea what the answer to the question was, or why it was relevant, but Labin's half-knowing grin promised further entertainment at the banker's expense.

"I'm not part of that organisation, sir, so it isn't for me to say what they did or didn't do with the money, Mr Chairman." He looked up at Labin trying desperately to hang on to any shred of respectability that he could before the Senator played the card that Whiteman now knew he would. He squirmed again in his seat, the movement sufficient to release a ripple of perspiration that traversed each undulating rib as it made its way down the inside of his shirt.

"Let me help you out, Mr Whiteman." Labin took his glasses off again. "Look at the man sat next you – does that jog your memory?" He was almost tormenting Whiteman now.

It was Sinclair's turn to squirm, but he continued to study the papers in front of him, desperate to avoid eye contact with anyone.

The uninitiated in the audience were beginning to catch on, but couldn't quite believe it. There were whispers and further gasps from around the room. The placards with SHAME written on them were being held up once again and Whiteman's peripheral vision picked them out as some sort of pink and black montage.

"Ladies and gentlemen, please," said Labin, as he raised a hand.

"No? That didn't jog your memory. OK. Let me remind you. Your ex-colleague Mr Sinclair here" – at this point, the Chairman pointed to the CEO of Silvermans – "received a cheque for $20 billion from USIG on 17 September."

The gasps were much louder this time and people broke out into excited conversations throughout the room. Several of the reporters ran for the exits, mobile phones at-the-ready in anticipation of calling their news desks. People in bars watching wall-mounted TVs were screaming at the plasma screens like their team were playing out the final seconds of Super Bowl.

Whiteman sat, trance-like – looking off at nothing in particular. The half-smile on his face distorted by a mixture of embarrassment and anxiety. He tugged the cuffs of his white shirt and took a deep breath.

Labin continued, "Did you know anything about that payment, Mr Whiteman?"

Whiteman found himself looking at the journalist with the psychedelic tie and bizarrely Monday Monday – the Mammas and Pappas track – immediately started playing in his head.

"Mr Whiteman – did *you* authorise that payment?" The Chairman's voice was louder now – emboldened by the lack of response from the one-time Secretary to the Treasury.

The Silvermans' attorney reached across and advised Whiteman that he shouldn't answer that question.

Whiteman didn't answer either man, because he hadn't heard either man; the tune kept playing, louder now. Everything else, for the moment at least, appeared distant. He just stared straight ahead, wide-eyed in a state of subliminal shock.

Oh, Monday morning you gave me no warning
of what was to be

It was the musical equivalent of a child's La, La, La! moment. Like a youngster trying to block out an admonishing parent by sticking his fingers in his ears: the music of his youth subconsciously trying to deny the harsh reality of the here and now. But images of Greenspan, Professor Rajan and the Jackson

Hole symposium forced themselves upon his vision and he recalled Greenspan's question from years earlier,

What if Rajan is right?

"Mr Whiteman, I don't know if I'm being particularly inarticulate or you're having a bad day, but you don't need artificial intelligence to understand what people will make of all this.

"I'll ask you one more time, Mr Whiteman, and remind you that you are under oath." Labin pointed an accusatory finger at Whiteman and his voice rose.

"Did you authorise a 'backdoor bailout' to Silvermans Investment Bank?" he demanded.

Even the stenographer managed a glance at Whiteman.

It was the chilling, almost menacing tone in Labin's voice that brought Whiteman back to the present. He looked at the senators, the journalists and then the placard-carrying awkward squad. The music then faded away as quickly as it had arrived and he found a new resolve to focus on the men in front of him. He cleared his throat and turned his head calmly towards Labin with a steely composure that contradicted completely his hesitancy of a few moments ago. Four decades of reputation was on the line; he wouldn't let this go – he couldn't let this go.

"*You* don't understand finance, do you, Mr Labin," he said in a manner that categorically made clear he wasn't asking a question. The voice was confident and the tone chilling – it brought the room back immediately to an arresting silence.

"Excuse me?" asked the Chairman. Mr Labin's own posture now stiffened and his grey eyebrows settled into a frown of confusion.

"Senator, in 2008, I had a responsibility way beyond what you can possibly imagine. The whole financial system was on the brink of total collapse and life as you, and everyone else knows it, virtually ceased to exist. If I failed, do you know what the consequences would have been?"

Another door could be heard creaking somewhere else in the building as the audience waited for Labin's response.

"Mr Whiteman, may I remind you that you're not here to ask the questions, I need you to—"

But Whiteman's fist came down so hard on the table that Labin stopped in his tracks. The half-empty glass of water hopped across the green baize a few inches. Even Sinclair looked up and joined everyone else in that room staring at the ex-Secretary to the Treasury. The Silvermans' attorneys shared urgent glances with one another.

"You don't have the first idea about what we were up against at the time these decisions were being made. None of you do" – he glared at each Senator, pointing at each in turn – "because none of you have ever had the responsibility." His voice was raised again. It was louder, but he wasn't shouting – just at a volume that let everyone in the room know that what he was saying was paramount.

"You want the truth, Senator? I'll tell you the truth."

The attorneys continued their sign language but none of them, it seemed, felt the urge to interrupt Chuck Whiteman.

"The truth is, you need banks like Silvermans – all of you need banks like Silvermans." At this point, he looked directly at the journalists and then the rolling TV cameras.

"If banks like Silvermans had failed, you wouldn't be here, Mr Labin. None of you would. There would be no mortgages; there would be no loans to corporate America that create the jobs. Without them being in a position to extend credit to homeowners and business alike, the financial crisis would have been much worse – millions more would have been unemployed."

"Mr Whiteman, will you answer my—"

"Bullshit! You can damn well be quiet and listen." Whiteman's voice now had an edginess to it that suggested he no longer cared where this conversation went. The TV audience and those in the room didn't have a clue about the direction of travel either – but that just added to their curiosity.

"You sit here with these other hypocrites" – at this point, Whiteman pointed at the press sat in front of him – "and try to make *us* out to be criminals. All of these people want to buy their own homes, they all want cheap mortgages, they want fancy new cars and six different credit cards to feed their never-ending desire to consume."

"Mr Whiteman, I must—"

But the ex-secretary to the Treasury wouldn't be denied.

"Who made that possible, sir? You, Senator Labin? You, Senator Smith? You, Senator Cole?" asked Whiteman, as he looked across at Labin's colleagues. "Do you think the government made this possible?" His voice was thick with bitterness; his face contorted by rage.

"No, sir. So whilst you put on a display for this media circus and portray us as some kind of grotesque band of greedy bankers that it is your responsibility to purge, it is just that – a display. Because deep down, Senator Labin" – Whiteman thrust his own finger back at the Chairman at this point – "you damn well know we didn't cause the crisis. We gave you ALL what you wanted and, when you over-consumed yourselves into oblivion, we damn well rescued you. We fixed it the best way we could so that the average American still had a job and a house. If we left it to the likes of you, Senator, it would have been a whole lot worse!"

This time, the Senator's voice rose above Whiteman's.

"Mr Whiteman! Did you or did you not authorise that payment to Silvermans?"

"Yes, sir! You're damn right I did, Senator Labin."

Lloyd Sinclair immediately covered his mouth and the photographers were rewarded handsomely for their patience; they caught the moment perfectly – the picture was on the front page of every newspaper for weeks.

Almost all of the information that Labin used during his examination was in the public domain, but nobody had ever pulled it together into one, simple narrative. Whiteman's collusion to protect Silvermans was laid bare for all to see. It was fatal for the reputation of a man that had once been revered by bankers and politicians alike. In one day, Whiteman had lost a reputation that he had spent almost four decades cultivating.

The journalist with the psychedelic tie predictably wrote his piece. The Washington Post wasn't the only newspaper to thank Labin for his eloquent performance, but its editorial was one of the most biting.

15 April 2010, Washington Post – Editorial

Henry Labin is a genius and exposed Chuck Whiteman for what he is. Financial derivatives – which Whiteman had made a career out of defending from regulation – came within a whisker of destroying the country, not just the economy.

Senator Labin demonstrated that Whiteman and his banking colleagues profited all the way up and, at the expense of their clients and the average

American, all the way down. They made money at every turn. And when eventually reality caught up with them, Whiteman had the audacity – born of arrogance – to force USIG to use its taxpayers' bailout to rescue his friends at his former employer – Silvermans Investment Bank. Without that 'backdoor bailout', Silvermans would have followed Lehman Brothers into bankruptcy. He relied on the confusion and panic of the financial crisis to hide his own subterfuge – but thanks to Senator Labin, we now know what happened. It really was a sordid tale of patronage, favouritism and market manipulation.

Unfortunately, Whiteman hasn't got a career to ruin any more as he's retired. But this man and some of his ex-colleagues should now be sent for trial. Perhaps, someone can persuade Senator Labin to return to prosecuting and repeat yesterday's performance: he'd surely persuade any court in the land of their guilt.

In July 2006, in the Cash Room at the Treasury Building, President Bush appointed Mr Whiteman as the 74th Secretary to Treasury. Readers may be interested in what President Bush said that day.

"...this historic space reminds us of our responsibility to treat the people's money with respect. And in a few moments, Chief Justice John Roberts will swear in a man that every American can have faith in – Chuck Whiteman."

The President could never have imagined the irony of his statement, and readers can decide for themselves if the people's money was treated with respect and whether they have faith in Chuck Whiteman II.

Chapter Seventy

"Well, thank goodness he made that train journey – that's all I can say, Ma!"
Laughed Alice. She was sat outside in the secluded back garden of Willow Tree
Cottage. Home was now a small village called East Bergholt on the
Essex/Suffolk border, just a few miles from Manningtree. Ma – the frizzy-haired
Mrs McGrath had invited her to call her that when they had first met – and Alice
were discussing Joe.

"If it wasn't for that journey, Joe and I would never have met. On that basis
alone, I consider it to be the luckiest day of my life; although at the time, it
certainly wasn't the happiest." Mrs McGrath looked at her daughter-in-law and
beamed, as if the train story was of great consequence to her own life.

Alice winced a little and moved in her seat to get comfortable. Joe had
already built a mountain of plumped up cushions around her and placed a small
footrest just in front of her seat. Her flip-flops had been discarded and she had
raised her swollen feet as per Joe's instructions. He'd told her not to move and
that if she wanted something just shout, but not to get up. Alice had reminded
him for the third time that day that she was pregnant not a 'bloody invalid'.

"Was he always so thoughtful, Ma?" asked Alice, as she nodded towards the
bottom of the garden. Beyond the apple tree and rose bushes, there was a small
decrepit jetty and an equally decrepit fishing boat tied to it. Alice couldn't see
them, but somewhere down in the thickets and undergrowth Joe and Megan were
playing. The garden, and the access to the water, had sold it to them both when
they came for the first viewing. They'd been in a year now and were even happier
in East Bergholt than they had been in London. Space was a big issue for an
expanding family and her bike didn't even have to reside in the hallway any
longer. A perfectly secure garage was attached to the side of the cottage that
housed the bike, Joe's well-worn punch bag and so much fishing tackle they
could open an angling shop. Joe had left the bank about a year before they moved

and was working as a surveyor for a local practice in Colchester; their slower pace of life now a reality.

"Yes, dear. He'd have been about two and half – Megan's age, I suppose – when I first noticed it," smiled Ma.

"I'll never forget it, we had a Sheep Dog called *Spike* and he'd herd Joe into a corner of the room and sit there and protect him. They'd be there for hours together playing with each other. Then one day, I came into the room to find Joe and Spike sat facing one another. Joe had an ice cream and he was taking a lick and then offering it to Spike before he took another for himself. As he did so, he was saying, 'one for you and one for me'. It was so bloody funny and so bloody Joe." She laughed, and a thousand wrinkles suddenly appeared around her bright-green eyes.

Alice chuckled and it reminded her of the photos they'd looked at last night. Megan was the absolute image of her father; the dark, wavy hair, the big, brown eyes and the high cheekbones all contributed to the similarity, but it was the smile that did it. Find a picture of Joe at two years old smiling and place it next to one of Megan and it was the same person.

Ma continued, the smile disappeared and her voice became quieter, almost subdued.

"But I don't think that train journey was just about Joe wanting to help you, Alice – in fact, I think it was more about his total lack of tolerance for bullies. And we both know where he got that from." Ma picked up her wine and closed her eyes as if fixing on some memories.

Alice knew exactly what she meant. Joe had told his wife the full story, and it turned out that her husband had a whole lot more to be grateful to Michael McGrath about than a debt-free University education. It was far more fundamental than that.

"The day Michael stood up to their dad you mean?"

Ma paused for a couple of seconds, opened her eyes and released a gentle sigh before she answered.

"Yes. I'm sure Joe has told you, Alice, but their father was an abusive bastard – firstly to me and then he worked on Michael I'm ashamed to say. On that day, he'd decided that at the grand old age of seven, it was Joe's turn to be initiated. He gave Joe a real beating for something so stupidly insignificant I can't even remember what it was. We argued and he went for me in the street. It tipped Michael over the edge. He was still only seventeen, still a boy really, but Joe isn't the only boxer in the family; he gave his father such a hiding that it took two fully grown men to get him off his dad. After that, we never saw the bastard again – Thank God."

Ma drained the last drop of wine and then continued.

"Joe didn't know the whole story for years, but eventually I felt I had to tell him. He knows without Michael standing up to his dad, he'd have taken a beating on a regular basis." Ma looked away towards the bottom of the garden.

Alice could feel her own eyes moisten at the thoughts swirling around her head. She now shared her husband's opinion that Ma had known about the physical but had no idea about the sexual abuse that Michael McGrath had endured. His brother's bravery had saved Joe from an awful lot more than the occasional beating.

The sound of trampling undergrowth and the excited chatter of a young girl broke the silence. Megan gave her mum and grandma a wave with the excitement of someone that hadn't seen civilisation for several months. Both returned the greeting with equal enthusiasm – grateful for the interruption. Alice looked at her husband, then Megan again and held her tummy lest she exclude her unborn child from the counting of her own blessings. She quickly wiped her eyes.

"Am I interrupting something?" Joe looked between his wife and mother. They'd stopped talking, as he approached.

"It's nothing, darling," replied Alice. A little too quickly, she realised.

"No, really? What's going on?"

Joe raised an eyebrow at Ma, but she wouldn't meet his eyes.

"OK. I assume it's nothing to do with me then. Now, does anyone want another drink, I'm going inside anyway?"

"Cup of tea would be great – thank you, Joe," replied Alice. She smiled reassuringly at her husband.

"Drop more wine when you're ready, Joe," replied Mrs McGrath. She had no problem meeting his eyes now and winked at her son, as she lifted her glass for him. He smiled and gently shook his head.

By now, Megan had climbed up onto Grandma's knee to give her an extra special hug after the successful excursion to the bottom of the garden. She showed her the beautiful stone that Daddy had found for her. It was a jet-black, water-worn pebble with veins of white quartz running through it. The contrast between the two colours produced an intense vibrancy that seemed to amaze the young girl.

McGrath was in the kitchen and pouring the wine when the knock at the front door startled him. They certainly weren't expecting anyone. He leaned so that he could look out through the back window and saw his 'three girls' chattering away. His mum was making funny faces and letting Megan pull her hair gently. He grinned and left them to it.

He opened the front door to three men. One was dressed in a police uniform and the other two were already brandishing their IDs.

Chapter Seventy-One

"Joseph McGrath?"

"Yes."

"Mr McGrath, may we come in please? It's rather a delicate matter to be discussing on the front door step."

"Of course gentlemen, please," replied McGrath.

He opened the thick wooden door to allow them to enter and warned them to mind their heads. He led them into the front room, as he began to worry about the purpose of the visit. His first thought was that something dreadful had happened to Michael in the 'home' but why would the plainclothes guys be here for that?

When they were seated and the introductions had been made, the older of the two plain clothed officers – a DI Child – spoke. "Mr McGrath, we'd like to speak to you about the fraudulent sale of properties from Allied English to various companies owned by a known business associate of yours – a Mr Andrew Longmire."

McGrath remained seated. Slowly, his head sank into his hands and he then pulled his hair, kneading his scalp as he did so. He was looking at the floor as the DI continued.

"We know you had responsibility for selling the assets and it would have been relatively easy for you to manipulate the process. We believe that on at least three occasions, you sold assets at up to 40% below the open markct value," continued DI Child.

McGrath slowly released his grip, but pulled down hard on his cheeks, contorting his expression in the process almost like a naughty boy making a scary face. His skin blanched where the pressure points of his fingers had been and he looked up at the DI; vertical, white streaks set against his otherwise dark skin.

After all this time, they'd found out. But how? What will Alice and Mum do? What about Megan?

The police officer continued.

"Although the buyers were always different companies, they were ultimately controlled by you and Longmire. Mr McGrath – can you hear me?"

He could hear, but he was too stunned to respond and if he'd wanted to speak, he doubted whether he would have been able to find the breath. The shock had, literally, taken it away.

There was a sound of plastic scraping along the tiled floor in the hallway; it sounded like a slow deliberate gait – like someone elderly or overweight was waddling along at a slow pace wearing plastic shoes.

"Joe, where's the tea you promised me…"

Alice had appeared in the doorway but stopped instantly when she saw the uniform and then the appearance of her husband.

"What on earth is going on?" asked Alice to no one in particular, as she made her way to McGrath. She managed to heave herself down onto the sofa beside him. The officers did a double take at Alice's 'baby belly' and exchanged nervous looks with each another.

"Joe, what is it? Has something happened to Michael?"

Joe quickly cleared his eyes with his hands and tried to collect himself. He took a deep breath and looked up at DI Child again.

"Excuse me, officer; may I have a couple of minutes with my wife please?" His voice hitched, as he spoke.

The officer looked at McGrath and then his wife.

"Two minutes, Mr McGrath. I'm afraid we have a job to do." McGrath thought he could detect an element of sympathy in the officer's eyes. DI Child led his team out, but as they were leaving, he popped his head back around the door.

"Mr McGrath, we'll be stood in the hallway and some of my men are in the front garden." He then closed the door behind him.

When they were on their own, he took Alice's hands and looked into her eyes. They were also swimming by this point. He hated himself at that moment, and the last thing he felt like doing was telling the truth, but that's what he did.

"I'm so sorry, Alice. I did something really stupid about two years ago. I found out that Allied English had robbed Michael. I can't explain fully for the moment, please just believe me. So I arranged for the bank to sell the three developments that they had 'stolen' from him to Andrew Longmire. We then sold them on at a profit a little later. My share of that profit is in a bank account.

The only time I use it is to pay for Michael's care. I know it was stupid, Alice, but I was so angry at how they'd treated Michael."

Alice didn't answer at first. An awkward smile built across her face as McGrath spoke. But after a few seconds, it was like a switch being flicked and she was able to process the significance of his confession.

"No, Joe. Not you. *You* didn't do this," she spluttered through the words, as she pulled away from her husband.

"Alice, I'm sorry, but I was just so bloody angry at what they'd done to my brother. That's why he's in the state that he's in!"

But it was no use. McGrath could see from his wife's expression that she was horrified by what he'd done. He couldn't get her to look at him.

"I can't believe it, Joe. I can't believe that *you* of all people could do this? I know Michael is ill, but there are other ways. What about us, Joe; Megan, and this one" – as she pointed to her stomach – "what about the house?"

"Alice, I just wanted to help my brother. I'm so sorry."

"You stupid, selfish bastard."

Alice forced herself to stand and moved away towards a wooden bookcase in the corner of the room – putting distance between herself and McGrath. She then turned.

"Joe, what's going to happen?"

McGrath didn't have the chance to respond. There was a tap on the door and DI Child opened it.

"Apologies, Mr McGrath, but I really do have to get on. Here is the search warrant," said the inspector, as he placed it on a nearby table.

"Joseph McGrath, you do not have to say anything, but…"

Alice gripped the side of the bookcase with one hand and covered her mouth with the other.

Chapter Seventy-Two

DI Child, McGrath and a second inspector from the specialist fraud division were sat in the interview room at Colchester Police Station. Joe was one side of a cheap, white table, the inspectors were the other and a tape-recording device sat in-between them off to one side. McGrath was still wearing his shorts and T-shirt he'd had on when the police arrived at his house. The room was poorly lit, cold and airless, and DI Child noticed the goose bumps appearing on the suspect's arms across the table.

Child had headed the Allied English investigation for over a year now. It had taken months of painstaking research to get them to where they were: just a few nuggets of information away from arresting Dave Arnold and the rest of the body snatchers. And securing Arnold's conviction would be a once-in-a-career coup for the arresting officer – the biggest fish the Serious Fraud Office had ever caught – and he'd be the man who landed it.

Every morning that Child looked in the mirror, he admitted to himself that he was interested in the glory and the profile of convicting Arnold. He was honest with himself about that. But as far as corporate fraud went, this was on a scale that even he had never come across. Arnold was a man who made decisions that ruined people's lives like most human beings made decisions about what to have for lunch. He was absolutely callous; provided the victims paid their fees that drove his annual bonus he didn't care what they lost, no matter how long or how hard they'd worked for it.

From everything Child had been able to gather, McGrath had been bloody stupid but he wasn't callous – he was a completely different animal to Arnold. They had McGrath banged to rights on the three deals he'd been involved with but he was curious as to why McGrath had stopped and why Longmire continued. More importantly, and Child was just about to test his theory, he believed that McGrath might have the missing piece of the jigsaw that would help him convict Arnold. They had evidence about the tricks that were used by Arnold to place unsuspecting clients into the Recovery Unit, but he was clever and there wasn't much explicit material about how he did it. Child needed to know if the man sat in front of him could help.

"Mr McGrath, let's cut to the chase here," said DI Child, as he spread some papers over the desk.

"These are the documents that demonstrate a company controlled by Mr Andrew Longmire bought three developments from Allied English Properties whilst you were in charge of transactions. We have also established that Mr Longmire then sold the three assets – all within a few months of purchasing them from you – and all at a considerable profit.

"Do you deny financially benefitting from the fraudulent sales out of AEP to Mr Longmire?"

"No," replied McGrath.

The other inspector immediately looked up from his notepad. DI Child stopped tapping his chin with the pencil and tried to read McGrath's expression.

"Would you like to expand, Mr McGrath?"

"Yes, I would actually," he replied. McGrath rubbed one of his arms as if to keep warm.

"Dave Arnold is a thieving bastard who robbed my brother of a company he'd spent twenty years building and took away his sanity in the process. I know what I did was wrong, but as far as I was concerned, I was taking money that didn't belong to the bank. I'm not going to deny it – I know it was technically illegal – but sometimes you just have to do the right thing. I'm sorry for what I've done and I accept there'll be a heavy price."

"How do you know he robbed your brother?" Child found himself bottling up his breaths in order to stay calm. The jigsaw in his mind was being rearranged, but the pieces were slotting into place bit by bit.

"Unknown to Arnold, my brother was a property developer and unbeknown to me, my brother used Allied English to fund his developments. After scheming and lying about valuations and breaches of bank covenants, Arnold and his cronies shoved the last three of my brother's developments into the bank's Recovery Unit. And once they'd chewed him up and spat him out, he was fit for nothing." At this point Child noticed McGrath's jawline stiffen. "My brother didn't know who I was the last time he saw me, inspector.

"Anyway, it was only a matter of time before I knew his case would come across my desk at the bank. I assume because it was done under the Virgil

Estates' banner, nobody bothered to look at his name or if they did, they didn't make the connection to me."

McGrath rubbed his other bare arm and continued.

"So when it did land on my desk, I found myself in a unique position, inspector. In one hand, I had the developer's version of events and the letters the bank sent to my brother and in the other, the bank's internal memos about what their real motivation was."

Bloody hell, this guy doesn't just have a piece of the jigsaw; he's the solution to the complete fucking puzzle!

"If you had read these documents, inspector, and seen the impact that it had on my brother's health, you'd also be a very angry man. It was all there in black and white how they screwed him for extra fees, how they adjusted valuations to put him in breach to get him to hand over more money. Money that the internal memos made clear would go straight to their profit centre. It was a totally callous exercise."

Child was battling to contain the grin; he covered his mouth whilst looking down to check his notes.

"And so when you had sold the three developments, that's when you resigned from the bank?"

"Yes. The arrangement I had with Longmire was clear – once I'd recovered the money from my brother's developments, I was gone. I had no interest in carrying on."

"Where is the money that you made, Mr McGrath?"

"It's in an account that I use to pay my brother's medical bills. He's still in a mental hospital after what those bastards did to him."

Child paused and made a couple of notes in his pad as his colleague took a sip of his coffee.

"And you can prove that, I assume, Mr McGrath?" asked Child, as he looked up.

"Yes, of course I can."

"Do you still have the files that prove exactly what Arnold did to your brother?"

"Yes: hard and soft copies. I also made copies of some of the other cases that landed on my desk because by that time, I knew what they were up to."

Child put down his pencil and then looked McGrath in the eyes.

"Then, Mr McGrath, this is what I suggest we do."

Chapter Seventy-Three

It had taken almost another year to get to this stage, and the Alferos appeal case had lasted two months. Lawyers from both sides retraced the arguments from the first court case and found several new ones for good measure. It had gone to the California Court of Appeal and the media interest had heightened even further, providing Hanlon with some further sleepless nights and adding considerably to the swelling skin under his eyes.

The morning of Judge Stanley Peter's decision at the Court of Appeal was a torrid one for Marina. Rodrigo didn't know what to do, but that his wife was nervous ahead of the judge's verdict could be clearly heard through the bathroom door. He gave her some privacy and walked downstairs. Ten minutes later, he was back.

"You OK, honey?"

"What do you think?"

Rodrigo rolled his eyes, as if to acknowledge his own silly question. He tried to recover whilst the sound of another empty heave escaped through the closed door.

"Can I do anything, honey?"

"Yes."

Another heave. Then silence.

"OK, honey, what do you want me to do?"

"Fuck off and leave me alone."

Rodrigo made a wry face at the bathroom door but didn't reply immediately.

"OK, honey. I'll be downstairs, but we do need to leave in the next twenty minutes." He smiled, as he walked to the stairs.

Marina just about made it and just about had the courage to put her best suit on. Now they were in the courtroom waiting.

The court attendant announced Judge Stanley Peters' arrival and everyone duly rose. After acknowledging the observance of courtroom etiquette, the judge sat down at his grand wooden bench that was raised on a platform above the rest of the courtroom. He wore his distinctive black judicial robes with the dignity of a man that had earned his elevated status, and he had done so as one of the first Afro-American judges to be appointed as the Chief Justice in the California Supreme Court. He used the ceremonial gavel in his right hand to bring the court to order. Obediently, the courtroom sat as one.

Marina watched a shaft of powerful sunlight locate the silver-plated seal of the State of California, which was embossed into the wooden panelling behind him. Its reflection transformed the ray into thousands of finer individual beams that shot out across the courtroom. It was fitting: today's decision by the California Court of Appeal would affect thousands of people, not just the Alferos.

As Marina sat, holding her husband's hand, she still had no idea where the funding had come from to launch their expensive appeal, but she did know this was the end of the road. There was nowhere to go after the California Court of Appeal.

Mrs Crabshaw was sat upright, as she faced the Alferos from across the courtroom. Marina couldn't believe how rude she had been to their attorney. She'd been in full-on super-bitch mode all the way through the hearing again.

Judge Peters began his ruling.

"We have heard counsel for Pinewood argue forcefully that the Alferos signed a contract that set out the terms of the mortgage that they freely entered into and that they should be bound by those terms. After all, a contract is a contract."

"I do have sympathy with that argument."

Marina's grip moved to her husband's arm and it tightened further.

The judge cleared his throat. "However, it appears to me that we also need to look elsewhere in a case such as this. Indeed, some of the discoveries that have been made on our journey through this hearing have persuaded me it was essential to look beyond the contents of one, single legal document."

Mrs Crabshaw's body remained perfectly still, but her head swivelled, slowly, changing her field of vision. Her eyes narrowed and locked onto the judge.

"Firstly, the spirit and intention of the HAMP legislation is to help people like the Alferos *despite* there being contracts in place. If HAMP were subservient to existing signed mortgage contracts, it would, by definition, never help anyone. This could never have been the intention of our legislators."

Hanlon looked up at the judge from his hitherto point of focus – the worn lace of his left shoe.

"Secondly, and in my opinion, there has been a change in financial circumstances. Disappointingly, the legislation is not clear on this point, and I fear the financial industry has taken full advantage of this ambiguity. However, it seems far more credible to me – particularly considering the overall aim of HAMP – that a near three-fold increase in monthly payments represents a change rather than not."

Crabshaw was completely focused on Judge Peters now – as if she was gauging the distance across the courtroom to him.

"Finally, there is no evidence that the Alferos were properly informed about the mechanics of the contract and the possible implications of future interest rate increases. This is a major failure of the mortgage company, particularly given the complexity of the mortgage documents. I have read the Alferos mortgage contract and I was shocked that I didn't understand much of the terminology. It seems to me to have been written by a company determined to confuse and obfuscate."

Marina found herself nodding furiously, as the judge lamented the complex jargon.

The judge paused and picked up a piece of paper.

"For example, I wonder how many people in this courtroom knew what an interest-only negative-amortising adjustable-rate subprime mortgage was before we started this hearing?"

The judge looked up and out across his audience. His question was rhetorical but he didn't hang around for an answer.

"My conclusion is that the application of HAMP to this case supports the plaintiff sufficiently for me to find in their favour. I am, therefore, ordering that the Alferos receive a mortgage modification," concluded Judge Peters. He opened his mouth to continue, but didn't get any further.

The courtroom erupted, as some in the gallery cheered and others scrambled to get outside and report the decision to the waiting TV crews on the pavements. Marina hugged her husband, laughed, kissed and cried in that order. The escape was immense. From the moment the first letter arrived two years ago demanding the higher payments, to the first confrontation with Crabshaw and the subsequent court cases, the pressure had become almost too much to bear. The threat of losing their home, the rising debts and the implications for starting a family had been her constant fear. Never more than one thought away from her.

Hanlon slumped into his chair. He removed his glasses and rubbed his tired eyes with the palm of his hands. After a few seconds, he replaced his eyewear and watched the happy couple and a slow smile emerged across his face.

Mrs Crabshaw's skin tone passed through, and went way beyond pale, as the blood seemed to drain from her face. She turned away from the judge and once again stared at her nemesis. Crying, hugging and kissing in the Supreme Court. She looked at them as if they were embarrassing themselves.

She then turned to face the Pinewood attorney sat behind her. He was gathering his documents like he'd just finished reading the Sunday newspapers.

It was the sight of his relaxed indifference that seemed to push her over the edge.

"What are you doing, you stupid man! You can't let these fraudsters get away with this. Tell them we're going to appeal!" Her shrill voice was accompanied by a thump of the table.

Judge Peters immediately slammed the gavel down on the hardwood sound block. "This courtroom will come to order whilst I finish my ruling," he continued, and he looked directly at Mrs Crabshaw, and then at her legal representatives. Slowly, the room fell silent.

"Indeed a cynical person may have concluded on the evidence that this Court received that Pinewood were deliberately denying the Alferos a mortgage modification for some reason other than their particularly stringent and literal interpretation of the HAMP legislation. This court has noted the conflict of interest that Pinewood has in this area and it has been a factor in my judgement.

"We have seen from the evidence put forward that organisations like Pinewood have a vested interest in stalling and denying modifications. This is because delinquent homeowners – although God-only knows why the industry thought such a term was a good idea – are charged extra fees whilst they are considered to be delinquent. I should like Pinewood and all of their peers to take note that this court has been alarmed by that conflict. I would urge them to take action before a court of law does so on their behalf.

"So, I'd like to thank everyone for their considerable time in presenting this case." Judge Peters smiled and looked at the Alferos. "I'd particularly like to thank Mr and Mrs Alfero. Both, I am sure it has been quite an ordeal—"

But before the judge could finish, he was interrupted again.

"And, I wonder why you hold these views, Peters, I really do?"

Her voice was not raised, but it was discharged across the courtroom with so much energy and bile everyone in the courtroom could hear Mrs Crabshaw's intervention clearly.

"Do you really think that's what HAMP was trying to achieve – help fraudsters like these *people*?" She almost spat out the last word. "Or are you just protecting your own? I wonder. You're allowing your own biases to undermine our legal system. You should be ashamed of yourself."

Mrs Crabshaw was stood up now and pointing a gnarled old finger at the Chief Justice of the California Supreme Court like she was chastening some errant schoolboy.

Hanlon watched open mouthed, as Crabshaw finally lost control. She had given evidence over a period of weeks with the balance and aplomb of a seasoned legal executive, but there wasn't a trace of that now.

It was the turn of Mrs Crabshaw's attorney to move beyond pale. He couldn't believe what was happening. He tried to interject in order to protect his client, but it was too late.

"Mrs Crabshaw, you're in contempt," declared Judge Peters.

The Court Attendant was instructed to take her into custody. She was shaking violently, as she was led away.

"You immigrant-loving son of a bitch. You're a disgrace to the United States," she said in a loud shriek of a voice. The door then slammed shut behind her.

Judge Peters once again resorted to the use of the wooden hammer on hardwood, as the courtroom buzzed with its reaction to Mrs Crabshaw's outburst.

A few minutes later, the formalities were over and the Alferos were leaving court; they were just about bringing their emotions under control.

"Well, honey, I'm not sure that the day could get any better than this, but why don't we try. Isn't it time for us to focus on that family thing again?" asked Rodrigo, wearing the suggestive grin that always accompanied one of his mischievous propositions.

Marina giggled like a schoolgirl and nestled into the arms of her husband on the steps of the court. She hadn't decided when to tell him. She had no idea whether they'd be looking for a new home or celebrating and she didn't know for sure what his reaction would be. *But, no time like the present,* she thought.

"Rodrigo, come with me, I think you better sit down, honey." She'd certainly had to sit down when she'd found out.

She led her husband away to a bench a few feet away as Hanlon was dealing with the press. She wanted to let Hanlon get on with it. As far as she was concerned, he was entitled to his moment of fame – he'd earned it.

"Honey, I'm sorry I swore at you this morning. I just haven't been right in the mornings for a week or so now. Do you know what I mean?" She looked at her husband straight in the eyes.

"That's OK, honey. I get it. I feel exactly the same way sometimes. This whole thing has made me feel queasy for more than a few weeks now. You don't need to be embarrassed." He was looking over her shoulder back at Hanlon; like he was thinking they really should be somewhere else.

Marina was fairly confident her husband was physiologically incapable of *feeling the same way* as she did each morning. She tried again.

She was smiling now. She loved the fact that the man who knew her better than anyone else on the planet was still capable of missing the obvious. "Rodrigo, honey. That's not why I was sick. It wasn't the court case."

Rodrigo forgot about Hanlon in an instant and turned to her as he took her by the arms. "Oh shit, Marina, what's wrong—"

But as her smile became a laugh and those eyes glistened, like the pristine black pearls of old, the penny finally dropped. The speed of change in his expression from concern to unbridled elation would stay with her forever. They laughed through tears together for the second time that day.

A few feet away, the eccentric gentleman who had bankrolled their appeal smiled, as he watched the young Mexican couple. He felt he'd got to know them in many ways via his briefings with Hanlon in the last twelve months and assumed that the laughing, crying and hugging was all about their legal victory. And why shouldn't they be happy? They'd just beaten a blatantly corrupt mortgage company and saved their home from being repossessed.

He turned and strolled along to his hotel whistling as he did so – chin up, shoulders back and feeling much taller than his five feet four inches.

Yes, there was still a lot of work to do, but this had been a good start – a small act of atonement for his part in all of this. When he got to his room, he opened the book he'd bought in hopeful anticipation earlier in the week. He'd read it before, many years ago, but he looked forward to catching up with George and Lenny – two other migrants who had once called California their home.

Chapter Seventy-Four

Hanlon was sat in his office, feet up on the desk – new shoelaces displaying a renewed optimism – as he read about his success in the newspapers. He was sipping his second cup of coffee, as he turned to the article in the San Francisco Examiner.

'Following the success in the Alferos vs Pinewood case, it has become known that the secretive Trust Fund which sponsored that appeal has apparently funded similar cases elsewhere in the country. A source close to the organisation said that it had spent at least $10 million on appeals and will continue to do so until innocent people who were mis-sold mortgages are able to secure modifications.

'The Alfero case is significant because it has set a precedent that could see millions of others granted a modification. Some are saying the Court's decision could have a greater impact than the HAMP legislation itself.

'The man behind the Trust Fund hasn't been named, but, ironically, is believed to be a Hedge Fund Manager who made billions of dollars betting against the subprime mortgage markets.'

Hanlon put the paper down and chuckled to himself. He knew exactly who the man was; he'd met him several times when they discussed the Alfero case. In fact, it was his idea to highlight the Pinewood conflict that almost certainly swung it for them with Judge Peters. But, unusually for the Examiner, they were way off the mark. There's no way that guy had been involved in finance – he was way too nice for that.

Chapter Seventy-Five

CI Smith was back where he belonged – sat in his new office in New Scotland Yard. He'd won a promotion – well kind of. He'd been appointed to head up a new unit that dealt with international criminals operating in London, but the important point was that he'd left East Anglia and Hanson behind and was back with the Metropolitan elite – in both senses of the phrase.

There was a knock at his open door. "Excuse me, sir, can I have a word?"

"Of course, sergeant, take a seat," replied Smith, pointing to the front of his desk. He continued to peruse the onscreen theatre-booking website.

The sergeant continued. "About three weeks ago, the Thai authorities got in touch. Seems some Brit – well, we think he was a Brit – was in the wrong place at the wrong time. He had an argument with a local villain in Bangkok and ended up taking a couple in the chest just outside the red-light district about three hours after the original altercation. He was killed instantly. The Thai authorities have arrested the main suspect."

CI Smith looked up from his computer for the first time since the sergeant had walked into his office. He regularly received information about Brits abroad that had died in suspicious circumstances – frequently, it didn't lead anywhere but sometimes there was a link back to organised crime in the capital.

"Why *might* be a Brit – he either is or he isn't surely?" asked Smith.

"Well, sir, that's the odd part, and one of the reasons why they contacted us. The name on the ID he was carrying all checks out in Thailand. He emigrated about three years ago and all the paperwork their end is fine."

"What's the problem then?" asked Smith, who had resigned himself to booking his theatre tickets a little later and was now tapping his fingers on the desk.

"It turns out his UK passport is false. From what we can tell, it was a bloody good and very expensive forgery, but the UK passport office certainly never issued it."

"What was the name on the passport?"

"Alan Williams, sir."

CI Smith shook his head. "Doesn't mean anything to me, sergeant. Have you got a photo?"

"These are the crime scene photos, sir. They're going through facial recognition now."

CI Smith took a sip of his tea, as the sergeant slipped them across the desk.

"Bloody hell – I don't believe it!" said Smith, as he crashed his teacup into the saucer.

Smith was looking at the man that had made him look like a fool during his time in Suffolk. He hadn't thought he was capable of a punch up, let alone committing murder – twice!

Twenty minutes later, Smith reluctantly emailed DI Jim Hanson in Ipswich. He couldn't quite face speaking to him, but it was a question of professional etiquette. He had a responsibility to let Hanson know what had happened to Paul Poorish.

Chapter Seventy-Six

3 April 2011 was an unseasonably cold morning in London. Andrew Longmire knew this because he was being led out of the meat wagon and across a small courtyard at the back of Southwark Crown Court. It was no more than twenty metres from the van to the security doors but it was cold enough for him to feel the halting chill seeping through the orange HMP overalls. A young female police officer smiled at him, as he hurried through the gated door and into the building; a small moment of warmth in what will otherwise be a desperately cold day, he thought.

The jury had apparently reached their verdict and he and Arnold were back here to face the music and the inimitable Judge Kenneth Walters, of course. After a trial lasting over four months, Judgement Day had apparently finally arrived.

As he was led into the dock in courtroom one, it was immediately clear there was standing room only. The tabloids that Longmire had tried to avoid claimed there were two main reasons for the heightened interest in the case. The first was the shock factor. Ordinary hardworking people, they argued, found it difficult to comprehend just how merciless Dave Arnold was in his treatment of people who were supposed to be his customers. The second reason was the convenient focal point that the two men represented. Here was a pair of 'evil bankers', who had actually been tried in a court of law for their crimes and, god-willing, could actually end up behind bars. Since the vast majority of bankers had 'gotten away with it', the vitriol that the public felt for bankers generally had become concentrated on the two men.

It was a further sign of the horrendous treatment Arnold had metred out that many in the court were relatives and friends of his victims rather than those he had preyed on directly. A number of the hitherto capable businesspeople simply couldn't be there; their health had deteriorated to such an extent that mentally or physically they were incapable. Michael McGrath was a case in point.

Now that Longmire reached the dock to hear his fate, a sea of resentment stared back at him. It felt like every fevered stare, each angry snarl was trying to bore through his skin to reach into his soul. He looked away and preyed the proceedings would start. He wasn't sure how much he could take of this.

He didn't have long to wait. Judge Walters arrived and the courtroom stood as one. He took his place on his platform and dealt with the administrators. He nodded to one of the clerks at the far end of the court and the 12 men and women of the jury filed back into the courtroom.

The judge cracked his gavel down hard to stop the frenzy of whispers and conjecture. It moderated and then stopped altogether within a few seconds. Longmire wiped away the perspiration gathering on his upper lip with his thumb and forefinger; the monogrammed white handkerchief was considered an unlawful luxury by HMP.

The judge nodded again – this time, to another clerk who now got to his feet.

"Has the jury reached a verdict in both cases?" he asked.

"Yes, we have," replied the foreman.

In the case of Regina versus David Arnold on the charges of fraud, money laundering, bribery and corruption, how do you find the defendant?

"Guilty."

There was a huge cheer in the courtroom. And then, the shrill competing voices descended from the gallery as relatives, friends and victims released their pent-up anger; anger that in some instances had been building for years. Everyone seemed to be screaming abuse at Arnold all at once. He just stood in silence staring ahead as the hideous cacophony grew.

The judge let it continue. He didn't appear, to Longmire at least, to be in any rush to call a halt to the braying. Perhaps as far as Judge Walters was concerned, this was part of the retribution process. Being allowed to listen to the anger of those that your crimes affected the most would cleanse the soul in some way.

Longmire pinched a sideward glance at Arnold. He was tense, but there wasn't a hint of remorse on his face. He didn't think there was much chance for Arnold's soul.

After the crowd had finally calmed down, the clerk asked the foreman of the jury, "In the case of Regina versus Andrew Longmire on the charges of fraud, money laundering, bribery and corruption, how do you find the defendant?"

"Guilty."

Another cheer went up, although less intense than the reception that Arnold had received.

Longmire looked up at his parents. His mum didn't see him. She had her face turned into her husband as she cried on his shoulder. His dad looked straight at him but didn't show any emotion.

"Thank you, ladies and gentlemen of the jury. This court and the British public owe you a tremendous debt of gratitude for investing the time to consider this complicated and, at times, harrowing case. You are dismissed. The Court will adjourn for sentencing in one week."

Judge Walters talked to the legal advisers of both men and asked them to make any submissions they felt necessary before sentencing. Since the next time the court sat, he would also be passing judgment on Joseph McGrath he asked for the legal team to be contacted with the same request.

Chapter Seventy-Seven

Judge Walters had been true to his word and, one week after the verdicts were declared, all three men were back in his courtroom to hear their fate. McGrath took his seat next to the other two men, as they faced a packed courtroom, and glanced at the judge.

Seated in his raised, leather-bound chair, Judge Walters appeared as an apparition of monochrome. McGrath considered the black robe and his black and white tortoise-shell glasses and their juxtaposition with the white horsehair wig, the stiff wing collar shirt and the ceremonial starched white bands jutting out from his neck to form the upside-down V. His wardrobe didn't seem to countenance the myriad of colours in between.

Apparently, as McGrath had been warned, his approach to sentencing was just as binary. The world came to Judge Walters, refracted, through those black and white glasses, and everything that funnelled past them appeared to him to be just that – black and white was right and wrong, was innocent and guilty. A jury couldn't find a man half guilty any more than it could deliver a half innocent verdict. You were one or the other. And once a jury had declared a man culpable, it was Walter's duty to apply the full force of the law. So even though he had turned Queen's evidence, McGrath knew that it was probable that he'd still receive a custodial sentence.

The judge cleared his throat and began. He had one of those voices that 'carried' – without straining his words seemed to resonate effortlessly across the courtroom and McGrath found an almost mesmerised audience staring back at him.

"Firstly, I have read all that counsel has submitted to me since last week. I would like to begin with these submissions and the pleas.

"To my complete astonishment, I have been asked by some to take into account the hardship that might be caused to their families by a sentence of imprisonment. I cannot help but think that the defendants should have thought about these things before they did what they did.

"Further" – and at this point Judge Walter's looked out at the gallery as if he was talking directly to the appropriate relatives – "if David Arnold's family believe that he is a 'pleasant and honest man', they are sadly devoid of all realism, and their submissions ignore the crimes that he committed and the damage he wilfully caused to his many victims."

Jesus, this guy's going to throw the bloody book at us, thought McGrath.

"Regarding pleas, only Joseph McGrath gets credit for pleading guilty. Unfortunately, the other two insisted on a trial and both have been found out."

McGrath looked at the judge and hoped to be able to acknowledge his observation, but Walters ploughed straight ahead.

"So much has been said about the events during the trial, that it is unnecessary for me to repeat much of it. However, this is not simply a case about a corrupt bank manager. It goes very much deeper than that. It is about an abuse of trust and lack of values on a scale that I have found breath-taking.

"And in two of these cases, the motive was the expectation of, and the very considerable realisation of, immense personal financial gain. That was at the cost of enormous losses to Allied English and the destruction of the livelihoods of a number of innocent, hard-working people.

"These are circumstances in which you, David Arnold and you Andrew Longmire, show not a shred of remorse.

"David Arnold.

"Stand up please," said Judge Walters.

In the gallery, an elderly couple were comforting each other and their intermittent sobs and sniffling became louder. *Parents of Arnold?* thought McGrath, and then looked away. The judge continued regardless.

"You are a thoroughly corrupt and devious man. For your own utterly selfish financial advantage, you have ruined the lives of hundreds of people.

"This case has exposed the department that you ran for what it truly was; an evil conveyor belt of wealth appropriation on an industrial scale. Hundreds of victims were swept into the department at one end in the belief that the GRU was there to help them, and then transported helplessly along your grim treadmill of corruption where they were bled dry and picked off by you and your cronies one by one. By the end of the process, they were almost always financially ruined and often mentally broken.

"The evidence has clearly highlighted that your pecuniary gains were then lavished on prostitutes, expensive boats, a string of houses and other material possessions.

"The abuse of trust here is absolutely immeasurable, Mr Arnold.

"I am sentencing you to fourteen years in prison."

The insults were instantly delivered with the same degree of ferociousness from many in the gallery as on the day the verdicts were declared. But there were other people that were stunned into silence by the length of the sentence. The elderly couple collapsed into each other's arms and wept openly.

McGrath sneaked a glance at Alice and Ma. They were huddled together in a silent embrace looking straight at him; both looked petrified now. He tried to reassure them, but sensed his own expression was one of terror. *How had it come to this?* he thought.

Judge Walters' matter-of-fact voice brought him back.

"Andrew Longmire.

"Stand up please.

"You are a devious individual who, with the help and assistance of David Arnold, facilitated the disposal of assets from the bank at prices consistently and substantially below their true open market value. Your actions have cost the Allied English shareholders vast sums of money, and their pecuniary loss was, quite literally, your financial gain.

"You have an exaggerated opinion of the value of money Mr Longmire. If you didn't, you would not have continued for as long as you did with these asset disposals to your immense personal financial advantage. Your financial gain was also lavishly spent on material possessions, prostitutes and much else besides as we have heard. This case has revealed your true character.

"You will serve twelve and a half years in prison."

McGrath knew it was his turn now. He took out the stone that Megan had given back to him from their river expedition on the day of his arrest – the two-tone pebble, jet-black with white quartz veins running through. He held it tightly in his grip and felt the moistness of his hand. He then looked back at the judge; a man who was certainly living up to his reputation – his decisions seemed as polarised as the stone with no room for the infinite shades of meaning in between. Hadn't Arnold and Longmire just discovered that?

So, there was little hope that Walters would rummage around in his conscience for the shades of greyness from which he might feel obliged to pluck out an element of leniency.

"Joseph McGrath."

Oh my God.

"Please stand."

McGrath could barely breathe. In the deal, he had agreed with DI Child, he had pleaded guilty, and had received assurances that it would stand in his favour. Now McGrath wasn't so sure. He tried to prepare himself but found it impossible to begin to imagine the mental anguish that a mind must go through once it's told that it will be locked away for a decade or more.

If his imagination was in need of assistance, all McGrath had to do was listen. Before sentencing, his co-defendants had continued with the façade that had accompanied them for the previous four months – no hint of remorse, stern expressions and arrogant smirks – worn as a badge of honour to demonstrate their pride at the ingenuity of their crimes. But Judge Walter's sentencing had reduced both men to blubbering wrecks within seconds. McGrath didn't dare look at them.

Judge Walters cleared his throat again.

"Mr McGrath, you have given me by far the greatest amount of difficulty in the past seven days as I have had to give consideration to sentencing in this case. To be frank, the other two were very straightforward."

"We cannot deny that you were a party to this horrific sequence of events; indeed, by your own admission, you instigated the first of the asset disposals and encouraged Longmire to aid you in your crimes.

"I cannot ignore this, Mr McGrath, and you should therefore prepare yourself for a custodial sentence."

McGrath closed his eyes.

Alice put her hand over her mouth, but not before the primal shriek had left her body. Ma tried her utmost to comfort her, but Alice's body was shaking terribly.

"However, there is a long list of mitigating factors in your case that are so powerful, that I have been forced to give them considerable attention."

At this point, Judge Kenneth Walters paused momentarily. He took off his spectacles, collapsed the arms and placed them very deliberately in a case to one side of him. He then placed his hands together on the wooden bench and stared at the defendant. McGrath looked up now. He'd never seen the judge without spectacles during the whole trial. He wondered, both half-jokingly and certainly half-heartedly, if it was a sign. Had the judge miraculously discovered a shade of greyness, a touch of empathy, which challenged his usual outlook?

"Firstly, and unlike the other defendants, your admission of guilt and your obvious remorse for what you did; I would like you to know that I have taken that, and your previous good character, into account in considering the right starting point for sentencing. It is also clear to this court that you have been instrumental in the CPS investigation. Indeed, it is not a stretch by any means to conclude that your cooperation has led directly to the successful conviction and therefore imprisonment of two very unscrupulous characters."

McGrath and DI Child exchanged a quick glance.

"Another factor, and this has been upper most in my mind, is the motivation for your crime. Unlike your co-defendants, you did not intend, nor did you at any point, benefit personally from your actions. As we have learnt, your crime was carried out in direct response to the predatory actions of your employer. In a cruel irony, and clearly unbeknown to you, your own brother suffered at the hands of David Arnold. He, like many others that had the misfortune to find themselves on Arnold's evil conveyor belt ended up losing everything. Unfortunately, he not only lost his business, and is still recovering in hospital from the trauma brought on by the catalogue of events that took his company and assets away from him. The proceeds from your actions, which have been reviewed and corroborated by the CPS, were used exclusively to pay for your brother's treatment and nothing else. This court recognises the stark contrast between what you, and the other defendants, chose to do with the proceeds of the crime."

Judge Walters then slowly moved his hands into a firm clasp in front of him and said, "I am therefore sentencing you to three years in prison, Mr McGrath – but all are to be suspended."

As he stopped speaking, the judge nodded his approval – briefly, but discernibly. On a different day and had it been a different person, such a modest show of respect would have gone unnoticed. But DI Child had clearly seen it; otherwise, he wouldn't have started to move his own head in agreement. The clerks looked at one another and shared knowing smiles. McGrath hadn't seen it, as all his powers of concentration were still focussed on what the judge had just said.

Alice covered her mouth and this time just about caught the scream of elation from escaping.

Ma had heard but appeared confused.

"What the fuck does that mean?" she asked, turning so quickly to face McGrath's lawyer that her Billy Connolly frizz collided with the man's spectacles.

"It means he's coming home, Mrs McGrath." He smiled back.

Allen, Geoff Finn and nine other boxers from the gym gave a massive roar as McGrath became aware of their presence for the first time.

When the cheering had died down, the judge tapped his gavel to signal it was his intention to continue speaking. McGrath was having difficulty standing, as his knees seemed to buckle once more. He tried to focus on the judge, but couldn't quite see the expression on his face – it was like looking through water.

"Mr McGrath, in some ways of course you are a very lucky man today. You could very easily be spending tonight in prison and not at home with your family. But we all know that there was an awfully high price to pay for you and your family. I'm certain I speak for everyone involved in the CPS and their specialist fraud division when I wish you, your brother and the rest of your family all the best for the future."

Ma went straight back onto the waterworks.

McGrath blinked furiously to clear his eyes and glanced at DI Child. The inspector smiled back at him and nodded to confirm the judge's assertion.

When McGrath looked back at the judge, he was sure that this venerable old man was sat a little less upright than he had been for the entire trial. He appeared a little different without the glasses – less severe somehow. Walters took a deep breath and looked up to the ceiling, as if to check in with some higher authority before proceeding. He then smiled in court for the first time anyone present could remember.

"Not for many, many years has anyone given me reason to recall my old professor from law school and his favourite maxim. But, Mr McGrath, you have, and for that, I am grateful. You, and indeed I suppose many others here" – at this point, Judge Walters looked out across the courtroom with open arms – "may find it difficult to believe that I was once a student. It was several decades ago but my memory and recollection of facts do, somehow, extend back that far."

There was a gentle ripple of laughter around the court and the judge permitted himself another smile. Two in one decade – he was getting rather carried away. You could sense the atmosphere begin to turn. Ma was now on her second packet of tissues. Alice was looking at her husband with complete admiration.

"He always assured me, Mr McGrath, that in life, one should be led by principle and not by principal. For those of you in the court a little confused, I suggest you think on that as you make your way home and if you're still confused invest in a good dictionary. The words are homophones – they're spelt almost identically, sound exactly the same but the peculiarities of the English language have awarded them entirely different meanings; as I think this case has demonstrated."

He looked at McGrath again and this time, their eyes met.

"I have tried to lead my life by that maxim, Mr McGrath, and from what I have seen, I think that you have too.

"As a result, I am beyond satisfied that you, any more than I, I hope, do not belong in a prison.

"This court is adjourned."

Only when he had finished his summary, did Judge Walter's attention return to the glasses case next to him. McGrath's was a grateful, yet puzzled expression, as he watched the judge take out the spectacles, buff the lenses with a cloth and then sit them, once again, on the bridge of his nose.

"All rise," said the Bailiff.

As Andrew Longmire was led away, his heavy, brown eyes scanned the galleries for one last time. He located his parents but not the person he was looking for. Back in Suffolk, she was signing her divorce application.